AGE TO READERS

ed under the auspices of

ULVERSCROFT FOUNDATION

(registered charity No. 264873 UK)

Established in 1972 to provide funds for research, diagnosis and treatment of eye diseases. Examples of contributions made are: —

A Children's Assessment Unit at Moorfield's Hospital, London.

•

Twin operating theatres at the Western Ophthalmic Hospital, London.

•

A Chair of Ophthalmology at the Royal Australian College of Ophthalmologists.

•

The Ulverscroft Children's Eye Unit at the Great Ormond Street Hospital For Sick Children, London.

You can help further the work of the Foundation by making a donation or leaving a legacy. Every contribution, no matter how small, is received with gratitude. Please write for details to:

THE ULVERSCROFT FOUNDATION,
The Green, Bradgate Road, Anstey,
Leicester LE7 7FU, England.
Telephone: (0116) 236 4325

In Australia write to:
THE ULVERSCROFT FOUNDATION,
c/o The Royal Australian and New Zealand College of Ophthalmologists,
94-98 Chalmers Street, Surry Hills,
N.S.W. 2010, Australia

Ann Cleeves worked as a probation officer, bird observatory cook and auxiliary coastguard before she started writing. She is a member of 'Murder Squad', working with other northern writers to promote crime fiction. In 2006 Ann was awarded the Duncan Lawrie Dagger for Best Crime Novel, for *Raven Black*. Ann lives in North Tyneside.

BLUE LIGHTNING

Shetland Detective Jimmy Perez is returning to the Fair Isles to introduce his fiancée, Fran, to his parents. But it's a close community: strangers are welcomed — with mistrust. And as the autumn storms rage, the island feels cut off from the world. The islanders are trapped; tension is high and tempers frayed. Enough to drive someone to murder . . . When a woman's body is discovered at the Fair Isles bird observatory, with feathers threaded through her hair, the islanders are fearful and angry. So, with no help from the mainland, Jimmy, assisted by Fran, investigates a cold, calculated murder. With no way off the island until the storms abate — Jimmy must work quickly. There's someone on the island just waiting for the opportunity to strike again . . .

Books by Ann Cleeves
Published by The House of Ulverscroft:

A BIRD IN THE HAND
COME DEATH AND HIGH WATER
MURDER IN PARADISE
A PREY TO MURDER
A LESSON IN DYING
A DAY IN THE DEATH OF DOROTHEA CASSIDY
ANOTHER MAN'S POISON
MURDER IN MY BACK YARD
SEA FEVER
THE MILL ON THE SHORE
HIGH ISLAND BLUES
THE BABY-SNATCHER
THE CROW TRAP
THE SLEEPING AND THE DEAD
BURIAL OF GHOSTS
TELLING TALES
RAVEN BLACK
HIDDEN DEPTHS
WHITE NIGHTS
RED BONES

ANN CLEEVES

BLUE LIGHTNING

Complete and Unabridged

CHARNWOOD
Leicester

First published in Great Britain in 2010 by
Macmillan
an imprint of Pan Macmillan
London

First Charnwood Edition
published 2011
by arrangement with
Pan Macmillan
a division of Macmillan Publishers Limited
London

British Library CIP Data

Cleeves, Ann.
Blue lightning.
1. Perez, Jimmy (Fictitious character)- -Fiction.
2. Police- -Scotland- -Shetland- -Fiction.
3. Fair Isle (Scotland)- -Fiction. 4. Detective and mystery stories. 5. Large type books.
I. Title
823.9′14–dc22

ISBN 978–1–4448–0652–6

Published by
F. A. Thorpe (Publishing)
Anstey, Leicestershire

Set by Words & Graphics Ltd.
Anstey, Leicestershire
Printed and bound in Great Britain by
T. J. International Ltd., Padstow, Cornwall

This book is printed on acid-free paper

For my wise, funny and indomitable daughters

Acknowledgements

Once again many people have contributed to the writing of this book and to keeping me organized and sane. Jean Rogers and Roger Cornwell do far more than look after my website. Julie Crisp and Helen Guthrie from Pan Macmillan and Sara Menguc and her associate agents round the world seem like family now. Helen Pepper advised on probably the most awkward crime scene I've yet devised for her. Visit Shetland and Shetland Arts continue to provide support and assistance with efficiency and good humour. Ingrid Eunson read the script, though any remaining mistakes in Fair Isle geography and customs are mine not hers. Although the North Light field centre is fictitious, I'd like to thank Hollie and Deryk from Fair Isle Bird Observatory for their hospitality and help. I look forward to visiting the new obs! Tim gave me the space and the time to write and lent his birding expertise to the book. Finally a big thank you to the glorious sisterhood of ex-bird observatory cooks.

1

Fran sat with her eyes closed. The small plane dropped suddenly, seemed to fall from the sky, then levelled for a moment before tilting like a fairground ride. She opened her eyes to see a grey cliff ahead of them. It was close enough for her to make out the white streaks of bird muck and last season's nests. Below, the sea was boiling. Spindrift and white froth caught by the gale-force winds spun over the surface of the water.

Why doesn't the pilot do something? Why is Jimmy just sitting there, waiting for us all to die?

She imagined the impact as the plane hit the rock, twisted metal and twisted bodies. No hope at all of survival. *I should have written a will. Who will care for Cassie?* Then she realized this was the first time in her life she'd been scared for her own physical safety and was overcome by a mindless panic that scrambled her brain and stopped her thinking.

Then the plane lifted slightly, seemed just to clear the edge of the cliff. Perez was pointing out familiar landmarks: the North Haven, the field centre at the North Light, Ward Hill. It seemed to Fran that the pilot was still struggling to keep the aircraft level and that Perez was hoping to distract her as they bucked and swivelled to make a landing. Then they were down, bumping along the airstrip.

Neil the pilot sat quite still for a moment, his hands resting on the joystick. Fran thought then he'd been almost as scared as she had.

'Great job,' Perez said.

'Oh, well.' Neil gave a brief grin. 'We have to practise for the ambulance flights. But I did think at one point we'd have to turn back.' He added more urgently: 'Out you get, the pair of you. I've a plane-load of visitors to take out and the forecast is that it'll get worse later. I don't want to be stranded here all week.'

A small group of people waited by the airstrip, their backs to the wind, struggling to remain upright. Perez and Fran's bags were already unloaded and Neil was waving for the waiting passengers to come on board. Fran found she was shaking now. It had felt suddenly cold after leaving the stuffy cabin of the small plane, but she knew this was also a response to her fear. And to her anxiety about meeting the waiting people, Perez's family and friends. This place, Fair Isle, was a part of who he was. He'd grown up here and his family had lived here for generations. What would they make of her?

It would be, she thought, like the worst sort of job interview, and instead of arriving calm and composed, ready with a smile — usually she could do charm as well as anyone she knew — the terror of the flight remained with her and had turned her to a shivering, inarticulate wreck.

She was saved the need to perform immediately because Neil had loaded his passengers on to the plane and was taxiing to the end of the airstrip to prepare for the return trip to Tingwall on the Shetland mainland. The noise of the engines was very close and too loud for them to have an easy conversation. There was a momentary pause, then the surge of the engines again and the plane rattled past them and lifted into the air. Already it looked as frail and small as a child's toy, tossed about by the strong wind. It turned over their heads and disappeared north, seeming more stable now. Around her Fran sensed a collective relief. She thought she hadn't been overreacting about the dangers of the flight. It wasn't a southern woman's hysteria. This wasn't an easy place to live.

2

Jane cut margarine into the flour and rubbed it through her fingers. She preferred the taste of butter in scones, but the field centre ran to a tight budget and the birdwatchers were so hungry when they came in for lunch that she didn't think they noticed. She paused as she heard the plane fly overhead and smiled. It had got off then. That was good. Half a dozen birders who'd been staying at the centre had gone out with it. Fewer centre visitors meant less work for the cook and when people were stranded here, stuck because of the weather, they became fractious and frustrated. It amused her to explain to a high-powered businessman that there was no way he could buy his way off the island — in a near hurricane neither the plane nor the boat would go no matter how much cash he offered to the skipper or the pilot — but she disliked the atmosphere in the place when people were marooned against their will. It was as if they were hostages and they reacted in different ways. Some grew listless and resigned, others became irrationally angry.

She added sour milk to the mixture. Although she made a batch of scones every day and thought she could do it with her eyes closed, she'd weighed the flour and measured the milk. That was her way: cautious and precise. There was a square of cheese that had been left unwrapped and needed using, so she grated it and stirred it in too. It crossed her mind that if the boat didn't get out tomorrow she'd have to start making bread. The freezer was almost empty. She pressed down the scone dough, cut it into circles and laid them, touching so that they'd rise properly, on the baking tray. The oven was hot enough and she slid in the tray. Straightening up she saw a figure in green waterproofs walk past the window. The walls of the old lighthouse cottages were three feet thick, and the spray had streaked the glass with salt, so visibility was limited, but it must be Angela, back from doing a round of the Heligoland traps.

This was Jane's second season in the Fair Isle field centre. She'd come the spring before. There'd been an advertisement in a country living magazine and she'd applied on the spur of the moment. An impulse. Perhaps the first impulsive act of her life. There had been a sort of interview over the phone.

'Why do you want to spend a summer on Fair Isle?'

Jane had anticipated the question of course; she'd worked in HR and had interviewed countless people in her time. She'd given an answer, something bland and worthy about needing a challenge, a time to take stock of where her future lay. It was just a temporary contract, after all, and she could tell that the person on the other end of the phone was desperate. The season was only a few weeks off and the cook who'd been lined up to start had taken off suddenly for Morocco with her boyfriend. The true answer, of course, would have been far more complicated:

My partner has decided that she needs children. I'm scared. Why aren't I enough for her? I thought we were settled and happy but she says that I bore her.

The decision to come to Fair Isle had been the equivalent of hiding under the bedclothes as a child. She'd been running away from the humiliation, the dawning understanding that Dee had actually found someone else who was just as keen to have a baby as she was, that Jane was alone and almost friendless. When she was offered the job in the field centre, Jane had resigned from her post in the civil service and because she had holiday still to take, had left at the end of the same week. There was a small ceremony in the office. Fizzy wine and a cake. The gift of a book token. The general feeling there was one of astonishment. Jane was known for her reason and her reliability, a cool intellect. That she should pack in her career, with its valuable income-linked pension, and throw everything away to move to an island, famous only for its knitting, seemed completely out of character.

'*Can* you cook?' one of her colleagues had asked, incredulous that the respected HR manager might be interested in something so mundane. And in the shambles of the telephone interview Jane had been asked that too.

'Oh, yes,' she'd said on both occasions with complete honesty. Her partner Dee had loved to entertain. She was a director with an independent production company and at weekends the house was full of people — actors and producers and writers. Jane had produced the food for all these gatherings, from the canapés for their famous midsummer parties to formal dinners for a dozen people. It had been a crumb of comfort to her, on walking away from the house in Richmond, pulling the large wheeled suitcase behind her, to wonder who would cater for these occasions now. She couldn't imagine Dee's new woman, Flora, who was sharp-featured and shiny-haired, in an apron.

Jane had arrived in Fair Isle without any real idea of what to expect. It was an indication of how disturbed she was that she hadn't researched the place beforehand. That would have been her normal style. She'd have checked out the websites, gone to the library, compiled a file of important information. But her only preparation had been to buy a couple of cookbooks. She would need to prepare hearty meals brought in to budget and she wasn't acting so completely out of character that she could contemplate doing a poor job in her new role.

She'd come in on the mail boat, the *Good Shepherd*. It had been a sunny day, a light south-easterly wind had been blowing, and she'd sat on the deck watching the island approach. There had been the excitement of discovery. It had occurred to her then — and it still did — that this was like meeting a lover. There was the first affectionate glimpse, then the growing understanding. Spring in good weather and it's easy to fall in love with Fair Isle. The cliffs are full of seabirds; Gilsetter, the flat grassland south of the havens, is covered with flowers. And she'd fallen head over heels. With the centre as well as the island. It had been converted from the North Lighthouse, now automatic, which stood in magnificent isolation on the high, grey cliffs. She'd grown up in the suburbs and had never imagined she would live somewhere so wild or dramatic. She thought that here she could be quite a different person from the timid woman who hadn't been able to stand up to Dee. The kitchen had become her place immediately. It was big and cavernous. Once it had been the senior lightkeeper's living room and there was a chimney breast and two windows which looked out over the sea. She'd ordered it to suit her as soon as she'd arrived, before even she'd emptied her case. It was too early in the season then for guests but the staff still needed feeding.

'What were you planning for supper?' she'd asked, rolling up the sleeves of her cotton shirt and slipping her favourite long blue apron over her head. When there'd been no immediate response she'd looked in the fridge and then the freezer. In the fridge there was a stainless-steel bowl of cooked rice covered with cling film, in the freezer some smoked haddock. She'd rustled up a big pan of kedgeree, using real butter despite the expense and big chunks of hard-boiled egg. They'd eaten it around the table in the kitchen. The talk had been of wheatear nests and seabird numbers. Nobody had asked why she'd decided to come to Fair Isle to be a cook.

Later Maurice had said it was like Mary

Poppins arriving and taking over. They all knew that everything would be all right. Jane had always treasured that remark.

She could tell from the smell that the baking was almost ready. She lifted out the tray and set it on the table, pulled the scones apart so they could cook properly inside, and put them back in the oven. She set the timer for three minutes though she wouldn't need it. In this kitchen things didn't burn. Not when Jane was in charge.

The door opened and Maurice came in. He was wearing a flannel shirt and a grey cardigan, cord trousers bagged at the knee, leather slippers. He looked like the crumpled academic he had been before moving to the Isle with his new young wife. Automatically, Jane switched on the kettle. Maurice and Angela had their own accommodation within the field centre, but he usually came into the big kitchen for coffee in the morning. Jane had a cafetière, ordered real coffee from Lerwick. He was the only person with whom she shared it.

'The plane got off all right,' he said.

'Yes, I heard it.' She paused, filled the cafetière, then lifted the scones out of the oven, just as the timer went off. 'How many guests are left?'

Maurice had given the departing visitors and their luggage a lift to the plane in the Land Rover. 'Only four,' he said. 'Ron and Sue Johns went out too. They'd heard the forecast and didn't want to be stuck.'

Jane was transferring the scones on to a rack

to cool. Maurice took one absent-mindedly, split it and spread it with butter.

'Jimmy Perez was in today with his new woman,' he went on, his mouth still full. 'James and Mary were waiting for them. Poor girl! She looked as white as a sheet when she got out of the plane. And I don't blame her. I wouldn't have enjoyed a flight like that.'

Maurice was the centre administrator. The place carried out scientific work but it also provided accommodation for visiting naturalists or for people who were interested in experiencing the UK's most remote inhabited island. During September the place had been full of birdwatchers. September was peak migration time and a week of easterly winds had brought in two species new to Britain and a handful of minor rarities. Now, in the middle of October, with the forecast showing fierce westerlies, the centre was almost empty. Maurice had taken early retirement from the university to act as a glorified B&B landlord. Jane wasn't sure what he felt about that and it would never have occurred to her to pry.

But she did know that what he loved about the place was the gossip. Perhaps that wasn't so very different from the slightly bitchy chat in a senior common room of a small college. He knew what was going on apparently without any effort at all. Jane had kept her distance from most of the islanders. She knew and liked Mary Perez, was occasionally invited to Springfield for lunch on her days off, but they were hardly close friends.

'He's the policeman, isn't he?' Jane wasn't very interested. She looked at her watch. Half an hour to lunchtime. She lit the Calor gas under a big pan of soup, stirred it and replaced the lid.

'That's right. Mary was hoping he might come back when a croft became vacant a couple of years ago but he stayed out in Lerwick. If he doesn't have a son he'll be the last Perez in Shetland. There's been a Perez in Fair Isle since the first one was washed ashore from a ship during the Spanish Armada.'

'A daughter could keep the name and pass it on,' Jane said sharply. She thought Maurice should be more aware of the dangers of gender stereotyping than anyone. All the visitors assumed that *he* was the warden of the place and that Angela organized the bookings and the housekeeping. In fact, Angela was the scientist. She was the one who climbed down the cliffs to ring fulmars and guillemots, she took the Zodiac out to count seabird numbers, while Maurice answered the phone, managed the domestic staff and ordered the toilet rolls. And Angela had kept *her* maiden name after they'd married, for professional reasons.

Maurice smiled. 'Of course, but it wouldn't be the same for James and Mary. Especially James. It's bad enough for him that Jimmy won't be home to take on the *Good Shepherd*. James wants a grandson.'

Jane moved out into the dining room and began to lay the tables.

* * *

Angela made her appearance after the rest of them had sat at the table. There were times when Jane thought she came in late just so she could make an entrance. But today there hardly seemed enough of them to make a good audience: four visitors plus Poppy, Maurice's daughter, and the field centre staff, who should be used by now to her theatrics. And Maurice, who seemed to adore her, who seemed not to mind at all his changed role in life as long as it made her happy.

Angela had helped herself to soup from the pan still simmering on the stove and stood looking down at them. She was twenty years younger than Maurice, tall and strong. Her hair was almost black, curly and long enough to sit on, twisted up now and held by a comb. The hair was her trademark. She had become a regular commentator on BBC natural history programmes and it was the hair that people remembered. Jane supposed Maurice had been flattered by her attention, her celebrity and her youth. That was why he had left the wife who'd washed his clothes and cooked his meals and looked after his children, nurturing them to adulthood — if Poppy could be considered an adult. Jane had never met this deserted wife but felt a huge sympathy for her.

Jane expected Angela to join them, to move the conversation quickly and skilfully to her own pre-occupations. That was the usual pattern. But Angela remained standing and Jane realized then that the woman was furious, was so angry that the hands that held the soup bowl were shaking.

She set it on the table, very carefully. Conversation in the room dwindled to nothing. Outside, the storm had become even more ferocious and they were aware of that too. Even through the double-glazed windows they heard the waves breaking on the rocks, could see the spray like a giant's spit blown above the cliff.

'Who's been into the bird room?' The question was restrained, hardly more than a whisper, but they could hear the fury behind it. Only Maurice seemed oblivious. He wiped a piece of bread around the bowl and looked up.

'Is there a problem?'

'I think somebody has been interfering with my work.'

'I went in to check the bookings on the computer. Roger phoned to see if we could fit in a group next June and for some reason the machine in the flat wasn't working.'

'This wasn't on the computer. It was a draft for a paper. Handwritten.' Angela directed the answer at Maurice, but her voice was pitched loudly enough for them all to hear the words. Listening, Jane was surprised by the image of Angela writing by hand. She never did, except perhaps her field notes when no other form of taking a record was possible. The warden was beguiled by technology. She even completed the evening log of birds seen with the aid of a laptop. 'It's missing,' Angela went on. 'Someone must have taken it.' She looked around the room, took in the four visitors sitting at their own table and her voice was even louder. 'Someone must have taken it.'

3

Perez had told Fran exactly what to expect of his parents' house. He'd described the kitchen with its view down to the South Harbour, the Rayburn with the rack above for drying clothes in the winter, the oilskin tablecloth, green with a pattern of small grey leaves, his mother's watercolours hanging on the wall. He'd talked about his childhood there, then listened to her tales of growing up in London; the intimate conversations part of the ritual of a developing relationship, absolutely tedious to any outsider.

'Mother will probably hide all her pictures away,' Perez had said. 'She'll be embarrassed for a professional artist to see them.'

And Fran supposed that she was a professional artist now. People commissioned her paintings and they were shown in galleries. She was glad that Mary had left her own work on the walls. The pictures were very small and delicate, not Fran's style at all, but interesting because they showed the small details of everyday Fair Isle life that it would be easy to miss. There was a piece of broken wall, with a few wisps of sheep's wool snagged on one corner, a sketch of one grave in the cemetery. Fran looked at that more closely, but the headstone had been drawn from the side so even if the model had had an inscription it would have been impossible to read from this angle. Alongside Mary's paintings of the Isle there were vibrant prints and posters reflecting the Perez family's Spanish heritage. Legend had it that Jimmy's ancestor had been washed ashore from a shipwrecked Armada ship, *El Gran Grifon*. It was probably true. The sixteenth-century shipwreck was certainly there, under the water for divers to explore, and how else was it possible to explain the strange name and the Mediterranean colouring of James Perez and his son?

Because the reality of the croft was so close to what she'd imagined, but not exactly the same — it was smaller somehow, more cramped — Fran felt rather that she'd wandered into a parallel universe. She sat at the table listening to Mary and James and it was as if she was an extra on a film set, disconnected, not involved in the main action.

Is this how it'll always be here? I'll never quite belong.

It hadn't been discussed recently, but Fran thought Perez might want to move back here one day. She loved the idea of that, the drama of being in one of the most remote places in the UK, of continuing the tradition of a family that went back to the sixteenth century. Now she wasn't sure how that would work out in reality.

Mary was talking about the wedding plans. Her son and this Englishwoman would be married the following May and she assumed Fran would be excited, eager to share her ideas for the day. But Fran had been married before. She had a daughter, Cassie, who was spending this week with her father in his big house in

Brae. Fran wanted to be married to Jimmy Perez but she couldn't get worked up about the details of the show. She hadn't expected Mary to be the sort of woman to fuss over flowers, invitations and whether she would need a hat. Mary had come to Fair Isle as the community nurse and since her marriage had shared all the work on the croft. She was a tough and practical woman. But Jimmy was her only son and perhaps she thought it would please Fran if she showed she was interested in their big day. It seemed to Fran that the older woman very much wanted to be friends with her new daughter-in-law.

'We thought we'd be married in Lerwick,' Fran said. 'A quiet civil ceremony. It's the second time for both of us, after all. Then a party after for family and friends.'

James had looked up at that. 'You'll need something here too. For the folks who can't get out to the mainland. And your family will want to see the Isle. You'll need a hame-farin'. This is Jimmy's home.'

'Of course,' Fran said, though it had never crossed her mind that they would have to bring the circus into Fair Isle. She imagined her parents having to endure the plane ride or the boat. And could she really allow Cassie to face that danger too? And if there were to be a celebration here she'd have to invite some of her close London friends. They wouldn't want to be left out. What would they make of it? Where would they stay?

'We were thinking we'd have a bit of a party

this week to celebrate your engagement,' Mary said.

'That'll be fun. But I wouldn't want to put you to any trouble.' Fran looked at Perez for support. He had been completely silent throughout this exchange. He gave a little shrug and Fran understood that the arrangements would already have been completed. Nothing they said would change things now.

'Oh, I wouldn't have it here.' Mary smiled. 'There's no room in the house. You couldn't have a proper Fair Isle party without some music, a bit of a dance. I thought we'd book the field centre. There's a good space in the dining room for dancing and Jane would do the food for us.'

'Jane?' Fran thought it was safest to focus on the detail.

'She works in the centre kitchen. She's a grand cook.'

'Fine,' Fran said. What else was there to say? *Oh, Jimmy*, she thought. *I'm really not sure I could live here, not even with you*. She turned to his mother. 'When were you thinking of holding the party?'

'I've booked the field centre for tomorrow.' Then in a rush: 'Only tentatively, of course. I wanted to ask you first.'

'Fine,' Fran said again. Mentally gritting her teeth.

* * *

After lunch she felt as if she'd go crazy if she stayed inside any longer. She'd helped Mary to wash up and afterwards they'd taken coffee into the living room, where a big window looked south over low fields to the water. Jimmy's father was a lay preacher for the kirk and had disappeared into the small bedroom they used as an office to prepare Sunday's sermon. The three of them sat for a moment in silence, mesmerized by the huge waves that rolled across the south harbour and smashed into the rocks. It had stopped raining, but Fran thought the gale was even stronger. The noise of it penetrated the thick walls of the house, a constant whining that stretched her nerves, made her even more tense than she would have been anyway. Just outside the window a herring gull was struggling to make headway against the wind; Fran was reminded of the plane and felt a little sick. She reached out to take her cup and drink the last of her coffee, thinking: *What's wrong with Jimmy? He's hardly said anything since we arrived. Does he regret his decision not to come back when he had that chance? We'd just met then. Does he blame me? Does he want to come home?*

Perez got to his feet and stretched out his hand to pull Fran up too. 'Come on. Let's go for a walk. I want to show you the island.'

'Are you mad?' Mary said. 'Why would you go out in this weather?'

'We'll go up to the North Light, talk to Jane about the catering for tomorrow.' A grin to show he knew there was no need, his mother would have done that already. 'Besides, the forecast is even worse from tonight. If we don't get out today we might not have the chance.'

* * *

They stood by the kitchen door to put on boots and waterproof jackets. It was sheltered there but she could still feel the taste of salt on her lips; when they moved away from the house a gust of wind took her breath away and almost blew her off her feet. Perez laughed and put his arm around her.

They walked north and Perez pointed out the places that meant the most to him: 'That's where Ingrid and Jerry used to live. I babysat their three lasses occasionally though I wasn't much older than they were. What a dance they led me! The wind turbine provides all the power for the island now. In my day every croft had its own generator. You could hear the sound of them starting when dusk fell. That place over on the bank is Myers Jimmy's house. There's Margo on her way back from the post office.'

They called in to the shop to buy chocolate and a pile of postcards for Fran to send to her family in the south — when the weather allowed for post to go. The talk there was all about the storm. The middle-aged woman in her hand-knitted cardigan leaned across the till. 'Any news on the boat, Jimmy?' And when he shook his head: 'I can't see it going tomorrow and the last of the bread's gone now. Just as well I bought in lots of dried yeast. The beer's on the low side too. Let's hope folks have stocked up for themselves.'

Further north again the settlements petered out. There was a rise in the land and Fran could see the road winding away, the hill and the airstrip on one side and an area of flat grassland on the other. To the right the sloping bulk of Sheep Rock, jutting into the sea, which gave Fair Isle its instantly recognizable shape from Shetland mainland and from the Northlink ferry.

'What's that?' Fran had stopped and turned her back to the wind. She'd thought she was fit but this was hard going and she was glad of the excuse to rest. She pointed to a wire-mesh cage built over the wall. It was shaped like a funnel with a wooden box at the narrow end.

'A Heligoland trap. It's where the wardens from the field centre catch the birds for ringing. There have been naturalists here since the fifties; they started off in some wooden huts near the North Haven. The place was set up by a couple of guys who were prisoners of war. Apparently they dreamed of coming back and founding a centre for studying birds and plants. When the North Light went automatic there was a huge fund-raising effort to convert it to a state-of-the-art field centre. In the spring there are organized courses for botanists. This time of year it's taken over by birdwatchers. Sometimes the Isle seems full of people with binoculars and telescopes chasing rare birds.' Perez paused. 'They're kind of obsessed.'

'How does it work, the people in the field centre and the islanders? Does everyone get on?'

'Generally. We all grew up with a centre on the island and everyone agreed with the lighthouse conversion — it's so far from the rest of the houses that you can't imagine ordinary folk wanting to live there. It provides business for the shop and the boat and the post office. There've been a few complaints in the past about visitors breaking down walls and flattening crops when they get onto folks' land, but one storm like this could do just as much damage as a horde of birdwatchers. Maurice and Angela have been there for about five years. Folk seem to like them OK.'

'I thought your mother said the place was run by someone called Jane.'

'Jane's the cook. Very good and scarily efficient. The island's started to have its parties there because the food's so good.'

He began walking again. Ahead of them was an isthmus with a sandy beach on one side, rocks and shingle on the other.

'That's the North Haven where the *Good Shepherd* puts in,' Perez said. 'In good weather she would be moored there, but they've pulled her up onto the slipway. Come on. Keep walking. There's still a long way to go.'

They came on to the lighthouse suddenly, rounding a bend in the single-track road. A row of white-washed cottages with the tower beyond and the whole complex surrounded by a low stone wall that had been whitewashed too, enclosing a paved yard, crossed at one end with washing lines.

Fran was tired after the walk in the wind. The sky was overcast now and there were welcoming lights in the small windows. She imagined tea, a fire, and an escape from the relentless noise of the storm. She wasn't sure she'd be able to make the walk back to the south of the island.

Perez pulled open a door into a porch with hooks for outdoor clothes, a bench holding odd boots and shoes. There was a smell of damp wellingtons and old socks, waxed jackets. In the distance they heard raised voices.

'I'm really sorry but that's impossible.' A clear, female voice, the voice of someone who expected to be taken seriously. Someone English and well educated. 'You had the opportunity to fly out on the plane this morning. We did explain that the boat was unlikely to go. The crew won't put their lives, and those of their passengers, into danger just because you've decided you're bored.'

Fran decided this must be Jane, the cook. Certainly the speaker sounded scarily efficient.

'Nobody told me about the plane!' This was another woman. Younger. The voice had the complaining whine of a spoilt teenager.

'An announcement was made at breakfast.'

'You know I never eat breakfast. You should have found me and told me. Why didn't my father tell me?'

'There was no point by then. The available spare places had already been taken.'

'Oh, God!' The words came out as a high-pitched wail, but Fran thought she sensed real panic behind it, the sort of panic she'd felt when she thought the plane was going to crash. 'I hate this bloody place. I'll die if I have to stay here for another day.'

4

Perez lay awake in his parents' guest bedroom, the room that had been his when he was a child. Beside him Fran was sleeping. Their sleeping arrangements had probably caused his parents some anxiety. One of the bedrooms in the house was tiny; now it housed the PC and a desk and a huge metal filing cabinet that Mary had taken when it was being thrown out by the school. There was no room for a camp bed. Perez had thought he might be expected to spend the nights on the living room sofa. His father had fixed ideas about sexual morality. But if there had been any argument over the propriety of their sharing a bed, Mary had won. She'd shown them into the room in the roof with an air of triumph.

'This is a bit different, eh, Jimmy? It's not like when you stayed here.'

And he saw that it had been transformed in their honour. There was a new double bed, fresh curtains with big blue flowers on them, and matching linen. A pair of blue towels folded on the old chest of drawers. He thought his mother must have been watching makeover programmes on daytime television when the bad weather made outside work impossible.

Lying there, listening to the wind tear at the roof tiles, Perez remembered the first woman with whom he'd had sex. The image came into his head, quite unbidden and remarkably vivid. She'd been a woman while he was still a boy. Beata. A German student, member of a National Trust for Scotland work camp; the camp had taken over the Puffin, an old stone fish store at the south end, for a month in the summer. He was sixteen, home for the long holiday. She was twenty-one.

It was the year all the construction work was done at the North Haven and the students acted as labourers, the year Kenneth Williamson had come to Springfield as a kind of lodger. One night there'd been a barbecue at the Puffin and Perez had been invited along. He remembered bottles of German beer in a row in the shadow of the hut, the smell of singeing meat. He was sitting on the grass talking to the woman and suddenly became aware that she was looking at him oddly. She half-closed her eyes and swayed slightly, lost it seemed to him now, in some erotic fantasy of her own.

'I want to swim,' she'd said, opening her eyes wide again. 'Where can I swim?'

By then the other students were rowdily drunk, singing songs in languages he couldn't understand. He'd taken her to Gunglesund, a natural pool formed in the rocks on the west of the island. It filled up on the very high tides and the sun warmed it, so it wasn't so cold there as swimming in the sea. But still cold enough to make the children who came there squeal when they first jumped in.

Beata hadn't squealed. Without any sort of fuss, she'd taken off all her clothes and slipped into the water. She had small breasts, a flat brown stomach, a white triangle where bikini bottoms had been. Her pubic hair was darker than he'd expected. She'd swum away from him with a languid crawl.

The sun had reflected from the water into his eyes and he'd felt faint. There was a weird shady light as if the sun had been eclipsed for a moment and would soon come out again.

'Aren't you coming in?' she'd demanded, turning back to him. Impatient. A little imperious.

He'd hesitated for a moment. What if someone should come? And he'd known even then that what was expected was more than a shared swim. She'd been looking at him greedily since he'd first arrived at the Puffin. He began to undress.

They'd lain on a pile of clothes on a large flat rock, in shadow now that the sun was so low. The woman's hunger for his body had scared and flattered him at the same time. And excited him. Of course he'd been excited. It had been like every adolescent's dream.

When he'd returned home that night, everyone was in bed. He'd half-expected his father to appear, to stand at his bedroom door ranting about sin. This had been such a momentous occasion for Jimmy Perez; how could the whole world not guess what had happened? But everyone had continued sleeping and in the morning his mother had given him breakfast just as usual.

Thoughts of Beata had consumed him for

months. While the work camp was still in the Puffin he'd haunted the place, but she'd taken no more notice of him than of any of the other island kids. The eyes that had been so predatory were now amused. 'It was nothing, Jimmy,' she'd said at last, irritated by his attentions. 'A little fun thing on a summer's night.' Her absence had allowed his dreams to become wilder. But they'd never been purely physical: in every scenario his imagination created they'd become a real couple, setting up home together in a bohemian city bedsit or walking across a moonlit beach hand in hand.

The storm must have lifted a tile from its place because there was the crash of it shattering in the yard; the noise was blurred by the sound of the wind but it brought him back to the present with a start. *Even then*, he thought, *I was an emotion junkie. I needed to be loved*. Fran stirred beside him.

He wondered now whether it had been right to bring her here at all. She was an independent woman and she must resent the interference in her life by his family. What right did his parents have to make assumptions about their marriage? Soon they would be dropping hints that it was time she considered having another baby: *Better not leave it too late. You might not have a boy first time round*. He hated to think what Fran's response to that might be.

The wind made everything a hundred times worse. Even the islanders who were used to the extreme weather started to bicker like toddlers. Most of them didn't leave the place for months at a time, but in fine weather there was the understanding that you *could* leave if you wanted to. In summer the mail boat went three times a week and there were regular flights. In an emergency it was possible to charter a plane. Now they, like the visitors, were trapped. The children who were studying at the Anderson High School in Lerwick wouldn't make it home for the half-term break and their parents were missing them. He should have waited until the spring to bring Fran here. Cassie could have come too and they would have seen the place at its best.

The walk up the island seemed to have exhausted Fran and she was in a deep sleep. He could feel her hair against the bare skin of his shoulder.

Maurice had given them a lift back to Springfield late in the afternoon, the three of them squashed together in the front of the Land Rover, windswept and breathless just after the run from the lighthouse to the vehicle. Perez had always found the field centre administrator an amiable man, relaxed and unflustered, but today he'd seemed infected by the general tension. He'd been quiet, gloomy, and there had been none of the easy conversation Perez remembered from previous meetings.

'Is anything wrong?' Immediately Perez had regretted the question. He was on holiday. If there were problems at the centre it was no business of his. Fran had flashed him a grin as the Land Rover rattled over a cattle grid. *You really can't help yourself, can you*? She thought his curiosity was a sort of affliction and that he'd only become a detective to give himself the licence to meddle in other people's lives.

Maurice had taken a while to answer. 'It's family trouble,' he'd said in the end. 'I daresay it'll sort itself out.' He'd been born in Birmingham and still had the Midlands accent. There'd been another moment of silence while he'd concentrated on keeping the vehicle on the road. He continued speaking but his eyes were fixed straight ahead. 'It's my youngest daughter, Poppy. She's always been a handful. My wife thought a few weeks on the isle might help to sort her out, keep her away from some of the bad influences at home, but it hasn't really worked as we'd planned. Poppy is desperate to leave. She can't, of course. I had to give priority on the plane to the visitors who wanted to get out. She feels like a prisoner here. She can't understand that there's nothing we can do. She's making life difficult for everyone, especially for Angela.'

Lying in bed, Perez thought about this. About problems within families and whether Fran's daughter Cassie would see him as a wicked stepfather when they were married and about what it might be like to have a child of his own. He loved Cassie with a passion that took his breath away at times. His marriage had failed partly because his wife had lost a baby late in pregnancy. If the child had lived she'd have been much the same age as Cassie. But would he feel the same affection if he and Fran had a baby? Would the girl feel rejected or put out?

He must have slept at last because he woke in

the morning to a grey light and rain like bullets against the window next to him.

Later he and his father went out and looked at the damage. A few slates down and the roof was right off the shed that had once housed a cow. Nothing too worrying. When they came back into the kitchen, drenched and scoured by the salt, sandy wind, Fran was up. She was sitting in his mother's dressing gown, her hands cupped round a mug of coffee. The women were chatting and from the porch where he stood to take off his boots, he heard a sudden outburst of giggling. His first wife, Sarah, had never been able to relax like that on visits to the Isle. He felt his mood lift. Perhaps it would be OK. Fran was strong enough to deal with his parents after all. He left aside the question of whether they might one day return to the Isle on a permanent basis.

They spent most of the day in the house. Mary worked at the knitting machine that was set up in the corner of the living room. All morning they heard the swish and click as she pushed the wool in its shuttle across the ratchets. Fran was reading. There was a fire made with scraps of driftwood and coal and the wind roared in the chimney. Later in the afternoon Fran went to get ready for the party.

'Come with me, Jimmy. Help me choose what to wear.'

And they made love very quietly, with the blue and white curtains drawn against the storm, like teenagers in their parents' home, listening out for the adults who might suddenly come in.

Afterwards she laid her clothes on the bed.

'What should I go for, Jimmy? Do people dress up here?'

He shook his head, bewildered by her sudden anxiety. She would look lovely whatever she chose. There was hardly a dress code for a Fair Isle party.

'It matters, Jimmy. I want them to like me. I want to do you proud.'

In the end she went for a long denim skirt and a bright red cardigan, little flat blue shoes. She stared at the mirror before nodding to herself. 'Not too formal, but dressy enough to show I've made an effort.'

Mary wanted them to be at the lighthouse early so they could greet all the guests as they arrived. She seemed a little tense to Perez. He'd never thought of her as a shy woman but she seemed awkward about acting as hostess in the field centre, away from her home ground. Perhaps she just wanted to make it special for him and Fran.

Everyone would be coming by car; this was no weather to take the three-mile walk north. Perez wondered how that would play out. There was hardly a strict adherence to the drink-drive laws in a place where the police only appeared if there was an emergency or to give a talk in the school. But everyone knew what he did for a living. He supposed there were sufficient non-drinkers in the Isle to provide lifts home. Mary never took more than a small glass of wine for a toast and they could squeeze someone else in their car.

In the field centre the tables had already been moved out of the dining room to make a space for the dancing. In the old keepers' accommodation, walls had been knocked through at the time of the original conversion to make big spaces for communal living. Jane was in the kitchen. Perez went in to thank her again for her work. She smiled and took his hand but seemed distracted.

'So we'll serve the food as we decided yesterday? About nine o'clock as usual?'

'How are things?' He realized he was like an old woman, desperate for gossip. How pathetic was that! Why couldn't he be content with his own business? But if he was hoping for more information about Maurice and his teenage daughter he was disappointed. Of course he should have known Jane would be discreet.

'It's been a very good season,' she said, with another brief, clipped smile.

In the dining room he heard the first sounds of the musicians. The fiddle player was tuning up. They swung into the first reel and he felt his feet tapping already. Looking out from the kitchen he saw Fran surrounded by a group of islanders. She had her head tilted to one side and was listening to them talking, her eyes wide open as if she was fascinated by the words. Then she said something he couldn't hear and they all began to laugh.

Of course they'll love her, he thought. She's so good at all this. How could they do otherwise?

He went to join her, took her hand and led her on to the floor for the first dance. He knew what was expected of him.

5

On the afternoon of the party Jane had sat in her room at the back of the field centre. She liked this space. With its high ceiling and narrow window, it made her think of a nun's cell. There was a single bed, a wardrobe incorporating a chest of drawers, a wash-hand basin. On the bedside table her wireless (this was how she thought of it, a legacy from her very old-fashioned parents) tuned to Radio 4, on the windowsill a row of books, spines facing outwards as if on a shelf. On the chest there was a pile of *Times* crosswords, carefully cut out of the newspapers by her sister and posted each week. The crosswords were the only things Jane had missed in her isolation. She wondered fleetingly if sisters in enclosed orders were allowed crosswords and then how many lesbians had become nuns in a less enlightened time. She supposed it would be one way to avoid marriage, the expectation that one would inevitably become a mother.

The simplicity of the room appealed to her. She'd gone south for three months over the winter when the field centre was closed for visitors and it was this clean, sparse space that she'd missed most. She'd spent Christmas with her sister's family and the good-natured chaos, the squawking children surrounded by wrapping paper and chocolate, had driven her slightly crazy. She'd fallen asleep each night, her senses dulled by the alcohol she'd needed to keep her sane, and dreamed of her room in the field centre, the ironed white sheets and the plain painted walls.

It was four o'clock, in the lull between clearing up after lunch and serving dinner. Dinner was already prepared; a casserole was cooking very slowly in the oven, potatoes had been scrubbed for baking. This evening a simple meal had been essential because of the Perez party later. Soon she would return to the kitchen to organize the buffet, but most of the work for that was already done. She took off her shoes and lay on her bed. She would rest for half an hour. This was a time of contentment. She loved the contrast between the drama of the storm outside and the peace of her room.

She was setting out the party food on big trays, before covering it with cling film, when Angela came into the kitchen. Jane was listening to the five o'clock news on the radio, but Angela's appearance made her reach over and switch it off. Angela never dealt with domestic matters and her presence in the kitchen was unusual, an occasion. Her natural habitat was outside. She strode like an Amazon across the hill with her telescope on its tripod slung over her shoulder and binoculars around her neck. Indoors she seemed constrained and restless.

Jane assumed that this was about Poppy. They both disliked Maurice's youngest daughter. It was the only matter they had in common. She hoped Angela had come up with a plan to control the girl. But it seemed there was something quite different on the warden's mind.

'I wanted to talk to you,' she said, 'about next year.'

Jane looked up from the tray of pastries. 'Of course.' She was astonished. Angela always left the staffing to Maurice. 'I was thinking I might come in early next season. The kitchen needs a good clean and we never get a chance once the visitors arrive. And I could fill the freezer with baking. Take the pressure off once the rush starts.' When there was no immediate response Jane added: 'You wouldn't need to pay me the full rate, of course.' Actually, she would have offered to do the work for nothing but she knew Angela would find that weird. Jane thought how much she would enjoy a few weeks here at the start of the season, imagined the kitchen after it had been thoroughly scrubbed, the red tiled floor gleaming, the cooker and the larder spotless.

Angela stared at her. 'That's the point. I'm not sure we'll need you at all next year.'

'You won't need a cook?' Jane knew she was panicking and that was making her obtuse. She stared at the younger woman, whose hair was loose today, a black cape down her back.

'Of course we'll need a cook. But not you.' Angela's tone was amused, slightly impatient. She had better things to do.

'I don't understand.' That at least was true. Jane knew she was the best cook the centre had ever employed. She didn't need the compliments from the visitors to tell her, or Maurice's comments after a particularly busy week: *I don't know what we'd do without you. I'm not sure how we functioned here before you arrived.*

'The chair of trustees wants us to employ his goddaughter. She's just out of catering college. Fully qualified.'

'Then she could come as my assistant.' Though Jane knew it would be a pain. Jane liked an assistant who did as she was told, who was happy to prepare vegetables and concentrate on the basics. The last thing Jane wanted was an assistant who thought she knew it all. In fact, she preferred to have the kitchen to herself. It had been a great relief when the latest help, a jolly Orcadian called Mandy, had gone off on the *Shepherd* the week before.

'We suggested that,' Angela said smugly. 'But it wouldn't do.'

'Surely that's Maurice's decision. Not the chair of trustees.'

'In theory.' Angela smiled. 'But Christopher has offered to make a substantial donation to the centre. It would allow us to completely update the library and replace the old computer in the office. In those circumstances we can't turn down his offer to find us a cook too.'

Christopher Miles had his own business in the north of England. Jane had met him briefly when the trustees came to the island for their annual meeting. She'd liked his enthusiasm and his lack of pomposity. She thought the offer of employment had come from Angela, a way of cementing the sponsorship deal. Nepotism wasn't his style.

'What does Maurice make of this?'

'As I said before, it isn't really Maurice's decision. We're appointed by the trustees.' She looked at Jane. 'You only have a short-term contract. We're not obliged to have you back each year. You're an educated woman. I'd have thought this sort of work would bore you eventually anyway.'

And Angela turned, her hair swinging, and strode out of the kitchen.

Automatically, Jane continued to arrange slices of quiche on a plate. It was some minutes later that she realized she was crying.

* * *

Usually Jane enjoyed the dances in the lighthouse. The experience reminded her a little of Dee's parties in the old house. It wasn't that Dee's media friends had gone in for fiddle and accordion music and they didn't dance eight-some reels or the Dashing White Sergeant, but Jane had the same sense that she was managing the event. She liked watching people having a good time and knowing that her cooking and her organization had made it happen.

Now she was determined that Angela shouldn't know she was upset. This was a celebration and it wouldn't do to spoil it. Besides, why should she allow an arrogant and manipulative woman any sense of victory? Jane couldn't believe that Maurice would allow Angela to sack her. Jane made his life easy and Maurice was all for an easy life.

She watched Perez lead his fiancée on to the

floor for the first dance, felt a moment of envy for the intimacy, the matching grins when Fran stumbled over a step. *I never had that. Not even with Dee.*

Maurice's teenage daughter Poppy appeared in the break, just as the food was coming out. Throughout her troubles she'd always kept her appetite. She was dressed entirely in black and had intended to shock. The skirt was very short. Jane thought she didn't have the legs to carry off the look and had made herself ridiculous, almost pitiable. She had a couple of young islanders with her — college students who'd got into Fair Isle for their reading week before the weather closed down. Jane thought Poppy had been entertaining them in her room; she'd got to know them on previous trips to the island. It was clear they'd all been drinking, but at the moment they were well behaved. The island kids wouldn't cause a scene in front of their parents and grandparents and at the moment Poppy was taking her lead from them. They joined the queue for food. From behind the counter Jane watched the girl and felt sorry for her.

The music started again and Maurice asked Jane for a dance. For a man who was rather unfit, who took very little exercise, Maurice danced well. He dressed up for these occasions, a parody of himself, in a bow tie and shiny black shoes. Jane had realized during her first season what a part traditional music and dancing played in island life and had determined to master the steps. She'd watched, taken notes and practised in her room. Now she could do them automatically. She no longer had to count the beats in her head.

'Angela says you don't want me back next year,' she said. They were in the middle of a circle of clapping people. They held hands, arms crossed, elbows bent, and began spinning, their bodies leaning out with the speed of the movement. He didn't have time to answer before they separated and skipped out of the circle, but with some satisfaction she saw a flush of anger. A moment later they came together again, linked arms, and promenaded around the room, following all the other couples. Ahead of them Mary and James Perez were light and easy on their feet so you could believe they'd keep going all night.

'Nothing's been decided,' Maurice said. 'She had no right to discuss it with you.'

'I think I have every right to know what's going on.' Jane thought she sounded very reasonable. 'I have my own plans to make.'

'Leave it to me. I'll sort it out.'

The music stopped and the dancers clapped and laughed. Outside, the storm grew even more fierce.

Poppy lost her temper at the end of the evening when many of the guests were leaving; by then Jane had been thinking they'd get through the party without a problem. The tantrum had been brewing for days. Jane thought Poppy was like an enormous two-year-old, chubby, demanding and inarticulate. She wouldn't have been surprised to see the girl lying on the floor kicking and screaming. How could you reach the age of sixteen and have so little self-control?

Angela had been taking her turn working behind the bar — all the field centre staff did a stint on open evenings — and had refused to serve Poppy a drink. Poppy had been clearly drunk, but Jane suspected the decision not to allow her one more can of lager had been a deliberate provocation. Angela disliked the girl and disliked Maurice's attention being distracted by her. The evening was winding up and perhaps Angela was a little bored. She did like a drama.

So suddenly Poppy started shouting abuse. She leaned across the bar and yelled at her stepmother: 'You have no fucking right to tell me what to do.' She took a full glass of beer that had been standing next to her and flung it at Angela. Jane saw with some satisfaction that it went all over the famous hair.

The lingering guests moved quickly into the lobby to collect their coats and change their shoes. They were clearly embarrassed. Jane went with them to say goodbye, to hold the door and warn them to take care on the drive south. Jimmy Perez was the last to go. He seemed intrigued by the scene being played out in the common room and stood watching through the open door. It took Mary to call him away. There was a flurry of thanks. Mary shouted back to her: 'You must come and have dinner with us in Springfield before Jimmy and Fran go home.' Then came the sound of a car engine over the gale, headlights showing it was still pouring with rain.

When all the guests had gone, Jane waited for

a moment. The wind caught the heavy outside door and it began to bang. The storm must have changed direction. Still westerly, which the birdwatchers hated, but with some north in it. She pulled it to again and locked it. The common room was quiet. She supposed Maurice and his strange dysfunctional family had gone through the kitchen to their flat.

She began the task of clearing up. The visitors would still want their breakfast the next day. Usually Maurice would have stayed behind to help her, but she knew he would have other things on his mind. Ben, the assistant warden, seemed to have rushed off too. Jane stacked plates into the dishwasher and cleared the glasses from the common room. The tables could wait for the following day. She felt oddly happy. Angela had miscalculated. It hadn't been clever to wind up Poppy so she made a show in public. Maurice wouldn't like that. Then there came a horrible thought, worm-like, entering her brain and refusing to leave. She couldn't let Maurice and Angela separate. If they were to split up Angela would stay at the North Light. She was the warden, the famous naturalist, the person who pulled in the punters. Anyone could take on Maurice's role. And there would be no place for Jane in Angela's new world.

6

That night Perez slept immediately, untroubled by memories of his first lover or anxieties about his current one. It was as if the first ordeal was over. Fran had survived the party, had even enjoyed it. In the car on their way back to Springfield she'd said what a wonderful evening it had been. 'Thank you so much, Mary, for organizing it.' And Mary, crawling at ten miles an hour as the wind buffeted the car, leaning forward for a better view of the road, had turned briefly to them and beamed.

He woke before it was light. The storm still there in the background, taken for granted now. There was a knock on the door, his father's voice as quiet as he could manage. 'Jimmy, you need to get up.'

He thought there must be some community disaster. He remembered being called from his bed as a young man, when old Annie had fallen ill and they'd needed an ambulance flight in the middle of the night. They'd lit fires along the airstrip to mark the way for the plane to come in, all of the island men working together, the women left behind to mind the bairns.

Fran stirred but she didn't wake. In the kitchen his father was making tea. He was wearing a cardigan over his pyjamas. That seemed odd to Perez. Why wasn't the man dressed? His father was the nearest thing the island had to a leader and he should be out there to supervise if there was a problem. Then he thought maybe his mother was ill and they were waiting for the nurse who was resident on the island. No way would a doctor get in this morning.

'They want you up at the field centre,' James said, breaking into his thoughts. 'You can take the car. I'll not be going far today.'

'What's wrong?' Jimmy drank the tea, helped himself to a couple of home-made ginger biscuits. He was still half asleep. 'Why do they want me?'

'You're the police, aren't you?' James looked up. 'There's been a murder.'

* * *

Perez had to bang on the lighthouse door to be let in, because it was locked. It was still dark and the beam from the tower circled way over his head. The locked door struck him as unusual, but perhaps someone had watched crime dramas on television and realized it was important to keep people away from the scene. Jane came at once to open up. She was fully dressed in jeans and a sweater, though it wasn't yet seven thirty. Inside, all the lights were on. The lighthouse was too far from the other houses to be on mains electricity and he heard the buzz of the generator in the distance. Jane looked very pale but quite composed.

'In here.' She opened a door that led directly from the lobby. 'In the bird room.'

He stood in the doorway and looked inside. It was a small square space with one window facing east. He supposed all the equipment was to do with the business of ornithology. There were plastic tubes covered with small metal rings of different sizes hanging from one of the shelves, pliers, a set of small balance scales, a pile of small cotton bags with drawstring tops. There was the base field centre smell of wood from the floors, but it was overlaid by something faint and organic, which he supposed came from the birds: the oil on their feathers, the muck left in the bags while they were waiting to be ringed.

Under the window there was a wooden desk and a swivel chair. Sitting on the chair was a woman. Angela was slumped across the desk as if she'd fallen asleep in the middle of her work. But in her back was a knife. It had an ivory handle that protruded through the scarlet silk top she'd been wearing the evening before. There wasn't a great deal of blood and no sign of a struggle. The knife had gone in just to the left of the spine and under the shoulder blade. Straight into the heart. Either the killer had known what to do or it had been a lucky strike. Lucky for him at least. Twisted through the black hair, like a garland, was a circle of white feathers. It gave Angela a frivolous air, reminded Perez of one of those flimsy hats that fashionable women wore to Ascot. She certainly hadn't been wearing feathers in her hair when he'd last seen her and he realized now that they'd all fall away if she stood up. The arrangement had been made after her death.

'Who found her?' Perez struggled to make this real. It was too close to home and the image was like the jacket of one of the old-fashioned detective stories his mother had enjoyed. Even the feathers belonged to a different era.

'Ben Catchpole, the assistant warden. It was his turn to do the trap round. He came into collect some bird bags on his way out.'

'Where's Maurice?'

'In the kitchen. I woke him to tell him. Ben's there too.'

Perez looked more closely at the still figure. 'Didn't Maurice realize something was wrong when she didn't come to bed?'

'He's in no state to discuss details.' The words were sharp, a reproof. 'I haven't asked him.'

'Do you always lock the main door of the centre?' Perez spoke as if he were only vaguely interested in the routine of the place, as if it could have no possible significance to the crime.

'No,' Jane said. 'Of course not. But the wind was so strong last night that it kept blowing open. I locked it before I went to bed to stop it banging.'

'Was Angela in the bird room then?'

Jane paused. Perez thought she understood quite clearly the implication of the question and was considering lying. At last she said: 'No, the bird room door was open and I could see inside. It was empty then.'

So this wasn't the work of one of the islanders. Whoever had killed Angela had been in the lighthouse when Jane locked the door.

Perez stood for a moment. Thoughts chased

through his head. First that he needed coffee. He'd not been drunk the night before, but he had a faint headache and his brain was sluggish and disengaged. He'd slept too heavily. Then that this was a complete nightmare. How long would it be before a crime scene investigator could get in to the island? Two days at least, according to the latest forecast by Dave Wheeler, Fair Isle's met officer. Would the body have to stay here until then? He'd need to phone the team in Inverness and get advice. But first coffee and a few words with Maurice. This would probably be very simple. A domestic row. He could understand how that could happen in the fraught and claustrophobic atmosphere that developed during a gale, though it didn't explain the feathers twisted through the long black hair.

'Is it possible to lock the bird room door?'

Jane looked dubious, disappeared and returned a few moments later with a bunch of heavy, old-fashioned keys. 'These have been hanging in the larder since I first came here.'

The third key he tried fitted. He locked the door and followed her through the common room, where the night before they'd all sat drinking and laughing, to the kitchen.

It was, he saw at once, Jane's domain. The men sitting at the table looked up when she came in and seemed comforted by her presence. She fetched ground coffee from the fridge and filled the kettle. Maurice was wearing pyjamas and a dressing gown. He was unshaven, red-eyed.

'I can't believe it,' he said. 'I want to see her

again. There must be a mistake.'

'I'm afraid there's no mistake.' Perez sat beside him. This didn't seem like a man about to confess to murdering his wife. And if it were a family affair, surely the daughter would be a more likely suspect? Maurice half-rose to his feet as if he were about to demand to be taken to Angela, then seemed to find the effort too much for him and sat down heavily again.

Ben Catchpole was skinny, with wild red hair. Perez had met him for the first time at the party the night before. He came from the West Country and had a soft rural accent. Perez tried to replay the conversation of the previous evening in his head. What had they discussed? The decline of seabirds. That had been the subject of Ben's doctorate, though it seemed to Perez that he hardly looked old enough to be an undergraduate, never mind to have gained a PhD. He'd been passionate, had railed against politicians and environmentalists for their cowardice in dealing with the problem. Fran had joined in the conversation and Perez had seen at once that she liked the young man. Later in the evening Perez had overheard Ben telling her he'd been an active member of Greenpeace as a student, remembered a description of a stint at sea monitoring the tuna fishery.

Now, nobody spoke for a moment. Jane poured water into the cafetière. Perez realized his brain was so accustomed to the sound of the wind outside that he no longer noticed it. It was starting to get light.

'The visitors will be down for breakfast in a

while,' Jane said. 'I told them we'd make it later today. Nine o'clock because of the party and the weather. What do you want me to do?'

'Give them breakfast,' Perez said. 'Of course. I'll talk to them then.' He wondered if Fran had woken yet, if she was sitting in Springfield eating the fancy organic muesli his mother had bought in specially. What would she make of his disappearance, the fact that work had followed him home to the Isle? 'But sit down for a moment please. I'd like to speak to you first.'

Jane poured out coffee, set a carton of milk on the table and joined them.

'If anyone knows anything about Angela's death,' Perez said quietly, 'now is the time to tell me.' They stared at him and he thought this might be harder than he'd expected. 'Where's Poppy?'

Now there was some response. Maurice looked towards the windows streaked with salt. 'You can't think she had anything to do with this.'

'There was an argument yesterday evening. It doesn't seem an unreasonable assumption.'

'She's a child,' Maurice said. 'She has issues with anger management. That doesn't make her a killer.' But Perez thought he could hear uncertainty in the voice. Perhaps Maurice had come to the same conclusion as him. What must it be like to believe that your daughter was a murderer?

'Talk me through what happened here after I left.'

'You heard the argument in the common room when Angela refused to give Poppy a drink?'

Perez nodded.

'A couple of our visitors were still up. I asked Ben to look after the bar and I took Poppy into the flat. You know we have our own accommodation at the west end of the centre.'

'Where was Angela?'

'She was already in the flat. She was drying her hair. Poppy had thrown beer over her.' He looked directly at Perez. 'She was drunk. It was childish, pathetic. But not malicious. Not murderous.'

'How was Poppy then?'

Maurice gave a little grin. 'Still angry. Unapologetic. She was here against her will. There'd been problems at school. Nothing serious, but she'd been excluded for a fortnight. Her mother decided a period away would be good for her. I thought she'd enjoy the island. She liked it here when she was younger, but I suppose a thirteen-year-old tomboy has a different outlook on life from a sixteen-year-old young woman.' He paused. 'There's a boyfriend at home. She has the melodramatic notion that we're trying to keep them apart. If anything her anger was directed at me, not Angela.'

'How did Poppy and Angela get on?' Perez finished his coffee and hoped there was more left in the pot.

'Angela didn't have a drop of maternal blood in her body. Poppy was an irritation to her. But she knew the irritation would be temporary.'

Perez was astonished by the honesty of the comments. People usually spoke more kindly of the dead. Especially dead partners. Maurice seemed to register the surprise: 'I'm a historian by training, Jimmy. Telling the truth has become a habit.'

Perez nodded. 'What happened when you got Poppy back to the flat?'

'I laid her on her bed and went to get her a glass of water. When I got back she was dead to the world. I took off her shoes and some of her clothes and covered her with the duvet. She hardly stirred. She was practically unconscious. There's no way she got out of bed and stabbed my wife. Or threaded feathers through her hair. Where would she get those?'

'Why didn't you look for Angela when she didn't come to bed?'

'She said she was going to do some work. She was young, Jimmy. She never seemed to get tired. There was a paper she was preparing and she was close to the deadline. I went to bed and straight to sleep. I didn't even notice she wasn't there.' He looked up with blank eyes. 'I loved her, you know, from the moment I first met her. She was a bright postgraduate student then. I knew it was madness but there was nothing I could do to stop it. My wife and I were happy, settled, and I wrecked all that, in a clear-sighted, self-destructive series of actions that alienated my children and my friends. And I wouldn't have changed it. Even now that she's dead, I wouldn't go back and do anything differently.' He stood up. 'I have to wake Poppy and tell her what's happened. That's all right, Jimmy? You will allow me to do that?'

Perez nodded again and watched him leave the room.

7

Dougie Barr came to Fair Isle for the birds, not the culture. The party on the previous evening had left him cold. He'd had a couple of drinks, then taken himself off to bed. He liked music, couldn't imagine a long drive without it blasting from the CD, but he was into techno, something with a strong beat. He'd never understood the attraction of folk music, of wailing fiddles and howling singers. He needed noise and rhythm to keep him awake on a long twitch and to get the adrenalin pumping before he arrived at the bird. When it came to his list of species seen in Britain, he was up there with the best of them. Respected. Whenever he turned up at a twitch people knew who he was. He couldn't afford to make a mistake.

He'd been coming to Fair Isle since he was a boy, staying in the old place down at the North Haven. He'd found the UK's first brown flycatcher here in 1992 when he was fifteen and had sneaked away early from school at the end of the summer term with a group of like-minded older friends, leaving his mother bewildered by his behaviour. On the estate where they lived kids got into drugs and car theft, not natural history. The memory of that glorious day in July, the sudden realization that he was looking at something truly mega, still lit up the gloomy hours in the call centre where he worked. Since then he'd had a kind of superstition about the place and had come back nearly every year. Waiting for another rarity to match the first. For him, the real thrill came in finding his own tick. There wasn't the same excitement chasing after other people's birds.

His mates mocked him. Why spend all that money? If you had to go birdwatching in Shetland it made much more sense to stay on the mainland and just get a plane into Fair Isle if you needed to, if the big one turned up. That way you kept your options open. But each season Dougie went back to the field centre, convinced that eventually his loyalty would be rewarded. He kept a blog and dreamed of the photos he'd post there, the description, very factual and precise, of the rarity he'd found on the Isle. It would be a first for Britain, maybe even a first for the Western Palearctic. Then his friends would read his blog and weep.

Dougie had never married. Some of his mates had gone to Thailand to find a bride, and at one time Dougie had been tempted to go down that route. He imagined a small pretty woman, mild-mannered and grateful to be in the UK. He would be her hero: after all, he would have rescued her from poverty, perhaps from a life on the streets. She would provide companionship, laugh at his jokes, come birding with him. There would be sex. Regular sex. But his acquaintances' Thai brides turned out to be strong and forceful women. They laughed at their men and made their lives a misery. Dougie had decided it would be better to continue alone. At least he had nobody else to consider when the pager beeped and there was a rare bird, a tick at the other end of the country. He could just put his binoculars round his neck, load the telescope into the car, and go.

Occasionally he had fantasies about a woman in the call centre where he worked. He was a supervisor now and most of the team he managed were women. He listened in to their calls, heard the soft persuasive voices talking to the anonymous customers on the end of the phone and imagined that they were trying to please *him*.

Once or twice he'd plucked up courage to ask one out, but that always seemed to end in disaster. Even if she agreed to go with him to dinner or a film, the fumbling advances at the close of the evening ended in humiliation. Then he would imagine her talking to the other women he supervised. During training sessions he sensed they were all secretly laughing at him. He'd decided it wasn't worth putting himself through that cycle again: the anxiety leading up to the invitation, the rejection, the resulting paranoia. Better stick to the soft-porn DVDs he brought back from trips to the continent. And birding. In that world at least he had achieved.

The wind had been westerly since he'd first landed on the island. Most rarities came in to Fair Isle on easterly winds, swept away from their usual migration routes through Scandinavia, Russia or Siberia. For the first few days he'd remained optimistic. Some of Fair Isle's rarities had arrived in westerlies after all. He'd got up at first light, walked miles, taken out a packed lunch so he could spend the whole day in the south of the island where most of the migrants appeared. He'd accompanied Angela and Ben on the trap rounds in case a rarity appeared out of nowhere in the catching box. Sometimes miracles like that happened. But now the westerly gales had taken their toll on his mood. He heard the shipping forecast each evening with increasing depression. He would return to work at the end of the fortnight with nothing to show for his dedication. If he could get off the island at all. This late in the season most of his friends were on the Isles of Scilly. There'd already been a smattering of rare birds from the States and they were sending him jubilant texts.

Dougie found it easier to think about birds than the other parts of his life. He hadn't slept well. These days, he didn't sleep much. Turning on his side he heard Hugh's breathing. Since the departure of the plane two days before, Hugh Shaw was the only other unmarried visiting birdwatcher left on the island and they shared the dormitory. Dougie lay awake, listening to the young man's breathing, and his thoughts wandered again.

Hugh was ambitious, sharp, a brilliant birder for someone so young. Ornithology was all they had in common. Dougie had done the local comprehensive and worked in a factory before he got into sales. Hugh had been expelled from some smart boarding school, then gone travelling. Despite the disgrace of the expulsion, his parents had funded the worldwide trip. Talking about it, Hugh had given a wide, slow grin. 'They hoped it would make me grow up. It just gave me a gigantic bird list.' On the long dark evenings while they waited for the wind to change, Hugh had told stories of his journey: being mugged in Vientiane, being chased by an elephant in India. He spoke with a laconic, old-fashioned, public-school accent that made the tales seem unreal. His hair was long and floppy and he had a self-deprecating smile, so it was impossible to tell how much was true.

'What will you do now?' Dougie had been fascinated by the young man's lifestyle. Dougie had always had to earn a living. He might throw the occasional sickie when a rare bird turned up, but he couldn't afford to lose his job.

'I was thinking I might get a job leading birding tours. How difficult can that be?'

There'd been the same grin. Dougie had thought of the responsibility of that work, the demanding customers in alien places, and had decided he was better off in the call centre. It would be weird to mix work and his passion for birds. Besides, he'd always been good at selling. He knew the gentle approach usually worked best, but he had a sense about when it was time to move in for the kill.

In the dormitory Dougie turned on to his back. Somewhere in the lighthouse below a door shut and there were muttered voices. Usually in these sleepless hours before dawn, he passed the time with sexy daydreams about Angela. She'd always terrified and fascinated him at the same time, with her brown legs, her full breasts and the long black hair that made him think of a witch or a vampire. Perhaps she was one of the reasons he'd kept returning to Fair Isle. She'd said once he was the best field observer she knew and he still remembered the remark, treasured it.

Today he found no comfort in thoughts of Angela and he was glad when his alarm clock went off. Although it rattled and jumped on the bedside cupboard, Hugh slept through the noise and stayed asleep even when Dougie switched on the light. Dougie thought the man looked younger lying asleep in the bunk. He had long, dark eyelashes. Dougie watched him surreptitiously for a moment, as if he were doing something shameful, and then he got up.

The dining room was empty though the table had been laid and through the serving hatch he could see Jane in the kitchen. There was the smell of bacon. The islander whose engagement they'd been marking the night before was sitting at the kitchen table drinking a big mug of coffee. It crossed Dougie's mind that he could have been in the centre all night. Now the lighthouse was almost empty there'd be plenty of room if some of the partygoers had overdone the celebrations and decided to stay over. The man looked at Dougie, stared at him, then gave a small nod. No smile. Dougie thought the islanders were all strange bastards. He helped himself to a bowl of cereal. Jane walked through to the dining room and rang the bell to let people know the meal was ready.

John and Sarah Fowler came in almost immediately. Dougie didn't really understand what they were doing in the centre. Everyone had heard of John Fowler: he'd been a big twitcher in his day. He wasn't much older than Dougie, but Dougie thought of him as part of an earlier generation, the gang that had hung around the north Norfolk coast in the early seventies. Now Fowler was more famous as a bookshop owner and collector of natural history books. You never saw him in the field much these days and if you did people just took the piss. Over the years he'd made a couple of really bad identification mistakes; on one occasion he had all the Shetland birders turning out to Virkie just for a dark meadow pipit! Of course everyone made mistakes but Fowler had gained the reputation as a stringer, as someone who regularly claimed to see impossibly rare birds. Dougie thought if people talked about him the way they spoke of Fowler he'd never go birdwatching again. He'd probably kill himself. In the field centre Dougie found it awkward to talk to Fowler — it wouldn't do *his* reputation any good to be too friendly. He was polite enough, passing the marmalade and the butter when required, but he showed no interest in the couple's lives away from the island.

Now, as the Fowlers took their places at the table, Dougie thought how similar they looked, more like brother and sister than husband and wife. They had the same faded brown hair, wispy and rather untidy, the same thin lips. And it seemed to him now that they didn't behave like any of the married couples he knew. They were too careful with each other, too polite. There was none of the banter and bickering he saw in his married friends. No laughter. Had they always been that way or had something happened to make them so tense? Sarah seemed to depend on her husband, without enjoying his company. With an unusual insight, Dougie thought perhaps they'd come to Fair Isle to mend their marriage.

Jane stuck her head round the door into the dining room and broke into his thoughts. 'Would you mind giving Hugh a shout, Dougie? Jimmy wants to talk to everyone.'

Dougie hesitated. He didn't think Hugh would be pleased to be dragged downstairs to hear what an islander might want to say. He was usually polite enough, but he did just what he wanted.

'Please, Dougie.' Jane had a way of speaking that made you respond immediately.

* * *

Jimmy Perez sat with them, but he didn't start talking until they'd finished eating. He didn't do anything. He just sat, watching and listening. Although Dougie had seen him the evening before at the party, he only recognized him now. He remembered meeting Perez when the man had worked occasionally on the boat. He'd always been quiet, dark-haired and dark-skinned like the skipper. Dougie usually came into the island on the mail boat. He didn't like small planes and anyway the *Shepherd* trip from Grutness was part of the ritual. It was how he'd come into the island that first time, the summer he'd found the flycatcher.

Just one table had been laid up so they all sat together. Jane was the only member of field centre staff present and Dougie thought that was odd. Where were Maurice and Ben? Perhaps because Perez was there, a silent observer, the conversation was stilted. Nobody asked why the man was with them or what he wanted. Even Hugh, who usually managed to keep the conversation going, didn't have much to say. It was a relief to them all when Perez stood up to speak.

He was strangely formal. 'I'm here in my capacity as Inspector with Highland and Islands Police.' He spoke slowly as if he was worried they might not understand his accent. Dougie remembered then that the man had gone south to become a cop. He'd heard old man Perez talking about it once in the *Shepherd*, grumbling because his son wasn't there to help on the croft or the boat. That was the day they'd seen the killer whales, just as they left Shetland mainland.

'Angela Moore is dead.'

The words cut into Dougie's memory of the huge mammals swimming beside the vessel. He looked at Hugh, who only blinked once. Then there was absolute silence in the room.

'I'm sure you'll cooperate with our efforts to find out what happened to her.' Perez leaned back against a table and seemed to be waiting for them to respond.

'How did she die?' Dougie was surprised that it was John Fowler who asked the question.

Usually he contributed little to the general conversation.

'She was murdered. I'm sure you'll appreciate why I can't give any details at this point.'

'Who killed her?' Fowler again.

'That's what I need to establish.'

'It's obvious, surely.' Hugh looked around the room and they all waited for him to speak. He had that way of getting people to listen to him. A storyteller, Angela had called him. Or 'my storyteller' when she wanted him to entertain her, to sit beside her in the common room and relive one of his adventures. Though Dougie had never been quite sure what Angela had made of Hugh. It was as if the pair of them had been playing a dangerous game. They were both chancers, adventurers. Now the young man's voice was relaxed and easy, as if he was about to start one of his traveller's tales. He was wearing denims and a grey rugby shirt. It was odd how the details of his fellow guests were fixed suddenly in Dougie's head. It was as if he was in the field looking at a new bird, branding the way it looked in his memory. Hugh continued: 'Poppy and Angela were arguing last night. We all saw that. Poppy lost her temper once and must have done it again.' He paused, repeated again, almost apologetically: 'Obvious.'

Perez hesitated and chose his words carefully. 'Oh, no,' he said. 'I don't think that's true at all. Not obvious. In a murder investigation, nothing's ever quite that simple.'

8

Perez stopped outside Maurice and Angela's flat and listened. Nothing. He tapped on the door and went inside, walking straight into a large room, with an original fireplace facing the door and windows on two sides. One looked south, through the gap in the surrounding wall, towards the pool the islanders called Golden Water, the other out to sea. For a moment he was aware of the outside reality of sky, wind and water. Talking to the visitors in the dining room, he'd been so focused on the people that he could have been in any of the bare rooms he'd used to interview witnesses during his career. There could have been city roads outside. He thought again that this case was too close to home. In normal circumstances he would have stepped away, handed the investigation to a colleague who was less involved. This was all wrong; it felt twisted and unnatural.

Maurice Parry and his daughter sat on a low sofa, which was covered by a woven throw. They were lit by a small lamp on the table beside them. It was barely light outside. There was a plain brown carpet, with a scattering of sheepskin rugs on the floor. The curtains were the same as in the public rooms in the field centre. Even though this was Angela and Maurice's personal space they'd done little to make it their own. Poppy was wearing a dressing gown, pink, too small for her. Perhaps it had been left here when she was a child. Last night's make-up was streaked on her face. Her hair was still stiff with gel. She was crying and Maurice held her in his arms. He frowned when he saw Perez looking at them.

'Couldn't you give us a little more time?'

Perez shook his head. 'Sorry.' If Poppy was going to confess to killing her stepmother, best that it happen quickly. He could be on the phone to the Fiscal and explain that there was no mystery here, no need for drama. A disturbed adolescent with a knife. In big cities almost a commonplace. They could make arrangements for Poppy's care on the island and decide what would happen to her once they were able to get her off. Then he could start worrying about what he should do with Angela's body.

'I'm so sorry.' The girl looked up at him with smudged panda eyes. He said nothing. Let her tell it in her own words and her own time. He supposed he should caution her, but this was hardly a formal interview and her father was with her to protect her interests.

'I spoiled your engagement party,' she said. 'I didn't mean to. It was stupid. Childish.'

'Angela's dead,' he said. 'More important than a party.'

'I'm sorry about that too.' She looked up at her father. 'I didn't like her much but she didn't deserve to be killed. I can't apologize for that, though. I didn't do it. I wasn't responsible.' Her voice was very quiet but it was reasonable. It was hard to believe that this was the overwrought young woman who'd caused such a scene the night before.

'I know, sweetheart.' Maurice stroked the hair away from his daughter's face. 'I know you couldn't do anything like that.'

Perez watched. He imagined how tense and claustrophobic it must have been in this apartment in the days leading up to Angela's murder. An enclosed space inside the enclosed space of the lighthouse. Sealed off from the rest of the island by two lots of walls. And inside, three people tied by family, but pulled apart by opposing desires and needs. The stress, he thought, must have been unbearable. There would have been little reason in the conversation then. His mind flicked again to the child who would soon be his stepchild. Fran's daughter Cassie was six and having a holiday with her father now. Would Perez still be able to love her if she was a large, awkward teenager?

'Did Angela want children?' The question was directed at Maurice, over Poppy's head, and was out before he'd had time to consider the tactlessness of asking it in the girl's presence.

'No. I explained earlier, she wasn't the maternal type. Far too selfish.' Maurice looked up at Perez and gave a little smile. 'I still thought of her as a child herself. A brilliant, adorable, precocious child.'

'I need to talk about Angela. About why someone might have wanted her dead.'

'Of course you do, Jimmy.' There was something patronizing in the tone. *Of course. Play your little games if it makes you happy.*

'It must be important to you too.'

'To find out who killed her? No, not right now. I'm trying to work out how I can survive without her. Revenge might come later.'

I'm not talking about revenge, Perez thought. *I'm talking about justice*. But he couldn't say that. It would sound impossibly pompous. He wanted to talk to Maurice and Poppy separately, but he could tell that individual interviews would have to wait. They were clinging to each other and he realized it would be impossible to prise them apart. It seemed to Perez that it wasn't grief that had brought father and daughter together now; the sudden absence of Angela in their lives had made the closeness possible, had somehow made them come to their senses. It was as if a spell had been broken. When he left the room, he thought they'd hardly noticed he was gone.

* * *

The centre's common room was furnished much as the living room in Maurice and Angela's flat, but there was a library in the corner: floor-to-ceiling shelves containing natural history books, with a pile of paper-back novels relegated to a low table. Perez checked that no one was sitting in the high-backed chairs, then he called a coastguard officer friend using his mobile phone. The reception was poor, but the field centre landline had a number of extensions and he didn't want to risk being overheard. He stood by the window and looked out at the sea.

'I know there's no possibility of a plane or a boat today, but I wondered about the coastguard helicopter.'

'No chance. I mean, it's hardly a matter of life or death, is it? I'm not prepared to risk my crew for a body.'

The next call was to Inverness.

'I've got a problem.' He'd asked to be put through to his line manager, a cheerful Englishman, who'd moved to the Highlands for the fishing and was even more cheerful now that retirement was approaching. Perez explained the position. 'I feel that I'm too close to the case, but none of my family members is involved and there's no chance of anyone else getting in to take it over at least for the next twenty-four hours.'

'It's yours then, laddie.' Frank had taken to using strange words that he thought sounded Scottish. 'And I'm assuming you'll have it all wrapped up by the time the weather improves. How many suspects can there be? You'd better let the Iron Maiden know.'

The Iron Maiden. Rhona Laing the Fiscal, based in Lerwick on Shetland mainland. A woman with political ambitions and the knack of covering her back in every situation.

'Put me through to Vicki Hewitt first.' Perez wasn't sure he could face Rhona Laing just yet. He needed to know exactly what he was doing before then. And that meant sorting out how he should manage the crime scene. Vicki was the Highland and Islands scene co-ordinator. She was a no-nonsense Yorkshirewoman with a sense of humour and experience of working with a big English force before taking up her present role. He thought she'd enjoy his dilemma: it would amuse her to think of him working without back-up.

'What have you got for me this time, Jimmy? Should I be packing my bags and taking my seasick pills?'

'Not yet. This one I have to deal with on my own. I have a dead woman with a knife in her back and no way of getting any forensic support.' He talked Vicki through the situation, imagined her sitting with her elbows on the desk taking notes, grinning at his dilemma, the inevitable can of Diet Coke beside her. 'So what should I do? I can't leave her there indefinitely. The chopper should get in tomorrow but there's no guarantee.'

'Remember your latest crime scene management training, Jimmy.' She'd led the refresher course, one of the few he'd felt it worth travelling south for. 'What do *you* think you should do first?'

'Take photographs,' he said. 'Lots of photographs.'

'Even more important if we can't get the experts in straight away.' He knew she was teasing but didn't care.

'What about the body?'

'Bag it up carefully and put it somewhere cold. Has anyone on the island got a walk-in chiller or a big fridge?'

'There'll be folk with freezers.'

'No,' she said. 'A freezer won't do. We don't

want ice crystals in the body. If you don't have a full-size fridge, put her in an outhouse. Somewhere watertight, where you can keep her cool.'

As he pressed the button on his mobile at the end of the conversation, he wondered where he'd find a bag big enough to take the body of a fit young woman.

Rhona Laing's secretary put him through to her immediately. Rhona demanded efficiency and usually got it.

'Yes?' The Fiscal was in her fifties, immaculate, dressed like the Edinburgh lawyer she had once been. He could picture her sitting at her desk. 'I thought you were on leave, Inspector. Visiting your parents.' That was the other thing about Rhona. She seemed to have spies everywhere.

'There's been a murder.'

'Where?' Her voice was measured. He'd never heard her express shock.

'Here on the Isle.'

'You're like the Angel of Death, Inspector. Violence seems to follow you around. First Whalsay, now Fair Isle.'

Perez thought that was unfair. His colleague Sandy Wilson had found the body in Whalsay.

'The victim's a young woman,' he said. 'The warden of the Fair Isle field centre. I'd met her but I didn't know her well. As I'm here and there's no chance of the Inverness team getting in, I think I can run the investigation without a conflict of interest.'

'Your victim is Angela Moore?' Her voice was sharp. 'She's a television celebrity. They seem to wheel her out to talk about everything from Shetland wind farms to the decline of the tiger. There'll be press interest.'

'If they get to hear about it — '

'Don't be naive, Inspector! Someone will already have tried to sell the story to the national press. One of the islanders or one of the guests. This has to be sorted out quickly. By the time the weather clears and the reporters can fly in, we need to have made an arrest.'

* * *

His last call was to Fran. In Springfield, Radio 4 was playing in the background. He recognized Kate Adie and *From Our Own Correspondent*. That would be something else she and Mary would have in common. Both women had it on all day, a background to their work.

'I'm so sorry.' He realized he'd repeated almost exactly the words and the inflexion of Poppy's words to him. 'I didn't bring you all the way to Fair Isle just to abandon you.'

'It's work. Nothing you could do.'

'What have you been up to?' At home she could occupy herself for hours on her own with her drawing and her painting. She had a concentration that he found enviable. He was too easily distracted. But he didn't think she'd be able to work with his parents around; Mary would want to chat and be full of questions. Perhaps that's where my curiosity comes from, he thought. I'm nosy, just like my mother.

'I asked Mary to teach me to use the knitting

machine. I've always wanted to learn. It's not nearly as easy as it looks.' She laughed.

Suddenly he felt as if he was as far away from her as when she was visiting her parents in London and he was left behind in Lerwick. It was hard to believe they were only separated by a couple of miles.

'I'll make sure I'm home for supper,' he said.

'Will it all be over by then?'

'I don't know. It seemed very simple. Now I'm not sure.'

9

Jane heard Perez talking in the common room while she was laying the tables for lunch. Despite herself she tried to hear what he was saying, but she couldn't make out the words. She couldn't even tell to whom he was talking. She thought she would have to tell him about that last conversation with Angela. In a place like this, there were no secrets. Someone would inform Perez that Angela had threatened not to renew her contract: Maurice, for example, would say anything to protect his daughter. It was best coming from Jane herself.

The smell of baking bread seeped out of the kitchen, reassuringly normal. Lunch would be soup and rolls, oatcakes and cheese, scones and cakes. Today they needed comfort food. It was eleven thirty. There was time to talk to Perez before she had to serve it. She tapped on the common-room door and looked inside. Perez was on his own, his mobile in his hand. He'd finished the conversation and seemed preoccupied. She followed his gaze out of the window. It was more exposed here, north facing, and the sound of the storm was louder.

'I wondered if I could talk to you. It's about Angela.'

'Of course.' It seemed something of an effort for him to drag his thoughts back to the present. 'Could we sit somewhere with a bit of privacy?'

She hesitated. 'We could use my room, I suppose. It's a bit cramped but nobody will disturb us.' She never invited anyone into her room, was shocked that she'd been the one to suggest it.

They passed the door of the bird room on the way to the stairs.

'Is Angela still in there?' Where had such a ghoulish question come from? Jane thought it was as if someone else had stepped inside her skin and was talking through her mouth.

He looked at her as if he was considering how much he should tell her. He must have reached the same conclusion as she had earlier: there could be no secrets in this place. 'I thought I'd go in when the rest of you are having lunch. I'll move Angela's body this afternoon. I'll take it to Springfield. There's a shed we can padlock. She'll be cool there. Then hope the wind drops tomorrow, at least enough to get a helicopter in.' He stopped for a moment. 'I don't suppose you have a digital camera I could borrow? It would save me going home.'

'Sorry.' Jane was going to ask why he might need a camera, but then she remembered an American TV programme beloved by her sister. Beautiful young men and women in designer clothes investigated brutal murders by swimming pools or in grand houses. They always took photographs of the crime scene. How excited her sister would be to know that Jane had been caught up in a real investigation.

There was only one chair in her room. She nodded for him to take it and sat on the bed. She saw him taking in his surroundings, the books and the newspaper clippings.

'Do you enjoy crosswords, Inspector?'

He smiled. 'I don't think my mind works that way.'

'I suppose I have a motive for killing Angela.' After all, she hadn't brought him here to make small talk. 'I thought you should know.'

He said nothing and waited for her to continue. *He sits so still*, she thought. *It's impossible to tell what's going on in his head*.

'We had a conversation in the kitchen yesterday afternoon, while I was getting food ready for your party. She said she wouldn't want me back at the North Light next year.'

'And that's a motive for murder?' He wasn't mocking her, but seemed genuinely puzzled. She wondered that he couldn't be as passionate about the place as she was.

'I would have killed her then if I'd thought I could get away with it.' Jane looked up, gave a little smile to show she was joking. 'I didn't. I'm not sufficiently brave.' She saw more explanation was needed. 'I love it here at the lighthouse. I suppose it's a sort of escape. There were things in my personal life . . . It was a mess . . . And Fair Isle captivated me from the moment I arrived.'

'Did she give you a reason for not wanting you back? Your reputation on the island is high. The best cook they've ever had, my mother says. I'd have thought she'd be bribing you to stay.'

'According to Angela, someone else was bribing her to get rid of me.' Jane explained about the chair of trustees, the massive donation to develop the library and replace the computers, the goddaughter straight out of catering college. 'But I'm not sure it happened like that. Angela might have been glad of an excuse to be shot of me and made the offer herself.'

'Why would she want shot of you?'

Jane hesitated a moment. She found it hard to be bitchy about a woman who'd recently been murdered. It was a matter of manners, etiquette. It seemed rather common to be unpleasant in these circumstances.

'Angela liked to be in charge, the centre of attention. She was accustomed to admiration.'

'And you didn't admire her?'

'I'm sure she was a very good scientist.'

'But?'

'I didn't like her as a person. She was capricious, wilful, determined to get her own way. I probably gave her less deference than she was used to. I'm sure that irritated her. After all, I'm only the domestic help. When the chair of trustees mentioned the possibility of finding a job here for his goddaughter, she'd have seen it as a good way of finding someone more biddable to take my place. Someone who owed her a favour.'

'I didn't really know her,' Perez said, 'though I've seen her on television, of course.'

'How did you think she came across?' Jane realized she was very interested in the inspector's opinion. He was a man whose judgement she'd trust.

He thought for a moment and it seemed as if

he would refuse to commit himself. 'As very charming,' he said at last. 'But only while the camera was running. I was never really convinced by it. She always seemed rather miserable to me.'

It was the last thing she would have expected.

* * *

During lunch she was aware of his absence, imagined him in the bird room. How would Angela look now? Just the same as when Ben Catchpole had found her? How soon did a corpse begin to decay, to look not entirely human? Jane had seen the body when Ben had called out to her, and the feathers woven into the hair had seemed to her grotesque, a bizarre show.

Before she began to serve the meal Fran Hunter arrived, blown in it seemed from another world, a reminder that life was continuing outside the solid field centre walls. She had a camera round her neck and a small rucksack on her back. She had arrived in Leogh Willy's truck and immediately joined Perez. Jane supposed that he'd summoned her to bring what he needed to record the crime scene and take Angela's body away.

In the dining room conversation was desultory. Again Maurice and Poppy stayed away, though Ben ate with them. Jane thought that all the people there wanted to talk about the murder, to enjoy the drama, share scraps of gossip about the dead woman, but no one could bring himself to start the discussion for fear of appearing callous. Jane wanted to give them permission to do it: *Come on. We all knew she was no saint*. But she was as frightened as the others of seeming unfeeling.

Later she knocked at the door of Maurice's flat. He came to open it. He was dressed now, but he still hadn't shaved and looked as he had when he'd had a bad bout of flu earlier in the year. Jane had looked after him then too. Angela had been far too busy with the seabird ringing. She'd never even had a cold in all the time Jane had known her and had no sympathy for people who were ill.

'I've brought a pan of soup,' Jane said. 'It'll just need heating up.'

He took the saucepan from her and stood in the doorway.

'How's Poppy?' Jane really wanted to ask what he would do now. She presumed that he would want to leave the island as soon as the weather improved. Then she would have the place to herself. To tidy and scrub and order. The new warden would be glad of a cook who knew the ropes.

'I've sent her back to bed,' Maurice said. 'She's exhausted. The shock, I suppose.' He looked up at Jane. 'I don't know what I'll do without Angela. I can't imagine life without her.'

It wasn't the sort of practical answer Jane was looking for, though she would have been happy to talk to Maurice, even about Angela, if that would have helped. But he shut the door without asking her into the flat, more distressed now, it seemed, than when he'd first learned his wife was dead.

Jane couldn't bear the idea of spending another minute in the field centre. It wasn't just the image she created in her head of Perez in the bird room, taking his photographs, collecting his samples, moving in his quiet, precise way around the dead woman. She needed to get away from the place for a while. She felt as if she'd been indoors for weeks. The truck was parked just outside the back door so she assumed that Fran was still in the bird room with him. Jane thought she'd walk down the island, talk to Joanne in the shop, and perhaps call in on Mary at Springfield as long as Perez and Fran hadn't returned. The wind would be behind her and she thought someone would give her a lift back. Jane wouldn't want to be thought curious or ghoulish, but Mary was the closest thing to a friend that she had in Fair Isle.

Outside, the wind took her breath away, but the rain had stopped and there were flashes of sunshine, sudden spotlights on the green sea and the sodden grass. For the first time she began to wonder who could have killed Angela, to work out how it might have happened. Like everyone else she'd assumed at first that Poppy had been responsible, but perhaps it wasn't that simple. Away from the tension and the raw emotion inside the building it was possible to regard the murder as an intellectual puzzle. Surely her intellect was as strong as the inspector's and she knew the people there better than he did. Angela had been right about one thing: Jane was ready for a new challenge. She imagined going to Perez and offering him the solution. She would enjoy his approval.

There were a couple of people in the shop, there not to buy, Jane thought, but to talk. They were delighted to see her, of course, and much less restrained about gossiping than the residents of the North Light.

'They say there were gallons of blood.' 'Has Jimmy arrested the child yet?' 'What a terrible thing to happen on the Isle.'

Jane said very little. She understood their voraciousness and their desire for information. They were outsiders looking in at the drama. No one was suggesting, for example, that they might be murderers. But still she was restrained. She told them there had been no arrest as far as she knew. And of course, she said, everyone at the North Light was very shocked and upset.

She wrapped her coat around her and went out again. The turbine blades of the windmill on the mound by the shop were spinning furiously and the machine gave off that low humming sound that meant the generator was storing power. The children must just have come out of school because they were making their way down the road, laughing and chasing, bent against the wind. There was no truck outside Springfield, no sign of Big James's car, so she opened the door and went in. Mary was standing at the kitchen table whisking egg whites.

'I hope you don't mind my turning up out of the blue,' Jane said. 'I just had to get away from the lighthouse.'

'Of course. Come in.' Mary shook the egg from the whisk. 'Just wait till I get this in the oven and I'll make us some tea.' She tipped caster sugar into the mixture and spooned it onto a tray. 'How's Jimmy doing?'

'I don't know,' Jane said. 'He's just getting on with it.' She paused. 'I suppose we're all suspects.'

'I worry about him,' Mary said. 'What must it do to a man to be mixing all the time with crime and violence? I thought he'd come back home and settle here on a croft. He always said it was what he wanted. But when Skerry was vacant and he had the chance he threw it away.'

'He seems very good at what he does.'

'He'll have a wife soon. She'll not want him away all hours, never knowing when he's getting home. I thought this week on the island would let her see what the place has to offer. Then this has to happen.'

'If she wants him to be happy surely she'll let him work . . . ' *But what do I know?* Jane thought. *I'm a lonely middle-aged woman and my idea of happiness is a couple of weeks' spring-cleaning in an empty field centre*.

'Ah.' Mary's voice was impatient. 'We all start off thinking we can change our men. It never happens that way.'

Suddenly there was a thunderous knocking on the door. Mary stood white and shocked, her hand resting on the kettle. She looked at Jane. The banging continued. 'Come in,' Mary shouted. 'Whoever you are, stop that noise and come in.'

The door was flung open.

'My God, man, whatever is the matter?'

It was Dougie Barr, flushed from running. His coat was flapping open and his telescope was still on its tripod, hanging from a strap on his shoulder. His binoculars hung round his neck.

'I need to use your phone.' The words came out in a pant. 'My mobile's not working. No reception.'

'What's happened?' Jane imagined another body. Her mind was racing.

'I have to call the lighthouse.' He saw they were staring at him. 'There's a bird in the South Harbour. Trumpeter swan. A first for Britain.' When they didn't answer he repeated, yelling at the top of his voice: 'A first for Britain.'

10

All morning Dougie Barr hadn't been able to stop thinking about Angela. Images of her swam in and out of his head. Of course he'd seen her on the television before he'd met her. She'd been famous before she married Maurice and was appointed as warden of the field centre, one of the new wave of young people brought in to present wildlife programmes, employed to make natural history more sexy and pull in a fresh audience. Dougie understood what they were doing. He knew about selling. Since then Angela had become a part of his life. A secret obsession.

Everyone remembered Angela because of her hair. Right down her back, sleek and beautiful even when she'd been camping out in the wastes of Alaska for a fortnight, or trekking across a desert. But it had been the hands, long and brown, that had stuck in his mind when he'd first seen them on screen. He'd noticed them at once, holding binoculars to her eyes, and later picking up a young razorbill as she prepared to ring it. When she first greeted him in the field centre he'd stretched out an arm to shake hands and looking down at the grip he'd been thrilled: the long strong fingers were just as he'd imagined. He'd thought that hand shake had been one of the most intimate experiences of his life. He was finally touching the woman he admired more than any other.

One evening, plucking up courage after a couple of beers, he'd asked her why she'd applied for the field centre job. She'd been sitting in the common room preparing to call the log of the species seen that day, squatting on a chair, her knees under her chin, drinking lager from a can.

'You're famous,' he'd said. 'You could travel all over the world for the telly. You could make a fortune. Why come to Fair Isle?'

She'd smiled. 'It's an addiction. I love it. Just like you do. I came to Shetland when I was still a student and was seabird assistant here for a season after I got my degree. I swore I'd be warden one day. The first female to run the place.' She'd set down the can. 'Television is just other people telling you what to do. I'm in control here. That's important to me.'

Dougie pictured her dead in the bird room and thought she wasn't much in control now. There were people who said she'd only married Maurice because she needed a partner to be administrator; it was the only way the trustees would appoint her. Dougie didn't know anything about that — he'd never had the nerve to ask her. They'd always seemed a strange kind of couple. Now, he thought her ambition to run Fair Isle Field Centre had killed her.

It was unusual for him to stay inside when it was light, even in weather like this. His office in the call centre was small and cramped and had no natural light. He joked with his colleagues that it was like being banged up in prison. On holiday he needed to be in the open air. Otherwise he felt he might just as well be working.

He found Hugh reading a trip report in the common room. The younger man held out the brochure. There were glossy photos of jungles and mountains, improbably coloured birds. 'I'm checking out the possibilities for work,' he said. 'I might apply to run this one. I quite fancy getting paid to spend three weeks in Argentina. I still need a few endemics there.'

Dougie wished he had the younger man's confidence. Hugh assumed the job would be his if he wanted it and that he'd do well at it. Perhaps that was what going to a smart school did for you.

'I'm going to the south end. Do you want to come?' Dougie liked company when he was birdwatching. It was part of the pleasure, the gossip as you walked down the island. He'd never been in a gang at school; his birdwatching friends had come from the more affluent parts of his town. Besides, he thought, conversation might distract him from thoughts of Angela.

Hugh tore his attention from the pictures. 'Nah, it's been westerly for weeks. It's a waste of time. I should have gone out on the plane when I had the chance.' He flashed the old smile that for a moment made Dougie want to lash out. Hugh of all people should show more respect. For this island and the craft of birding. 'Anyway, I don't want to miss the excitement. You don't get involved in a murder every day.'

Dougie supposed he meant the policeman

poking around in the bird room — although the door was shut Dougie had heard movement inside and soft voices when he went to put on his boots — and Angela's body being carried away. That was excitement he could do without. Hugh's attitude was ghoulish, weird.

Walking down the road towards the crofts Dougie saw nothing but a couple of meadow pipits being blown over the double dyke trap and a hooded crow close to the cliff, but he felt his mood lighten. He caught a glimpse of a figure on the hill and for a second assumed it was Angela, not imagining a ghost, but having forgotten she was dead. That was how she'd moved, purposeful as if she could carry on at the same pace all day. Immediately he knew his mind was playing tricks on him. This must be Ben Catchpole, doing the hill survey because Angela wasn't there. In waterproofs most of the birders looked the same. He raised his binoculars to check, but the figure had disappeared over the horizon.

Dougie knew he was unfit. He lived on takeaway food and drank too much beer. In his local pub on quiz nights he could believe he had friends who weren't birders. Weekends were spent twitching: long trips in the car with his birding mates, a brief burst of activity to see the rarity, then nights on the sofa, sharing more beer, more stories of great twitches in the past. Though often these days he spent the evenings alone with his laptop on his knee catching up on *Surfbirds* or writing his blog. There weren't so many single men birding now and the married ones sloped back to their wives and their kiddies as soon as the twitch was over, with excuses for being late and promises to be more considerate in the future. Times like that Dougie was pleased he still lived alone.

Now, with the wind behind him, he enjoyed feeling the stiffness ease out of his joints as he walked. He should join a gym, play sport. Lose some of the weight round his belly and the girls at work might take him more seriously. He always felt better when he came into Fair Isle, took a bit of exercise, ate healthy food.

Where the road split south near the school he chose the lower westerly path with Malcolm's Head to his right. It seemed a little more sheltered there or maybe the wind was dropping slightly. In the field below Midway, there was a flock of redwings, new in. As he passed they rose into the air, calling. The sight of the birds lifted his spirits again. They'd reached the island within the last twenty-four hours; no reason why something rarer shouldn't be with them. He started to run through the possibilities in his mind. More daydreams.

The sea out from the south harbour was still dramatic, huge rolling waves and white breakers against the grey rocks. The sun came from behind a cloud, lit up a rainbow of spray, then everything was dark again. He walked past the small graveyard, which was so close to the sea that spindrift blew across it, tucked himself behind one of the boulders to catch his breath and keep his telescope out of the wind and the salt. A squall of rain pitted the water a little way out to sea, and he raised his binoculars to look at the storm, then focused again so he was looking closer to the shore.

There was a swan near to the beach where the water was calmer. It was back on and its neck was tucked beneath one wing, so he couldn't see the head. He thought it would be a whooper; it was big and mute swans were hardly known on the Isle. Then the bird extended the neck as if it were preparing to fly. The beak was black. It took a moment for the detail to register and Dougie set up his telescope, fumbling with the tripod mechanism. God, why had nobody in the world invented a decent tripod? He needed to check this out. Perhaps a piece of weed had become tangled around the bill. Best to limit expectations. He'd been disappointed so many times before. But through the scope the beak was still black.

The huge bird flapped its wings slowly and raised its chest. It seemed to be running over the surface of the water, then it sailed slowly into the air. On one leg there was a thick metal ring. There would be numbers on it. Dougie was muttering a kind of prayer under his breath: *Please don't disappear. Nobody will believe this. I need someone else to see it too*.

Dougie jumped to his feet and followed the swan north through his binoculars. It was flying strongly enough but not too high. With any luck it would land on one of the pools at the far end of the island. Whooper swans often settled on Golden Water. *God*, he thought, *what would Angela have made of this? She'd have loved to put trumpeter swan on the British list.*

He fumbled in his pocket for his mobile phone. He was wearing gloves and pulled them off to speed things up, dropping one in a rock pool in his hurry. Phone reception in the island was patchy but he might be lucky. He had to call the centre to get some people out to look for the bird. This time of year it got dark so early and they'd need to have it pinned down for the following day. If a plane could get in tomorrow, there were birders from all over the UK who'd want to charter flights. And Dougie Barr would be a hero. But his phone had no signal. And the swan was no longer in sight.

The nearest house was Springfield where Big James and Mary lived. He slung his telescope over his shoulder and began to run up the bank towards it, into the full force of the wind. His feet slipped on the shingle and there were tears running from his eyes.

I care more about this bird than the fact that Angela Moore is dead.

The thought came out of nowhere and stunned him more than the storm and was followed by another even scarier:

I'd kill to find a bird like this.

He reached the house. There was a light on in the kitchen. He banged on the door and was aware that he was screaming to be let in, heard the noise in his ears as if someone else was making it.

The two women inside stared at him as if he were a madman. The phone was in the living room. It was the first time he'd been in any of the island houses but he took no notice of the surroundings. He dialled the number of the North Light.

Ben Catchpole answered. The assistant warden hadn't been out long and he couldn't have done a proper survey of the hill. But that hardly mattered now. Ben would have access to the field centre's Land Rover and Dougie was in no state to walk the three miles north to Golden Water.

'I've just had a trumpeter swan.'

There was a silence on the other end of the phone.

'Did you hear what I said?' Dougie was tempted to swear but knew the women in the kitchen were listening. He couldn't understand the lack of excitement, the lack of urgency.

Still no answer.

'Can you pick me up? It flew north. It could be on Golden Water. And tell the others. They could walk down there, find it for us, while you come to get me.'

At last Ben spoke. 'I don't know — '

'Just fucking do it!' Ignoring the women, he screamed so loud that the back of his throat hurt.

'Right,' Ben said. 'Right.'

* * *

Hugh relocated the bird and it was just as Dougie had pictured it, alone on the pool close to the North Light. The gale had whipped the water into waves and it bobbed on the surface. The sky was overcast again; the lunchtime weather forecast had predicted another depression coming in from the west, the tail end of Hurricane Charlie. So the swan looked very white against the grey water. Hugh must have run down the bank from the field centre because when they arrived he was still panting. Ben had picked the Fowlers up halfway along the road; Sarah seemed mystified by the desperation of the chase but John was as excited as they were. 'To be in on a bird like this,' he said. 'It's every lister's dream.' Dougie thought the man might be a stringer, but at least he understood how important the moment was.

Hugh was lying on his stomach in the grass with his telescope focused on it. He heard them approaching but he didn't turn round. 'Did you see it was ringed? It walked out onto that patch of sand and I could see the ring then.'

'Did you get any details on it?' Dougie held his breath.

Before Hugh could answer Ben interrupted. 'Doesn't that mean it was a captive bird and escaped from a collection?' Escapes couldn't be ticked. They all knew that. Dougie wanted to tell him not to be a prat and to let Hugh finish. How did someone as stupid as Ben Catchpole get to be assistant warden on Fair Isle? Because he had a degree, Dougie thought. Because he talked nicely and would be polite to the visitors.

Now Hugh did turn round and his grin lit up his face.

'This was no captive bird. That's a USGS band. You can read the unique number through the scope. The swan was ringed in the wild in the

States and we'll find out the date and the exact location of its ringing. There's no doubt about this one, Dougie. Congratulations, you jammy bastard.'

Later, as he bounced along the track to the North Light in the back of the Land Rover, Dougie found himself resenting Angela. He would never have thought it possible: she'd been important to him for so long. But this was the biggest find of his life and he wasn't going to be able to celebrate. They could hardly have a party the day after a woman had died and a find like this deserved a party. He just hoped they'd already taken her body away.

11

Perez's call, asking to borrow her camera, came as a relief to Fran. Mary was great. Good company. She could see that they might become friends. But by lunchtime Fran was starting to get so bored that she wanted to scream. What must it have been like for island women before electricity and flights to the mainland? Fran thought she could have coped in the summer. Then there'd have been shared work in the fields, light nights, music. But at this time of year when the stormy weather kept folk indoors, you'd go slightly mad by the end of it. There'd be nothing to do but gossip and knit. She imagined knitting all day in poor light in a room filled with stir-crazy children and thought that at the end of it she'd feel like committing murder.

Could I live here now? If I had my own work and my own house, could I make my home here? She didn't come up with an answer.

'I'll bring the camera up to you,' she said as soon as Perez had explained what he wanted. 'I'm sure you're busy there.'

'I don't know . . . ' He was thinking rules, she could tell. Procedures. He was a great one for going by the book.

'Please, Jimmy.'

He must have heard the desperation in her voice.

'OK then, but could you come up in Leogh

Willie's truck? Mum will arrange it for you. You could take Dad's car back. And there's a big roll of polythene at the back of the shed at home. The new bedroom carpet was delivered in it. Could you bring that too?'

'Sure,' she said. 'Sure.' No questions. She always asked too many questions and she didn't want to give him time to change his mind.

* * *

She loved driving the truck up the island towards the North Light. The vehicle was so eaten away by rust that it was hard to believe it would go at all, but perched in the cab, she felt as she'd done as a child on a fairground ride. There was the same engine noise and smell of diesel and she had a new perspective on the landscape around her. There was a joyous sense too that she was playing truant. She was such a kid. Perez was waiting for her.

'The keys are in Dad's car,' he said. 'You'd better get straight back.'

'Jimmy!'

'You shouldn't be here,' he said.

'I could help. Hold things. Take notes. Everyone else here is a suspect. You know I couldn't have killed the woman. I wouldn't get in the way.' She could tell she was wheedling like Cassie on a bad day and was certain he'd send her away. But he relented. Perhaps this was such an unusual situation that rules weren't so important. Perhaps he felt isolated in the field centre, where everyone was English and he was like an impostor in his own land. And she was a much better photographer than he was.

'I'll need to phone the Fiscal and check that it's OK. I couldn't do anything to prejudice a possible case.'

He left her standing in the lobby, unlocked the bird room door and went inside. She realized he would feel awkward talking to the Fiscal in front of her. She wondered if he would stretch the truth? Would he tell the woman he couldn't possibly manage without an assistant? He wouldn't want Fran to hear him lying. She imagined him standing next to the body of Angela Moore, conducting a normal conversation with Rhona Laing, and wondered how he could do that. Did she really want to work with him after all? She'd seen a dead woman before and the sight had haunted her for weeks. Perhaps Perez had only been trying to protect her.

The door opened. 'Are you sure about this?' As if he'd been tuned in to her doubts.

She nodded. This was his work and she wanted to be involved in it. She wouldn't have another chance. He stood aside to let her in and locked the door behind them. She looked at the figure as if Angela were a subject for a painting; it would be a big canvas because this was a strong woman. There was the texture of the hair, the muscular shoulders. The handle of the knife, smooth, cream-coloured, in contrast to the hair. The long, bony hands that already looked skeletal, lying on the desk. The strange arrangement of feathers resting on the head. *The piece of art could be a collage*, Fran thought.

Glorious and three-dimensional.

'What's going on with the feathers?'

'I don't know,' Perez said. 'They must have been arranged after death, I think. But I haven't a clue why.'

'It makes her look like a child who's been dressing up.'

'Do you think so?' Perez seemed surprised. 'The first thought that came into my head was that they look like those silly hats smart women wear to Ascot. Then I wondered if they might be sending a message. Something about cowardice, maybe? Didn't women hand out white feathers to men who wouldn't sign up to fight in the First World War?'

Fran thought that seemed too elaborate. Too preachy. This was about decoration. 'Were the feathers already in the room?'

'I don't know,' Perez said. 'Something else to check.'

'What about the knife?'

'It was hers. Maurice said she brought it back from one of her trips abroad. India, I think. Apparently she used it to cut a net if a bird got caught while she was trapping. She kept it in her belt when she was out, otherwise here in the bird room. The assistant warden said it was always very sharp.'

'She bit her nails,' Fran said. 'Strange, you expect nervous people to bite their nails and she didn't come across that way at all.' She looked up at him. 'Does that mean they won't find anything under them?'

He shrugged. 'They'll take samples at the p-m.

We don't have the facilities to do it here and we can't leave the body here in the centre for another night. It would mean me camping out outside the door to make sure no one tampers with her. Besides, I need to get her somewhere a bit cooler. The radiator's switched off here now but it was on all night — Angela would have been the person to switch off the generator before she went to bed — and the room's still quite warm.'

'What would you like me to do?' She refused to play the little woman and go all squeamish on him, but suddenly she imagined the stink of decomposition and felt faint. She needed to concentrate on the practical.

'Take photographs,' he said. 'Loads of photographs. Of everything here. The whole room from as many angles as you can and then everything in detail. Have you got gloves?'

She grinned and took a thin woollen pair from her jacket pocket. 'Just call me Dr Watson.'

'Mm?' He looked at her and she saw he was so preoccupied with his own thoughts that he hadn't understood the bad joke.

'Doesn't matter.' She took her camera from its case and positioned herself to take the first photograph.

'I don't have a fingerprinting kit,' he said, 'but I don't suppose it's important. Everyone staying in the lighthouse would have been in here at some point. It's where Angela ringed the birds and apparently the visitors are invited to watch.'

Through the camera lens she looked at the room in detail. There was the ringing equipment, a shelf of bird books, a PC and printer. There was dust on the shelf and the floor was mucky.

'They haven't cleaned in here recently,' she said. 'Not as recently as in the common room at least. That was spotless last night. I suppose they must be allowed in here in their boots.' She guessed that was Jane's job too. It seemed overwhelming, to be cook and housekeeper for the whole place.

'No point looking for footwear impressions then.' Perez was talking almost to himself. 'Again, any of the staff or visitors would have had a reason to be in here, and the killer would have come straight from the party. He'd have been wearing indoor shoes and wouldn't have left a mark.'

'He?' Fran looked up from the camera.

'Or she,' he said.

She couldn't tell whether he had any idea who the murderer might be and she didn't ask. She thought of the people who'd been at the party the night before; she'd been chatting and laughing with them. When she said goodbye, she'd touched them, held their hands and kissed their cheeks. One of them had stuck a knife in the back of the young woman who lay in front of them, then carefully laid feathers over her hair. She tried to imagine being so angry that she might do that. *I might lash out*, she thought. *If someone had hurt Cassie or Jimmy, I might even kill. But afterwards I'd come to my senses. I'd want to put things right. I'd fetch help. I couldn't stand here and watch a young woman bleed to death, knowing it was my fault.*

She shifted position, so she could take a photograph of the desk. Angela's head was twisted, so one cheek lay against the wood. Fran found herself looking into the staring eyes that were only partly covered by the long hair. She took the picture quickly and turned away.

Perez was unplugging the computer. 'I'll take this back to Springfield and check it out there.'

'Won't it have personal stuff on it?'

'Of course,' he said. 'It's the personal that interests me most.'

She suddenly found it slightly distasteful, his preoccupation with the private lives of dead people. He enjoyed the prying and the privileged knowledge of their domestic affairs. It was the enjoyment that was the problem for her: she'd find it acceptable if he considered it a duty and a chore. She wondered if that was all she was to him. An interesting specimen and someone else to investigate. Then he caught her eye and smiled at her, a brief flash of affection. She saw him as she'd seen him first — the dark, untidy hair, the tired eyes. She felt a deep and inappropriate moment of lust and thought everything would probably be all right.

Outside in the lobby the phone rang. She sensed Perez tense. 'It won't be for you, surely,' she said. 'Work would use your mobile.'

'Angela was a bit of a media star. I'm worried Maurice and Poppy Parry will start being hassled by reporters once the news gets out.'

He opened the bird room door, but came back when he realized Ben was already answering. He left the door ajar and they stood quietly so they could overhear the assistant warden's side of the conversation. As soon as he realized the conversation was about birds, some rare swan, Perez turned away.

'Have you recorded this?' He nodded to a pile of books and papers on the desk. 'It all seems a bit random. What do you think she was doing?'

'Maybe it isn't related at all. Could be stuff she's been working on over the past few weeks and just hasn't put away yet. It seems she was hardly obsessively tidy.'

Fran took a photograph of a book that was lying face down, close to one long hand. The book had been written by Angela Moore and there was a photo of the woman, the trademark hair clipped away from her face, on the back jacket. '*On the trail of the slender-billed curlew*,' Fran read from the blurb. '*The species everyone thought was extinct, rediscovered on the silk trail of Uzbekistan. A modern tale of adventure and exploration*.' She looked up at Perez. 'Didn't they make a television series about that?'

He looked up briefly. 'Yes, it was the first programme to make her famous. She led the expedition into the desert and found a small number of the birds. Soon after the series was broadcast she moved here to Fair Isle. It caused a bit of a stir on the island, having someone who was almost a celebrity moving in.'

'Why would she want to read her own book?'

'I'm not sure.' He straightened up and considered the matter seriously. 'Perhaps she was writing an article and wanted to check a fact. Or perhaps she just wanted to cheer herself up. It was her moment of glory, after all.'

He went back to his methodical investigation of the papers on the desk, carefully marking the page where the book had been opened, before adding it to the black bin bag.

Outside in the lobby, they heard the ring that showed the phone had been replaced and there was a sudden flurry of activity. Ben Catchpole was shouting something unintelligible up the stairs and they heard running footsteps, the sound of the Land Rover being started. Through the window they saw the youngest of the visiting birdwatchers running across the yard and out onto the hill.

'What's all that about?' Fran thought it sounded urgent and wondered why Perez was being so relaxed. 'Shouldn't we go and find out?'

He looked up briefly from sorting through a bunch of printed papers. 'It'll be a rare bird,' he said. 'It happens all the time. I told you, they're kind of obsessed.'

* * *

Big James came to the North Light to help Perez move Angela's body into the lorry. Fran was relieved. All the time she was taking photographs she'd been wondering how she and Jimmy would manage to roll the woman in the polythene and carry her outside. She didn't have much strength and imagined spilling Angela on the grass among the sheep droppings and rabbit holes, the indignity of a farcical pantomime trying to manoeuvre her into the back of the lorry. At least with the field centre empty of guests and Maurice and Poppy hidden away in the flat, they wouldn't have an audience.

But when James came he took charge and the whole thing was managed quickly and without drama. All Fran had to do was hold the door and let down the back of the lorry. While Perez was talking to his father, his accent changed and she hardly understood what they were saying. Not many words were exchanged. She supposed they'd worked together before on the croft and loading the boat. James drove the lorry away and they stood watching at the back door of the field centre.

'Wait in the car,' Perez said. 'I need to tell Maurice what's happened.'

She expected him to be a long time. There would surely be other questions. Perez was a meticulous investigator. But he came out very quickly. It seemed to her that he was distressed.

'What happened?'

'Maurice was heartbroken,' he said. 'Much worse than when he found out that Angela was dead. I thought something new had happened to upset him. But it's the fact of her leaving the North Light. While she was in the bird room, there was still something of her there. Now he realizes that she won't be coming back. Ever.'

12

On her way back to the North Light, Jane passed the lorry and the Springfield car. The vehicles were going south, in the opposite direction to her. She stood on the grass by the side of the road and saw first the lorry driven by Big James and then Perez and Fran in the car. All three waved to her, but they didn't stop to speak and on the island that was unusual. She waited for a moment and watched them disappear over the rise by the entrance to Setter. It came to her that Angela's body would be in the lorry, and she wondered what the woman would have thought of making such a lowly exit from the North Light. Usually it was used for carrying sheep to the boat for the abattoir. She remembered what Perez had said about Angela always appearing miserable to him. *I never really knew her*, Jane thought. *I took against her without any real reason and I never made the effort to understand her*.

Almost at the lighthouse she saw Ben Catchpole walking towards her. Even in the gloom she could make out his red hair at a distance, the only colour visible in the grey landscape.

'Did you see the swan?' she asked. 'Dougie came into Springfield to use the phone while I was having tea with Mary. Such a fuss.' *You'd have thought someone was being murdered*. She stopped herself speaking the words just in time.

'It's roosting at Golden Water.' He turned and began walking back to the field centre alongside her. She realized he'd come out to find her. He was out of his depth and she was the only person he could ask for advice. 'I don't know what to do. Dougie's already put the word out on the pagers. Every lister in the country will be desperate to get in to see it.'

'While the weather's like this, we don't have to do anything.' Jane could see he found the 'we' reassuring. Despite all his experience, the green activism, the doctorate, he seemed out of his depth. 'We can make a decision when it clears. Perhaps by then the investigation will be over.'

Ben kicked a piece of shingle off the road. 'Who do you think did it?'

'I don't know.'

'She treated me like shit,' he said. 'But I would have died for her.'

In the centre, Jane dropped off her coat in her room and closed the curtains. The wind had dropped a little, or perhaps she'd become accustomed to it. The light had gone. In the kitchen she lit the Calor gas under the vegetables she'd prepared earlier and put plates to warm. The table was already laid. Just for the six of them: four visitors, Ben and her. With the main lights on she couldn't see outside — just her reflection in the big windows, looking pale and thin. She was a dried-out middle-aged woman. *I need a lover*, she thought. *Someone warm and big-breasted with a deep laugh to breathe some life into me*. The potatoes had come to the boil and she turned down the heat. She'd mash them to serve with the gammon she was roasting. Ben was the only veggie left in the place since the last plane went out and there was a quiche left over from the party that he could have. She knew there was a packet of broad beans still in the freezer and she'd serve them with a white sauce. Shame the last gale had killed the parsley in the little field centre garden. But all the time she was deciding the trivial domestic details that so calmed her, she was thinking about Angela's murder. *An act of anger*, she thought. *Or revenge*.

She walked down the corridor that linked the kitchen to Maurice's flat. Her leather shoes slapped on the tiles and echoed so they sounded like following footsteps. She knocked at the door and when there was no reply she went in. Maurice was sitting hollow-eyed, alone in the dark. She switched on a table lamp, and took a seat beside him.

'Where's Poppy?'

'I'm not sure,' he said. She saw he couldn't care about anything. He was entirely wrapped around in his own grief. 'She might be in her room.'

When Jane stood up to look he called after her. 'They've taken Angela away.'

'I know.'

Poppy was lying on her bed watching television, an Australian soap. On the screen, two impossibly beautiful teenagers were lying on a sandy beach staring at each other. For a moment Jane thought it was crass and insensitive for the girl to be engrossed in a sentimental love story while her father was so miserable. But the girl's presence wouldn't make things easier for him and she'd never pretended to be fond of Angela. The birdwatchers had been chasing all over the island after some rare bird and that was just as inappropriate. As inappropriate as Jane taking a secret delight in her attempts to unravel the mystery of Angela's death.

'Are you hungry?'

Poppy switched down the sound, but continued to stare at the sunny landscape, the young lovers.

'Starving.' She turned abruptly towards Jane. 'Is that really gross? To want to eat when there's a dead woman lying in the bird room?'

'Of course not. And she's not there any more. Jimmy Perez has taken her away.' Jane sat on the bed. 'Where do you want your dinner? In the flat or with us?'

There was a pause. 'Do they all think I killed her?'

'I don't know what *they* think. I don't believe it was you.'

The soap opera ended and the titles rolled silently towards a blue horizon. Poppy lay back on the pillow. 'Could I have something here? I can't face Dad either. He keeps crying. I've never seen him cry before.'

'I'll bring something through.'

'Is there pudding too?'

'Lemon meringue.'

'Can I have a piece?'

Jane smiled and nodded.

* * *

At the table the talk was all about the swan. There was a pile of reference books between them. Dougie Barr was manic. It was as if he were on speed, the words tumbling out one after another. 'Sometimes you see a bird and you just *know*! Like, that it's the best bird you'll ever find in your life, the thing you'll be remembered for.' He set down his knife and fork and turned a page in the big book beside him, then picked up a can, not of beer, but a highly coloured fizzy drink. Jane thought the sugar in it, added to his mood, had turned him into a hyperactive child. 'I wasn't even sure trumpeter migrated, but it does. Look. The Alaska population is migratory. So my bird came all the way from Alaska.' *My bird*. As if he'd given birth to it. He began to eat again, very quickly, and occasionally small pieces of food flew out of his mouth. Perhaps he finally remembered that there'd been a death in the centre because he added: 'Angela would have understood that. She knew what it was like to find a rarity. Her reputation was built on it.'

'That and her hair,' Sarah Fowler said.

The interjection was so unexpected, so bitchy, that for a moment Jane wasn't sure how to respond, or even if the implied criticism was intended. She'd chatted to the Fowlers when they first arrived at the field centre on the *Shepherd* and found them pleasant, in a quiet, inoffensive way. She couldn't remember if John had said what he did for a living; Sarah was some sort of social worker, dealing with kids and families. Now, surprised, she looked up and caught Sarah's eye and they grinned at each other. Two women sharing a moment of cattiness, enjoying it all the more because of the circumstances, because they were restrained, polite women of a certain age and no one would have expected it of them. Sarah began to giggle, very quietly into her napkin, and Jane thought they were all close to hysteria.

Around them the conversation about the swan continued.

'The wind's supposed to drop tomorrow afternoon.' This was Hugh Shaw. Jane knew his charm had been practised from birth. You could tell he'd always been adored by women — his mother and grandmother, certainly, and there'd probably been a nanny too — but still she found herself seduced by him. He was so pretty and his smile was so languid and appealing. He had to work hard to achieve the desired response and so she felt he deserved her admiration and amusement. 'Birders are already travelling to Shetland on the chance that they'll get to Fair Isle to see the swan.'

Jane looked at Ben, but he hardly seemed to be following the conversation.

'Even if the wind does drop, there probably won't be time for the plane to come in tomorrow,' she said. 'It's starting to get dark so early.' She hoped that was the case. It would be worse if the plane arrived late in the afternoon with a full load of visitors and immediately took off again without them. She'd have to find rooms for the incomers and feed them. She didn't see how that would work — an influx of people with Maurice and Poppy hiding away in the flat. And if birdwatchers could get in, so could journalists. She had a sudden image of hacks surrounding the lighthouse, pointing their cameras through the windows, of Maurice, his head in his hands, appearing on the front pages of tabloid newspapers. Perhaps she should take the decision to close the field centre to new guests, but the reporters would probably find somewhere on the island to stay. Jane hoped that the weather would close in again, at least for the next few days, at least until Perez had discovered the murderer. Or until she had.

There was a lull in the conversation and she took in the scene. Dougie had moved on to pudding and was cramming his mouth full of lemon meringue pie. The Fowlers were talking quietly to each other. Jane saw that under the table John had taken Sarah's hand and again she felt a stab of loneliness. *I have nobody to touch, nobody to wrap me up in her arms to comfort me*. Hugh was leaning back in his chair, his eyes half closed and a smile of contentment on his face. Ben was fiddling with his paper napkin and staring out into the darkness.

Someone in this building is a murderer, she thought. *I could be sharing a meal with a murderer*. There was an Agatha Christie book she'd read when she was a kid. A bunch of people on an island. Dying, one by one. It was warm in the dining room. She'd lit a big fire of driftwood to cheer them up here and in the common room. But she shivered.

She went into the kitchen to make coffee. While the kettles were boiling she stacked the plates in the dishwasher and then spooned instant granules into a big Thermos jug. Her evening ritual. The final task before the end of the working day. She thought suddenly that this would be her last year at the centre. She wouldn't come back to the Isle once the season was over. It wouldn't be the same and, anyway, she was ready now to move on. By becoming a victim of violence, Angela Moore had done that for her.

There was a movement behind her and she turned, expecting to see one of the visitors, Sarah perhaps, offering to help with the coffee. But Perez stood there. He'd taken off his boots and his coat and was standing very still, just by her shoulder. She felt her pulse quicken. Did everyone feel scared when the police arrived? Did everyone remember the misdemeanours, the unkind acts, not criminal perhaps but inhumane, when confronted by a detective like Perez? *We all think he can see right through us. He knows what we're thinking. It's like standing before God on the Day of Judgement.* Carefully she poured boiling water into the flask. Her hand was quite steady. *I'm being ridiculous. It's the weather and the melodrama of the situation.* She thought again that she could have walked into a novel, if not Christie then something else Gothic and overblown.

'I'm sorry to intrude,' Perez said.

'You're not intruding. Come and have coffee with us.'

He followed her into the dining room. They were all sitting just as she had left them. Another squall had blown up and the rain was hitting the window. Nobody was speaking. Jane felt a responsibility to put people at their ease. It had been the same at the parties in Richmond: Dee had invited strangely mismatched people to her home and then ignored them and it had been Jane's role to make the introductions and bring the guests together.

'Everybody's rather excited,' she said. 'There's a very rare bird on Golden Water. A trumpeter swan. It's never been seen in the UK before.'

Still Perez said nothing. He pulled a chair up to the table and sat between Dougie and Hugh.

'This is an unusual situation.' Perez seemed to be weighing his words. Jane wondered if he already knew who'd killed Angela. Perhaps there was some magic test of technology that had made it clear during the hours he'd spent in the bird room. Was he here to make an arrest? She realized she'd be disappointed as well as relieved if that were the purpose of his visit. She was still intrigued by the puzzle. She felt as she did when she was attempting to complete a crossword and someone leaned over her shoulder and gave her the answer to a cryptic clue.

But it seemed Perez was no further forward in the investigation than she was. 'Usually, in a case like this a big team would be working it, taking statements, checking the background of the witnesses. Here, there's only me. I'd be grateful for your cooperation. I do need a statement from each of you and I'd like to speak to you individually.' He looked round the table. 'As soon as possible while your memories are still fresh.'

'What about Maurice and Poppy?' Hugh said. 'I assume you'll be talking to them.' He shrugged and gave the diffident little smile to signal he intended no offence.

Really, Hugh, Jane thought. *You're rather poisonous after all. And I thought you were such a nice boy.*

'I'll be talking to everyone,' Perez said sharply. 'And I'll run the investigation in my own way. I'll begin the interviews this evening.' He handed sheets of paper around the table. 'In the meantime, I'd be grateful if you could write down everything you can remember about yesterday evening. I'll need a timetable of your own movements after the party, but anything else that might be relevant. Perhaps there was an overheard conversation that has become more significant in the light of Angela's death. Or perhaps you noticed someone moving around the lighthouse late last night. Please don't discuss the matter with fellow guests. It shouldn't be the subject of speculation. And be honest. As I said this is an unusual situation, but it isn't a game.'

He turned to Jane and for the first time since arriving he smiled. 'Would it be possible to have more coffee? It's going to be a long night.'

13

Perez thought this was the most difficult case he'd ever worked. Here, stranded in the North Light, it was as if he was working in a strange country; it even seemed that the witnesses spoke a foreign language and he was groping to make sense of the words. He understood for the first time how difficult it must have been for Roy Taylor, his colleague from Inverness, to come into Shetland and take charge of an investigation there. The place would have seemed quite alien to him. Perez knew how Shetlanders thought. He could see the world through their eyes. The field centre staff and guests were English and had different ambitions and preoccupations. In a sudden fancy, he thought that the building was like an outpost of Empire during the time of the Raj; he felt like a native official bridging the gap between both cultures.

He moved everyone from the dining room to the common room. They would be more comfortable there and he could use the dining room to interview his witnesses. He preferred to sit on an upright chair with the table between him and his interviewee, rather than slouched on a sofa, his knees touching those of his suspect. Because of course they were all suspects. That was the only way he could consider them at the moment. He knew it was unlikely that the field centre residents would sit in silence in the common room; they would discuss what was going on as soon as he left the room. Their written statements would be compromised. But it was the best he could do.

Fran had offered to come back to the field centre with him: 'I could help. I'm observant. I could watch them and listen to what was said. Make notes without their realizing.' But he wasn't sure information gathered in that way would be considered admissible evidence. And one woman had been murdered already. He wasn't going to place Fran in danger again.

He asked John Fowler to join him first in the dining room. Why had he made that choice? It was a random decision made partly because quiet people always interested him, and Fowler had hardly spoken over coffee. Also, he seemed amiable and Perez could do without a hostile conversation to kick off the evening.

They talked with the churning of the dishwasher in the kitchen as a background to the conversation. Perez set a small tape recorder on the table between them. He'd borrowed it from Stella, the schoolteacher, when he'd gone down the island to store Angela's body.

He nodded towards the machine. 'You don't mind? This isn't a formal interview, but I don't have anyone to take notes.'

Listening to the recorded conversation later, the background sound of the kitchen appliance, kicking in before the speech, would immediately make him feel uneasy and remind him of his struggle to ask the important questions.

He began with the factual details he already

knew: he'd found guests' names and addresses on the bird room computer and colleagues in Lerwick had already done a check for criminal records. Fowler's was clean. The couple lived in Bristol. John was forty-nine and Sarah was forty-one. Now the man sat in front of him, quite unmoved, it seemed, by the situation. His hair was slightly long for a man of his age and he wore denims and a knitted jersey. There was nothing unusual or impressive about him. He was the sort of character always passed over in an identity parade.

'What brought you to Fair Isle in the autumn?' Perez asked.

'Birds.' Fowler smiled. 'We're just like the other mad people who come all this way. I've spent a couple of autumns in Shetland, but I've never been to Fair Isle. It's been a dream, you know. For birdwatchers the place has an almost mythical status. It's a place where almost anything can happen. And today it did, of course, with the trumpeter swan. Besides, Sarah needed a holiday.'

'Why did your wife need a holiday?'

'Does it matter?' The smile vanished, replaced by a small frown, as if Perez had committed some unfortunate breach of manners.

'Probably not.' Perez wasn't sure what had led him to ask the question, but now Fowler's response intrigued him. 'But I'm interested.'

Fowler shrugged. 'She'd lost a baby. We'd given up hope of conceiving. Tried everything — had all the tests, IVF. Then there was that wonderful moment when she realized she was pregnant. But there was a miscarriage. Nobody can tell us why. Her baby would have been due this week. It's been a strain for both of us. I had to get her away.'

'I'm sorry.' Perez's first wife had been called Sarah too and she'd had a miscarriage. He'd thought it had been at the root of the breakdown of his marriage. Certainly he had never been more unhappy than when they lost the baby. Now he felt like an insensitive oaf for prying into private grief.

'You won't say anything to her.' Fowler looked earnestly at Perez. He had the air, Perez thought, of an academic, gentle, a little unworldly.

'Of course not.' The dishwasher beeped to show it was at the end of its cycle. 'Had you met Angela Moore before you came to the field centre?'

'Once, I think, at a publisher's party. I used to write features for specialist journals.'

'You're a journalist?' Perez looked up sharply. 'These interviews are confidential. I wouldn't want what's said here to appear in a newspaper.'

'I wouldn't do that to her family.' Fowler was staring out of the window. 'Besides, I'm never asked to write anything these days. I seem to have gone out of favour. And I didn't write much for the dailies: only occasionally features on natural history.'

Perez supposed he would have to trust the man but he thought every journalist would like a story in a big paper, his name in bold, next to the headline. And Fowler would be very quickly back in favour if the nationals realized he was here. 'So why was Angela at the publisher's party?'

'It was to celebrate the launch of her book. They were hoping for publicity. A review.'

'That was when Angela's book on the curlew was published?' Perez felt he was having to prise information from the man. Perhaps the tape recorder was a mistake and there would have been a more relaxed conversation without it.

'Yes.'

'Did you write a review?'

'I did. I'm afraid it was less than generous.'

'It's not a good book?'

'You'll have to read it, Inspector, and judge for yourself.' He looked up and gave a brief smile.

'Did Angela recognize you when you arrived at the lighthouse?' Perez asked. He still didn't know where these questions were leading. Again he thought this was a world about which he knew nothing. He could talk to crofters about their sheep and fishermen about the piltock, but these writers and birdwatchers were strange and incomprehensible to him.

'She knew my name, but probably didn't remember having met me.'

'And you got on all right, despite the poor review?'

'Of course, Inspector. She had become a famous woman. She had no reason to bear a grudge. She no longer needed my approval.'

It seemed to Perez that Angela was a woman who might bear a grudge for a long time. He looked at the sheet of paper on the table in front of him and saw he'd written nothing.

'How do you make your living now?' he asked.

'Still through books, Inspector. But now I collect them and sell them, I don't write about them. I have a little natural history bookshop. Most of my work is done over the Internet these days of course, but there are still devoted customers who like to browse. I'm very fortunate to be able to indulge my passion and call it work.'

Perez wondered if that was what *he* did. Did he indulge his passion, his curiosity at least, and call it work?

'You were at the party here last night,' he said. The Fowlers had introduced themselves, offered their congratulations and said how lovely it was that all the guests had been invited, but he had no memory of them dancing. Perhaps they'd stayed long enough to be polite, then gone to bed. 'How did Angela seem to you then?'

Fowler shrugged. 'Much as she always was. Driven, abrasive, entertaining.'

'Why would anyone want to kill her?' It had seemed to Perez, despite the strange show with the feathers, that this was a crime with a rational motive. Apparently, there'd been no sexual assault on Angela. He didn't believe they could blame a madman enraged by the storm.

'I don't think I'm the right person to ask, Inspector.' Fowler's voice was quite distant now, though he was as polite as ever. It was as if the interview was beginning to bore him. 'I hardly knew the woman.'

* * *

Perez took a break before calling the next witness into the dining room. He poured another mug of coffee and on impulse carried it outside for a moment in an attempt to raise his energy level. He had to put his weight behind the door to get it open and even in the lee of the building, the force of the wind made him gasp for breath. The noise of the sea thundered and echoed, driving speculation about the case from his brain. It was replaced by a moment of despair. *I can't do this. Not on my own*. He'd never found formal interviews, the sterile question-and-answer session with the witness defensive and on guard, particularly useful. Here, he thought, he had no control at all and no sense of what the suspects were thinking. This was his island, but in the North Light the writer, the scientists and the birdwatchers were on home territory. They had the advantage. Somehow he had to shift the balance of power.

He walked briskly into the common room. They had heard his approaching footsteps on the wooden floors and when he entered the place was quiet; everyone seemed to be concentrating on the papers in front of them. They looked up. Who would be next?

'A change of plan,' he said. It seemed to him that his voice was unnaturally loud. 'I have to go back to Springfield. There's been a call from Inverness. We'll continue tomorrow, but I'll set up base in the community hall. Then I disrupt the working of the field centre as little as possible. I'll phone when I'm ready. If I could collect your statements now . . . '

He stalked away, the papers in one hand, feeling like a teacher in a rough school struggling to maintain authority in his class. He had reached his car when Jane called after him. He saw her in the light that spilled out from the lobby. She had thrown a coat over her shoulders but was still wearing indoor shoes. She ran to join him. 'Jimmy, can I talk to you? I've remembered something. Probably not important, but I thought you should know.'

They sat in Big James's rust-pocked car, battered by the wind. Occasionally he had to ask Jane to speak up so he could hear her.

'It was something Angela said at lunchtime the day before she died.' Jane was looking ahead of her through the windscreen, though it was quite black outside. Perez had switched on the interior lamp, had been astonished when it worked, so they talked in that pale, rather flickering light. 'She said someone had been into the bird room and disturbed her papers. Something she was working on. She was furious. I mean, incandescent. It wasn't unknown for her to manufacture rage, just because she was bored, but this was the real thing.'

'Can you remember anything else about the conversation?'

'I think a paper was missing. She accused one of us of having taken it.'

'Anyone in particular?' Perez asked. He turned to look at the woman, at the thin, intense face. Why did this matter so much to her?

'I don't think so,' she said. 'At least it didn't seem so to me at the time.'

'Thank you.' He assumed she would get out now that the conversation was finished, but she sat where she was. He waited, thinking that waiting was one of his skills. He could do it better than anyone else he knew.

'You should speak to Ben Catchpole,' she said at last. 'Hugh too, perhaps. Angela liked pretty young boys.'

'You're saying she slept with them?' He heard the surprise and disapproval in his own voice. How Fran would mock him if she'd been listening in! She was always telling him he was narrow-minded, prudish. And if they'd been talking about a man, would Perez be equally shocked?

There was no direct answer. 'She was predatory,' Jane said. 'She needed admirers. I don't know for certain about Ben and Hugh, but it certainly happened last year. She took up with a young visitor and really screwed him up.' She continued to stare ahead of her into the darkness.

'What did Maurice make of the arrangement?'

'I would guess,' Jane said, 'that he pretended not to know. Maurice likes an easy life. And more than anything he wanted Angela to be happy.'

'Thank you,' he said again, and this time Jane did get out of the car. Through the back windscreen he watched her run towards the lights of the field centre.

* * *

In Springfield they were watching television. The thick curtains were drawn against the storm.

There was a fire of peat and driftwood and he could smell that as soon as he walked into the house. His mother got up when she heard him come in and made him coffee, brought out a plate with oatcakes and cheese. His father poured him a glass of whisky. Fran was alone on the sofa, her legs curled under her, and he bent and kissed her head. He smelled the shampoo she always used, along with the peat smoke.

'We weren't expecting you back so early,' she said. 'Is it all over?'

'No, but I couldn't go on this evening. I wasn't getting anywhere. Plenty to do tomorrow though.'

'We've just seen the forecast,' his father said. 'The weather should start to change in the morning. There's a high pressure coming in.'

'You'll get the boat out then?'

'Not just yet. There'll still be too much of a swell. And I can't see the plane making it either. The chopper might be OK. And the day after should be fine. Everything should be back to normal by then.'

Except, Perez thought, *that there's a dead woman padlocked in our shed and I still have to find her killer. Not normal at all.*

14

Dougie Barr listened to the late-night shipping forecast on the old transistor radio in the dormitory. At home, the precise voice listing the sea areas sent him to sleep.

When he was working, what did it matter which way the wind was blowing? Here, it mattered very much. In the next couple of days the weather would change. There'd be a still, cold period. A time of fieldfares and redwings and snow buntings. The birdwatchers gathered in Shetland waiting for the wind to drop, so they could charter boats and planes to get to Fair Isle, would have heard the forecast too. He almost wished he could be with them, sitting in the bars in Lerwick or in the Sumburgh Hotel, reminiscing over other crazy twitches, near misses and serendipitous finds. He would like to share the mounting excitement and tension. But then he wouldn't have found the trumpeter swan. His name wouldn't appear in the British Birds rarity report. He wouldn't be the envy of every birder in Britain.

Sitting on his bed, he unbuttoned his shirt and caught snatches of conversation coming from the common room below him. Ben and Hugh were sitting up drinking; there was a sudden outburst of laughter. Dougie felt excluded, frozen out. The old paranoia: *They're laughing at me. Because I'm not as bright as them. Because I have to work for a living*. It had been the same since he was a child, the chubby boy in the playground, teased and bullied. He stood up and looked out at the window, had an almost overwhelming impulse to force his fist through the glass. He imagined the noise, the pain as shards pierced his skin, almost to the bone, the sensation of wind rushing through the splintered gap. With a great effort, he took off his trousers and folded them on the back of a chair, climbed under the duvet, shut his eyes very tight and thought of Angela's silky black hair and long, brown hands. He pictured her naked body. But the image failed to work its old magic. Instead he thought of her staring through her heavy polythene shroud — because of course details of her leaving the lighthouse had leaked out — with lifeless eyes.

Downstairs, the conversation continued. There was another explosion of laughter. On an impulse, Dougie got up and dressed. He stormed downstairs, just as his mother had done on occasion when he was still living at home and had been foolhardy enough to invite friends round. She'd appear at the living room door in her dressing gown and slippers, her face blotchy with indignation and embarrassment: 'Do you mind keeping the noise down, our Dougie? Some of us have got work to go to in the morning.' As if he hadn't worked for a living.

The big generator had been turned off for the night and he used a torch to see himself down the stairs. In the common room a Tilley lamp stood on the table and someone had put candles on the mantelpiece. The fire had been banked up with peat but the central heating had gone off and there was a chill in the room.

He'd only expected to see Hugh and Ben, but John Fowler was there too and Dougie was thrown by that. The man was older than him and it didn't seem right to make a fuss, to complain about the noise. He'd make himself look bad-tempered, stupid even. Instead Dougie poured himself a whisky and went to join them, as if he'd been up all the time. He didn't drink much; he preferred the taste of the soft drink Jane got in specially when she knew he was staying. Perhaps it was the whisky that made the whole episode seem like a dream when he thought about it later.

He thought Hugh must have started the game. It was his style. There was an empty wine bottle on the table and Hugh turned it on its side and began to spin it. The light from the Tilley reflected in the moving green glass.

'Have you ever played the truth game?' Surely that must have been Hugh? There'd be the easy smile. They'd all been drinking though, and later Dougie thought it could have been any of them. Except Dougie himself. He'd never have suggested playing that sort of game. He remembered the taunts he'd endured when he was still at school, the questions he'd refused to answer: 'Have you ever had a girl, Fat Dougie? Or are you still a virgin? Who'd want you, after all?'

None of them answered, but Hugh took no notice. He twisted the bottle again, more violently. When it stopped, the neck was pointed towards Ben.

'You're the first victim, Ben,' Hugh said, grinning. 'The rest of us get a question each.'

'Surely there's no guarantee that he'll tell the truth.' John Fowler was leaning back in his seat and his face was in shadow. 'How would the rest of us know if he was lying?'

'Oh, we'd know,' Hugh said. 'Most people are very bad liars.'

Perhaps it was the situation. The candlelight flickering in the inevitable draughts, the memory of Angela's body lying for most of the day in the room next door. Perhaps they were afraid of provoking Hugh. But none of them refused to play. Nobody said: *This is ridiculous, childish, let's just go to bed*.

We should be celebrating a new bird, Dougie thought. Instead we're sitting round like mad old ladies at a seance. After his dad died, his mother had got into spiritualism for a while and she'd brought some seriously weird people back to the house. They'd sat with their fingers touching in the dark, crouched in the front room of their suburban council house, believing they were conjuring up spirits.

'I'll ask a question,' John Fowler said. He leaned forward and the buttery candlelight slid down his forehead and over his chin. 'Did you kill Angela Moore?'

Ben's head shot up. For a moment Dougie thought he would hit the man. 'No! I'd never have hurt her.'

'Your question, Dougie.' It sounded as if Hugh

was laughing. Dougie didn't look at him, but he knew the smile would be there, the white teeth gleaming out of the shadow.

Dougie didn't know what to ask. He was just dreading his turn as victim. 'Have you ever done anything you're ashamed of?' Where had that question come from?

Ben turned to face him. 'Once,' he said. Then: 'I betrayed some friends.'

'When was that?' It was John Fowler. Dougie thought you could tell he'd been a journalist. You could imagine him sniffing out stories.

'I've answered the question, haven't I? No need to go into details.' In the candlelight it looked as if Ben's hair was on fire. 'What about you, Hugh? What do you want to know?'

'Did you love her?'

'Who?'

'Angela, of course. We're all thinking about her.'

No hesitation. 'Yes.'

Oh, Dougie thought. She'd have enjoyed that. Nothing Angela liked better than unquestioning devotion. And nothing she despised more.

John Fowler reached out and twisted the bottle, a deft movement that Dougie in this heightened mood thought looked like someone wringing the neck of a chicken. He watched the spinning glass, saw it stop. It was halfway between him and Hugh but he wanted this over. He couldn't stand the waiting. 'My turn then,' he said. He felt he couldn't breathe. The questions would be about sex. Or about Angela, which came to the same thing.

Hugh stared at him. 'Did you kill Angela Moore?'

Dougie relaxed. 'No.' An easy question. And Hugh was the mischief-maker. If any of them was going to turn him into a figure of fun, it would be Hugh.

He turned to face the others. Now the worst was over he was almost enjoying being the centre of attention. John Fowler was watching him. It was out of character for the man to be here, playing a stupid adolescent game. Usually Fowler went to bed early with his wife. Straight after the cocoa and the biscuits and the calling of the log. Why was he here? Did he think they'd like him, accept him and believe his records again, just because he stopped up drinking with them? But Fowler didn't speak and it was Ben who asked the next question.

'Do you know who killed Angela?'

Dougie paused for a moment, but suspicion wasn't knowledge. 'No.' He looked at John again, waiting for the last question.

'Have you ever strung a bird?' Fowler asked. 'Have you claimed a record you weren't sure about?'

It was the last thing Dougie had been expecting. Fowler was the stringer, not him.

'Well?' Fowler said gently. Hugh looked on, smiling.

Dougie was tempted to lie, but he could feel himself blushing.

'Yes,' he said.

'Will you tell us about it?' Fowler again. Like some priest, encouraging confession.

'No.' Dougie reached out and spun the bottle. It jerked and bounced on the table. When it stopped it was pointed directly at Hugh.

Dougie found that stupid, demeaning questions were running through his head. The sort of questions the bullies at school might have asked. 'Have you ever pissed yourself? Fancied a bloke?' But in the end, the worst question he could think of was the one he'd just been asked.

'Are *you* a stringer?'

'Not to my knowledge.' *He's lying*, Dougie thought. *We've all exaggerated a record at some point in our birding life*. Hugh seemed as still and white as if he'd been carved from ice.

'Have you ever been in love?' That from Ben, who was leaning forward across the table.

'No!' The answer swift and contemptuous.

'Do you hate anyone?' Fowler's question was courteous, interested.

Hugh paused for a moment. Dougie thought he wasn't considering the answer. It was clear he had that immediately. He was wondering whether he should share the information with them.

'Yes,' Hugh said at last. 'I hate my father. I always have.'

He reached out and Dougie thought he was planning to spin the bottle again, though surely it was Fowler's turn to be the victim and there was no need. Instead Hugh picked up the bottle and set it upright on the floor beside him.

'That's enough,' he said. 'It's time to go to bed.'

'Hey.' Fowler looked round at them all. 'What

about me? Don't I get a go?'

'We're not interested in you.' Hugh sounded like a spoilt toddler. 'We don't care what you have to say.'

15

As soon as it was light Dougie was at Golden Water to check that the swan was still there. He'd left Hugh asleep. The boy's mobile phone was on the table by the side of his bed, set to silent, but it had vibrated just as Dougie was getting up. Dougie had looked at the caller ID, thinking it might be a birder he knew wanting more information. *Dad*, the display read. The father Hugh claimed to hate. The father who'd paid for his travels and his smart school and was probably subsidizing his stay in the North Light. *Spoiled brat*, Dougie thought again.

The clouds were higher, less dense, and the wind wasn't quite as strong: the water on the pool was ruffled but not as choppy as the previous day. The swan was at the east side of the pond. He saw it immediately and tried to decide what he thought about that. Was he pleased that the waiting birdwatchers still had a chance to see it? Or disappointed? Would the bird be devalued if it was seen by more people? He thought he was pleased. The worst scenario would be for it to fly on to Shetland mainland, where the birders would see it without having to make the pilgrimage to the Isle.

He attached his digital camera to his telescope and took photographs of the swan. The image stabilizers factored out the windshake. These would be good, clear photographs and there'd be a market for them in birding magazines. He'd make enough in fees for another trip to the island. On his way back to the lighthouse he met Ben and Hugh; they were walking south, presumably hoping to see the swan too.

'Hey,' Hugh said. 'You should have woken me up. I'd have come with you.'

It was as if the evening game, the strange episode of the spinning bottle, had never happened, as if this was another man altogether.

'The bird's still there,' Dougie said. He heard his voice sounding curt, the anger underneath it. He nodded at the two younger men and was just about to continue back to the North Light to breakfast when he remembered the phone call.

'Your dad rang. Did you see?' Dougie knew it was malicious, but he couldn't help himself. He was curious too. What was it with Hugh and his father?

'You didn't answer it?' Hugh almost spat out the words.

'Of course not. It was your call.'

* * *

Dougie was shocked when he got to the field centre to see Poppy in the kitchen, leaning against the workbench with a bowl of cereal in one hand and a spoon in the other. He'd almost forgotten about Maurice Parry and the girl, they'd been hiding out in the flat for so long. She looked younger than he remembered, less aggressive, almost attractive without the make-up and the stuff in her hair. He stared awkwardly for a moment, then he called through from the dining room: 'Are you OK?'

She nodded very quickly but she didn't speak. Perhaps her mouth was full of food. Jane came bustling through with tea and toast. She was wearing a long blue apron over jeans. Dougie thought she could have been working in one of those smart cafe bars in the city centre, where sometimes he took a woman from work. 'You're late,' she said. 'The others have all finished.' He wondered if she was having a go at him, but he didn't think so. 'Bacon and egg?'

He nodded. 'If it won't put you out. Sorry, I've been down to Golden Water to see the swan.' He poured himself a mug of tea, but remained standing, so he could talk to her through the kitchen door. She had bacon keeping warm, but moved a frying pan on to the cooker to do his eggs.

'It's still there then?' Jane splashed some oil into the pan, but looked at him and seemed genuinely interested. Poppy just stood, filling her face, saying nothing. 'I've already had some birders on the phone,' Jane went on. 'There won't be any flights today, but tomorrow looks good for the boat and the plane.' She cracked two eggs. The oil spattered and hissed. Dougie suddenly wondered if it would be possible to frighten the swan away. Maybe there was an islander with a gun, who might fire very close to it and scare it off the island. He thought of all the smug birders tipping out of the plane and running up to Golden Water, only to discover that the swan had just left. He felt himself smile, but tried to control his expression. After all, that wasn't what he really wanted.

Poppy set down her bowl and her spoon and walked out. Jane frowned but didn't try to stop her.

'Jimmy Perez wants to see you,' she said to Dougie. 'In the hall. Ten o'clock.'

'I can't tell him anything.' He sat down at the table.

'Can't you?' Jane set his breakfast in front of him. 'I thought Angela always used to confide in you.' She stood for a moment beside him, as if she wanted to make a point, or perhaps she was waiting for him to answer. But he didn't. He stuck his knife into the centre of the yolk and watched it spread out across the plate.

* * *

Dougie arrived at the hall early. Punctuality was one of his curses, inherited from his mother, who was anxious about everything and particularly about being late. Dougie had laughed at her when he was a boy. 'What's going to happen, do you think? Will you get locked up for missing the dentist's appointment by two minutes?' But now he understood how she'd felt, had the same sensation of panic when time seemed to pass too quickly or he was delayed and he was scared he might be late. Then it did feel as if the sky would fall in and his whole world would collapse.

Perez was there already. He'd set up a small table in one of the corners, close to the stage. The building smelled of wood polish and disinfectant. Dougie wondered if the hall had been cleaned specially for the occasion, if one of the island women had been in early with dusters and a mop, just to get it ready for Perez.

The detective waved him over. 'Would you like coffee? I can run to that.' He seemed more relaxed than he had in the lighthouse the evening before. Dougie nodded. He was always wary when people tried to make friends with him. Only Angela had got under his defences and look where that had led.

Perez pulled out the statement Dougie had written, sitting in the lighthouse common room. Then everyone had been so tense and Dougie had been infected by the mood. A sort of collective guilt, Dougie thought now. As if they'd all been responsible in some way for Angela's death. *We were all scared of her. Fascinated, but terrified at the same time. Because none of us could stand up to her*.

'Tell me about Angela,' Perez said.

Dougie hadn't been expecting that. He'd thought there'd be a list of questions, a bit like the script he prepared for the call centre staff.

'I mean, you must have known her quite well,' Perez went on. 'You've been coming to the island for a long time.'

'She was a very good birder.' It was what came first into Dougie's head. He realized it was the tribute Angela would have wanted. No, he thought. *She would have wanted more than that: brilliant. The best of her generation*. He didn't think he could go that far.

'But competitive,' Perez said. 'Not a team

player. Not an easy person to get on with. That's the impression I have.'

'She knew how good she was,' Dougie conceded. 'She didn't suffer fools gladly.'

'Did you like her?'

Dougie thought about that for a moment. Had he liked her? She'd been a kind of obsession, but that wasn't the same thing. 'We got on OK.'

Perez leaned forward across the table. 'You see, in this case motive is important. Any one of you staying in the centre had the opportunity to kill her. You all had access to her knife. It didn't have to be a premeditated crime. The knife was there in the bird room. But why would anyone do it?'

'She could wind people up,' Dougie said. He finished the coffee and carefully set the mug on the table.

'How do you mean?'

'She'd prod and poke until she got a response. She enjoyed making people angry. She thought it was a laugh.'

'And you think she just went too far? She provoked someone to kill her?'

'It could have happened that way,' Dougie said. 'Everyone was tense anyway. Stranded here because of the weather.'

'Did she ever make you feel like that? Angry.'

'Nah, I was never worth provoking. Fat Dougie. Too easy a target. She took me under her wing.' Dougie struggled to explain the relationship he'd had with Angela. 'You know how sometimes really fit women have an ugly friend. Someone who's not a threat. Someone to confide in. That's how Angela was with me. I was the ugly friend.'

'Even though you only came to the field centre once a year?'

Dougie hesitated. He wasn't sure how much to tell Perez. He'd decided to stick to answering the questions, not to volunteer any information, but the questions were more wide-ranging and personal than he'd expected. And he thought Jane had guessed how things were between Angela and him. She'd probably tell Perez anyway. 'We kept in touch,' he said at last. 'Email mostly. Sometimes by phone.'

'Didn't you resent it?' Perez asked. 'The way she used you, I mean.' When Dougie didn't answer at once, he added: 'Or perhaps you didn't feel used? You didn't mind being the ugly friend?'

'I knew I could never be anything else,' Dougie said. 'It was better than nothing.' He paused. He had never thought he'd tell anyone about his feelings for Angela. And in five minutes this strange islander with the dark hair had wheedled information out of him that he'd always kept secret. Dougie thought this was what it must be like to be under hypnosis. Perez said nothing. He waited for Dougie to continue and Dougie felt compelled to speak.

'I loved it when she phoned me. It was always late at night. I imagined her in the bird room, looking down over the cliffs to the sea. It was exciting. She knew she excited me. Perhaps she only did it when she needed a boost for her ego. I didn't care, even when she just wanted to talk about her marriage, other men. I was flattered that it was me she'd chosen to talk to.'

'Were there other men?'

Dougie nodded. He expected other questions, a demand for specifics, but Perez didn't follow that line of inquiry.

'What did she say about the marriage?'

'That Maurice was a sweet man but sometimes he bored her so much that she thought she would die. She wasn't sure she could stand living with him any more. 'And he's crap in bed.' That was what she said.' Dougie felt he should apologize for Angela. *She wasn't malicious, not really. Sometimes she said outrageous stuff just to make me laugh*. But he had the feeling Perez understood anyway.

'Do you think she was seriously considering divorce?' Perez asked.

'Nah! Maurice was just what she needed: someone to look after the domestics so she could spend all her time birding. He was too convenient to have around. And he was besotted with her. She knew he'd let her get away with anything.'

'Did you go and see her in the bird room the night she died?'

Dougie was astonished. Was the inspector some sort of magician? Could he read men's thoughts?

'Because it's the sort of thing a friend would do,' Perez went on. 'There'd been that scene with Poppy. Angela might have been upset. I thought you might call in to check that she was all right.'

'I heard her go into the bird room,' Dougie said. 'I couldn't sleep. I'd brought a bottle of whisky to the island with me. I don't drink much, but other people do.' *And you still feel the need to buy friendship, don't you, Dougie?* 'I took it down. I offered a drink but she didn't want one. 'Not for me, Dougie. You have one if you like.' I didn't stay for long. She was working. She made it clear I was disturbing her. If we had any sort of friendship it was always on her terms.'

'Did you have a drink? Was there a glass on her desk?'

'Nah, I didn't bother either. Like I said, I don't really like it.'

'Did she tell you what she was working on?'

'No. We talked about Poppy. Angela said if the wind didn't change soon, so she could get rid of the teenager from hell, there'd be a murder.' Dougie looked up at Perez. He didn't want the Shetlander to think he'd made some sort of crass joke, but Perez still focused on the notes on the paper before him.

The detective looked at him. 'Was she alive when you left her?'

'Yes!' Dougie felt himself flush. Would Perez assume that was a sign of guilt? He couldn't help himself. He always blushed like a girl when he was nervous. In the distance he thought he heard the sound of the plane coming in. Jane had said there'd be no flights today, but perhaps she'd got that wrong. Would it be full of birders? He wanted to be on the hill to meet it, to show the incomers his find.

But Perez still had questions: 'Were there any feathers in the bird room? Was Angela working with them?'

'That night? No.'

'Any time?'

Dougie knew what this was about. Ben had described the feathers in the hair. 'I don't understand why there should be. Unless there was some special study I knew nothing about.'

'Was Hugh asleep when you went back to the dormitory?'

'Yes.'

'Would you have heard him if he left the room in the night?'

'No,' Dougie said. 'It takes me a long time to get to sleep, but when I finally go off, I sleep like the dead.'

16

In the field centre kitchen Jane made a cottage pie. Easy to prepare and also Maurice's favourite. She'd do a veggie chilli for Ben. Jane was starting to worry about Maurice, who was still holed up in the flat and who hadn't really eaten anything the previous day. The community nurse had come up to the lighthouse the morning that Angela had been found dead and offered sedatives, but Maurice had refused to see her: 'I don't need her pills. I don't need tranquillizing. I don't want to forget my wife.'

Now, Jane wondered if she should get the nurse back. The woman was chatty, easy-going and she was probably the source of many of the rumours floating round the island about Angela's murder. She'd be happy enough to call in. But it was unlikely that Maurice would be persuaded to see her, and Jane didn't want to provide more fodder for the Fair Isle gossip machine. She put the pie in the larder to keep cool and phoned Mary Perez. Mary had been the island nurse before she became a full-time crofter and Maurice had always got on well with her. No reason why Jane shouldn't invite her to the North Light for coffee and try to persuade Maurice out of the flat to meet her.

While she waited for the woman to arrive, Jane went upstairs to make beds and tidy rooms. In the height of the season they'd employed a young woman from Belfast to do the cleaning, but now Jane looked after all the domestic chores. It wasn't too onerous this week. Two rooms: the small dormitory where Dougie and Hugh slept and the twin belonging to the Fowlers. The staff looked after themselves, though sometimes Jane took pity on Ben Catchpole and did his laundry.

The dormitory had the stuffy, sweaty smell of men living in close proximity, even though two of the beds were empty and the men were sleeping at opposite ends of the room. Jane straightened sheets and folded duvets, cleaned the sink, opened the sash window just a little to let in fresh air. She wondered if Perez had searched in here. Would that be the normal procedure in a murder investigation? Surely he'd have to get permission first and he certainly hadn't asked her if he could look round her room. She thought she would have known if he'd been there, looking through her drawers, prying in her things. Again she felt the investigation as a sort of challenge, an impersonal puzzle that had nothing to do with the reality of the murdered Angela. Jane had always been competitive and now she wanted to pit her intelligence against that of Perez, to come up with the identity of the killer before he did. She'd become an amateur sleuth, like a character in the detective stories she'd read as a child.

Of course it was presumptuous to think she might succeed ahead of the police, but she could get away with behaviour that would be impossible for the inspector. Who would know, for example, if she looked through guests' personal belongings? She had every right to be in their rooms.

The chest of drawers next to Dougie's bed contained underwear, a couple of folded T-shirts and a pile of socks. On top, next to a bottle of whisky that was three-quarters empty, there was a field identification guide to the birds of America. This, it seemed, was Dougie's only bedtime reading. Hugh's possessions were more interesting. They were still piled in his rucksack and in such an untidy and random way that he would never tell that anyone had been looking. A torn envelope file made of pink card had been slipped end on by the side of a tangle of clothes. Jane pulled it out. There was a moment's hesitation before she opened it. Really, what right had she to pry? But by now she was so curious that it was impossible for her to replace it before reading the contents. Besides, she had a sense that here, in the lighthouse, they were living outside the normal rules. She knew Hugh would be on his way down the island for his interview with Perez. She wouldn't be disturbed.

The file seemed to contain all Hugh's recently received correspondence. There was a bank statement still in its envelope. It had come in on the plane with Jimmy Perez and Fran, redirected from home; Jane had collected the mail from the post office that day. It was unusual for visitors to receive post and she recognized the envelope. It showed that Hugh had been seriously overdrawn until the week he arrived in Fair Isle, when £2,500 had been paid into his account. The indulgent parents bailing him out again, Jane thought. There were a couple of copies of his CV. Jane had worked in HR and picked up the lack of experience, the unexplained gaps, despite the creative description of his short adult life. She wouldn't have hired him as a tour leader. At the bottom of the file there was a handwritten letter from Hugh's father, saying he felt he had supported Hugh financially for long enough. They would continue, of course, to provide advice and support but Hugh would have to earn his own living. The letter had been written some months before. Why had Hugh kept it? And where had the £2,500 come from? Had Hugh charmed his parents into providing one last handout? Or had he actually done some paid work? She looked for a name on the statement but it seemed to have been paid in cash. It was something the police would be able to check easily enough and as she straightened she supposed she should pass this information on to Perez. But then she'd have to confess to snooping and the thought of it made her blush. Surely if the police were looking for a motive they'd look into their suspects' bank accounts.

The Fowlers' room was always orderly. They made their own beds each morning. Sarah's nightdress was folded on one pillow. There were matching tooth-brushes in the glass on the shelf by the sink. In the top drawer next to Sarah's bed there was a diary. Jane left it where it was — despite the temptation to read it, she thought that was a step too far. There was something about Sarah's closed expression, her jumpiness, which made Jane think there had been a tragedy in her personal life. They'd never visited Fair Isle before and it was unlikely to have anything to do with Angela Moore. It seemed that John had brought work with him. A laptop computer in a case leaned against the wall and a pile of files and books were piled on the bedside table. The files contained magazine articles, printed pages that looked like work in progress. After reading halfway down the pile Jane stopped. She couldn't spend too long here; she might be missed and although she knew Perez was interviewing the Fowlers, she couldn't bear the thought that she might be caught snooping. There was a catalogue for Fowler's bookshop. He'd called it something fancy in Greek, that meant nothing to her. *How pretentious*, she thought. She blinked at some of the prices being demanded for rare and out of print books. She supposed he must operate mostly with dealers.

Jane opened the laptop and switched it on. There was no password and she clicked on 'recent documents'. There was a letter from John pitching an article about the diet of wading birds for a scientific magazine. He seemed excited by a new study of mole crickets in saltpans in the Middle East. The rest of it made little sense to her. There was no Wi-Fi in the field centre so she couldn't check his emails, which was rather a relief. That would have seemed a terrible intrusion.

In the corridor outside the room a door banged. It was the fire door at the top of the stairs. Even though she had every excuse to be here, Jane felt the sort of glorious terror she'd not experienced since playing hide and seek as a child. What if the Fowlers had come back early from their interview with Perez and were on their way into the room? She replaced the computer in its case, wiped a cloth around the sink to justify her presence and left. The corridor was empty. It must have been Dougie or Hugh on his way to the dormitory.

Mary arrived just as Jane reached the lobby. She'd brought Perez's fiancée with her. Jane thought Perez and this Englishwoman made a strange couple; Perez was so straight and silent, very Shetland despite the dark hair and olive skin, and Fran so full of energy and questions, stylish in a bohemian sort of way. She could quite easily have been a colleague of Dee's, would have fitted in perfectly at one of the Richmond parties.

'You don't mind me turning up too?' Fran said now. 'I don't want to gatecrash.'

'Of course I don't mind. It's a treat to have someone new to talk to.' She thought she and Fran might become friends and the thought cheered her. She led them through to the kitchen, put the kettle on for coffee. 'I'll see if I can persuade Maurice to join us.' She looked at Mary. 'I'm worried about him. He's not eating and he hasn't been out of the flat since Jimmy took Angela's body away. I thought you might have a chat with him.'

Mary nodded and Jane saw she wouldn't have to explain her misgivings about calling in the regular island nurse. Mary had understood.

Jane knocked at the door of the flat and when

there was no answer she went in. The curtains in the living room were still drawn. She opened them and was almost blinded by a sudden flash of sunshine. The clouds had parted to let a biblical shaft of light onto the sea. She could hear the television in Poppy's room.

'What are you doing here?' Maurice's voice seemed unnaturally loud.

She started. Maurice had been sitting in one of the armchairs; perhaps he'd been there all night. He was wearing the same clothes as the day before.

'I did knock,' she said. 'I'm making coffee and thought you could use some.'

'No, thanks.' The words were aggressive, almost violent.

'You can't sit here all day. You'll make yourself ill and you've got Poppy to think about.' *I'm a bossy cow*, she thought. *I always sound like a middle-aged nanny*. She saw he was crying, that tears were rolling silently down his cheeks. She took a tissue from her apron pocket and wiped them away. He sat quite still like an obedient child having his face cleaned. 'Come on. A change of scene will do you good. Mary Perez is here. You've always liked her. But everyone else belonging to the centre is out on the island. You won't have to face them.' She took his arm and helped him to his feet, giving him no real choice. She felt the stiffness in his joints, thought again that he'd probably been there all night.

In the kitchen she poured coffee, cut a freshly made scone in half, buttered it and set it before him.

'The boat's going out tomorrow,' Mary said. 'James and the boys will be up later to get it into the water.' She turned to Maurice and asked gently: 'Will you go out with it?'

'I don't know.'

'Maybe it would be for the best if you and Poppy got away for a while.' Mary reached out to pour herself another mug of coffee. 'Is there somewhere you could stay?'

'Poppy will go back to her mother's,' Maurice said. Jane saw how clever Mary was, gently persuading him to consider the practical, to form constructive thoughts from the mess of emotion in his brain. 'They've already discussed it. Someone will come up to Shetland to collect her. I'll phone her this afternoon and make sure it's arranged.'

Fran had finished her coffee and was on her feet, looking out of the window down past the low wall all the way towards the havens. Jane thought Fran would rather be out there, walking along the beach, climbing out on the rocks at the point of Buness. She wouldn't get on with the endless round of social calls that made up island life, especially in the winter. She wouldn't settle here.

'Would Poppy like to spend the rest of the day with us, do you think?' Fran asked, turning back to the room. 'She might be glad of some time on the island, especially if it'll be her last day. That'll be all right, Mary, won't it? She could have lunch with us? It would get her out, away from the lighthouse for a while. It must be weird for her here. There's no one of her own age.'

'Yes,' Maurice said. 'I think she'd like that. I've been no help to her.'

'I'll go and ask her then, shall I? Is it just through here?' Before Maurice could reply she was away, down the corridor towards the flat. Jane wondered what Fran was up to. Had Perez set her up to this? Or was she playing her own game? *But you won't come to the solution before me*, Jane thought. Because an idea had come to her suddenly when she was talking to Maurice, like the flash of sunlight on the green waves.

There was a moment of silence in the kitchen. Mary turned back to Maurice.

'And what about you?' she asked. 'What are your plans? You must have friends who'd put you up?'

'I don't know. I lost a lot of friends when I married Angela. They thought I was mad: to leave my wife, to give up my job and move up here. They thought she'd put some sort of spell on me.'

'But they'd be glad to help you now,' Mary persisted.

'Now she's dead, you mean?' Maurice looked up and his voice was bitter. 'Oh, yes, there'll be lots of people glad that she's dead.' But he drank his coffee, picked up the scone and ate it.

The field centre phone rang. It was Perez to say the coastguard helicopter was on its way to take out Angela's body; he wondered if Maurice would like to be there to see her off. When Jane passed on the information Maurice shook his head. 'I couldn't,' he said. 'I can't face it.'

17

Perez stood at the South Light and watched the helicopter circle to land. He'd wondered, when the coastguard had first phoned, if his sergeant Sandy Wilson would travel in with it, but the helicopter had come from Sumburgh and the flight had been too quickly arranged to allow for passengers. At least Angela's body would be off the island. The forensic examination would begin. The plane should make it the following day. As the helicopter took off again and he closed his eyes tight against the wind from the rotor blades, Perez wished for a moment he was going with it. He had a sudden desperate desire to leave Fair Isle and the complications of this particular case behind.

On the way back to the community hall, he noticed that the weather was changing. The wind was still there but it was intermittent, dropping at times almost to nothing, and the sky was brighter behind the cloud. In the hall he had to wait twenty minutes for Sarah Fowler. She'd arrived at her appointed time, but after hearing the helicopter overhead when he was interviewing Dougie, Perez had sent her back to the field centre.

'Have a coffee. I don't know how long I'll be. I'm sorry.' He hadn't wanted sightseers when Angela's body was being lifted into the aircraft.

Now she hurried in with a tight little smile of

apology for keeping him waiting.

'We got a lift back down the island. The lighthouse is such a long way from everything else, isn't it?' Her husband stood at the door of the hall looking in and she turned and gave him a wave as if to say she was fine. Perez thought the man would have liked to come in with her, to sit beside her holding her hand while the questions were being asked, but Fowler turned and shut the hall door behind him. Throughout the interview, Perez caught glimpses of him waiting outside. He stood there patient and still, occasionally raising his binoculars to his eyes.

Inside, Perez sat opposite Sarah Fowler and tried to find a way to make her relax. He felt constrained; perhaps it was the name, but she reminded him too much of his first wife to push her for answers about Angela Moore's death. It wasn't her physical appearance — his Sarah had been softer and rounder — but the air of anxiety, unhappiness even, that she carried around her. Her tension was contagious and when he took up a pen to make notes he saw his own hand was trembling slightly.

'I'm sorry to have disrupted your holiday like this.'

She looked up sharply. It wasn't what she'd been expecting.

'You didn't commit the murder, Inspector. You're just doing your job.' The words sounded brusque but he thought she was abrupt only because she was so nervous. He understood why her husband felt the need to protect her.

'Has it been very awkward for you to extend

your stay? I presume you too have work to get back to. Or are you involved in your husband's business?' To Perez, this felt less like a formal interview than an attempt to make small talk with a reluctant stranger.

'Good lord, no! He hardly earns enough from selling books to keep himself.' She paused. 'I manage a Sure Start children's centre on a council estate in Bristol. Challenging but I enjoy it.' She paused. 'At least until recently, when things got on top of me. The management thing is rather stressful, though the children make up for the bureaucratic hassle. I have great staff. They'll cope without me.'

He stumbled to find something to say. The loss of a baby must have been almost unbearable for a woman who so much enjoyed the company of children. He found it hard to imagine this shy woman in charge of a bustling, noisy centre.

As if she was reading his mind she continued. 'They're used to managing without me. I've had a couple of months off work sick this year. Depression.'

'I'm sorry.'

'My husband and I have been under a lot of pressure recently, Inspector. This holiday was an attempt to mend the relationship, bring us back together. I wasn't sure coming to Fair Isle was a good idea. John's rather a figure of fun in the birdwatching world. He made a couple of highly publicized mistakes. Embarrassing when previously he had such a high profile. I know I shouldn't care what people think but I find all that more awkward than he does. But we'd enjoyed our stay very much until Angela died.'

She looked up at him. He saw she was waiting for the real questions to begin. Perez would have liked to know more about the events that had brought the couple to the island, but of course he should move on.

'Did you know Angela Moore before you came to Fair Isle?'

'I'd never met her,' Sarah said. 'I'd heard of her of course, seen her on the television.' She paused. 'I read her book.'

'What did you make of it?'

'It was interesting.' She paused again. 'If somewhat egocentric.'

'And Fair Isle,' he said. 'What do you make of that?'

She gave a sudden smile so unexpected that it changed the character of her face. 'It's beautiful now the sun's shining. You're very lucky to have been born here.' The sudden switch of mood disturbed him. He found it impossible to pin her down. How would he describe her to Fran, for example?

'Tell me what you thought of Angela Moore.'

The smile disappeared as she considered the question, frowning. Precision mattered to her. He wondered what her background was. Health? Teaching? Social work? 'She didn't take much notice of us. She was obviously involved in her work. Very charismatic, of course, as you'd expect from the television performance, but she wasn't very kind. I'd guess she could be a bit of a bully to the people who worked for her.'

'Did you realize she'd gone into the bird room to work after the party?'

'No. It was a lovely party and we felt honoured to be invited, but I did sense we were intruding on a private celebration. We went to bed straight after supper was served.'

'Do you have any idea who might have killed her?' Perez thought that of all the guests, this woman might have an idea. Her business was about watching people and understanding them. She wouldn't participate. She'd have sat in a corner throughout the dancing, watching the dynamics of the group playing out.

'As Hugh said, I suppose the most obvious suspect is Angela's stepdaughter. I could see her throwing an adolescent tantrum and lashing out with whatever was at hand. She seems rather unhappy, unpredictable.'

Perez said nothing. He thought it would suit all the adults if Poppy were found to be responsible. Most of them had disliked Angela Moore and that would be making them feel guilt as well as shock and sadness in their response to her death. A speedy resolution to the case would allow them to move on and feel better about themselves. He had nothing else to ask the woman and watching her walk away he felt the interview had been a failure. He wanted to call her back and start again, to ask her all the irrelevant questions that were rattling around in his mind. To understand her better.

* * *

Hugh Shaw had been waiting outside, smoking a cigarette. He must have seen Sarah Fowler leave the hall, but although he knew it was his turn to be questioned next he still waited to be summoned. Perez saw him through the open door and felt a sudden impatience. Was the young man's indolence, his leaning against the wall and finishing his cigarette although he knew the detective was waiting for him, an attempt to make a point? Or had the pose become so much of a habit that he couldn't help himself? Perez couldn't face sitting here, prising answers from this arrogant youngster who acted as if he owned the place. He grabbed his coat and rucksack and went outside.

'Come on. Show me this rare swan. We can talk as we go.'

Perez felt better just in the physical activity of walking. After the rain, the colours of the landscape — the grass and the muddy bog water and the lichen on the walls — seemed very sharp and bright. He led Hugh away from the road and towards the airstrip. He didn't want to meet anyone else from the field centre and he also wanted to prove to the man that this was his place. If Hugh came here every autumn for the rest of his life he wouldn't understand the island as well as Perez. Hugh wasn't at all disconcerted by the unusual interview technique. He seemed perfectly at ease as they made their way north over the hill and kept up with Perez stride for stride over the heather.

'Were you sleeping with Angela Moore?'

Again, perhaps he'd hoped to shock the boy,

to jolt him from the self-assured confidence that Perez found such a barrier. It didn't work.

'Well, we didn't do a lot of sleeping.' Hugh stopped and looked down over the island. They could see each of the croft houses, set out like a child's drawing. The clarity of the light made the perspective look wrong. Everything was flat and too close. Hugh took out another cigarette, the only sign that he might be nervous. 'How did you know?'

'Someone told me Angela liked pretty boys.'

'She picked me up the first night I was here.' Hugh had a smile, wide and welcoming, but fixed; there was somehow, even when he was talking, a shadow behind the words. It gave Perez the sense that he would take nothing seriously. 'I was last up in the common room. I'd been drinking all evening. I'd wanted to visit since I first heard about the Fair Isle field centre; it was so cool to be there finally. I felt like celebrating. And Angela wandered through from the flat and found me there. 'Let me give you a tour of the island.' It was a clear, still night, just before the westerlies started. Cold. There was ice on the windscreen. Unusual so early in the year, apparently. She took me up to the west cliffs and pointed out the lights of Foula right in the distance.'

'You had sex?'

'Twice that night. Once in the back of the Land Rover, parked on the airstrip, and once in an empty room in the North Light when we got back. It was three in the morning when she left me.' He paused, added with admiration: 'She was up at dawn to do the trap round.'

'And on other occasions?'

'Not every night. She'd made it quite clear we met up on her terms. She'd come and find me when she wanted me.' Hugh spoke without apparent resentment. He wasn't like Perez with his first lover; it seemed Hugh had no interest in forming a permanent relationship. The smile remained in place.

They'd reached the peak of a ridge and now had a view north. The only sign of habitation from here was the lighthouse and that was almost obscured by a fold in the land; only the tower and the lens were visible. Perez remembered when the lighthouse was manned: there'd been a Glaswegian couple with a little boy who'd come to the island school, a bluff retired merchant seaman as senior keeper and they'd all lived in the whitewashed buildings at the foot of the tower. Then the field centre trust had taken it over, raised the money to convert it. From this position he became aware again of how isolated it was.

'Did she come to find you?' Perez asked.

'Oh, yes. At odd times. Once in the middle of the day when everyone else was having lunch. We were in the dorm. Dougie could have come in at any time. But that was what she liked. The excitement. The danger.'

And you? Perez wanted to ask. *Did you like it too?*

But he could see that Hugh would have found the question ridiculous. Of course he liked it. Sex without complications. Wasn't that the dream of every young man? And why shouldn't a woman enjoy it too? Perez would have liked to discuss Angela's attitude to men with Fran. He suspected Fran would accept it without question. Very little shocked her. He found Angela's need for pretty boys not so much shocking as depressing. What did it say about her marriage? That it bored her? That she had to find her excitement elsewhere? Did that make Perez boring too, with his plans for marriage, a settled family? Would Fran think him tedious after a couple of years?

Now they were both out of breath and they stopped. Perez took a flask of coffee from a small back-pack and handed Hugh a slice of the sticky chocolate concoction that the islanders called peat. His mother had made a batch the evening before. They sat on a flat rock that stuck out of the heather, looked down on the bright blue sea and the wild white waves.

'Did Angela talk to you?' Perez asked.

'Of course we talked.' Hugh regarded Perez with patronizing amusement. 'We got on. We were good mates.'

'You didn't seem very upset by her death.'

Hugh shrugged. 'To be honest, it was never going to be a long-term thing, was it? I mean, I can't imagine we'd have kept in touch once I'd left the Isle. I'm sorry she's dead, but I can't pretend to be devastated. I can't bear shallow sentimentality.'

Perez wondered if that was what he was. Sentimental and shallow. A brief affair followed by no contact didn't fit his definition of being a good mate.

'Did she seem anxious about anything? Concerned for her own safety?'

Perez had expected an immediate flip remark, but Hugh considered the question. 'Something was bugging her,' he said eventually. 'The last couple of days she'd seemed tense, not her usual self.'

'What was the problem?'

'She wouldn't talk about it,' Hugh said. 'Told me it was none of my business. That was OK with me. I didn't want to pry. I thought the weather was getting her down. The lack of good birds. Or Poppy. The girl really got under her skin.'

'Did she discuss her husband with you?' Perez looked out over the blustery water. The air was so clear that he could see Shetland mainland, the outline quite sharp on the horizon, the first time it had been visible since they'd arrived on the island. He found the sight reassuring, a connection at last with the outside world. The next day the boat would go out and Vicki Hewitt and Sandy Wilson would come back in with it. He would no longer be working alone.

'Oh, Maurice wasn't bothering her,' Hugh said with a little laugh. 'Maurice would let her do whatever she wanted as long as she stayed married to him.'

'He knew about her affairs?'

'Probably. Or didn't look too hard at what she was doing because he didn't want to know. As I said, she resented Poppy being here. I think it was the first time Maurice had ever stood up to her. Angela had said the autumn was a bad time for the girl to visit — after the seabird ringing it was her busiest time. He'd insisted, said his daughter had to come first for a change. Angela was shocked. She usually got her way. But I'm not sure that was what was worrying her. It was only temporary, after all. Eventually the wind would change and the girl would get out.'

Hugh stood up and brushed the crumbs from his jacket. 'I thought you wanted to see this swan.' He turned on the inevitable smile and walked very quickly down the bank towards Golden Water. Perez had almost to run to catch up with him.

The swan was on a shingle beach at the side of the pool. It looked to Perez like any of the swans that came into the island in long skeins in the winter. 'Show me what all the fuss is about,' he said again.

Hugh set up his telescope on a tripod and let Perez look. 'It's the black beak that's important. That and the American ring, which proves it hasn't escaped from a collection somewhere.' He straightened. 'There'll be hundreds of birders in Shetland mainland waiting to come here to see it.'

Perez had a sudden image of an invading army preparing for battle. How would a sudden influx of visitors affect the investigation into Angela Moore's murder? And was there anything he could do to prevent it?

'Will folk really go to all that effort?'

'Believe me,' Hugh said. 'People would kill to get that bird on their list.'

18

Fran found Poppy in her bedroom, plugged into her iPod. She was lying on the bed, still in pyjamas, staring up at the ceiling. The curtains were drawn, so there was little light, but Fran saw a pile of dirty clothes in the corner, a dressing table covered with girlie debris — make-up and bangles, long strings of black beads. When she saw Fran come in, Poppy took the plugs from her ears and sat up, but she didn't speak.

'How do you feel about getting away from here?' Fran stood close to the door. She didn't want the girl to feel crowded.

'Is the plane coming in?' The urgency of the question made Fran realize how miserable Poppy was. She was hiding out in the bedroom, just waiting to make her escape from the island.

'Not today. Tomorrow maybe. And the boat will certainly go in the morning. I meant getting away from the centre. I wondered if you'd like to spend the day with Mary and me.'

There was a hesitation. It took Poppy a moment to work through the disappointment that she wouldn't be leaving Fair Isle immediately. 'Sure,' she said at last. 'Why not?'

'I'll give you a minute to grab a shower, shall I?' The girl could certainly do with a good scrub. 'I'll wait in the kitchen with Jane.'

When Poppy emerged she was wearing jeans

one size too small and a long grey sweater. Her hair was still wet from the shower but she didn't look very much cleaner. She hadn't bothered with make-up and looked very young — an overweight child with an unhealthy pallor and poor skin. *But we all looked like that when we were growing up*, Fran thought. *Or we believed we did*.

She found herself thinking of Poppy as a slightly older version of Cassie. *She needs some fresh air, a bit of exercise*. 'We'll walk, shall we?' she said. 'We can meet up with Mary at Springfield for lunch. I need to stop off in the post office to buy some stamps.' And perhaps Poppy was too tired to object or perhaps she was glad for someone else to take decisions for her, because she followed Fran out of the lighthouse without speaking.

They walked for a while in silence. Poppy was hunched in her jacket, her hands in her pockets.

'What's it like going out with the filth?' The question came out of nowhere just as they were approaching the turn in the road by the North Haven, Poppy's attempt to reassert herself or to provoke a reaction.

'I don't think of him as the filth. He's a good man doing a hard job.' Fran kept her voice easy. After all, some of her London friends had asked her the question in almost the same words. They lapsed again into silence.

Further south, Fran's attention kept returning to Sheep Rock to the east. It had been painted and photographed many times, but something about the shape, the sloping green plane at the top of the cliffs, the way it dominated that side of the island, attracted her to it nevertheless. When Perez was a boy, they'd grazed sheep there; the men had gone over in a small boat and climbed a chain to get on to it. Would she be able to bring something fresh to the image? She'd asked Perez what she should give Mary and James as a gift. 'Do a painting for them,' he'd said. 'They'd value that more than anything.' She'd found nothing suitable to bring. Now she thought she'd draw something that would give her take on Fair Isle, on the iconic Sheep Rock. It would have to be in this light, she thought. Very clear, after rain.

She had the picture in her head, was so engrossed in fixing it there, that Poppy's second question startled her. She'd almost forgotten that the girl was with her.

'They all think I killed Angela, don't they?'

'I don't know what they think.'

'I hated her,' Poppy said. 'I'm glad she's dead.'

'It must have been hard, your parents splitting up. You were still quite young.' *But not as young as Cassie when Duncan and I separated and she seems to have survived. I hope she's survived.* The perennial guilt of the lone parent.

Poppy stopped in the middle of the road. 'I didn't hate her because she made my parents divorce. I mean, that was a pain. I thought my mum and dad were happy. But it happens all the time. I could cope with it. There aren't many of my friends who live with both parents now. I just hated her.'

'Why?'

'She was a cow and she treated my dad like shit.'

Fran didn't know what to say. She was curious, of course. For the first time she could understand Perez's fascination with the detail of his work, this voyeurism into other people's problematic lives. But really, what right had she to pry? She didn't have the excuse of work. In the end, she didn't have to say anything. Poppy was already continuing.

'You know Angela only married my dad so she could get the job on the island? I mean, look at him. What else could she see in him?'

'He's kind,' Fran said. 'Understanding.'

'He's old and worn out. He wears corduroy trousers and cardigans. He's going bald.'

Fran grinned. Poppy caught her eye and began to giggle too. Fran thought it wouldn't be so bad having a teenage daughter. Mary drove down the road behind them. She stopped and shouted to ask if they wanted a lift back to Springfield.

'We're OK to carry on walking, aren't we?' Fran asked.

'Sure.' Poppy smiled again. 'My mother's always saying I need more exercise.' *Just like you*.

'Why were you so desperate to leave the island?' Fran asked. 'Was it just that you didn't get on with Angela?'

There was a pause. 'I used to love coming here when Dad first moved up. I mean, it was a sort of adventure. Mum would come with me on the train to Aberdeen and Dad would meet me there. We'd get the ferry. I was the youngest kid at home and always felt a bit left out, so it made me feel special to have that time with him. The overnight ferry, then the plane into Fair Isle. And Angela made more of an effort to get on with me then. She'd take me out ringing with her. Out in the Zodiac to count the seabirds.'

'What went wrong?'

Poppy shrugged. 'I guess I grew up. I could see how she treated my father. Like he was some sort of servant. He was a senior lecturer at the university, important in his own right, before he married her. She had no right to talk to him like that.'

'So you hadn't wanted to come to the Isle this time?'

'They wanted me out of the way.' Poppy's voice was becoming shrill.

'Who did?'

'My mother, the school. I was becoming a nuisance so they decided to banish me to the far north. Like it was some sort of Russian prison camp. Like I'm some political fucking prisoner.'

Fran didn't say anything. *This is what Jimmy would do. He'd wait. She's so angry that she'll just keep talking*.

A raven appeared overhead. Fran heard it croaking before she saw it and the noise made her shiver and remember past horrors, distracted her again from the girl ambling along beside her.

'They don't like my boyfriend,' Poppy went on. 'He's older than me. Different background. They pretend to be open-minded, but they look down on him because he gets his hands dirty when he works and he doesn't talk like we do.

Just because his parents couldn't pay for him to go to a smart school. They blame him because I lose it sometimes. But they're the ones who make me angry. They make me want to lash out.'

'Sometimes it doesn't hurt to spend a bit of time apart.' *God*, Fran thought, *I sound like the agony aunt from a tabloid newspaper*.

'I've been trying to text him,' Poppy said. 'And phone him. But he hasn't answered. He's probably found someone else.'

Fran saw this was at the root of the girl's misery. It had affected her more than Angela's death and her father's grief; she felt abandoned. She had been desperate to leave the island to find out why her older man was refusing to respond to her. When she was mooning in her bedroom, listening to depressing music and watching endless television, it was the man she was thinking of, not the violence of her step-mother's death.

'Angela knew,' Poppy said. 'She knew that Des hadn't been in touch. She laughed about it: 'What would a grown man see in you?' She didn't do it when Dad was around, but when we were on our own she'd pick away at me: 'Heard anything from the boyfriend yet? Still no news?' I think it drove me crazy. In the flat with the wind howling outside. Nobody to talk to. I dreamed of killing her. When it actually happened I could almost believe I'd done it, I'd wanted it so much. I was drunk and I couldn't remember much about the night of your party. Perhaps it was me after all.'

She turned so Fran saw her face and realized

how scared she was. She wanted a reassurance Fran wasn't able to give. Fran tucked her arm around Poppy's and they walked together into the shop. 'Chocolate,' Fran said in the no-nonsense tone she used to Cassie when she woke with nightmares. 'That's what you need.'

They sat on the bench outside the shop to eat the sweets they'd bought. 'Do you have any idea who might have killed Angela?' Fran asked. She couldn't help herself. 'You were there all day, every day.'

Poppy shook her head. 'She was in a weird mood all week,' she said. 'I mean, even weirder than usual. Something was freaking her out. She treated them all like she did me — poking and prying. It could have been any of them.'

* * *

Later Fran and Mary distracted Poppy with long games of Scrabble and Cluedo. They sat at the kitchen table and at last could hear the sound of sheep and herring gulls over the wind. James was at the Haven supervising the return of the *Good Shepherd* into the water. In the croft, Poppy shrank back into herself and there were long periods of silence. She could have been sulking. It seemed to Fran that the girl switched from a woman to a child and back again in seconds. She wondered how any parent could deal with these mood changes. She could see why Poppy's mother had needed a break.

At four o'clock Fran offered to drive Poppy back to the North Light. She hoped she might catch up with Perez there, even for a few minutes, and thought she was as star-struck about him as the girl was with her unsuitable boyfriend. But Poppy said she would walk.

'Are you sure? It's a long way. It'll be almost dark by the time you get there.'

'Like you said, I need the exercise.'

'I'll come with you then.' Fran was already on her feet.

'No,' Poppy said. 'I could do with some time on my own.' Suddenly she became almost gracious. 'You can understand how I feel. I've been trapped inside with all those people for almost a week. But thanks for today. It's been great. A real help.'

Fran went out to the track and watched her take the east road past Kenaby. A small dark figure, the hood of her cagoule pulled over her head, disappearing into the distance. The light was beginning to fade and just before Fran lost sight of her, she was tempted to run after her. Perhaps she should have insisted on accompanying her back. Perez might disapprove of Fran allowing her out alone. But Poppy needed the chance to make her own decisions and Fran went back into the house.

19

While the field centre staff and guests were having lunch, Perez walked down to the Haven to talk to his father. There was the habitual anxiety before the encounter. He'd grown up with the sense that he'd never match the older man's expectations. Big James wanted a son who was an islander, who understood the traditions and sensibilities of the place. Most of all he'd wanted a boy who wouldn't question his own authority.

The crew were lowering the boat from the slipway into the water. Perez would have been glad to help but the operation was over before he arrived at the jetty. Old school friends grinned up at him.

'You arrived just in time then, Jimmy. Are you volunteering to come out with us tomorrow?'

They knew he suffered from seasickness if the water was very lumpy. More teasing. Had he always been the butt of their jokes? It wouldn't have been because he was a Perez — here in Fair Isle that was a mark of honour — but because he was different, more thoughtful. They'd all been surprised when he said he wanted to join the police. It was the last thing they would have expected of him. He'd joined up for all the wrong reasons: not for car chases and action, or even a regular salary. He'd had a romantic notion of making things right.

'The body of the murdered woman went out

on the chopper,' Perez said, smiling at them, because really there was no malice in the teasing. 'No point me coming out with the boat. And you won't have to deal with her.'

'That wouldn't have caused us any bother. It's the living that make the fuss.'

Mary had made Perez sandwiches, enough to feed an army. He stepped onto the deck of the *Shepherd* and handed them round. His father was in the wheelhouse and though he waved to Perez he didn't come out to join them; even on the boat he kept himself apart. He was the skipper and they all knew it.

'What did you make of Angela Moore?' Perez leaned against the rail. The sun had come out again and he could feel the faint warmth on his face.

The young men looked at each other and then at James in the wheelhouse to make sure he couldn't hear. The skipper disliked lewd jokes and bad language.

'She knew how to have a laugh,' one said. Careful. After all, Jimmy Perez was police, also his father's son.

'That's one way of putting it.' Tammy Jamieson was the youngest crew member, a clown, easy-going, generous. Not given to discretion. 'She'd shag anything that moved. If he was fit enough.'

Then they were all jumping in with stories of Angela's wildness, the flirting and the drinking. They'd been talking about her among themselves since they first heard of the murder. There was the day the cruise ship put in and she disappeared below deck with the head purser. The politician who'd flown in for an hour to speak to a meeting of the island council, and was still in the North Light two days later, and most of the time spent in her bed. 'At least her husband was away that time.'

'Has she ever had an affair with an island man?' Perez asked.

Now they were careful again. They shuffled and giggled but they wouldn't speak.

He pressed them: 'There must have been rumours.'

'Oh, you know this place. There are always rumours.' And he could get no more out of them than that. It was already two o'clock and he had an appointment in the community hall with assistant warden Ben Catchpole. He might get Tammy on his own later. He might talk with a few beers inside him.

On the way south Perez thought about Angela. He hadn't realized the reputation she'd gained on the island. His father would call her a scarlet woman. Perez had known her as a celebrity, someone the place was proud to acknowledge as a resident. This was another woman he couldn't get a fix on. Sarah Fowler and Angela Moore: two unfathomable women. He was losing his grip. He thought maybe he should speak to Angela's family. They had no record of her mother's whereabouts, but there was a father, who'd brought her up. He lived on his own in Wales. The local police had informed him of Angela's death but Perez had no information about how he'd taken it. He wished he could have been there when the constable had knocked at the father's door, but what would he have asked? *Was your daughter always a sexual predator?* He made a mental note to track down the Welsh officer who'd notified Angela's father of her murder.

Ben Catchpole was waiting for Perez outside the hall. Perez saw the tall figure as he walked from the road. It was playtime in the school and the children were playing in the yard; a couple of the girls were swinging a long rope for the others to jump over. Perez waved to the individuals that he recognized. They giggled and waved back.

Inside the hall, he set the tape recorder on the table and asked if Ben had any objections. The man shook his head. Then Perez realized he was terrified, so scared that he was almost frozen and could hardly speak.

'How long have you been working at the North Light?' Factual, unthreatening.

'This is my third season.'

'Isn't that unusual?' In Perez's experience most of the assistant wardens just stayed for one year. He looked at Ben's statement. Although he looked so young he was nearly thirty. 'I mean, it's only seasonal employment. Aren't you looking for something more permanent?

'You think I should be settling down, Inspector?'

Perez didn't answer and after a pause Ben continued: 'I grew up in a weird kind of family. I mean it didn't seem weird when I was growing up, but it was different from other kids'. My mum was one of the Greenham women and she couldn't settle to domesticity when she left the Common. There was always a battle to fight, strangers coming to stay, discussions into the night about politics and justice and the environment. I suppose for me communal living seems kind of normal.'

'I've checked your criminal record. You were found guilty of criminal damage. Lucky not to get a custodial sentence, according to the notes. That was here on Shetland?'

Ben must have been expecting the question, but still he hesitated before answering. 'It was the anniversary of the *Braer* disaster. You know, the tanker that went aground at Quendale, leaving a slick of oil miles wide?'

Perez nodded. The disaster had made national news for weeks. Shetlanders had made a fortune out of the visiting media.

'Nothing had changed! I mean, still people don't take environmental issues seriously. I broke into the terminal at Sullom Voe.'

'And did thousands of pounds' worth of damage to oil company property.' Perez had been working in the south at the time, but the Shetland police had still been talking about it when he joined the service there.

'How much damage did they do to Shetland wildlife?' Ben sat back in his chair, not really expecting an answer. 'My mother came to court. She'd never been so proud of me.' Perez couldn't tell what he made of that. Would he have preferred a more conventional mother?

Perez slid Ben's written statement across the table.

'Is there anything you'd like to add to this?' Perez asked.

'I don't know what you mean.'

'I think you were close to Angela. She was more than just your boss, wasn't she? Yet you don't mention that in the statement.' For a moment Ben just stared at Perez and it seemed he would maintain the poise, the pretence at confidence. Then he seemed to lose control of the muscles in his face. It crumpled. He screwed up his mouth and frowned like a child trying not to cry. Perez went on. 'Why don't you tell me about it?'

'I can't stop thinking about it,' Ben said. 'Finding her in the bird room. At first I thought she'd fallen asleep there. She worked so hard that sometimes that happened. I'd go into the bird room before starting the morning trap round and find her still in front of the computer. I haven't been able to sleep since she died.'

'That isn't quite what I asked you.' But Perez saw now that Ben would talk to him. The strain had come through pretending he didn't care too much what had happened to the woman. 'Tell me about your relationship with Angela.'

'I worshipped her.'

And suddenly Perez saw himself as a schoolboy, intense and passionate, following his German student around the island, declaring his devotion. 'What did Angela make of that?'

'I expect she thought I was pathetic, ridiculous, but I didn't care.'

'Did she say you were pathetic?'

'No, she called me sweet.' Ben spat out the word.

'You had sex with her?'

Ben flushed suddenly and dramatically. 'Yes!' Then, forcing himself to be honest: 'Though not so often recently.'

'She had sex with other men in the field centre too. And not just in the centre. Visitors, islanders even.'

The assistant warden didn't answer.

'How did that make you feel?'

'I didn't have the right to feel anything,' Ben said. He seemed to have composed himself. Perez thought he had been through the same argument in his head many times. 'I didn't own her, I couldn't dictate how she behaved with other men.'

'That's very rational,' Perez said.

'I'm a scientist. I am rational.'

Perez wanted to laugh out loud. There was nothing rational in this infatuation.

'When did it start?'

There was a beat of hesitation. 'My first season. I couldn't believe it. I'd never met anyone like her.'

'You hadn't met her before you started work at the field centre?'

Ben stared directly at him. 'No. Where would I have met her?'

'Is she the reason you keep coming back?'

'No!'

'Where did you get together? It must have been hard in the lighthouse, with other staff and visitors about.'

'In the Pund. That was our place.'

Perez nodded. The Pund was a ruined croft

house. Once it had been set up as a bothy for campers, with a loft bed. Aristocratic naturalists had stayed there before the war but it had fallen into disrepair and was no longer used. It would be a romantic place for an illicit meeting and he could see how the young man would love the excitement of hiding away there, the sun slanting through the gaps in the roof, the charge of expectation when he heard Angela approaching.

'You do know she was sleeping with Hugh too?' he said.

'He dropped hints.' Ben kept his voice unemotional. 'There have been other visitors and Hugh was her type.'

'You didn't discuss it with him?'

'Of course not! None of my business.'

Perez had a picture of life in the North Light in the week running up to Angela's death. The wind and rain making people feel trapped inside the building. Angela manipulating events for her own amusement, playing the young men off against each other, fuelling Poppy's resentment, suggesting that Jane wouldn't be welcome to return to the isle the following year. And Maurice? How would he have reacted to the mounting tension, to Angela's games? Would he have welcomed them as one way of relieving her boredom, of ensuring that she would stay married to him? Perez thought the situation must have been intolerable.

'Do you know which of the islanders was her lover?'

'No!' Ben was shocked. 'It wasn't something we discussed. She would have hated me prying.'

He paused. 'If I'd asked about anything like that, she would never have seen me again.'

'Was Angela undertaking a particular study at the moment?'

'She was writing up the summer seabird census. I don't think there was anything else.' Ben frowned. How was this relevant? He seemed almost to resent the conversation moving away from his affair with Angela. He longed for the opportunity to talk about her.

'Anything involving the collection of feathers?' Perez asked.

'You're thinking about the feathers in her hair?'

'I wondered if they'd have been in the bird room already.' *Otherwise the murderer must have brought them with him*, Perez thought. *And why would anyone do that? What sort of point was being made?*

'I don't think so. I can't remember seeing them. But that doesn't mean they weren't there. Angela was quite private about her own research. She was paranoid about people stealing her ideas, getting into publication before her.'

'What could she hope to prove through a study of feathers?'

Ben shrugged. His interest was only marginally engaged. He was still more concerned about his own feelings. Perez thought how self-absorbed some people were. How they liked to create dramas with themselves playing the leading role.

'An analysis would prove identification,' Ben said. 'Through DNA. You can also get an idea where a bird might have come from. That's to do with trace elements found in the environment.'

There was a moment of silence. Perez found his concentration slipping. He looked around him. The hall was the place for wedding parties. He imagined bringing Fran back here as his wife for the traditional 'hame-farin'. She'd be wearing the dress she'd worn for the marriage ceremony — that was the custom. The place would be decorated with flowers and balloons, a big banner across the stage: '*Jimmy and Fran*'. There'd be music and dancing. *I wanted to marry her from the minute I saw her*. That idea was new to him and the sudden realization took his breath away. He didn't think he'd ever be able to say the words to Fran. She'd laugh at him. *Shallow and sentimental*, he thought. *That's me*.

'Why were you so scared to talk to me?' he asked. 'You were scared?'

Ben shrugged again. 'It was the waiting. It felt like waiting for an exam to start. I've never been good at exams. I nearly passed out before my viva.'

'Is that all?'

'I thought you must have found out about us. About her men. I suppose I have a motive for murder.'

'Jealousy?' Perez asked. 'Were you jealous?'

'Horribly.' Ben's initial fear had quite gone. He was almost cheerful. *Have I missed something?* Perez wondered. *What was making him so worried, so guilty?* Ben went on: 'I'd have killed Hugh Shaw if I'd thought I could get away with it. But not Angela. I'd never have harmed her.'

20

Perez remained in the hall after Ben Catchpole had walked away; he was thinking about Angela. Her mischief, her games, her meddling with the emotions of the men in the field centre, all these could explain the outburst of violence that had led to her death.

What am I saying? That she asked for it? The idea shocked him. He'd always been dismayed when colleagues suggested that victims, especially women, had contributed to the crimes against them. But he was curious about Angela Moore and he wanted to understand her better. He tried to picture the woman he'd met at island functions. He'd never had the sense that she was flirting with him. Although she'd been lively and confident, he'd never been attracted to her, and he found it difficult to explain Ben Catchpole's infatuation or to see how she caused such chaos in the lives of the men in the lighthouse.

Perhaps I wasn't her type. Too old. Too boring. Despite himself he felt a sting of envy.

After a couple of calls he tracked down the home number of Bryn Pritchard, the officer who'd notified Angela's father about her death.

'He's the community plod,' the station sergeant in Newtown had said. 'Been there for years. No ambition. But he knows the place like the back of his hand.'

The phone was answered by a woman. She

put her hand over the receiver, but still Perez could hear her shouting. 'Bryn, it's for you. Work. Sounds like a foreigner.' A voice like a foghorn.

Bryn would have stayed chatting all day. At one point his wife must have brought him a drink, because Perez could hear him slurping in the occasional gap when Perez could insert a question.

'They're not local, not really. They moved to the village when Angela was eleven or twelve. There never was a mother. At least, I suppose there must have been once, but we never saw her. Gossip had it that she ran off because the prof was such a difficult bastard to live with, but that could have been speculation. There was a lot of speculation because nobody could find out what had really gone on. They didn't mix. Angela didn't go to school, for instance. The prof taught her at home. Not that unusual here with English families, home schooling. We tend to attract the hippy dippy crowd.' He paused for breath, a gulp of tea.

'The prof?'

'That's what he was. A professor. Or had been before he retired and moved out to live with us. Professor of biological sciences at Bristol University.'

'He must have been quite old then, to be bringing up a daughter of that age.' Perez tried to imagine what that would have been like for the girl. Cooped up in a house with an elderly academic. No friends of her own age.

Bryn had his own opinions about that. 'Archie

Moore was about fifty-five when they moved here. It wasn't right. I don't know what the education welfare were thinking about allowing it. How could he provide for the needs of a teenage girl? Because that's what she was when she left home. But they said she was receiving balanced schooling. She took all her exams a year early, passed with some of the highest marks in the country. But education isn't only about exams, is it? He pushed her and pushed her. Not just in her school work, but music too. He sent her to Newtown for piano lessons and if you walked past in the evening you'd hear her practising. She didn't have any sort of social life, not even with the other home-school kids. I don't know where he bought her clothes for her but she dressed like a middle-aged woman. Who knows what sort of monster he was creating?'

Perez didn't answer and Bryn continued: 'No wonder she went a bit wild in the end.'

'Wild in what way?'

'It was the last summer, before she went off to college. She hung around with some of the bad lads in the village. The girls never seemed to take to her. There was nothing criminal, not that she was ever done for, at least. But drinking. Probably drugs. One night Archie reported her missing; she turned up a couple of days later with a hangover, looking as if she hadn't slept for a week.'

'Where had she been?'

'She would never say. But with a man. There were rumours that she went off early to college so she could get an abortion.'

Perez didn't ask how Bryn could know that. He too lived in a community where personal information leached into the public domain.

'Did she come back to visit her father?' Perez asked. 'In the university holidays? After she graduated?'

'No.' There was a moment of silence. 'That was the last time anyone here saw her, when she went off to uni on the coach from Newtown. I always thought that was very hard. I don't like the man, but he'd done what he thought was best for her. Given her an education. She'd never have had all those chances without him. He didn't even get invited to her wedding.'

'Do you have any thoughts about why she might have stayed away?'

Another silence. 'You're thinking abuse?' Bryn said. 'Is that the way your mind's working?'

'I did wonder.'

'So did I,' Bryn said, 'at the time. But no, I don't think that was the reason she didn't come home. She didn't suffer the sort of abuse you're thinking about anyway. She had nothing to bring her back. There was no more to it than that. The old man's turned into a bitter old soak. He props up the bar of the Lamb from teatime to closing, talking to everyone who'll listen about his famous, ungrateful daughter. She had no real friends here. She probably just put the place out of her mind.'

'How did he take the news of her death?'

'I went to see him as soon as I heard. It was about lunchtime, so at least he was almost sober. He lives in the same house where he'd brought up the girl. An ugly sort of bungalow on the edge of the village. It must have been built in the fifties — you'd never get planning permission for it now. Lily Llewellyn goes in every now and again to clean, but you'd never think it. Such a mess. He can't throw anything away. Piles of newspapers all over the living room. And he still seems to be carrying out experiments. The kitchen bench is covered with jars and test tubes, with stuff growing inside. There's a microscope. No telly. They never had a telly.'

Perez thought if Sandy Wilson were doing this interview he'd be hurrying Bryn along, urging him to come to the point. But Perez was grateful for the detail. He could see the house in his head, was with Bryn when he stepped into the room, cleared a seat so he could sit down, felt the stickiness underfoot.

'I just told him straight,' Bryn said. ' 'Angela's dead. It seems as if she was murdered.' He sat there looking at me. He was a big man in his day and he's still tall, though he's lost a lot of weight. Then he started crying. 'I thought one day she'd understand what I'd done for her,' he said. 'I thought she'd be grateful. Now she won't have the chance.' He'd always been a hard man. No compromise with him. Angela was his project, after he gave up the university. It made me a bit queasy watching the tears. But I had the feeling he was crying for himself and not for her.'

'Didn't he want any details?' Perez would have expected a scientist to need to know the facts of his daughter's death. He had brought his child up to be rational. Even in old age, wouldn't he need the facts to hang on to?

Bryn hesitated for a moment. 'He just said he wasn't surprised. 'She wasn't the sort to live a quiet and easy life. She was her father's daughter, after all.''

Perez switched off his mobile. Was this what he'd expected? An eccentric upbringing for Angela. Loveless, driven. It was hardly surprising that she hadn't turned into a woman who made friends easily. She'd had no practice as a child. He tried to imagine what it must have been like for a girl growing up in a small community, looking different, sounding different. No mother. No television. If there were other kids around, she'd be the subject of their jokes and their gossip, an easy target, a scapegoat. Hardly surprising that she'd developed other ways of getting attention and affection. But he wasn't sure the conversation with Bryn Pritchard brought him any closer to explaining her violent death.

Through the window he saw a couple of mothers waiting in the schoolyard for the nursery children to come out. Angela's mother would surely have been younger than Archie Moore. Where was she now? Had she followed her daughter's career at a distance, seen the news reports of Angela's death? Perez hit the number for the police station in Lerwick and got through to Sandy Wilson.

'Are you all set for coming into the Isle tomorrow? Make sure you're at Grutness early. I've asked the boys to take the *Shepherd* out ahead of time to bring you back. There's a rare bird on the island and I don't want the place swamped with birdwatchers.' He'd hoped to outwit the reporters too, though if the wind continued to drop they'd have no problems chartering planes. 'There's something I want you to do this afternoon. I need you to trace the deceased woman's mother. They've had no contact as far as we know since Angela was eleven. The father was a professor at Bristol University so you could start there.'

Sandy yawned. Perez knew this was the sort of task he hated. The folks on the other end of the phone could never understand his accent and anyone with a higher education intimidated him. He'd grown up a bit in the last couple of years but he still had a low boredom threshold.

Perez felt the need to explain why he couldn't track down Angela's mother himself. 'I'm going back to see Maurice. I'll ask if he knows where the woman might be, but you've got access to records I won't have.'

'Is it so important to track down the mother? I mean, she could hardly have committed the murder, could she? Not if she wasn't there. You said yourself it had to be someone staying at the field centre.'

'Surely she has a right to know her daughter's dead!'

But in terms of the investigation, Perez thought Sandy was probably right. This was a waste of time, a distraction activity. He didn't want to admit to himself that he had no idea who had killed Angela Moore. But Maurice had lived with Angela for five years. He'd put up with her affairs, and continued to adore her. He must understand her better than anyone and with Poppy away from the North Light at Springfield with Fran and Mary, Perez at last had the chance to talk to him on his own.

21

Perez bumped into Maurice Parry in the field centre kitchen. The man showed no surprise at seeing him there. He looked grey and gaunt.

'I was looking for Jane,' Maurice said. 'I don't suppose you've seen her. Perhaps she's in her room. Dinner's all ready but I can't find her. There's nobody here to ask. They all must be out.' He seemed put out that Jane wasn't available for him. He looked around like a petulant child, demanding attention or reassurance. Perez found it hard to remember the competent, affable man who had run the centre.

'Is there a problem?'

'No,' Maurice said. 'Not really. I was hoping she might help me pack for Poppy. I'm sending Poppy out on the boat tomorrow and I thought I should get her stuff together. She went out with your fiancée and she hasn't come back yet.' Again there was a faint tone of complaint as if he blamed Perez for his daughter's absence.

'You're not planning to go south yourself?'

'No,' Maurice said. 'I'm not sure where I'd go. This is the only home I have now.' He looked around the room. 'I suppose there are friends who'd put me up, but I'd be terrible company.'

'Can I help?' Perez was a decent packer, better than Fran at least. And it would give him the chance to talk to Angela's husband in an informal way.

But Maurice seemed unable to make a decision. 'Perhaps I should leave it to Poppy. It doesn't really matter if something gets left behind and she should be back soon to do it herself.' He looked vaguely at Perez. 'Perhaps you'd like some tea?'

'Yes,' Perez said. 'Tea would be great.' He expected Maurice to take him through to the flat, but the man turned round and switched on the kettle there. Perhaps he saw the big lighthouse kitchen as neutral territory. Perez thought Maurice might have questions about the investigation; instead this was the sort of polite conversation you'd have with an acquaintance, about the weather forecast and the prospect of a quiet spell at last. The tears and depression that had formed his first response to the murder had given way to a mindless focus on small details. Another way, Perez supposed, of coming to terms with Angela's death.

'I was wondering if you could help me fill in some gaps in Angela's background.' Perez interrupted Maurice's description of the high-pressure system that was due to settle over German Bight.

There was a moment of shocked silence. Maurice dropped teabags into mugs.

'I don't know much about her life before she took up with me,' he said at last. 'She didn't get on with her family.'

'She must have told you something about them.'

'Her father was a scientist. An academic. He had strange ideas about education and taught her at home instead of letting her go to the local school.'

'Do you know why her parents separated?'

'Angela never discussed it,' Maurice said. 'She resented her mother leaving, said she grew up feeling abandoned.'

'How did she get on with her father?' Perez asked. He cupped his hands round the mug of tea.

Maurice shrugged. 'They were very close when she was young, but later Angela found him controlling. I had the impression he was a bit of a bully or at least that he tried to live his life through her. When she left home to go to university they lost contact.'

'That was her decision? Not to see him again? It seems extreme, especially if they got on together when she was young.'

'I didn't mind,' Maurice said. 'It was Angela I cared about. I hadn't married her family.'

'What about her mother? Did Angela keep in touch with her?'

'I don't think so.' Maurice opened a tin of Jane's ginger biscuits and handed one to Perez. 'She never talked about her and I didn't ask.'

* * *

Walking back towards Springfield, Perez realized that the wind had dropped almost to nothing and suddenly it seemed very cold. Maurice had been right about the high pressure. The sky was clear and that night there would be a frost. What weird weather they were having this year! Storms followed by this sudden chill. The light was fading quickly. Soon it would be the shortest day, followed by the madness of Up Helly Aa, Lerwick's fire festival. Another Shetland winter. He'd first met Fran in midwinter and liked to think of her in the snow, flushed with the effort of pulling Cassie on a sledge up the bank to the Ravenswick house.

On impulse he turned away from the road by the Feelie Dyke and walked west towards the Pund. If Angela took her lovers there perhaps it might hold other secrets, a diary perhaps, information about her parents, scraps of her life that she hadn't wanted Maurice to see. Perez imagined how *he'd* feel if he'd given up on his mother and father, deciding he wanted to have no more to do with them. There were times when he'd thought that would make his life less complicated, but he knew he could never turn his back on them. Guilt was part of his make-up, part of what his first wife had called his emotional incontinence. There was a connection he had no way of breaking. He felt miserable if he left his mother's phone calls unanswered even for a day.

The Pund was even more dilapidated than he remembered. Once it had been solid and weather-proof, lined with wood. There was still a loft bed reached by a ladder, but the place smelled damp. He pushed the door open. By now it was too dark to see much inside and he didn't have a torch. In the last of the daylight coming through the open door he saw there was a candle stuck in a grubby saucer on a makeshift table made of a packing case. The place looked like a child's den. Next to the saucer sat a box of matches. He lit the candle. In the first flare of the match being struck, he picked up details — there was a fire laid in the grate: white twisted pieces of driftwood and a few lumps of coal; a rack of wine stood in one corner, two glasses and a biscuit tin on a shelf. The candle caught and the light became more even. He stood in the centre of the room and looked around.

Again he had the impression that this was a Wendy house, a space for playing. The floor had been swept. There was a jam jar containing dried flowers on the windowsill. But he didn't think the island children had been in here. This had been Angela's room, the place where she escaped from field centre life, where perhaps she had lived out her fantasies with her young lovers. It threw a new perspective on the woman. Here, he saw, she had been domestic, even romantic.

Perez walked around the walls, carrying the candle with him, looking for a hiding place for her treasures. The Angela who was a media star and warden of Fair Isle field centre would have nothing to do with sentiment or nostalgia, but the woman who had created this space might have kept mementos from her past. Perez hoped for a letter from her mother. It still seemed inconceivable to him that the mother had abandoned her daughter entirely. But there was nothing. He tapped on the panels, thinking he might find a space between the stone wall and the panelling, was excited when he came across a polished wooden box hidden behind the wine rack. But when he opened the lid, there was only a pair of silver earrings and a plain silver bangle. Presents perhaps from one of the lovers.

He began to climb the ladder into the loft, struggling to keep his balance with the candle held in one hand. He'd brought Sarah, his wife, here before they were married. It had been summer, a mild day with the scent of cut grass and meadow flowers coming through the open door. He'd thought he would never love anyone else in his life. They'd covered the old straw mattress with sheepskins and lain there for most of the afternoon, stroking each other, kissing and whispering. They hadn't made love there. Sarah was religious in an old-fashioned, matter-of-fact way and had asked that they might wait. He'd thought himself magnificently restrained in agreeing, but in fact the delay had only added to the excitement, to his view of her as the perfect woman. When sex had been allowed it had been something of an anticlimax. He hadn't been able to admit that at the time, even to himself. Certainly not to her.

There were still sheepskins on the bed. White ones and black ones, piled in profusion, more of them certainly than had been there when he'd spent the lazy afternoons here with Sarah. Perez saw them while he was still standing on the ladder. He reached in to set down the candle, so he could use both hands to climb into the loft. At the same time he saw the woman's body lying, as if in abandon, on the rugs, and the blood that had turned the sheep's wool pink, as if it had been dyed. He saw the small white feathers that covered the skin like flakes of snow.

Perez stood for a moment, so shocked by the scene in front of him that it was as if his hands were frozen to the ladder rungs. A draught caught the candle flame, made it flicker and then burn more brightly, and he saw the patterns of blood spatter on the wooden walls of the loft: at some point the killer had pierced an artery. This was quite a different murder. The first had been planned and calmly executed. This was wilder. If it had been committed by the same person, the killer was beginning to panic or to lose control.

22

Sitting at the makeshift table in the ground floor of the Pund, Perez made phone calls. His voice was abrupt and urgent. The colleagues on the end of the line hardly recognized it. The Perez they knew was relaxed and softly spoken. He didn't bark out orders or shout down their objections.

The first call was to Sandy. 'Is Vicki Hewitt in from Aberdeen yet?'

'Aye, she's ready for the boat in the morning.'

'I need you to charter a plane and get into Fair Isle now. Bring Vicki with you.'

'You'll not get a plane tonight.' Sandy would have liked the drama of the emergency flight; Perez could tell that. He just didn't see how it was possible. 'It's almost dark.'

'There's no wind to speak of and there'll be a moon. We'll light the airstrip. They'd do it for an ambulance flight.'

'What's the rush?'

'There's been another murder. I need the crime scene assessed by an expert before it gets contaminated. This doesn't look to me like the same sort of killing. This victim's been stabbed, but it's not such a clean job. More wounds. More of a struggle, I'd say, though the scene's been posed like the first time.' Perez paused for breath. 'And I want suspects properly interviewed. I can't do that on my own. I need you both here tonight. Within an hour if possible.'

Perez switched off his phone before Sandy could argue. He sat in candlelight. The candle was tall and fat. Occasionally a pool of melted wax threatened to douse the wick so he tilted it to pour out the liquid, but it would provide light for him until the plane came in. Then they'd have a generator and powerful torches, the equipment and the manpower needed to prevent another murder.

He phoned Springfield next, hoping his father would answer. He would need a team of men to light fires along the airstrip to guide in the charter plane and his father would organize that. Just now he didn't want to speak to Fran. She'd be full of questions and he wasn't sure what he would say to her. *You see, you get violence everywhere. Coming back to Fair Isle wouldn't protect us from that.*

Mary answered. 'Jimmy, we started tea without you. When will you be coming home?' Ordinary words that seemed almost blasphemous when he thought of the scene in the loft above his head. Before he could answer her she shouted: 'Fran, Jimmy's on the phone for you.'

'Hi, sweetie.' Her usual greeting.

He struggled to find words and her response to the silence was immediate. 'What's wrong?'

'There's been another murder.' It came out as a confession, as if it were his fault. *And of course it is*, he thought. *If I were better at my job I'd have prevented it.*

'Who?' she demanded. And before he could reply: 'It's Poppy, isn't it? I let her walk back to the North Light on her own. She wouldn't let me go with her.'

'No!' The last thing he wanted was for her to feel guilty. He could do that well enough for the both of them. 'No, it's Jane Latimer, the field centre cook.'

Another pause. No hysteria. 'I liked her,' Fran said at last. 'I wanted to know her better. I thought we might be friends. Is there anything I can do?'

'No. Stay in Springfield. Tell Mother to lock the door. Now I need to speak to my father.'

Perez explained to James what had happened and what he needed. 'You'll have to meet the folk from the plane and bring them up to the Pund. There'll be a lot of heavy gear, so sort out a vehicle to bring them as close as you can. Borrow the centre's Land Rover if you need to, but don't tell Maurice why you need it. I'll have to wait here. I can't leave the scene unprotected.'

'Would you like to meet them yourself? I could stay at the Pund for you, once I've sorted the team on the airstrip.'

For a moment Perez was tempted, but he'd broken enough rules already in the Angela Moore murder. If he'd been in a position to follow procedures perhaps the killer would already be caught.

'No,' he said. 'I have to stay here. But thanks.' It was the first time his father had wanted to participate in his work.

Perez's next call was to Rhona Laing, the Fiscal. She was still in her office. 'You've just caught me, Jimmy. I was on my way out. Dinner at the Busta House Hotel with a group of lawyers.' Her voice was posh Edinburgh, the tone as ever faintly accusatory.

'I've arranged for an emergency flight into Fair Isle this evening. I thought you might want to be on it. There's been another murder.'

'That sounds expensive, Jimmy. Have you cleared it with Inverness?' Thinking of the politics before even asking the identity of the victim.

'I thought I'd leave it until the plane was on its way. Then they couldn't object.'

She gave a little laugh. 'My, my, Jimmy. You're learning. I'm a great teacher, am I not?'

* * *

Still he sat. It was quite dark outside now. He would have liked to go back to the loft, to look again at Jane Latimer, lying on her bed of sheepskins. Although the image was printed in his brain, perhaps there was a detail he'd missed. Something that would point immediately to the killer. The thought tantalized him. He was a patient man but it was driving him slightly crazy to be sitting here, in the strange cold light, inactive, nothing to do but wait. If he were to climb the ladder he might contaminate the scene again with his fingerprints, the fibres of his jersey, his breath. This time things would be properly done.

He got up and stood at the door of the Pund and looked out across the hill. He couldn't see the airstrip from here. Earlier he'd thought he'd heard vehicles along the road past Setter, heading north. He imagined the island men working, building fires, lighting hurricane lamps, all under his father's supervision. The volunteer fire crew would be there; someone was always on duty when a plane came in and that would be even more important in these special circumstances. Dave Wheeler would be in charge of them. This was what Fair Islanders did best, pulling together in times of emergency.

The sky was quite clear and there was a halfmoon, a scattering of stars. He realized how cold he felt and he stamped his feet to bring back the life to them. *But not as cold as Jane Latimer*, he thought. And he pictured her again, like the Snow Queen, resplendent on her sleigh, resting on the sheepskins, covered with a dusting of feathers that looked like crystals of ice.

There was a red glow behind the dark line of the hill. The fires were lit and ready. Then he heard the plane's engine to the north and saw its lights approaching. He looked at his watch. It had been an hour and a half since he'd phoned Sandy. *Not bad*, he thought, with something approaching admiration. Sandy's drinking friends were in positions of power throughout Shetland. He must have called in some favours to get an aircraft out this quickly. The plane came lower. Perez could see the light in the cockpit and the silhouette of the pilot. Then it dipped out of view on to the airstrip and the engine stopped.

Perez went back into the croft house and tried to warm his hands by holding them close to the candle flame. It would take some time to unload the gear and bring it here to the Pund. But he felt as if the cavalry had arrived. He was no longer working alone.

Sandy arrived first, much sooner than Perez had expected, in Tammy Jamieson's van. Tammy was obviously keen to hang around — this was the most exciting thing to happen in Fair Isle since the Queen had visited in his parents' time — but Perez sent him away. Sandy was flushed with the success of getting the plane out to Perez's deadline: 'What a nightmare,' he said. 'Some reporters must have got wind of the fact that there was a flight coming into Fair Isle. They were waiting for us at Tingwall. I thought they were going to stand on the runway in front of the plane.' Tingwall was the small airport close to Lerwick from where the inter-island planes operated.

'Had they heard there was another murder?'

'No,' Sandy said. 'All the questions were about Angela Moore.' He paused. 'There was a film crew there from BBC Scotland. I might have my picture on the television tonight.' Perez thought Sandy wouldn't mind about that. He'd quite like the idea of being a celebrity, of his Whalsay relatives pointing him out on the evening news.

'Where's the Fiscal?' Perez knew the Fiscal would have flown in with them despite her dinner date. She was a control freak and she wouldn't resist the chance to take charge on the ground.

'She's coming up with Vicki Hewitt and the gear.' Sandy was interrupted by the roar of the plane taking off again. It climbed steeply above their heads before banking and flying north again. 'Your mate's van stinks of fish and she didn't fancy it. She wanted to know where she'll be staying tonight.'

'There'll be plenty of room at the North Light,' Perez said. 'She'll have to feed herself though. They all will. The cook's dead.' For the first time he began to consider the implications of the second murder. Surely now the field centre residents would insist on leaving on the morning boat. How would he keep a hold on the investigation if half his suspects disappeared to the south on the Aberdeen flight the next day? He thought Poppy should go. She was hardly more than a child and she needed her mother. She would be at home and under supervision. He'd talk to her this evening. The rest he'd invite to stay. He could hardly hold them here against their will, but he would make them understand that their leaving might compromise the case. It would look better if they remained where they were until the investigation was over.

The Land Rover headlights shone on the heather above them and they heard it straining over the rough grass. His father was driving. He got out first and helped the women from the vehicle, handing them down with a gesture that Perez found strangely gallant. The Fiscal was wearing a warm waterproof and walking boots, but she still managed to look elegant. 'Two women dead. What's going on here, Jimmy? I'm assuming the same killer?'

'Either that, or a copycat.' He explained about the feathers.

'Who knew about the feathers?'

'All of them. The assistant warden found the first body and word was out before I could stop him talking.'

'Any sign of sexual assault?' Rhona asked. 'That must have been your first thought.'

'No, in both cases the women were dressed and their clothing hadn't been disturbed.'

James was helping Sandy and Vicki carry the generator from the Land Rover. Although she was tiny, the CSI always insisted on pulling her weight. She'd strung crime scene tape from metal poles to mark a path into the Pund and now she and Sandy joined Perez and the Fiscal, leaving James to set up the lights. Vicki had made him wear a scene suit and bootees and Perez was aware of him, working in the shadow just inside the door of the ruined croft.

'Do you want a hand to set that up?' Sandy shouted over to James.

'No, no, I can manage fine.' The response sharp, as if Sandy were suggesting the task was too much for him. A couple of minutes later the Pund was lit from inside by a bright, white light.

'I have to get to the lighthouse,' Perez said to Rhona Laing. 'Each of the residents is a suspect and I haven't had the chance to talk to them yet. Do you want to come with me? We can leave Sandy here with Vicki and you can look at the scene in the morning when she's finished.'

Usually the last thing he would have wanted was to conduct interviews with the Fiscal sitting in. She made him nervous. But now he thought he could do with a different perspective. She was an educated incomer like most of the field centre residents.

James drove them north to the lighthouse. 'I've left my car there. I'll pick it up and go straight back to Springfield. What'll I tell Fran?'

'That I probably won't get back tonight and she's not to worry.'

23

Dougie had spent a lot of the day at Golden Water. The swan was still there. He'd already started writing his account of its discovery for *British Birds* and as the light had improved he'd taken more and clearer photographs. Of course there were other things at the back of his mind — anxieties about murder and the police investigation — but he'd always been able to focus completely when he was birdwatching. It was his usual means of escape.

Now the light was fading and he made his way back to the lighthouse. On the way he stopped three times to answer his mobile phone. There'd already been half a dozen missed calls when he'd been watching the swan. The north end of the island had very patchy reception. All the calls were from birdwatchers on the Shetland mainland, checking that the bird was still there, making plans for coming into the Isle to see it the following morning.

'I've been watching it all day,' he said. Jaunty, exaggerating too, of course: he hadn't spent all day at Golden Water. 'Mind-blowing views . . . Yeah, if you like, I can meet you at the plane and walk up with you.' He sensed a new respect in their attitude. He'd always be remembered as the guy who found the UK's first trumpeter swan. The storm and the wait in Lerwick would only add to the mythology.

It was quite dark when he got to the centre. He dumped his gear in the dormitory, then went to the common room and helped himself to a can of pop, putting the money in the honesty box, because nobody was running the bar. The place had a deserted feel and he realized that was because there was no sound coming from the kitchen. Jane usually had the radio on. Not music but talk and the discussion seeped through as a background hum into the common room. The quiet unnerved him and though he still felt awkward when he remembered the truth game, he was relieved when Hugh and Ben wandered through. Something about the empty lighthouse spooked him.

'We met up on the road north,' Hugh said. He caught Ben's eye. Dougie wondered why Hugh had felt the need to explain the meeting. Was there something conspiratorial in the way they looked at each other?

Again he felt like the fat boy in the playground, never invited to join a gang. He wondered what they'd been chatting about, suspected that there might have been jokes at his expense. Ben reported catching a few migrants on the trap round and they discussed the possibility of another rarity on the following day.

'I've done all the crofts at the south this afternoon,' Hugh said. He stretched as if the exertion had exhausted him. 'Nothing special but it's looking good for tomorrow. Especially if there's a bit of drizzle at dawn.'

It was the sort of conversation they would have had with Angela.

'How did you get on with Perez?' It seemed odd to Dougie that everyone was carrying on as if she hadn't been murdered, as if there wasn't a detective camped out in the hall conducting interviews.

'He made me show him the swan,' Hugh said. Dougie thought Hugh seemed almost jubilant. 'Really, I'm not sure how bright he is. Now the weather's cleared, surely they'll send someone in from the mainland to take over the case.'

'I think he's bright enough.' Ben was drinking beer too. 'He pretends he's slow, but he seems to have a pretty good idea what's been going on here. I wouldn't underestimate him.'

The Fowlers arrived then, showered and changed for dinner as always, as if this was some smart hotel. They always looked scrubbed clean. Everyone sat waiting for the bell to go for the meal. There was an odd tension. There was no more talk about Perez and the questions he'd asked them. They just sat, looking at each other. Only Hugh seemed relaxed, lounging in his chair, reading an old Shetland bird report.

'Jane's a bit late tonight.' John Fowler looked at his watch. 'Not like her. It smells good though.' Then they lapsed into silence again. Sitting beside her husband, Sarah had twisted her handkerchief into a ball, and was passing it from one hand to the other, incapable, it seemed, of sitting still. The constant movement frayed Dougie's nerves. *If she doesn't stop soon, I'll scream*.

A couple of minutes later they heard a noise in the kitchen, the door from the staff quarters being opened, and there was a moment of relief. Dougie only realized then how dependent they'd all become on Jane. It was the routine of the field centre — trap rounds and mealtimes, the log being taken each evening — that had prevented them falling into panic after Angela's murder. Without Jane in the kitchen, the reassuring ritual was falling apart. Now she was here, all would be well again.

But instead of Jane, bustling in to lay the table and apologizing for the delay, they saw Maurice and Poppy.

'We thought we'd eat with you tonight,' Maurice said. 'It's Poppy's last night. Where's Jane?'

Before they could answer they heard the plane going over. It seemed very low, even more noticeable because it had been several days since they'd last heard the engine noise.

'Perhaps she's been arrested.' It was Hugh, making a joke of it. Dougie thought any more jokes like that and one of them would slap him. 'That's the plane coming in to take her away.'

'Don't be ridiculous!' Maurice's voice was more assertive than Dougie had ever heard it. Perhaps the man couldn't bear the thought of life on the island without Jane to make things run smoothly for him. 'She's probably down at Springfield with Mary and Fran. She needs some time off, for goodness' sake. Dinner's all ready. I think we can help ourselves.'

It occurred to Dougie that none of them had expressed any concern over Jane's safety. She was one of those efficient women who could always look after themselves. And nobody speculated about the arrival of the plane. They assumed it would be police business. They'd watched dramas on the television. Now, it seemed getting fed was the most important thing in their lives. It was at least something to focus on, just as he gave all his attention to birdwatching when he was troubled.

So they all went into the kitchen and the Fowlers took control, setting Poppy to lay the table and asking Ben to put out the plates. John Fowler found rice keeping warm in the oven, almost as if Jane had expected to be delayed. Sarah carried the big pot of chicken casserole to the serving hatch and began to dish it out, acting just as Jane would have done, even wearing Jane's apron.

They were so quiet when they ate that they heard a vehicle coming into the lighthouse yard.

Again there was a collective sense of relief. 'Jane must have got a lift back,' Poppy said, the words unnecessary, because it was what they were all thinking. She'd put on the black eyeliner and the gel in her hair so she looked almost back to her normal self. They heard the outside door of the lighthouse open and then the door into the dining room. Dougie thought they were all preparing things to say: *You see, we managed without you. Did you have dinner at Springfield? I bet it wasn't as good as this*. Words so Jane wouldn't know how thrown they'd been by her absence.

But it wasn't Jane who came into the room. A strange woman stood there, looking at them. She had the groomed hair and subtle make-up of a television news presenter. Jimmy Perez stood behind her. The woman moved aside and obviously expected Perez to speak.

'This is Rhona Laing,' he said. 'The Procurator Fiscal. She's supervising the police investigation here. The Scottish legal system is different from the English and she'll be involved through to the prosecution.'

'Have you seen Jane?' Maurice spoke for them all. At the moment Jane's whereabouts seemed to concern him more than the appearance of a lawyer from Lerwick. Who would make the coffee? 'She seems to have disappeared. We thought she might be at Springfield with you.'

Dougie saw a look pass between Perez and the Fiscal.

'Jane Latimer is dead,' the woman said briskly. 'That's why I'm here.'

They all stared at her.

'What happened?' Hugh's smile had disappeared. Dougie thought his face looked quite different without it.

'We're here to ask questions, not to answer them,' Rhona Laing said. 'Her death is suspicious. That's all you need to know for the present.'

Dougie thought her approach was very different from Perez's. But probably easier to deal with, he thought. More straightforward. He found Perez's silences, his quiet understanding, terrifying. This woman would bluster and bully but she wouldn't have the detective's ability to read minds.

'When did you last see her?' Rhona demanded. She stood at the head of the table and looked at them all. She didn't have to ask them to introduce themselves. Perez must have described them to her. It seemed to Dougie that she was enjoying herself. Perhaps she spent most of the time in an office, and the flight through the dark to the island, this confrontation with possible suspects, was a great adventure to her.

'She was here for lunch,' John Fowler said. 'She served it and cleared it up. I haven't seen her since then.'

'Did anyone see her after lunch?'

Nobody answered. 'This is a small island,' Rhona said. 'There are few places to hide. It seems she walked away from the field centre at some point in the afternoon. It didn't look as if she drove. Surely somebody saw her. Who was outside?' She sounded like a teacher trying to elicit a response from a particularly unresponsive class.

Still there was no reply. Dougie's phone began to ring. The call was from one of the Bristol birders, a member of the rarities committee.

'Switch that off!' Rhona snapped at him without looking round. She pulled up a chair and sat at the table. It was Perez's turn.

'We have to decide how to proceed from here,' Perez said. 'The boat will go tomorrow. We've agreed that Poppy should be on it. Her mother will be meeting her in Grutness to take her home and we'll know where she is if we need to talk to her again. Was anyone else planning to leave?'

'I'm contracted to be here until the middle of

November,' Ben said. 'Someone should carry on ringing throughout the migration season. I'd like to prepare the annual report as Angela's not here to do it.'

'I want to stay,' Dougie said. He still resented not being allowed to take the call from the birding celebrity. The wind was light south-easterly. Who knew what other vagrants might turn up? American birds were all very well, but they weren't as exciting as the rarities from the east. Anyone with enough money could go to the US to see trumpeter swan. Birds from Siberia weren't so easy to track down on their breeding grounds. 'And there'll be loads of birdwatchers turning up tomorrow.'

'We should decide how we're going to manage that.' Perez looked at Rhona.

'You can't stop them coming!' Dougie said. 'They'll come anyway. If you stop the flights they'll charter boats.'

'We can't allow them to get in the way of the investigation,' Rhona said.

'They won't! I'll bring them up to Golden Water and then back to the airstrip. They don't need to stay overnight.'

Rhona looked at Perez: 'Would that work?'

'I don't see why not.' He paused. 'The press might be more troublesome.'

'Don't worry about the press,' she said. 'I'll cope with them. It'll be best to get them all in together and give them the same story.'

She'd enjoy dealing with the media, Dougie thought.

'There must be somewhere we can hold a

press conference. The community hall, perhaps?'

Perez nodded.

'I was hoping we could go out on the boat,' Sarah Fowler said. Still her hands moved in her lap. 'We're booked to stay for another week, but I'm scared now. Two murders. Two women. I want to go home.'

'I can't keep you here,' Perez said. 'But it would make life easier for me if you stuck to your original plan. We'll need to talk to everyone again in the light of this afternoon's discovery. Another police officer came in on the plane this afternoon. He'll be staying here at the lighthouse. I'm sure you'll be quite safe.'

'Of course you'll be safe,' Rhona said. 'I'll be staying here too.' As if she would be far more effective than Perez's colleague at preventing another outrage.

The Fowlers looked at each other. Dougie thought it would take more courage to stand up to the Fiscal and insist on going than to decide to stick it out. Sarah put her hand on her husband's arm. 'Please, I don't think I can stand it here any longer.'

Fowler frowned. Dougie thought he was torn between meeting his wife's request and doing what he'd see as his duty. 'Just a few more days,' he said. 'If the inspector thinks it'll help.'

Sarah looked at her husband and saw that she was defeated 'OK. We'll stay.'

'Who'll do the cooking?' Dougie asked.

For the first time that evening Perez smiled. 'I'll ask someone from the island to help out. We'll make sure that you're fed.' He turned to

Hugh. 'What about you? Do you need to get home?'

The trademark grin had already returned. 'I want to stay until this is all over. Until the killer's caught. Of course.'

24

In Springfield, Mary and Fran waited for news. Fran thought: *Throughout history, it's been the women who've waited. The men have it easy. They see the action and they know what's happening. The women sit, imagine disaster, and peer through gaps in the curtained windows for the men to return*. Then she thought she was being ridiculously melodramatic. She was hardly the French Lieutenant's Woman, staring out from the end of the pier. These days there were mobile phones. She could always phone Perez and ask him what was going on.

Waiting would have been more bearable if she could have had a proper drink. She was drowning in tea. Perhaps because of James's puritan influence, Mary seemed to think alcohol was sinful and corrupting, especially for women. If James took a dram she considered that almost medicinal, but she never joined him. Fran had bought a bottle of wine in the shop when she was last there, to have with dinner when they all got together. It seemed that was unlikely to happen in the near future, and the bottle was still in her room, tempting her. It had a screw top. She wouldn't even have to steal a corkscrew from the kitchen. Already, in her head, she was forming this as an amusing story to tell her London friends. They'd be in a bar somewhere and she'd be talking about her first visit to Fair Isle and the religious in-laws, about sneaking into her bedroom, drinking the wine straight from the bottle. She was a good storyteller. She'd have them in stitches.

She phoned Cassie as she did every evening. Duncan had taken the girl to Whalsay with him on business and Fran sensed she'd been bored. 'When are you coming home?' Cassie demanded. 'Jimmy promised to take me swimming.'

'Just a couple of days. I promise. Not long now. Get Dad to invite Jenny to play tomorrow.' Jenny was Cassie's new best friend.

Fran had just replaced the receiver when Big James arrived home. She knew Perez found it hard to get on with his father. They'd discussed the relationship: parents and how to survive them. But Fran thought James was a sweetie. He'd been pleasant enough to her at least. When Perez was busy he'd walked round the croft with her, explained the crops he was growing, told her how they worked the sheep. It had seemed to her that he was a man who enjoyed the company of women.

Now she thought he looked very tired and quite old. She'd always considered him a strong man, muscular and fit, but this evening she saw the lines on the back of his hands and the slackness in the skin around his eyes and his jaw.

'I don't know how Jimmy does that work,' he said. 'It would be too much of a strain for me.' He sat in his usual chair by the fire and pulled off his boots.

'The plane got in all right?' Mary asked.

'No problem at all. It was the new pilot, but he knew what he was doing.' James got to his feet and poured himself a glass of whisky. He lifted the bottle towards Fran. 'Will you take a dram?' A sign that these were indeed unusual times.

She hesitated for a moment and then she nodded. He poured her a measure that was as large as his own.

'Have they made an arrest?' Fran asked. It had occurred to her that at least a second murder might have brought a fresh impetus to the investigation. Surely now Jimmy would have more idea what had happened.

'I don't think so,' James said. 'Jimmy couldn't talk about the case. I understand that.'

'So you have no news at all.' It was Mary, looking up from her knitting. She set it down on the floor beside her. 'I can't understand why anyone would want to kill Jane. That Angela was a different matter. I never took to her.' She looked up sharply at James. 'You know what I thought of her.' Fran had never heard her speak ill of the woman before and thought this a sign of how the murders were affecting everyone on the island. 'But Jane? What harm was there in her?'

'We never knew her,' James said. 'Not really.'

'I knew her enough to know that I liked her. She was in here the other day when the birdwatcher came banging at the door with news of the rare swan. We laughed together about the obsessions men have. We decided that women had more sense.'

They sat for a moment in silence.

'That new Fiscal came in on the plane,' James said at last, an attempt, Fran thought, to distract Mary with a snippet of gossip. 'She seems a fine woman.'

Fran was going to say that Jimmy didn't get on with her so well, but stopped herself. It wasn't the sort of subject Jimmy would want to discuss with his father.

James turned to her and his voice was unusually gentle. He could have been speaking to a baby. 'Jimmy wants you to come out with us on the boat in the morning. He thinks you'll be safer at home.'

'No!' How much harder would the waiting be, if she were at home in Ravenswick. Even with Cassie to keep her company, she couldn't bear it. 'Absolutely not.'

He shrugged, as if that was the answer he'd been expecting, as if he'd told his son already that she wouldn't be persuaded.

'Have you any idea when he'll be back here?' Mary asked.

'He said not to wait up for him. He could be out all night.'

Fran felt desolate. Was this how her life would be? Jimmy would have his work. She'd be at home worrying. Perhaps she couldn't deal with that. Perhaps they'd be better moving on to Fair Isle. If he were working on the croft and the *Shepherd* he wouldn't be poking around in the private lives of killers. She wouldn't spend her time thinking he was in danger.

* * *

She was still awake when Perez came in. It must have been after three in the morning; she'd glanced occasionally at the alarm clock by the bed. Now the wind had stopped she heard a vehicle approaching, a couple of whispered words, and then the sound of the engine disappearing north again. Sandy Wilson would have driven him home. Perez must be exhausted. She hadn't appreciated before his ability to do without rest. The relief of his return made her relax and she thought now sleep would be possible.

He came to bed immediately. No whisky for him, no tea. She switched on the bedside light when she heard him come in. He blinked. She thought he was disappointed she was still awake and tried not to feel hurt. He was too tired to talk. So, no questions. No recriminations about him wanting to send her away. She lay in silence and watched him take off his clothes, opened her arms when he climbed into bed beside her.

His whole body was cold. He couldn't have driven straight from the North Light; he wouldn't be that chilled. She rubbed his arms to bring the life back into them and twisted her legs around his. She felt herself drifting into sleep, but could sense him lying beside her, rigid and quite awake. It was as if he'd suffered a personal grief; it didn't feel as if he were a professional investigating the death of a stranger.

She woke again when it was still dark. There were domestic noises in the house — a tap being run, the clatter of pans. James was up early to take out the *Good Shepherd*. She was alone in the bed. It was hard to believe that Perez had come back at all, that she had held the cold and silent man in her arms.

25

In the North Light with Rhona Laing after the plane came in, watching the residents reacting to the news of Jane's death, Perez felt disengaged from the process. It had already been a long evening. Perhaps because he hadn't been present to see the arrival of the plane flying in through the darkness and could only imagine the sight — the silhouettes of the men, black against the orange lights — its appearance seemed part of a strange dream.

He sat with Poppy in the warden's flat. The curtains hadn't been drawn and he saw the hill lit by moonlight and by the hypnotic regular sweep of the lighthouse beam. At last he was alone with the girl. Maurice was still in the common room with the guests. They sat together on the sofa. The grate hadn't been cleaned and was full of ash and the remains of a piece of driftwood, some charred paper. The room was cold. Poppy had pulled a fleece jacket over her jumper.

'You walked back from Springfield this evening,' Perez said. 'Did you meet anyone on the way?'

It seemed that she hadn't heard the question. 'Jane was really kind to me,' she said. 'I didn't care about Angela dying. It made my life easier. But why would anyone want to harm Jane?'

'Can you think of a reason?'

Poppy shook her head. 'Angela was the only

person who didn't like her.'

'Why didn't Angela like her?'

'Because Jane didn't care about her being famous and stuff like that. Angela needed people to tell her how great she was all the time and Jane wouldn't play those sort of games.'

Perez returned to his original question. 'Did you see anyone while you were walking back from Springfield?'

'There was someone walking on the hill beyond the airstrip.' Poppy hunched into her jacket. 'For a moment it freaked me out because I thought it was Angela. You'd always see her walking like that. Like she could go on for miles without stopping. But of course it couldn't have been. I don't believe in ghosts.' She shivered.

'Who was it?' It could have been the murderer, Perez thought, on his way north from the Pund.

She shrugged. 'It could have been anyone. It was just a silhouette against the hill. And they all look the same, don't they, the birdwatchers? Waterproof jacket, hat, gloves.'

'Man or woman?'

'Well, I thought at first it was Angela so it could have been a woman. But more likely a man.'

The only woman staying at the centre was Sarah Fowler, but she was as tall as her husband, and in a bulky jacket and a hat, from a distance it would be impossible to tell the difference. But from the hill the walker would have seen Poppy clearly, especially if he had binoculars. Perez was pleased the girl would be out on the boat early the next morning.

'Did Angela say anything to you in the week before she died? Anything to explain why she was killed?'

'Nah, she didn't pay much attention to me. I mean, she poked away about my boyfriend and what a loser I am, but looking back I don't think her heart was in it. She had something else on her mind.' There was a pause, a moment of honesty. 'That's probably why I tipped the beer over her. Better that she hated me than acted as if I wasn't there.'

* * *

At ten o'clock, Perez decided he would leave the residents in the company of Rhona Laing and return to the crime scene. She was untroubled about being abandoned and as he left, she was organizing sleeping accommodation for herself, Sandy and Vicki.

'Absolutely *not* a dormitory,' he heard her say to Maurice. 'At least not for Ms Hewitt and me. Single rooms. Preferably with showers. You can put DC Wilson wherever you have room.'

Perez walked through the moonlight to the Pund. There was already a frost and a thin shell of ice on the water in the mire. His earlier conversations with the field centre residents ran through his mind. What had he missed? What had provoked another murder? Perez still thought the killer was rational. These weren't the actions of the tabloid psychopath. There'd been no sexual assault and, certainly in Angela's case, no more violence than was needed to kill. That had been controlled, not the outburst of a spoiled teenager. He thought again he could safely send Poppy away from the island to her mother. After their conversation he had no sense of her as a murderer. It seemed to him that Jane had been stabbed because she posed a threat to Angela's killer: she'd seen something or heard something or worked out the identity of the perpetrator. But even if she hadn't been a victim in her own right, there'd been a ferocity in the attack that was different and Perez found that confusing.

If Jane had discovered Angela's hideaway, that might provide a motive for the death. Perhaps there *had* been a diary there, a letter or a photograph, which would have pointed to the killer. Jane had been killed for it. And now the item had been taken away and probably destroyed. That was the theory that he'd been developing since the discovery of Jane's body. Before leaving the field centre, he'd sat in the bird room with Rhona Laing and discussed it with her; now it was firmer in his mind and he ran through the implications. They would pull in a specialist team to search the North Light. While whatever had been taken from the Pund probably no longer existed, they had to make the effort to find it. He knew it would be possible to bring planes in all the next day and if the charters had been taken by the birdwatchers, they'd call in the emergency helicopter again.

When he arrived at the Pund, he found Sandy smoking outside. Perez saw the glow of the cigarette end as he approached the building and then the white halo of condensed air.

'It's weird,' Sandy said. 'I thought this would be like Whalsay, but smaller. But it isn't, is it? It's much more remote.' Whalsay was the island where he'd grown up. It was only a few miles from Shetland mainland and linked to it by a regular roll-on roll-off ferry service. He rubbed out the cigarette and put the butt in a bag in his pocket, stamped his feet to keep out the cold. 'I couldn't take this. It would drive me crazy after a week.'

'You'd get used to it.' But Perez wasn't really sure he would get used to it again if he moved home. Perhaps he'd been away for too long. 'How's the CSI getting on?'

'She says she's finished the photographs,' Sandy said. 'She was bagging up the evidence. I was getting in the way.' He spoke as if he was always in the way.

Perez left Sandy where he was and stood at the Pund door. He couldn't see Vicki, so she must be in the loft. He shouted in to her: 'Is it OK if I have a look up there?'

'Yeah, I'm about finished. Just put on a suit and walk between the tapes. You don't need to bother with the bootees. I'll need to take a print of your shoes before I leave anyway.'

Perez found a paper scene suit just inside the door, put it on and climbed the ladder. He stood halfway up and looked inside. Jane's body remained just as he remembered it, lit up by the fierce white light. Vicki was crouched in the corner of the loft, to avoid an outstretched arm, and was running her hands under the sheepskins.

'I was looking for the murder weapon,' she said.

'It's another stabbing, isn't it?'

'Certainly looks that way to me. But it won't be the same knife, of course. That went out in the helicopter with the first victim.'

'There's more blood this time.'

'And more wounds,' Vicki said. 'I think Jane heard the killer climb up the ladder. There'd have been no escape for her but she put up a struggle. There are defensive cuts on her hands and arms.'

Perez wondered what the murderer had made of that. Had he been sickened by having to face the woman he was stabbing? Or had he enjoyed it?

'Could a woman have done it?' Surely a woman wouldn't have been excited by the violence?

Vicki shrugged. 'I don't see why not.'

'Any idea what sort of weapon we should be looking for?'

'Hey, ask the pathologist. He gets paid a lot more than me.'

But she grinned. She was never precious, and he valued her judgement more than that of the eminent doctor who performed the post-mortems in Aberdeen.

'Something with a narrow blade,' she said. 'Very sharp. The murderer pulled it out afterwards, which is one reason why there's more blood here than there was at the first scene.

Looks like he hit an artery. Of course, the feathers are very different too.'

'Are they?' He was surprised. He thought feathers were feathers. 'I suppose there are more of them here. In the bird room a few were woven into Angela's hair. And those were longer.'

'Here someone's just slit open a feather pillow and spilled out the contents,' she said. 'Didn't you ever have pillow fights in that boarding school of yours?'

'The hostel at the Anderson High was hardly a boarding school.' He made the same point every time they met, but it was a running gag: that he'd been to a posh boarding school while she was at the local comprehensive. 'What about the feathers in Angela's hair then?'

'I've sent them for DNA analysis, but they're not the sort you stuff pillows with, that's for sure. Looks like they might have come from a couple of different species.'

Perez considered that. He couldn't understand what the implication might be. 'Have we found the empty pillowcase?'

'It's not here.' She stretched. The spotlights shining up from the ground floor threw strange shadows on her face. 'Definitely no murder weapon either.'

'I'm going to ask the search team to come in. They can pull this place apart and go to the North Light too. I'll sort it out first thing.'

He climbed down the ladder and Vicki followed. He'd brought a flask of coffee with him from the field centre. Now, standing with Sandy just outside the house, he took it out of his rucksack and pulled out of his pockets, like a magician conjuring brightly coloured ribbons from thin air, several rounds of sandwiches and half a fruit cake. 'Jane's fruit cake was famous. Make the most of it.'

They sat in Tammy Jamieson's van to eat. The man must have walked home. There were fingers of ice on the windscreen, but the cold hadn't driven away a background stink of fish. Perez sat in the back on a grubby cushion. He drank some coffee but left the food to the others.

He asked: 'Where have you fingerprinted?'

Vicki took her coffee like he did, strong and black. There was milk in a screw-top jar for Sandy, and a couple of tablespoons of sugar, twisted into the corner of a polythene bag. She took a gulp, spluttered because it was so hot, then turned round to where he was sitting behind her. 'The shelf, the wine rack, the mugs. There are a couple of smudges on the ladder but I've pulled a good one from the planks in the loft. Could be Jane's or Angela's, of course.'

'I opened that wooden box, before I found her body.'

'I tried that for prints. There was nothing. Not even yours.'

He thought that was odd because he hadn't been wearing gloves, but maybe he'd just touched the edge of the lid and the prints hadn't taken.

He leaned forward to ask her another question. By now the back windows of the van were running with condensation. 'Have you bagged up the stuff that was inside the box?'

'What stuff?' She took a slice of cake and put it in her mouth.

Perez shut his eyes and felt for a moment as if he were drowning. He pictured his father, dressed in the crime scene suit, setting up the strong lights inside the Pund, the sharp response to Sandy's offer of help. When Perez looked up again, Sandy was asking about plane times and the practicalities of bringing up the search team. 'Do you think we could fly them direct from Inverness?' Perez held his breath and waited for Vicki to repeat the question: *What stuff?* But when he hadn't immediately replied, she'd answered Sandy instead, too tired and overwhelmed by the detailed work, it seemed, to hold the thought in her mind.

What will I say if she asks me again?

In the van the conversation continued, passing backwards and forwards between Sandy and Vicki, but he hardly heard it.

Will I answer with the truth? The silver earrings and bangle. Jewellery made in the Isle by that Scottish woman who set up business in the South Light. I recognize the style. I bought some for Fran.

'I hope they've got some heating on in the lighthouse,' Vicki was saying. 'What's the accommodation like, Jimmy? OK?'

'Fine.'

What stuff? She didn't repeat the question again. And he didn't remind her.

They decided then to call it a day soon. Vicki said she just wanted to have a quick look for footwear prints on the muddy track outside the

Pund. If the weather changed overnight they might lose them. 'And shouldn't one of us stay here to keep an eye on the scene?'

'We'll tape it,' Sandy said. 'And I'll be back here before it gets light. Surely it'll be safe enough if I have a couple of hours' sleep. Jimmy?'

And Perez, distracted, only nodded. While Vicki and Sandy were busy, he went into the ruined house. He opened the shiny wooden box himself and saw that it was empty.

By then Sandy had the engine running. Perez turned off his torch, ran outside and climbed into the back of the van. Still he didn't speak of the empty box. He paused before he got out at Springfield, and he might have said something then, but Sandy shouted from the driver's seat: 'Come on, man, I want my bed.'

Perez let himself into the silent house. When he pushed open the bedroom door, Fran turned on the light. There was nothing to say to her, so he remained quiet. She wrapped him around with her body to warm him, but long after he heard the regular breathing that meant she was asleep, he stayed as cold and stiff as if he were lying outside on the frozen ground.

26

Perez stood on the bank above the Pund and looked down on it. He thought the building was crumbling back into the hill. The stone that had once formed the surrounding wall had been scattered and was indistinguishable now from the rocky outcrops that grew out of the bog. The building itself sagged at one end. There was a pool of mist covering the low land from Setter to the Pund, so in the dawn the house looked almost romantic. An ideal place for lovers to meet.

Perez hadn't slept, had turned occasionally during the early hours to look at the alarm clock, surprised at how slowly time was passing. The implication of the empty wooden box had struck him as soon as Vicki had given the puzzled frown, had turned to him in the stinking van and murmured: 'What stuff?' It had stayed with him all night, going round and round in his mind.

He had known his father had taken the jewellery. Who else would have done it? Not Sandy or Vicki. Why would they? They hadn't any personal connection with the investigation. And nobody else had had the opportunity. He had realized his father must be involved as soon as Vicki had asked the question, but he hadn't answered. Did that make him as corrupt as the people he despised? The politicians who found work for their children, the businessmen who paid for planning rules to be overlooked. The Duncan Hunters, who blackmailed and bribed their way to success.

James had got up at the same time as Perez. They'd stood in the kitchen at Springfield drinking tea, eating toast made from his mother's home-baked bread. But Mary had been there too and besides, tense and confused after a sleepless night, Perez wouldn't have known what to say to the man. He wouldn't have been able to control his anger. Because after the first realization of what his father had done, rage had swamped his brain and drowned out reason. How could his father, who blethered from the pulpit in the kirk about righteousness and morality, live with himself? How could he be such a hypocrite? Perez, who'd never really understood the impulse to physical violence, was scared of what he might do. He imagined how it would feel to smash his father's face with his fist until the blood ran through his fingers. So he'd stayed silent and just nodded when James offered him a lift up the island on the truck with the rest of the *Shepherd* crew.

They'd dropped him at Setter and he'd walked to the Pund from there. It was just starting to get light. Every blade of grass and head of heather was covered in hoar frost. As he got closer to the house he disturbed a snipe in the grass. He stopped for a moment and watched it zigzag away across the hill. In the old days, he supposed, men would have shot it, though it wouldn't have provided more than a mouthful of food.

After the first shock, Perez wasn't even surprised that his father had taken the earrings and bracelet or by the betrayal that the theft implied. It made sense, explained details that had previously seemed irrelevant. Perez remembered the embarrassed shuffling of the boys on the boat when he'd asked if Angela had an island lover. His father's offering to help by staying with Jane's body if Perez wanted to meet the plane. Later, James must have taken the opportunity to steal the jewellery when he was setting up the lights in the Pund and their attention was elsewhere. He wouldn't have realized Perez had searched the ground floor of the building before finding Jane's body.

And James had always liked younger women. He'd been flattered by their attention. He liked to dance with them. They liked him too, were taken in by the old-fashioned courtesy. Even Fran, the most discerning of people, had been seduced by his charms.

How many women have there been? Perez thought now, watching the sky lighten over Sheep Rock. *How many lies has he told my mother?* Then it came to him that Mary must surely have known about his father and Angela Moore, guessed at least that something was going wrong. She was a perceptive woman and they'd been married for more than thirty-five years. James would be the worst sort of liar. Perez wondered that he hadn't realized there were problems in the marriage; between them his parents had managed to keep the crisis secret from him.

He saw that Sandy was already at the ruined croft. He was sitting on the threshold watching Perez approach. Perez hoped that Vicki was still in the lighthouse catching up on some sleep. He'd ordered the helicopter in with the search team at ten o'clock. She could take the body and her evidence back on that and would be in Aberdeen by lunchtime. Now he wanted to talk to Sandy alone.

Again he had coffee in his bag, and bacon sandwiches and sticky date slices. His mother had got up before James to prepare food for him and the crew and had made up a parcel for Jimmy too. Every boat day was the same. *Why would you do that if you knew he'd been sneaking here to the Pund and having sex with Angela Moore?* Perez thought it would be about pride and presenting a united front in the face of island gossip. She must still care for his father and wouldn't want him to look a fool.

Perez sat on the doorstep next to Sandy. 'How were things at the field centre?'

'Fine. The Fiscal said she'd be here to see the body away. She'll borrow their Land Rover. Vicki will make sure it's all done right.'

'I need your advice.' Despite himself he smiled at the surprise and pride on Sandy's face. People usually offered Sandy advice, whether he wanted it or not; they didn't often ask for it.

Perez told his story. About finding the silver earrings and bangle in the wooden box, while he was searching the Pund before finding Jane's body. About the implications of their disappearance.

'What does your father say about it?' Sandy

had lit another cigarette.

'Nothing. I've not asked him.'

'Maybe you should. You could have got the whole thing wrong. Do you not think you could be jumping to conclusions?'

'I wasn't sure how that would look. If we were to charge him . . . '

'Ballocks.' Sandy blew smoke into the cold air, watched it rise above him. 'You're not saying the man's a murderer?'

'No.' That at least was something Perez had discounted almost immediately. His father had been at Springfield when Angela Moore had been killed and if he'd stabbed Jane Latimer to prevent her from talking about his affair, he could have taken the jewellery out of the wooden box then. Besides, the show with the feathers wasn't his style.

'Then charging doesn't come into it,' Sandy said. 'But if he knew the woman then he might have something useful to tell you. It would be wrong not to ask him about her. He's an important witness.'

'He's tampered with a crime scene,' Perez said. 'Perverted the course of justice.'

'Maybe,' Sandy said, 'if you *have* got this right, he's trying to save his marriage.' He paused. 'And his son from embarrassment.'

They sat in silence and watched a huge orange sun rise over the sea beyond Sheep Rock. In the distance there was the sound of an approaching plane.

* * *

Perez went to the airstrip to watch the plane arrive. It must have left Tingwall at first light and it certainly wasn't a regular scheduled flight. He met Dougie Barr, the fat birder, on his way; the man was flushed despite the cold and out of breath.

'I've just been up to Golden Water,' he said, the words coming out in short, painful bursts, 'to check that the swan's still there.'

'And is it?' After a night of anxiety about his father, Perez saw the birdwatchers now as an amusing distraction. He'd always found the obsession of these men faintly ridiculous. He realized that they *were* mostly men. Angela Moore was a rarity.

'Yes. Just where it went to roost yesterday evening.'

'You'll take them straight up to the north end and then back to the plane. No detours. Otherwise the flights will be stopped.'

'I've explained all that to them.' They both stepped off the track to allow Dave Wheeler to drive past.

There were still signs on the airstrip of the preparations for the emergency flight the night before — piles of ash where the fires had been lit, scorched grass. The plane circled the strip and came in low to land, smooth and easy. Tammy Jamieson's wife turned up, not in the van — Sandy was still using that — but in a gold Ford Capri with the wheel arches eaten away by rust. She parked just where Perez was standing and wound down the window. She was a Fetlar woman; she and Tammy had met at school.

'Glad to have Tammy out with the boat?' Perez asked.

'Aye, he's like a bear with a sore head if he doesn't get on to the water every week. And I'm glad of the peace. I love him to bits but we all need some time on our own.'

'Anyone you know coming in on the flight?'

She grinned. 'Nah, I'm here as a taxi. Maurice phoned last night to ask if I'd give the birdwatchers a lift to the north end and bring them back. I'll be at it all morning, it seems. A kind of shuttle. He said they'd pay and it'll be something towards the holiday fund.'

Perez thought Maurice must be slipping back into his role of field centre administrator. Perhaps Jane's death had forced him to pick up the reins again. Or maybe Rhona Laing had something to do with it; few men would have the nerve to stand up to her and Maurice had always taken the easy course. Almost immediately after thinking about the Fiscal, his mobile rang and her name flashed on to the screen.

'Jimmy. Where are you?'

'At the airstrip seeing the first lot of birdwatchers in.' He watched them climb out of the plane, laden with telescopes, tripods and cameras. Dougie shepherded four of them into the waiting car. Even from where he stood he could sense their excitement. They stuffed their equipment in the boot and piled into the back. Dougie took the front seat. 'You can start walking up the road,' he said to the remaining four. 'We'll pick you up as soon as we've dropped this lot off.'

'Jimmy?' The Fiscal, impatient, waiting for an answer.

'I'm sorry, I didn't catch what you said.'

'I've fixed a time for the press conference. Two o'clock in the hall.'

Perez couldn't hear what else the Fiscal had to say, because the plane rolled past him on its way to take off. He supposed the aircraft was doing a shuttle too. It would bring another lot of birders in and take out the folk already here.

'Sorry,' he said again. 'Could you repeat that?'

'I'd like you there, Jimmy. At the press conference.' He sensed her growing irritation. She was used to getting an immediate response.

'How are the reporters getting in?'

'We've arranged one special charter. The rest will come on the boat. I'm hoping we'll have got rid of most of the day-tripping birdwatchers by then.'

He thought she'd choreographed the whole procedure very well.

'Well, Jimmy?'

'Sorry?'

'You will be at the press conference?'

'Yes,' he said. 'Yes, of course.'

* * *

In the North Light they were eating breakfast. Dougie was missing, but all the other suspects were there: the Fowlers, Hugh Shaw, Ben Catchpole, Maurice Parry. Perez stood at the door watching them before they noticed he was there. *One of you is a murderer*. They all looked so ordinary, so unthreatening, that the idea seemed a ridiculous exaggeration.

Again Sarah Fowler had taken up Jane's place in the kitchen. Now Poppy had gone, she was the only female long-term resident left. Perez wondered what Fran would make of the assumption that she'd do the cooking, but he saw that she'd taken over the role with enthusiasm. The desperation of the night before seemed to have dissipated. She stood behind the counter just as Jane had done, sliding bacon and fried eggs from the warm tray on to plates, looking up occasionally to talk to the other guests. Again he wished he could find a way of understanding her better. What lay behind her switches in mood? Of course, last night, they'd all seemed to be in a state of shock. This morning, it was as if they'd determined to ignore the violence and continue as normal. Perhaps the fact that Jane's death had occurred away from the centre made that more possible.

'Would you like some breakfast, Inspector? Or coffee?' Sarah Fowler had seen him and called him over.

'Coffee,' he said. 'Please. So you're left doing all the work?'

'I'm much better having something to do. Really, there's no need to organize anyone else to cook. I'd prefer to be busy.'

There was no sign of Vicki or the Fiscal in the dining room.

'You've just missed your colleagues,' Sarah said. 'They took the field centre Land Rover.' *To the Pund to collect Jane's body, then to the helicopter landing pad near the South Light*.

He nodded, took his coffee and sat at a table next to Maurice. 'Poppy went out OK with the *Shepherd?*'

'Yes.' Maurice was tidier than Perez had seen him for a while. Had he shaved before seeing his daughter on to the boat? Made a last effort to hold things together for her sake? Or was it the Rhona Laing effect again?

'In the end she seemed quite reluctant to go,' Maurice went on. 'She said she was worried about me.' He looked up. 'Did you get in touch with Jane's relatives?'

'Her sister,' Perez said. 'Jane's parents are quite elderly. The sister will pass on the news to them.' He looked over to the birdwatchers on the other side of the table. 'Why aren't you at Golden Water with that American swan?'

'The work of the field centre has to go on. We're not all on holiday.' Ben flushed and Perez wondered what had provoked such an angry response. Did he resent the plane-loads of birders tramping across the island? 'Fair Isle isn't just about rarities, despite people like Dougie. We're doing real science here.'

'Of course.' Perez drank his coffee.

'I've walked round the traps and now I'm going to do the hill survey. Without Angela someone has to keep things going.'

'If you're up on Ward Hill you'll have a good view of the Pund.'

'So?' Another flash of anger and defiance.

'I wondered if you were there yesterday. Someone was out on the hill and you might have seen something.'

'I was on the hill in the morning. Jane was still in the lighthouse then.' Ben stood up and walked out, almost flouncing, tossing his red hair like a young girl. Poppy had gone but it seemed Ben had taken her place as token petulant teenager.

'We're all rather short-tempered, I'm afraid,' John Fowler said. 'It's the stress. You mustn't take it personally.'

On the table beside him lay a notebook, the top page covered in squiggles of shorthand. Again Perez suspected his motives. Would all this become an article in a grand Sunday newspaper? It would make a good story, he could see that. The group of witnesses gathered together in the same building on a wind-swept isle, wondering which of their number was a murderer.

The journalist muttered something about helping his wife and wandered into the kitchen. Hugh said he'd go to Golden Water; it would be a good chance to catch up with his friends and he might as well make the most of his moment of glory. Perez and Maurice were left alone.

'She was gay, you know,' Maurice said suddenly. Then, when Perez didn't respond immediately: 'Jane Latimer. She was gay. Probably not relevant and it didn't make any difference to me, but I thought I should tell you.'

'Was it something she discussed?'

'She didn't make a big deal of it, but it wasn't a secret. She talked occasionally about her partner — her former partner. She works in the media: television, film. Something like that.'

'Did she form any relationships while she was here?'

'Not to my knowledge, but then I might not have known. She would have been discreet. It seems unlikely though. We don't get many single women staying at the North Light.'

Perez thought Sandy would be excited by this revelation. He would find it significant. But Perez didn't believe that Jane was the primary victim in this case. She was killed for what she knew or what she had guessed, not for who she was.

Outside, there was the sound of an engine and through the long window he saw the helicopter arriving to take the dead woman back to the mainland. There would be no dramatic send-off for her, but he thought she would have preferred it that way.

27

Dougie looked at his watch. Another twenty minutes and he'd have to get this last load of birders back to the airstrip. One lot had already gone. They were all experiencing the post-tick high, not really looking at the bird any more — they'd been concentrated enough when they'd first arrived, staring through telescopes, taking notes, drawing sketches. Then, everyone had been whispering. Now, they'd turned up the volume: they were laughing, catching up on the news, sending texts and photos to friends not lucky enough to be there, gripping them off. Hugh was in the centre of them. You'd have thought it had been him and not Dougie who'd found the swan and because he'd been the second to see it, his name would be in the British Birds rarity report too. Dougie resented that.

Soon the plane would be in. In the distance he thought he could hear Tammy's car on the return trip to collect them. That was a relief. He felt responsible for getting the newcomers down the island on time. It was all very well Hugh holding court with his stories — everyone wanted to hear about the murder and Hugh was happy enough to oblige — but it would be Dougie who'd get the blame if they weren't on the airstrip when the plane landed. If Angela had been here she would have laughed at him. *For fuck's sake, Dougie boy, lighten up a bit*. She'd laughed at him a lot — about his obsession with being on time, the boring nature of his job, taking himself too seriously. But she'd taken herself seriously, Dougie thought. At least, when it came to her work.

The gold Capri driven by Sally Jamieson appeared round the corner and a sort of cheer went up. There were comments about the rust and the smell but none of them would have wanted to walk. The group started to move away from the edge of the pool towards the road. The Shetland birders would be glad to get back to Lerwick, to lunch in a bar and a few beers to celebrate. The rest had to make their way south. Dougie walked behind them. He turned for a last look at the swan. It stretched its wings, ran over the water to take off and sailed into the air. He expected it to circle and return to the water. It had done that a number of times since it had settled on Golden Water. But it flew high into the air and disappeared to the north. The birders fell silent and watched it until it was out of sight. They knew it wouldn't return now.

28

The hall was very warm. Rhona must have arranged for the heating to be turned on and the sunlight was flooding in through the windows, reflecting on the camera lenses, picking up a swirl of dust in one corner. Chairs had been unstacked and set out in rows. The Fiscal stood with Perez at the front of the room. He was still distracted by the thought that he should confront his father. The *Good Shepherd* had arrived back into Fair Isle and he couldn't put it off much longer. But Perez was already having doubts. What if Sandy was right and he was misreading the whole situation? What if he accused his father of adultery only to find he'd made a huge mistake? The man would never speak to him again.

Rhona took the press conference. She read out the statement she'd prepared in the lighthouse while they were eating lunch. The news of the second murder came as a surprise to most of the reporters. The helicopter had come in and out with Jane's body before they'd arrived. There was a gasp, almost of glee, when she gave the facts in her dry, measured voice. Perez supposed he couldn't condemn the press for enjoying the drama of the story. Many of the Fair Isle folk had reacted in the same way. It was as if the little community at the North Light were a living soap opera, being played out for the audience's enjoyment.

The Fiscal looked around the room, squinting a little against the sunlight. 'Are there any questions?'

A big man wearing an old Barbour jacket raised his hand. Perez didn't recognize him. He must have come in from the south. 'Two women dead on an island this size. I'd not have thought it'd be hard to track down the killer. Why has it taken so long to make an arrest?'

The Fiscal stared at him icily. 'I've explained about the unusual situation here. The weather prevented the usual forensic support. We have every expectation that an arrest will be made shortly.'

'Will you be calling in the Serious Crime Squad from Inverness?'

'I have every confidence in the local officers, assisted by the specialist search team that arrived from the mainland today. Of course, should it become necessary we'll ask for additional support.'

No pressure then, Perez thought. He understood the subtext of her words. *Sort this quickly or we'll take the case away from you*. Two days ago that wouldn't have bothered him. He'd have been glad to hand it over and take Fran away from the Isle. Now his father seemed to be involved. If it came to light that he'd had a relationship with Angela Moore, the press would make his family's life a misery.

A dark-haired young woman stood up. 'Angela Moore was a celebrity. Do we know if she'd received unusual attention from any individual?'

Again the Fiscal took the question. Perez had

only spoken to clarify a few points of fact.

'Are you talking a stalker? No, we have no evidence of that.'

'Have Mrs Moore's relatives been informed of all the circumstances surrounding the case?' A slight man, with prominent front teeth that made him look like a rat. Perez supposed the national press were already tracking down Archie Moore. Were they camping outside the run-down bungalow Bryn Pritchard had described? Perez imagined the old man sitting in the pub, taking drinks from reporters, talking about his famous, ungrateful daughter.

This time he replied to the question before Rhona could step in: 'We have informed Mrs Moore's father, but we still have to trace her mother. I'd be very grateful if she could contact me through Highland and Islands police.' He was surprised by a camera's flashlight and felt foolish.

There were no further questions. Perez thought the media wanted to be away from the island as quickly as possible. This might be a huge story for them but they didn't want to be stranded on a lump of rock for the night. He thought they were less concerned about there being a murderer on the loose than the fact that there was no pub here. As they waited at the airstrip for the planes to come in, the main topic of conversation was where they could get their first drink.

Rhona Laing went out with them, pushed her way past the reporters to get on to the first plane back to Tingwall. Perhaps she'd rearranged her dinner date at the Busta House Hotel and wanted to get home in time to change.

'Keep in touch, Jimmy.' A little regal wave. No last-minute instructions, no insistence that he wrap up the case quickly. She realized he understood the pressure. Another couple of days and the press would be demanding that someone else, someone from the city, should take over.

The second plane took off just as it was getting dark. He watched it disappear across the horizon. Now all the day visitors had gone. Apart from the North Light residents the only strangers on the island were members of the specialist search team. They would stay at least for another day. He decided to get home and speak to his father. The *Shepherd* would have been long unloaded and Big James would be at home, in front of the television, waiting for the football results. Perez felt a brief moment of pleasure at the thought of disrupting the sacred household ritual of *Final Score*.

He was walking down the track to pick up his borrowed car, and wondering where Sandy was, when his mobile rang. He was so certain that it would be Sandy, reporting on the results of the search, that he didn't check the screen and was surprised to hear Maurice.

'Are you busy, Jimmy? Could you spare a few minutes?'

Maurice was waiting for him in the flat. The place was untidier than Perez had seen it, untidier certainly than when he'd been there with Poppy the night before. Maurice might have cleaned up his act for public appearance but in private things were still falling apart. With Poppy gone, perhaps he no longer felt the need to put on a show. On the table in the living room there was an ashtray full of cigarette ends. Maurice shrugged. 'I'd given up. Angela hated it. Now . . . ' He went into the kitchen and came back with a bottle of whisky and two glasses. 'Have a dram with me, Jimmy. I'll drink alone if I have to but I don't like it.'

Perez nodded. Had Maurice called him back to the North Light just because he was lonely? He sipped the whisky and waited.

'The mail came in on the boat today,' Maurice said. 'You know what it's like when the weather's been bad. You get a heap of the stuff and most of it junk.'

Perez nodded again. 'And some of it's for Angela?'

'Of course I should have realized it would be, but it threw me, seeing her name on the envelopes.'

'I'd like to take the mail with me, if that's OK,' Perez said. He should have thought about it and asked Joanne at the post office to set Angela's mail to one side. 'I'll bring it back. Have you opened it?'

'Not the letters addressed to her!' Maurice sounded shocked.

'But there was something that worried you? That's why you phoned.'

'It was the bank statement.' Maurice stood up and pulled a sheet from the pile of paper on the table. 'Our joint current account. I don't understand it.'

'What don't you understand?'

'I don't usually deal with our personal account. Of course, I manage the field centre budget, but most of our joint income came from Angela — from television and from her books. So really the joint account was always hers and she dealt with it.' Perez wondered what that might be like — to have a partner who earned so much more than you. It might happen to him when Fran became really famous. He told himself that of course he'd be fine with it, but deep down he wasn't sure. And it occurred to him for the first time that Angela might have been quite wealthy. The couple had no real expenses. They lived rent-free and the trust paid all their living expenses. Money was a powerful motive for murder.

Maurice was continuing: 'Angela went off for the day just before the weather closed in. A dentist's appointment. She had dreadful toothache one night and arranged it urgently. The statement says she took three thousand pounds in cash from our joint account. Why would she have done that? Why would she want so much money? All we use cash for here is for the occasional drink at the centre bar and maybe chocolate from the shop. Everything else is settled on account.'

'Is the cash here? Has the search team been through the flat yet?' Perez had asked it to start at the Pund and move on to the North Light.

'No.' Now Maurice just seemed confused. He still stood with his back to the window, looking in at Perez.

'Where would Angela have kept money? Handbag? Wallet?' There had been no handbag in the bird room when the body was found.

'She used a small rucksack instead of a handbag,' Maurice said. 'Her purse would probably be in that.' But he made no move to find it.

'Should we look?' Perez spoke gently. Again he thought that although Maurice was managing to hold himself together to keep the field centre running, he was struggling to cope when he was alone. 'Where might the rucksack be?'

'In this cupboard with the coats.' Maurice was already on his feet, scrabbling through a pine cupboard that stood in the entrance to the flat. He threw out odd boots and shoes and emerged with the sack. By the time Perez got to him, it was too late to suggest that it should be bagged up and regarded as evidence. Maurice squatted where he was and tipped the contents on to the floor.

The burst of manic energy seemed to have left him drained and he just sat, looking at the pile of objects on the carpet. Perez knelt beside him.

There were scraps of paper, including a couple of till receipts, which Perez would look through later, a small diary, a packet of tissues and a large leather purse. Maurice saw the purse at the same time as Perez did and reached out for it before the detective could stop him. It was fat with a wad of rolled notes. Maurice counted them out.

'Three hundred and fifty pounds,' he said. 'And a bit of loose change. What did she do with the rest of it?'

'Maybe early Christmas shopping?' Perez suggested. His mother always went into Lerwick in November to stock up. Most of the islanders bought presents online, but she said she enjoyed her trip out to the shops. As much as anything it was a time to catch up with old friends.

'Angela? Are you joking? Angela didn't do Christmas!'

But we will, Perez thought suddenly. *This year it'll be me and Fran and Cassie in the house in Ravenswick*. He was ashamed then of thinking about his own happiness in the face of the man's misery.

Maurice looked up at him, his eyes bright and feverish. 'I need to find out what was going on here. I know I said I didn't care, but it's making me crazy. The speculation. The possibilities. It just goes round and round in my head.'

Perez replaced all the items in the bag. 'I'll take this with me too. It'll help me sort this out for you. It's probably got nothing to do with Angela's murder. All kinds of things come to light during an investigation. As soon as I know anything I'll be in touch.' He stood up. Maurice remained on the floor. Perez bent down and carefully helped him to his feet.

* * *

Sandy was using the bird room as an office and Perez found him there on the phone. He must have been talking to one of his girlfriends because as soon as he saw Perez he ended the conversation quickly.

'Did the search team come up with anything?' Perez asked.

'Not yet.'

'I need you to get back on the phone. Apparently Angela Moore went out to Lerwick to the dentist just over a week ago. Find out if she did see her dentist in town. I've got a feeling the toothache was just an excuse to allow her off the island. She also withdrew three thousand pounds in cash from the Royal Bank of Scotland. She wouldn't have been able to get that much from the hole in the wall. Talk to the cashier who served her. Did Angela mention why she needed that amount of cash? And see if you can track down what else she did that day. The cash doesn't seem to be here. What did she do with it?'

Perez could have answered these questions himself, but he knew it would take him weeks to do it. He'd grown up in Shetland, but still he was considered something of an outsider in the town. People would be reluctant to talk to him about the trivial details that would help trace Angela's movements while she was off the Isle. Perhaps it was because he'd worked in a city in the south for part of his career, perhaps because he came from Fair Isle. Sandy might be a Whalsay man, but he was completely at home in Lerwick now. He had contacts everywhere.

'I'll get on to it now.' Sandy leaned back in his chair and looked up at Perez. 'I might as well. There's nothing else to do. Did you know there isn't even a television for the guests here?' It was as if Perez had brought him to the edge of the world.

29

The next day was Sunday and suddenly everything was still. All activity ceased. No planes filled with bird-watchers and media folk. No helicopters. No murder. Even the weather was quiet. The island woke to a clear, cold dawn. On the bank by the shop, the wind turbine was motionless.

Perez asked Sandy to spend the day at the field centre: his role to reassure the remaining residents and to continue taking statements about Jane Latimer.

When Perez was a boy Sundays on Fair Isle were sacred. Every week he was taken to church twice — once to the kirk and once to the Methodist chapel. Before he was born, the islanders had decided they couldn't live with sectarianism and this was their way of dealing with it: whatever denomination they'd been born into, they'd all go to both services, kids scrubbed, men in suits or fancy hand-knitted sweaters, women in skirts and proper shoes. Sunday was a day of rest then. There was no work on the croft. No fishing. It had been different for the women, of course. There had to be lunch and the pans had to be cleaned, but they couldn't hang washing on the line — even if it was a good drying day — or the neighbours would talk.

Perez took Fran to the morning service in the

kirk. He knew it would make his mother happy to have them there and he needed time for reflection, away from the investigation. Let Sandy take the lead for a while. He felt too that Fran should understand what living in the Isle was about — she still had romantic ideas of a harmonious community existence. He wasn't sure she'd stomach the part religion played in bringing about the cohesion — the sort of religion preached by his father at least.

Thoughts of his father had been with him, reminding him of his cowardice, since he'd woken up. Perez still hadn't confronted the man about his relationship with Angela Moore. The night before, the moment had never been quite right. Perez had got back to Springfield in time for a late supper and the family had spent all evening together. To take his father outside and say he had something important to discuss would have alerted Mary and even if she suspected anything about her husband and Angela she would hate to think the relationship had become part of the inquiry. Over the meal James had been jovial, a good host. Perez thought his father was probably relieved. He'd taken the jewellery from the Pund and thought his secret was safe. What had he done with it? Thrown it out of the *Shepherd* on the way to the mainland? Or perhaps James was pleased Angela had died. The temptation to sin had been removed.

They left early for the kirk because James would be preaching, and took the long way round by the road because the ground was still sodden. Fran thought God was about as real as the tooth fairy. She came from a family of unbelievers and, to her, religious faith was incomprehensible. But today she behaved herself. She was soberly dressed in a long brown skirt and a little tweed jacket, brown leather boots. Just as they went in through the kirk door, she whispered to him: 'I hope you know I'm only here because I love you, Jimmy Perez. You owe me.'

Then after a quick grin she followed Mary to her seat.

Whenever they discussed religion, Perez always ended up agreeing with Fran. Stories and metaphors, that was the Bible. But in his gut he couldn't dismiss his father's teaching so lightly. He'd grown up with the notion of sin and had spent his adolescence haunted by guilt. He thought guilt was like a tapeworm living — and growing — inside him.

They'd just sat down when John and Sarah Fowler came in. The congregation turned to look at them; visitors were always welcomed to services but were something of a novelty. John beamed amiably around him, but Sarah still seemed tense. Perez thought she'd been most happy in the field centre kitchen. Away from the lighthouse she seemed lost.

His father took as his text Galatians 5:22 on the fruits of the spirit. At first Perez let the words wash over him. He was still thinking about the double murder, looking for connections between the women. He'd assumed at the beginning that Jane's death had come as a direct result of

Angela's but it wouldn't do to close his mind to other possibilities, to dismiss altogether an irrational killer targeting women. The team in Lerwick should do a more detailed check on the North Light visitors and staff. Were there unsolved crimes of violence against women in the areas where the incomers lived? He felt in his jacket pocket for a pen, so he could jot down a few notes.

Then the meaning of his father's sermon seeped into his consciousness. Perez set down the pen and the scrap of paper and began to listen more carefully. As he laid the pen on the narrow shelf built into the seat in front of him he saw his hand was trembling. Anger. It was all he could do not to walk out.

James had moved on to talk about self-control. One of the fruits of the spirit. It might be the last in the list but it was by no means the least important. James leaned forward and repeated the words for emphasis: 'By no means.' He turned over a sheet of paper on the lectern. James took his preaching seriously; he always made notes.

'In Proverbs, we learn that controlling one's own passions is harder than conquering a walled city fortress. A man must have mastery over his own behaviour. If he can't control himself, he'd be like the city after its walls are destroyed. Defenceless.' The last word came out in a thundering roar, but seemed to have little impact on the audience and James sought to find an image closer to home. 'Think how it would be if you were out in a small, flimsy kind of boat in the gale we've had in the last couple of days. Bad enough in something like the *Shepherd*, which is built for the job. But imagine one of those small dinghies the bairns play in close to shore in the mainland on summer days. And a force ten wind battering into the hull. You'd be drowned by the waves. Lost.' The audience nodded then in understanding and looked at their watches. Fifteen minutes. Big James never went on for much longer than that. And it seemed he was coming to a close: 'Without self-control the other fruits of the spirit would be impossible. Kindness, gentleness, patience and peace. All those would be swept away and drowned by selfish desires and emotions.'

The music started and they swung into a hymn. Sarah Fowler had a sweet voice and seemed to know the words. The couple were sitting just in front of them and Perez could make it out over the rest of the congregation. Beside him, Fran was singing too, but she could never hold a tune. It was something they laughed about.

After the service the islanders stood outside in the sunshine and chatted. No talk of the murders. The conversation was about when the bairns would get in from the Anderson High, a sixtieth birthday party to be arranged in the hall. Perhaps the Fowlers' presence constrained them. The couple stood for a moment too on the edge of the crowd, rather awkwardly.

Fran went up to talk to them: 'Did you walk all the way from the North Light?'

'It's a lovely day,' John said. 'And we wanted

to get away for a while. I'm sure you understand.'

'I'll give you a lift back,' Fran said. 'That is OK, Mary? I can use the car?'

Mary looked for James as if the decision wasn't hers to make, but Perez answered for her. 'Sure, no problem. Take it. But come straight home or you'll be late for lunch.' He didn't like the idea of Fran without him at the lighthouse.

He was still furious at his father's hypocrisy; how dare James preach about self-control? Perez thought he couldn't sit down for another meal with the man until the matter of Angela Moore had been discussed. Even if he'd got the whole thing wrong, if he made a complete fool of himself, he had to know.

Mary hurried away after a few words with her friends. She had the meat to get into the oven. Fran went with her, followed by the Fowlers. She muttered to Perez as she went: 'If I don't get out of these clothes soon, I'll almost believe I'm a Sunday school teacher or a member of the WI.'

'I'll hang on for my father,' Perez said. 'You don't mind?'

'Of course not. You don't see him often enough.'

James was still playing at being minister, shaking hands and asking after his flock. At last the rest of the congregation drifted away and the two men were left in the bright autumn sunshine, their long shadows making strange shapes on the boggy grass.

'That sermon.'

James turned to face him. They'd started to

walk slowly away from the kirk. 'Yes?' Pleased that his son was showing an interest.

'I really don't know how you've got the nerve.'

'What do you mean?' Big James's face was dark and impassive. No reaction other than a slight frown.

'Did you show much self-control when it came to Angela Moore?'

His father stopped suddenly in the road. What had Perez been expecting? Bluster and denial? A plausible explanation, which would make *him* seem ridiculous? Certainly not this stillness. He stopped too, waited for a moment for some response, then looked into the man's face. James was struggling to compose himself. There was no sign now of the fluent preacher, the spiritual leader of the island. James could find nothing to say.

Perez waited. All his life he'd been scared of this man and now his father was stuttering like a child caught in some petty mischief.

'You were having an affair,' Perez said at last.

'No!'

'You slept with her.'

'Once,' James said, his voice high-pitched with stress. Then, more controlled: 'Yes, I slept with her once, but there was no sort of relationship.'

'You gave her presents. Jewellery.'

'I fancied myself in love with her.' The man paused. 'But it was lust. I see that now.' He began walking very quickly down the road. Perez followed until they were marching in step.

'And what did my mother make of that? She was happy, was she, that it was only lust?'

James stopped abruptly. 'You have no right to pry into another man's marriage.'

'I have every right!' Perez realized he was yelling so loudly that the back of his throat hurt. 'I'm investigating a murder and you're a witness. You've corrupted a crime scene!'

'Always the detective, aren't you, Jimmy? Can't you leave the police out of this for once?'

They stood for a moment, staring at each other, the hostility sparking between them.

'All right then,' Perez said eventually. 'Let's leave the investigation out of it. For a while at least. Let's keep it personal. All my life you've given me the morality lecture, the guilt trip. Tell me how you justify sleeping with another woman. How can you live with yourself after that?'

'With my head I knew it was a shameful, stupid thing, but it was that woman.'

'So you're blaming her? She forced you to have sex with her, did she?' Perez felt the anger returning. He couldn't bear to see his father so cowed, so pathetic. The least he could do was take responsibility for what had happened.

'It was after a do at the North Light,' James said. 'About this time last year after all the visitors had left. A bit of a party, music. Jane put on a magnificent spread — a real sit-down supper. It was to thank the island for its support over the season. Angela claimed it was her idea, but I think Jane and Maurice hatched it up between them.'

'Go on.'

'There were a few drams before the meal and

wine with it. I'm not really used to wine.'

Perez said nothing. Let his father make his excuses.

'She took me into the bird room, made a big show of locking the door behind her. I . . . '

'Mother was still in the building!' Perez interrupted because he couldn't face hearing the details of his father and Angela Moore having sex. That was more information than he needed. But still he imagined it. The smell of wood and birds, the hard desk, the excitement and the urgency, the need to have it over before they were missed.

'And that was the only time?' Perez asked. He supposed his father was right. One hurried encounter hardly counted as an affair. Fran and her London friends would probably dismiss it as a trivial mistake.

'I dreamed about it happening again,' James said. 'I wanted it to. But it never did.'

'You tried to persuade her?'

'I made a fool of myself. I see that now.' He looked at Perez. 'We'd chatted at parties before it happened, flirted a bit. I hadn't thought she would do *that* with me if she didn't care for me.'

Perez saw for the first time that his father was an unworldly man. Throughout his childhood he'd thought of James as having great knowledge and experience. But of course his father had never lived away from the Isle. He'd been too young for National Service, had never been to university. Angela would have found him an easy target.

Perez found his anger was already starting to fade, replaced by the inevitable understanding. He didn't want to understand — that was for social workers, for weak indecisive people who made excuses for criminal behaviour. But he could never quite find it in him to condemn. Perez saw that as a failure, a kind of cowardice. Now he began to see how his father had been tempted. A long marriage. A life of routine — the rhythm of the croft, the boat, the kirk. And along had come a young woman, sexy and famous, appearing to find his father attractive. Of course he'd deluded himself.

James continued: 'She was all games. This was a boring place for her. She needed more excitement in her life. I told her I loved her, bought her presents. I suppose it was a kind of amusement for her. Maybe she was flattered by it.'

'Did she ever talk about her other men?'

Silence.

'You must have known there were others.'

'It seems that I knew nothing about her.' James paused, turned to Perez again, his face scarlet. 'I told her I'd leave my wife for her.'

Just like Maurice, Perez thought. He'd said all those things too. Had he come to his senses finally? Had he decided he could no longer live with a woman who made a fool of him?

'And what did my mother make of all this?' Perez asked, keeping his voice cold and hard, because Mary had been tempted in the past too but had never betrayed his father.

'She forgave me,' James said. 'She said it might

even have brought us closer together. We'll get over it in the end.'

Perez wondered how his mother could do that. James had made a fool of her. Surely no woman could forgive that. *She'll live with you and even be happy with you. But she'll never forget what you did.*

30

Driving north with the Fowlers after the church service, Fran found herself intrigued by the middle-aged couple. John was full of questions, about her family and Perez and why she'd decided to make her life on Shetland. And about her art. She was flattered that he'd seen her work and could talk about it with such knowledge and enthusiasm, but found it odd to be the object of his attention.

'Why all the questions?' she asked at last, laughing. 'Are you planning to write a book?'

'You never know. Perhaps one day I will. I'm interested in the nature of celebrity.'

Despite herself she felt a thrill that he considered her famous.

It was only when she was on her way home after dropping them off at the lighthouse that Fran realized Fowler's wife had hardly spoken at all. Fran had female friends who were much the same age as Sarah, but she could have belonged to a different generation. Fran's middle-aged London friends dressed flamboyantly, held strong opinions, laughed a lot. There was something almost Victorian about Sarah Fowler's dependence on her husband, in her anxiety and her timidity.

* * *

After lunch Fran and Perez went out for a walk. An island Sunday ritual, it seemed, because on their way north they met other families promenading in the sunshine. A middle-aged couple, arm in arm. Then a child with a bicycle, wobbling, the stabilizers off for the first time, and a girl pushing a doll's pram, followed by their parents, all still dressed for church.

Fran could tell that something had happened between Perez and James, but Perez wouldn't talk about it. Fran's parents were liberal, generous, easygoing. There'd been times as a teenager when she'd wished there'd been more rules — boundaries to batter against when she wanted to rebel and to hold her up when she was floundering. She thought Perez's childhood had all been about rules — James's rules — and wondered what had happened now to shift the balance of power. Over lunch James had seemed subdued, almost penitent.

Earlier she'd had a long telephone conversation with Cassie: 'Not long now, sweetie. Only two more days till I'm back.' Fran had decided she'd go out on Tuesday's boat as planned whether the investigation was over or not. 'I do miss you.' She worried occasionally about whether she'd got the balance right in bringing up Cassie. Too many rules or too few? Duncan let her get away with murder.

The walk ended up back at the North Light, as Fran had known it would. Perez would want to talk to Sandy; he couldn't take a whole day away from the investigation. The place was quiet, the common room empty. In the kitchen they found Sarah Fowler, scrubbing away at a roasting tin too grubby and too big for the dishwasher. She stood at the big sink, her sleeves rolled up to her elbows, again wearing one of Jane's aprons. There were soapsuds on one cheek. When she heard them behind her she turned round, anxious for a moment.

What is it with that woman? Fran thought. *Does she enjoy playing the martyr? The pathetic little wifey?* Then she thought: *Of course they'll all be jumpy. If I were staying here, I'd be just the same.*

Sarah gave a little smile. 'Your colleague's in the bird room.'

Perez nodded but stayed where he was. 'How's everything going?'

'Fine.' Satisfied at last that the roasting tin was clean, she set it upside down on the draining board. 'Actually, it's a dreadful thing to say, but it seems more relaxed here without Angela and Poppy.' She frowned. 'I miss Jane though.'

'Did you get a chance to talk to her much?' Perez leaned against the workbench. Inviting confidence. *If I were a murderer I'd confess to him*, Fran thought. *I wouldn't be able to help myself. I'd want so much to please him*.

'A bit,' Sarah said. 'She was a great listener. She didn't give away a lot about herself.'

'You had no impression that Jane felt scared, threatened?'

Sarah gave herself time to think, squeezed out the dishcloth and hung it over the long tap.

'No,' she said. 'Nothing like that.'

* * *

In the bird room Sandy was talking on his mobile. Fran could tell it wasn't work. Some woman, she thought, confirmed when he began to blush. There was always some woman.

'Rushed off your feet, Sandy?' Perez said. 'What have you got for me?'

Sandy kicked his legs off the desk and gulped the tea remaining in the mug in his left hand. 'Not much. I've talked to all the field centre residents now. Nobody admits to seeing Jane Latimer once she left the lighthouse on the day she died.'

'Someone's lying then. Because one of them slashed her with a knife and left her bleeding.'

'Could it not be one of the islanders? I mean this bunch, they all seem kind of civilized.'

Watching Perez, Fran saw him jump in to reject the idea immediately, then reconsider.

'Someone staying in the field centre killed Angela Moore,' he said. 'But you're right. It's important to keep an open mind. Anyone on the Isle could have murdered Jane. Is there anything from the search team yet? They haven't found the knife?'

Sandy shook his head. 'But then they wouldn't, would they? You'd just walk a hundred yards and throw it over the nearest cliff.'

'Who knew Angela kept the Pund as a love nest?'

'Ben Catchpole and Dougie Barr.'

'Not Hugh Shaw?'

'He claims not. He admits he had sex with

Angela Moore, but says it was either in the Land Rover or here in the centre.'

Fran tried to think herself inside the head of the dead warden. It had been Angela's dream to run this place and she'd achieved her lifetime ambition before she was thirty. What was left for her? A marriage of convenience and the adoration of young men flattered by her attention and attracted by her celebrity. She must have been bored witless. Had she decided it was time to move on? She was sufficiently ruthless to walk away, leaving Maurice and the other centre staff to make the best of it. It would have been different if she'd had a child, Fran thought. Everything would have been much more complicated then.

Perez was still speaking. Fran thought both detectives had forgotten she was there. Usually Perez was careful about what he said in front of her: he knew she would never betray a confidence but it was about sticking to the rules. Doing the right thing.

'I wonder if I've been looking too hard for a motive. Maybe after all this is just a man who likes to kill women.'

'Strong, competent women.' It wasn't Fran's business, but she'd never been much good at being seen but not heard. 'Women who subvert the stereotype of femininity. Jane was a lesbian and Angela a sexual predator.'

'So they were both women who could appear threatening to men.' At least Perez was taking her seriously.

Sandy just looked confused. 'Come off it! You

can't have any of the guys here as a psychopath.'

'Why not?'

'You've read the case histories and the profiles; psychopaths are loners. They're all poorly educated weirdos. These people have degrees, wives, proper jobs.'

Perez gave a tight little grin. 'Not all of them and maybe only the stupid ones get caught. We don't get to know about the bright ones. They get away with it.' He looked down at Sandy. 'Have you found out what Angela was doing in Lerwick on her day off the Isle?'

'Well, she didn't go to see her dentist. Nor any of the others in town.'

'Have you checked the banks?'

Sandy grinned. 'You do know it's the weekend and they're all closed?'

'But I know you have contacts, Sandy. Like that red-headed lass that serves behind the counter of Maurice Parry and Angela Moore's bank. The one you brought to the staff party in the summer.'

'Angela went into the Royal Bank of Scotland in the street and withdrew three thousand pounds in cash from the joint account.'

'We know that! Give me something useful.'

Sandy shook his head. 'It was lunchtime. The place was busy and there was a queue. There was no time to chat. She took most of the money in fifty-pound notes — almost cleared the bank of big denominations. She folded them in half and put them into a pocket in her rucksack.' He looked up at Perez. 'You did check all the pockets?'

'What do you think?'

'Then she walked out.'

'She came home on the afternoon plane,' Perez said. 'Where did she spend more than two thousand five hundred pounds in a couple of hours?'

'Maybe she didn't spend it,' Fran said. 'Maybe she had her own account with another bank and she put it into that. Cheques can take ages to clear. If she wanted the money to cover a cheque she'd already written, cash would have been more efficient.'

Perez turned back to Sandy. 'Can you check that out in the morning?'

'Angela was seen again that day,' Sandy said. 'About two in the afternoon, in the street. Coming out of Boots.'

'Who saw her?'

'Just an old school friend of mine. That was her I was talking to on the phone when you came in.' He grinned again.

* * *

Fran wanted to put off their return to the south of the island and Perez's parents. She couldn't face Sunday tea, Sunday television, bland and boring conversation. She and Perez stood outside the centre, preparing for the walk back down the island, when she found a possible distraction.

'Have you ever been up the lighthouse tower?'

'Once,' Perez said, 'when I was a bairn. They had an open day and showed everyone round.'

‘Any chance we could have a look, do you think? There’d be an amazing view from the top.’

She saw he was considering the matter. There were times when she wanted to scream at him. *Don’t you ever do anything on impulse, Jimmy? What is it with the caution? If I hadn’t proposed to you I’d still be waiting*. But it seemed that he too was in no hurry to rush home.

‘Sure, if it’s open. I know Bill Murray from the Koolin has a key. He holds it for the Northern Lighthouse Board. They come once a year to paint it and service the light.’

‘Won’t Maurice have access to it? In case of emergencies?’

‘Let’s check if it’s locked before we trouble him.’ She felt he was indulging her as he might have done Cassie. There was a small arched door at the foot of the tower. The handle was stiff but eventually it turned. Inside, a stone staircase spiralled around the outer wall. There was no light, except from the door that Perez had propped open — and that grew fainter as they climbed — and then from a small window further up. Fran felt the muscles in the backs of her legs strain and stopped for a moment to catch her breath. Ahead of her Perez seemed not to feel the exertion. He continued and must have reached the top and opened a door into the lens room because suddenly the shaft of the tower was flooded with light. She followed him.

She’d been right. The view was astounding and the island was spread out beneath them like a three-dimensional map. The jagged forks of cliff made sense, the road twisted past the northernmost crofts, which she could now recognize by name. *Even if we never come to live here*, she thought, *this is always going to be a special place for me. I kind of belong*. She saw the Land Rover being used by the search team making its way back to the field centre. Then, turning to the west, she saw Sheep Rock again, from a different and arresting perspective. She took a sketchpad from her bag and began to draw, very quickly, her forehead pressed against the glass.

'You don't mind the height then?' Perez said. 'After the plane I thought you might have a problem with vertigo.'

She turned briefly to smile. 'In the plane I thought I was going to die. A reasonable fear in the circumstances.'

Perez looked briefly over the island but soon turned his attention to the north and west. 'You can see the lighthouse at Sumburgh Head and the Foula cliffs.' Fran was so focused on her sketch that she hardly heard him.

When she saw him again, conscious of a silence, a lack of movement, he was peering under the wooden bench that ran round the room, under the windows. He must have sensed her looking at him. 'What do you think that is?'

'Don't know. A bit of rag.' Her head was still full of the painting she was planning. She thought it might be her best work ever. Would it be possible to exhibit it before she gave it to James and Mary?

'White cotton certainly. A pillowcase, do you think?'

'You're thinking it might have held the feathers scattered over Jane's body?'

'It's possible. Even the automatic lights are kept immaculate. The guys who come to check the working wouldn't have left that here. The search team haven't found the pillowcase yet and I asked them to look. I'll get them up here to check the place out. Don't touch more than you have to now. There might be fingerprints.'

Fran expected Perez to climb immediately down the stairs to fetch Sandy and the other officers but he didn't move. 'I think the murderer has been up here spying,' he said. 'I wondered how he tracked down Jane to the Pund. From here you can see everyone's movements at least in the north half of the island. He knows exactly what we're all doing and where we are.'

She reached out and took his hand.

* * *

As they walked south again, the late afternoon sun was almost warm. Almost. They were still holding hands, like seven-year-olds pretending to be grown up, exchanging a few words. All about themselves, how lucky they were to have found each other, plans for the future. Sentimental stuff that had nothing to do with the investigation. Fran had assumed Perez would want to stay in the tower to supervise the search, but he'd decided to leave them to it. Fran was grateful for that, and for the knowledge that the murderer could no longer be up there, looking down at them. She felt ill whenever she thought that their intimate moments together could have been observed.

Perez's phone hadn't rung all day. Too good to be true, Fran thought suddenly.

'Is your mobile actually switched on?' His phone was a standing joke. An alternative form of contraception, she said. Always ringing at the most awkward time.

'Shit! I turned it off for the kirk and forgot to switch it back on.' He pulled a face, pressed a button. 'Five missed calls.' And the romantic walk through the warm autumn light was over. He was a cop all over again.

'So tell me . . . ' His phone pressed against his ear with his left hand, scrabbling for a pen and paper with the other. They'd stopped and he leaned the paper on a piece of dry-stone wall. She squatted on a flat rock, looked back towards Sheep Craig, remembering the perspective of it from the tower, thinking again about the painting she'd make. His words were like background music in a bar. She heard them but didn't take in the meaning. Perez scribbled on the paper, filled one side with his crabby, repressed writing and turned it over. His questions weren't much more than promptings to persuade the caller to continue talking.

'How long? So she would have known?'

Fran was thinking about the shadows formed by the different planes of the cliffs. In this light the rock was almost pink. Perez ended the call and pressed the buttons again, listened to a message on his voicemail. The sun had disappeared behind Ward Hill, on Sheep Rock the shadows had deepened.

Another phone call. As the sun had set the air grew colder. Fran stood up, stamped her feet, pulled her coat around her. Perez mouthed at her that he wouldn't be long. This time there was a more even conversation. Perez asked questions and listened to answers.

'What's she doing now?'

Fran heard the indistinct reply, a woman.

'Did she say when she last spoke to Angela?'

Eventually the call was over. Complete silence. He took her hand again. *Don't ask*, she told herself. *It's not your business*. But Perez was talking anyway.

'The first call was the pathologist from Aberdeen with initial post-mortem results on Angela Moore.' He focused on a hooded crow, flapping over a fence post. 'She was pregnant. About eight weeks. She must have realized.'

'Maybe that's what she was doing in Boots,' Fran said. 'Buying a pregnancy test. A confirmation.'

For more than a year now Fran had been broody. There were times when she was so desperate to feel a baby kicking in her belly that she thought any child would do, but the longing was also about Perez. She imagined a baby with black hair, strong limbs, a tight grip. Looking like its father. She had brought up the subject with Perez. Elliptically, not wanting to put him under pressure. *Of course, a child*, he'd said. He wanted nothing more than that. *But let's wait until after the wedding. The wedding night if you like*. And she'd agreed, because she understood his need for rules and order, and besides, how romantic would that be, to conceive on their wedding night! But the longing had become a quiet and aching frustration, always with her.

Now, she thought of the body she'd seen in the bird room, cold, the colour of putty. Inside it, a dead baby.

Had Angela been feeling broody too? She'd been of an age when the most unlikely women can become obsessed with the notion of motherhood.

'Maurice had no idea,' Perez said. 'I'm sure of that.'

'Are you? I don't feel I know him at all. And it might not be his child.'

'I suppose it's a motive,' Perez said uncertainly. 'Though we don't know she was planning to keep it. Perhaps the trip south was something to do with that.'

'She wasn't drinking at the party,' Fran said. 'I noticed, wondered if she had some rule about drinking on duty. If she was planning a termination, why would it matter?'

The colour had seeped out of the landscape. They walked together down the middle of the road.

'Another piece of news,' Perez said. 'Morag has tracked down Angela's mother.'

31

Back in Springfield, Perez spoke on the telephone to Angela's mother. He wished he could go to visit her, but she was still living in the south-west of England, a small village in Somerset. She was called Stella Monkton. Perez didn't know if she'd remarried after her divorce from Archie or gone back to using her maiden name. She had the same sort of accent as Ben Catchpole, the assistant warden in the field centre. Soft, round vowels. But educated, Perez could tell that. There was precision in her words. She made every one count.

'You didn't see about your daughter's death in the media?' He was still surprised that it had taken Morag to find her, that the woman hadn't approached *them* for details.

'I belong to a choir,' she said. 'There was a week's music school in Brittany. It was rather a wonderful experience and in the evening the last thing one wanted was to look at the television news.'

He was curious about her work, how she'd earned her living after running away from her husband, abandoning her child, and she told him without his having to put the question.

'I work in a school for children with special needs. I was fortunate that the trip with the choir happened in half term.'

'I understand that Angela has made contact

again with you recently.'

There was a moment of silence. 'Look, Inspector, I find this extraordinarily difficult to discuss over the telephone. Would it be possible to come and see you there? I'd very much like to see where Angela lived and died. I've looked at the possibility of travelling up. I could get to Shetland tomorrow lunchtime if I leave Bristol on the first plane to Aberdeen. Perhaps you could meet me there?'

'There's a small plane into Fair Isle tomorrow afternoon if you'd like to come to the field centre.' Perez wondered briefly what the woman would make of the ride, hoped the weather stayed fine. 'I can book you on to that.'

Another silence. 'Thank you, Inspector. That would be very kind.'

Then, although it was Sunday he called Vicki Hewitt, using the private number she'd given him in her message on his mobile.

'What have you got for me, Vicki?'

'It's about those feathers, the ones on the first body. Not the stuff emptied from the pillow over Jane Latimer.'

'What about them?'

'I've got them to an expert. Some he's pretty sure he can identify. There are kittiwake feathers, herring gull, a couple from waders — he's fairly certain they're curlew but he'd like to do a DNA test to be completely sure. Another from a swan.'

'All those you'd find on the island,' Perez said. But he didn't think there'd been whooper swans yet that autumn. The only swan he'd heard about was the rare one that had caused all that fuss.

And Angela had been dead when that was discovered.

'Can you get your chap to get a DNA test on the swan too?' he said. 'Pin down the exact species.'

'It'll come out of your budget.'

He thought he really didn't care.

Back in the small bedroom in the roof he went through the letters that had been addressed to Angela. He'd looked at them quickly the evening before, after Maurice had handed them over. Most of the mail was junk, circulars and advertising. There was a letter from her publisher, but it seemed designed to give away as little information as possible: 'I agree we should meet to discuss the matter. Perhaps you could let me know when you're planning to come south.' Perez made a mental note to talk to the editor the following day. Then there was a thick white envelope containing a set of train tickets. First class advance National Express from Aberdeen to London dated the beginning of November. Had Angela already made an appointment to meet the publisher? The letter was so delayed that it was possible. Or maybe there was another reason altogether. Perhaps Maurice would know.

* * *

Later, he drove back to the North Light. There'd been a proper Sunday high tea. Cold meat and salad followed by one of his mother's fruit cakes; although the lettuce had come in on the recent boat it was still limp and unappetizing. Fran seemed content enough to stay in Springfield, though she'd given him a wistful look when he said he had to go back to work. She'd brought out her sketchbook and made notes in charcoal, now she was roughing out a drawing, oblivious to *Songs of Praise* in the background.

He went straight to Maurice's flat, using the staff door through the kitchen. He didn't want to get caught up in a conversation with the guests until he'd talked to Angela's husband. In the flat the television was on too. This time football. Maurice got up and switched it off when Perez came in. His response to the knock had been a shout to come in.

There was the inevitable bottle of whisky and a glass on the table. 'You will join me, Jimmy?' Maurice nodded towards it. Then: 'Don't look at me like that, man. I'm not a drunk, but I find it helps dull the edges a bit. Now Poppy's gone, what does it matter?'

'Maybe a small dram,' Perez said and Maurice went off to find another glass.

'What about Angela?' Perez asked. 'Did she like to take a drink?'

'Red wine. That was her tipple. And lots of it if the mood took her.'

'But not recently,' Perez said. 'At our engagement party, for example. She didn't have a lot to drink then.'

'What are you saying, Jimmy? Where is all this leading?' Maurice wasn't drunk, but as he'd said the hard edges were blurred, his thoughts a little slow and fuzzy.

'I spoke to the pathologist today,' Perez said.

He paused to make sure he had the man's attention. 'Angela was pregnant.' Maurice blinked at him. 'You didn't know?'

Slowly Maurice shook his head.

'She'd arranged to go south,' Perez persisted. 'I was wondering maybe for an abortion. But if she'd stopped drinking, was looking after herself, that doesn't quite make sense.'

Maurice looked up. 'The baby wasn't mine. I had a vasectomy years ago. Maybe you should talk to the father.' The first hint of bitterness since Angela had died.

'Who would that be?' Perez asked. 'Who should I talk to?'

'Maybe you should look close to home, Jimmy. Big James followed my wife around like a love-sick puppy.' Then he shrugged, a sort of apology for loading his pain on to the other man. 'No, it couldn't be him. If anything happened there it was nearly a year ago.'

'A more recent admirer then.'

'Oh, they all admired her,' Maurice said. 'And who could blame them? The more difficult question is which of them might she have fallen for. Enough to carry his child. I didn't think she cared for any of them that much.'

'It could have been a mistake, an accident.'

'Angela didn't make those sort of mistakes, Jimmy. I found the morning-after pill in her bag once.'

'Not a maternal bone in her body,' Perez said. 'That's how you described her to me.'

'So I did. But perhaps biology overtook her in the end. Perhaps she'd decided she wanted a child even if she couldn't have one with me. Angela was used to getting what she wanted.'

Perez looked at the man. He didn't seem as astonished by the news of Angela's pregnancy as Perez had expected. Had there been signs? Sickness? After all, he'd had three children of his own. Had he guessed she was carrying a child, but not asked, not really wanting his suspicions to be confirmed? Or was the information just too much for him to take in?

'I wonder if Jane guessed that Angela was having a baby,' Perez said. Jane had been observant. Nothing much happened in the field centre without her knowing about it. If Jane had worked this out, could it be a reason for her death? 'Did Jane drop any hint about it to you? Maybe after Angela died?'

'No!' It came out as a shout. Maurice held up his hands. 'I'm sorry, Jimmy, but I didn't know Angela was pregnant.'

He hadn't drawn the curtains and Perez looked out into the darkness. There were the lights of a ship, a big tanker from the shape of it, moving steadily south. Maurice had turned his body away, as if to make clear that the discussion was over. It was time for Perez to leave.

'We've traced Angela's mother.'

No reaction.

'She's coming into Fair Isle tomorrow. I've booked her on to the afternoon plane.' He paused, but still Maurice gave no sign that he'd even heard. 'I think she'd like to meet you, but that's your decision.'

At last Maurice turned his head. 'Of course I'll

meet her. You'll make the arrangements, will you, Jimmy? You'll bring her here.'

'Why had Angela booked train tickets to go from Aberdeen to London at the beginning of November? It seems she had a meeting with her publisher, but do you know what that was about?'

'No! It seems to me now that I didn't know anything about her. She was my wife, but she could have been a stranger.'

He looked up at Perez, now obviously expecting him to leave, but still Perez sat where he was.

'Is the lighthouse tower always kept unlocked?'

'Of course not, Jimmy. It'd be a health and safety nightmare. We have kiddies staying here in the summer. You couldn't have them running up and down the stairs, tampering with the light.'

'But I found it unlocked this afternoon.'

Maurice shrugged. 'Is it important?'

'It could be. Did you have a key here?'

There was a pause. Maurice looked up from his whisky. 'It was kept with the big bunch on the hook in the larder.'

'The same one as the key to the bird room?'

'Yes, but we never used most of them.'

'But anyone staying in the centre would know where they were kept?'

'Only if they'd asked Jane. She was the keeper of the keys.' Then Perez thought at last he'd found a motive for the cook's murder. She'd known the killer had been in the tower. Had he hidden something else there?

They sat for a moment in silence. 'Were you

never tempted to go up there?' Perez asked at last. 'To see where Angela was going, to see who she was with? You'd get a view from there of everything that was going on.'

Maurice set down the glass so violently that some of the liquid spilt on to the polished table. 'You don't get it, do you, Jimmy? I didn't want to know where she was going or who she was meeting. As long as she came home to me every evening I didn't care.'

* * *

Sandy was in the common room, drinking beer, talking to the three single men. Perez hoped Sandy realized he was in the North Light to work; this wasn't a few days' unofficial leave from the routine of the office. Immediately he decided that the thought was unfair; these days the Whalsay man took his job seriously. No one would be better than Sandy at getting these men to discuss Angela Moore and her relationships.

Perez helped himself to a coke at the bar and slipped some money into the honesty box. He took a seat just outside the circle of chairs. There was a pyramid of empty beer cans built on the coffee table in the middle. Hugh Shaw was at the end of a story — something about a birdwatcher in a brothel in Tashkent. He nodded to acknowledge Perez's presence and continued to the tagline. Sandy almost choked, he was laughing so much. The others were more restrained; Perez guessed they'd heard it before.

Sandy saw Perez look at the empty cans.

'These aren't all ours,' he said. 'The boys from the search team were here earlier. They've only just gone to bed.'

'Could I have a few words, Sandy?' No point his sitting there drinking with them. They'd never accept him as one of the boys.

They returned to the bird room, the closest thing they had to an office here, the memory of a woman's body still lying over the desk between them.

'Did the team find anything in the tower?'

'You were right. That was a pillowcase and the lining of the pillow itself. There are small fragments of feather still left inside. Nothing else. No fingerprints. The handrail going up the steps and round the lens had been wiped clean.'

'The screwed-up pillowcase would have gone in a pocket. The killer must have gone straight up to the tower after murdering Jane.' Perez pictured the killer, looking down the island. Had he seen Perez walking towards the Pund? Had he been already aware that the body had been found before Rhona Laing and the rest of the team arrived in on the plane?

Perez nodded vaguely in the direction of the common room. 'Do any of them admit to having been up the tower?'

'No, they all claim to have assumed it would be locked.'

So all it would take, Perez thought, would be one piece of forensic evidence linking a field centre resident to the lens room and we'd have our murderer.

'What do your drinking pals say about Angela

Moore?' Perez wondered if the three men had considered themselves rivals. They'd all been bewitched by the woman. Had the spell been broken now she was dead?

'That she was a cruel and wonderful woman.'

'Specifics would be good, Sandy.'

'I have the feeling that they're all relieved she's dead. Like, they say how fantastic she was, but I think they were a wee bit scared of her. They didn't know how to stand up to her.'

'Did they all feel like that?'

'Maybe Dougie, the fat one, a bit less than the others.'

'Why do you say that?'

Sandy shrugged. 'I think he enjoyed her company. He wasn't so intimidated.'

'He wasn't having sex with her,' Perez said. 'It was more about the shared interest. The birds.'

'But occasionally she got things wrong.' Sandy had brought his beer with him and took a swig from the can. 'That's what Dougie told me. 'She was a great birder, but not quite as great as she thought.''

'He didn't tell me that.'

'Well, he'd not have wanted to look disloyal. He said it wasn't unknown for her to take credit for identifying a bird found by someone else. And the others agreed. Not really a motive for murder but you said you wanted the detail.'

Perez considered, tried to imagine this flawed, driven woman. She wouldn't bear being wrong. She would hate it. Perhaps that was a motive for murder after all.

'What did they make of Jane Latimer?'

'That she was a brilliant cook. Nothing else about her mattered to them.'

'Angela Moore was pregnant,' Perez said. 'Which of those boys would you put down as the father?'

There was a moment of silence while Sandy considered. He was much better these days at keeping his mouth shut until he had something worth saying. 'Hugh,' he said at last. 'I mean, she wasn't looking for a man to stand by her, was she? She had that already with Maurice. If it was just the sperm she was after, Hugh would make less of a fuss.'

'It couldn't be him,' Perez said. 'He's only been here for a few weeks and Angela was two months' pregnant. Unless he's telling us lies and he'd known her before. I suppose she could have met him on one of her trips south.'

'Couldn't we get them to do a blood test? That way we'd know for sure.'

Perez supposed they could but he wasn't sure it would help them discover who had stabbed the women. He always thought of the victims as women in the plural. Because, despite his warning that they should all keep an open mind, he was convinced there was just one killer.

* * *

When Perez arrived home, Fran had gone to bed but his mother was still up, on the computer in the office that had once been a small bedroom. Recently, she'd become a demon Internet freak. She emailed friends all over the world and had even started her own blog: *Notes from a Fair Isle*. James had at first felt threatened, then become resigned. He was happy for Mary to save the croft accounts on the PC and to order in feed and seeds online. He still resented the time Mary spent on the computer though, the notion that she had an exciting life in which he played no part. Perez sensed it had caused arguments.

Perez pushed open the office door. Mary's glasses had slid down her nose and there was a mug of tea, cold on the desk beside her.

'Mother, you're obsessed,' he said, only half joking. 'Go to bed.'

'I thought you might be interested in this . . . '

He pulled up a kitchen stool, ready to indulge her. He knew she enjoyed the times they had alone together. The two of them had always been close. He was grateful she'd taken so easily to Fran. Some mothers would become petty and jealous. He was tempted to ask her about James. How could his mother be so generous about his encounter with Angela? But she wouldn't want it discussed and would hate to think that Perez knew about it. Better to leave it to his parents to deal with in their own way.

'What is it?' He thought his voice sounded forced, unnaturally cheerful.

'An article about Ben Catchpole.'

'How did you find it?'

'I Googled him.' She blushed. 'I tried it with all the folk staying at the North Light. Just out of interest, you know. You can't blame me for that.'

'Did you come across anything else?'

'Some bits and pieces,' she said. 'I'm surprised

you've not tried it yourself. But this seemed the most important.' She pushed her chair out of the way so Perez could read the screen. The article was in the Scottish edition of *The Times* online and had been written six years before. The piece ran:

Green Activist Arrested in Braer Protest

To commemorate the environmental disaster caused by the running aground of oil tanker the *Braer* in southern Shetland ten years ago, Benjamin Catchpole, research student and green activist, broke into the oil terminal in Sullom Voe and caused tens of thousands of pounds' worth of criminal damage. He received a suspended custodial sentence when he appeared in court earlier this week. Police sources say they believe Catchpole had help within Shetland to carry out the crime, and it seems likely that other charges will be brought.

'I know about the conviction, Mother. It's one of the first things we do: check the criminal records of suspects.' He hadn't known that Ben had received a suspended sentence though. Or if he had known, he'd forgotten. He remembered the case, even though he'd been working in the south when the offence was big news in Shetland. The protesters had had some support locally, the effect of the *Braer* still fresh in people's memories. He read on to the end of the article and couldn't prevent a small gasp when he saw the byline. *John Fowler*. So all these apparent strangers, turning up in the North Light for the same week in late autumn, had been in contact in the past. Catchpole was quoted in the article, so Fowler must have spoken to him at least over the phone. Coincidence? Birdwatching was a small world. Or had the autumn gathering in the Fair Isle field centre not been random at all, but planned? For the purpose of murder?

32

Monday. Fran's last day on Fair Isle. She found herself looking forward to being back in the small house in Ravenswick. Her own space and her own rituals: working in the early morning while she was still in pyjamas, catching up with her friends over more than the one glass of wine she felt she could take in front of Jimmy's parents, cooking for herself and for Cassie. And being free to swear when the mood took her. They'd decided they would sell Perez's place and the Ravenswick house and buy somewhere bigger before they got married. Fran had enjoyed driving around Shetland mainland looking at prospective homes. The west side was so pretty, she thought, but if they moved somewhere like Walls, it would be a long trek into work for Jimmy and to school for Cassie when she started at the Anderson. Now she wondered if she could bear to leave Ravenswick. Maybe they could build on to the small house there. She imagined something wonderful, very light and spacious to contrast with the original space, new and old Shetland together. And a purpose-built studio. Would that be too much of an indulgence? It would be a project and she loved projects. She'd discuss it with Jimmy when this case was over. Now it would be pointless; he'd never concentrate.

He'd been back late the night before and when

she'd asked how things were in the centre he'd been noncommittal, not uncommunicative, but not sure himself what to make of events surrounding the case. It seemed to her that he brooded about it all night. She woke to find him already up and dressed, a shadow in the room, though it was dark still outside.

'Shall I bring you tea?' Usually she adored tea in bed. It was his way of pleasing her.

'No. I'll get up,' she said. 'Our last day before I go back.'

They had the kitchen to themselves. They giggled and whispered, supposing Mary and James to be still in bed. Again she thought there was something exciting, illicit in their being alone together in his parents' house. She fancied herself like a heroine in a nineteenth-century novel maintaining the proprieties. But not like Sarah Fowler, she thought. Fran would always have more spirit than her. Perez was standing behind her chair, watching the toast on the Rayburn. She reached up, put her arms around him and kissed him. By the time they'd finished breakfast the sky was getting lighter.

'What are your plans for today?' She'd always promised herself that she wouldn't interfere with his work. She had her own life; she didn't need to meddle in his to stop herself being bored. But here on the Isle things were different. Boredom had crept up on her over the last two days. Another hour alone with his parents and she'd go stark staring mad.

'Angela's mother arrives on the midday plane,' he said.

'And this morning?'

He gave her a sudden, wide grin, so she realized he knew how she was feeling.

'I'm going back to the North Light. Come with me. I promised Sarah I'd find her someone to help in the kitchen.'

'So it's a skivvy you're after?'

'I thought you might talk to her,' he said, serious now. 'Find out if her husband knows more about Angela than he's letting on. He admits to having met her. I sensed something. A tension.'

'You think he'd had an affair with her? His wife's not going to know about that, surely. She would never have agreed to come here with him if she thought there was something going on. And even if she had suspected they were lovers, she's not going to talk to me. It's not something she'd want to chat about to a stranger while we're washing the dishes.'

'You don't want to come with me, then?'

'Hey, Jimmy Perez. Just try and stop me.'

* * *

The wind had increased again, buffeting the car from the north. Fran tried not to think of her trip back to Shetland mainland in the boat the next day. As they approached the lighthouse there was a sudden shower of hail, ferocious, so the balls of ice bounced off the windscreen and the noise in the car meant they had to stop speaking. The yard was white as if it had snowed. Fran remembered her first meeting with Perez.

The ground had been white then too.

The residents were still sitting in the dining room over scraps of toast and cold coffee. They were all at one table and the rest of the room looked empty and bare. Maurice was with them. He wore the same clothes he'd had on when Fran had last seen him. There was a small grey splash of what might have been porridge on his jersey. She had a sudden urge to shake him. *Pull yourself together, man, and have some pride. Bad enough that you let your wife make a fool of you*.

Perez, she knew, would only feel sympathy. She thought again he was more like a social worker or a priest.

Maurice looked up with sad, red eyes. 'If you're looking for your colleagues from Inverness, they went out early. They wanted to look at the ground near the Pund one last time. They said Ms Blake took footwear impressions from the track, but the heather's long and they still haven't found the knife. Sandy's in the bird room.' Then he rested his head in his hands as if the words had exhausted him.

Sarah got to her feet and began to clear the tables. Fran found a tray and began to help. 'I'm your assistant for the day.'

'Really, there's no need.' Sarah gave a quick, sharp smile. A touch of panic? What would she be frightened about? Sharing the place with a murderer. Of course that would be reason enough.

'Trust me, there is. Another day at Springfield with Jimmy's folks and I'd go quietly crazy.'

So Fran found herself in the field centre kitchen, peeling carrots to make soup, while Sarah was kneading dough for pizza.

'Doesn't it feel weird doing all this?' Fran asked, the first thought that came into her head. 'I mean, doesn't it feel like stepping into a dead woman's shoes? It always seemed to me that the kitchen was entirely Jane's domain.'

Sarah stopped for just a moment and then returned to work, pressing the heel of her hand into the dough. Her sleeves were rolled up to the elbows.

'I'd never thought of it like that,' Sarah said. 'I don't have that sort of imagination. Maybe I need to work because it stops me worrying about what's happened here. I mean, if you really thought about it, how could you carry on?'

'Sharing supper with a murderer, you mean?' Fran looked up but she didn't stop slicing carrots. Nosy neighbour, that was the tone she was aiming for. And really, she'd once worked for a women's magazine: she could do gossip as well as any Shetlander.

Sarah shook her head. 'I really can't believe anyone here killed two women. They seem so pleasant, so . . . ' she paused, 'civilized, ordinary.'

'So you don't sit here in the evenings with a glass of wine, all looking at each other, wondering which of you is going to be the next to die?'

'No!' Sarah looked horrified and Fran wondered if she'd gone a bit too far. She could occasionally be flippant and felt liberated — and a little wicked — after a week of watching her words carefully. The chopping board was full and she pushed the sliced vegetables into a pan, before continuing with the neeps.

Sarah rolled the dough into a ball and lifted it into a bowl. She took a clean tea towel from a drawer and covered the dough. 'Now I've just got to wait for it to rise.' Fran thought she seemed very happy in this domestic role. Did she prefer it to her work with disturbed families? Had she made so little fuss about returning to the mainland because she was happy to escape her career for a while?

'Obviously, you can't help wondering,' Sarah said. 'I mean, I suppose some of us make more probable murderers than others . . . '

'So who's your preferred candidate?'

Sarah shot a sideways glance that was almost conspiratorial. Fran thought she'd probably missed the company of other women. Since Jane's death and Poppy's departure, Sarah had been stuck here surrounded by men, and although some men could gossip, none was as good at it as a woman.

'Of course, I can't imagine what the motive might be . . . '

'But?'

'Hugh,' Sarah said. 'He has that streak of cruelty. I can imagine any of the others killing Angela . . . '

'Even your husband?' Fran expected an immediate denial, but Sarah took the question seriously.

'Perhaps even him,' she said. 'Angela had this knack of winding people up. For her own amusement. Or perhaps just because she had no social skills at all. She knew what she wanted and just went for it. But although I can imagine John, and any of the others, killing Angela in a fit of rage, I can't see them stabbing Jane. She was lovely. Completely inoffensive.'

'Even if she'd discovered who the murderer was and threatened to expose him?'

'Even then,' Sarah said. 'Surely it would be a step too far.'

Fran leaned heavily on the knife to cut a particularly dense piece of turnip. Is this how much strength it would take to stab a person, to push through muscle, fat and bone?

'But you think Hugh might have done it?'

'I'm not saying that exactly, but of all of us I think he's the most likely. He seems to have no morality, no qualms about using people. A bit like Angela herself, I suppose.'

'But as you say, he has no motive.'

'No,' Sarah said. Fran thought the answer came too quickly. 'No,' Sarah repeated, then paused. 'Look, we're all done here for lunch and for dinner. There's no need for you to stay.'

'What were you planning for the rest of the morning?' *You're not getting rid of me that easily*.

'I thought I'd strip the beds in the big dormitory where the policemen from Inverness have been staying. Apparently they're leaving today and it'll be one less thing for Maurice to think of.'

'Sounds like unskilled work,' Fran said. 'Just my bag.'

The big dormitory held six beds in two rows of three. With the high ceiling, Fran thought it looked like an old-fashioned hospital ward. The search team had already packed and their bags were stacked close to the door. The room was on a corner and there were two long windows. Outside, the sky was grey. Fran thought winter had come early this year.

There were two pillows on each of the beds, so it seemed unlikely that the killer had stolen one from here, but as Fran stripped off the cases she felt the sharp shafts of the small feathers inside. One just like this, she thought. It was taken from the centre. Then: *But how would anyone carry a pillow to the Pund without being noticed?* In the rhythm of folding blankets, of pulling fitted undersheets from the mattresses, it was the practical that occupied her mind. *Does that mean the murderer drove there? Of course not. All the bird-watchers carry small rucksacks. It would be quite easy to squeeze one of these thin, rather mean pillows inside. And that's where the knife was too, of course. Once Jane had been stabbed, the pillowcase would be removed and the same knife used to slash the lining. Then the feathers could be scattered over the corpse. But why? Why go to all that trouble?*

Now all the beds were stripped and the sheets were piled in a heap in the middle of the floor.

'What now?'

'There's a laundry next to the kitchen,' Sarah said. 'We could make a start on the washing if you really want to stay.' She made the sheets into two bundles and the women carried them down the stairs.

The room was small and hot. There were two big industrial washing machines and a tumble dryer, a sink under the window, a press iron and a domestic iron and ironing board. Along one wall there were rows of wide shelves with sheets and towels. And spare pillows.

'Are the guests allowed in here?' Fran asked.

'I don't know. I've never used it, but the whole place is pretty relaxed.' Sarah started to load the first machine.

Looking around the room, beautifully organized, sweet-smelling, with its neatly folded linen, Fran thought this was more of a tribute to Jane than a grand memorial.

'What exactly do you do in the real world?' Fran asked.

'I run an early-years centre, working with babies and parents.' Sarah looked up. Her face was flushed from the heat of the room. She switched on the machine and it started to churn.

'Interesting. How did you get into that?'

'I trained as a nurse, then worked as a health visitor. I always enjoyed the community stuff most.'

So she would make a natural confidante for Angela. But if the field centre warden had told Sarah she was pregnant, why hadn't Sarah passed on the information to the police straight after the woman's body had been found?

The door opened and Perez was standing there. 'So this is where you've been hiding.' His voice was light, but Fran could tell he'd been worried. He didn't like her being on her own in the North Light. Well, tough. No way was she going to spend another day with his parents. 'I'm just going to fetch Angela's mother from the airstrip,' he said. 'Do you want to come?'

'No, thanks.' She grinned at Sarah. 'All this domesticity, I think we deserve a coffee.'

They had coffee in the kitchen to the background smell of yeast from the rising pizza dough.

'Did Angela ever talk to you?' Fran asked. 'She didn't get on with Jane or Poppy. You'd have thought she'd be glad of another woman around the place.'

'I don't think she liked women very much.' A pause. 'I don't think she liked anyone.'

Outside, the sky was dark and another storm of sleet passed over, rattling against the windows, bouncing inside the chimney breast.

'Is your husband out in this? Jimmy said the birders were obsessed, but they must be mad.'

'John loves being out.' Sarah looked at her over the rim of her mug. 'Even in bad weather. Birdwatching has been his passion since he was a child. Sometimes I resented it. It took up so much of his time. It was as if he were defined by it. I felt rather excluded.'

'And now? Do you still resent it? You're here after all.'

'I suppose if you love someone, you don't stop them doing the things that make them happy.'

'That's just what I think.' Fran looked up, smiling. 'I feel exactly the same way about Jimmy and his work.'

'But it's not easy,' Sarah said. 'Sometimes you feel you come second place to an obsession.'

'What do you make of the other guys here? Are they all obsessives?'

'I'm not sure about Ben. He's more into the science, the conservation, than the rare birds. John did a piece on him once when he worked for Greenpeace. Ben was very radical then. I think he's calmed down a bit, but the passion's still there. He lives what he preaches. He's vegetarian. He doesn't wear leather. Angela used to tease him.'

'She was a meat-eater?'

'Oh, yes,' Sarah said. 'A predator in every sense.'

'Did she prey on your husband?'

'What do you mean?' The woman looked up, shocked.

'Well, she seems to have had a go at all the other men in the place. And Angela was a writer too, wasn't she? Perhaps they met before.'

Sarah gave another of her strained little smiles. 'Oh, no!' she said. 'Can you imagine it? Angela and John! She liked her men young and pretty as far as I could tell, unless they could be useful to her. Besides, she'd scare John rigid.'

Fran smiled too as if she were sharing a joke, but she thought John might have been useful to Angela when her book had first been published. And in fact, John didn't seem to her to be the sort who would be easily scared.

33

Perez stood at the airstrip waiting for Angela's mother to arrive, his hood up against the hail. Fran would be leaving the next day. He'd told her the sea might be a bit lumpy but she'd decided to stick with her decision to go out on the boat. He hadn't realized how much the plane trip in had scared her. 'I don't care if I'm sick. I'll feel safer.'

The search team was already there, eager to be leaving. Frustrated because they'd contributed nothing to the case. Perez turned his back to the weather and chatted; occasionally they had to raise their voices to be heard against the breeze.

'Nothing,' the leader repeated. 'Complete sodding waste of time. You found the only piece of useful evidence in the lens room of the tower.' As if it was Perez's fault that they'd spent a couple of days on a bleak lump of rock where the Atlantic met the North Sea. 'I mean, we did the field centre. Although Miss Hewitt is sure the second victim was killed where she was found, we treated the whole of the lighthouse as a potential crime scene — except the lens room, obviously. It never occurred to us that anyone could have access up there.'

Perez said nothing. No point in recriminations now.

'The woman was moved around a bit in the loft after the attack,' the man went on. 'Posed, like Miss Hewitt said.'

'The killer would have had bloodstained clothes?' Perez asked.

'Almost certainly. There was that arterial spatter. Unless he wore protective gear.' Perez had a picture of the oilskins the *Shepherd* crew used. 'Not that we found anything. The clothes could have been burned, I suppose. Or ditched over a cliff.'

'And nothing else of interest in the field centre.' Perez didn't pose it as a question, just repeated it to himself.

'Of course, that doesn't prove much.' A younger man, dark-haired, spoke now. 'They all knew we were coming. He'd have dumped anything he didn't want us to see.' That assumption again that the killer was a man.

As the noise of the plane approached, the conversation moved on to their families, what they'd be doing for half-term, plans for Christmas.

Stella Monkton was small and neat, dressed in a long camel coat and brown leather boots. The only other passengers were Anderson High kids, late home for the mid-term break. They took the plane for granted: it could have been the school bus. They sauntered away to meet their parents, super cool. Angela's mother followed them away from the plane, then stood and looked around her. The waiting families stared. They'd noted Perez's presence. News of the stranger's arrival would be all over Fair Isle before teatime. He wondered how many would guess her identity. At first glance there was no physical resemblance to

Angela, who had been tall and strong. Perhaps she'd chatted to the kids on the way and word would get out through them.

Perez had already decided to take her back to Springfield before they went to the field centre. She'd be tired after her early start, would have only been given snacks on the flight into Sumburgh. And he'd find it easier to unpick the complicated family relationship in a more domestic setting.

She stood again by the car and looked east towards Sheep Rock. 'It's very beautiful here. Very dramatic. I can see what appealed to Angela.' Then she sat beside him, with her seat belt fastened and her hands clasped primly in her lap.

James was working and Mary had gone to visit a couple of elderly spinster aunts. The kitchen had been tidied specially for a visitor. There was a lasagne bubbling in the bottom of the Rayburn. New bread. The last of the fruit cake. They sat across the table from each other. He'd given her the seat with the view, a politeness he regretted later in the interview. There were times when she seemed distracted.

She knew what was expected and began her story as soon as the meal was over.

'Of course I should have taken Angela with me when I left my husband. But at the time I thought he would be better for her. I was ill, severely depressed. Only partly his fault. He had a good job. We were still living then in the home where Angela had grown up. I thought, if I could think clearly at all, that the house would provide stability. And she was bright, determined — much more like her father than me in most ways. It never occurred to me that he'd sell up and move her out into the country, that she'd become one of his projects. His experiments. He said she didn't want to see me and I believed him. They had always been very close.'

Through the window something seemed to catch her attention. Perez turned to see what had interested her, but there was nothing out of the ordinary.

'But Angela did make contact with you later?'

'Much later. Yes. I wrote to her twice a year with brief snippets of news. That I'd qualified as a teacher. With my address if I'd moved. New phone numbers. At Christmas and on her birthday. I always sent money. Not a great deal at first, but as much as I could afford. I never knew whether she received the letters, but Archie must have passed them on, because at last there was a reply. She was eighteen, just about to start university. She asked if we could meet.' The woman paused. 'I'm not quite sure what I was expecting. Perhaps not someone quite as big. It was ridiculous, but I still thought of her as a child. She was very assertive. Forceful. She knew just what she wanted. From her life and from me.'

'What did she want from you?'

The woman paused.

'At first she just wanted me to listen. To understand what I'd put her through. To be sorry. Of course I could see why she was angry. She told me what it was like growing up alone with her father. 'I had no friends. How could you do that to me?' Her passion for natural history grew out of her loneliness, I think. At least when she was watching the wildlife around the house in Wales there was a connection with something living. She was always going to be a scientist of some persuasion; her father had brought her up to believe that anything other than rational thought was ludicrous. She developed projects of her own — a study of a family of badgers, for example. She watched them from when she was ten until she left school and talked about them at that first meeting. 'People speak of badgers as if they're playful children. They can be really aggressive.'' Stella smiled. 'She told me she'd learned a lot from badgers.'

'So she studied biology at university?'

'Ecology,' she said. 'Later a PhD. Research into wading birds.'

'And she dropped contact with her father?'

'Apparently.'

Perez replayed the conversation in his head. 'You said at first she just wanted you to listen and to be sorry. What came later? What did she want then?'

'Money.' She looked up at him, seemed to feel a need to explain. 'Not for things. Angela was always ambitious but never materialist. For experience. The experiences she'd missed out on when she was growing up with her father. I paid for travel mostly and always gave her as much as I could. It never stopped me feeling guilty, but it helped.'

'So you developed a relationship,' Perez said.

'An understanding at least.'

'I'm not sure I ever understood her.' Stella Monkton's eyes were drawn to the garden just outside the window. It had been surrounded by a wall to provide shelter from the wind, but everything there had been ruined by the previous week's storm. She seemed particularly fascinated by the row of sprouts, blackened by the salt spray, flattened. 'And I didn't like her very much. But occasionally there were moments of kindness and humour, a sudden vision of the girl she might have been in different circumstances.' Stella corrected herself. 'If I'd behaved differently.'

'How could you ever know what she might have become?' Perez said. 'Nature and nurture. An old argument.'

'In either case, surely, I was partly responsible.' She gave a wan smile. 'After Angela completed her PhD all contact stopped. It was as if I'd never existed.'

Perez didn't know how to respond. It wasn't what he'd been expecting. He felt an ache of sympathy for the woman. She'd thought she had her daughter back — even if Angela wasn't the daughter she might have chosen — only to lose her again.

'Was there a row?' he asked at last.

'Nothing like that. Perhaps it was what she'd planned all along. Revenge. To drop me as I'd abandoned her. Perhaps she just felt she didn't need me any more. After all, her disappearance from my life coincided with her success: the discovery of a rare bird on one of her travels, a best-selling book. The television series followed soon after.'

'Did you try to get in touch with her?'

'Of course. By email and by phone. But she didn't reply and I knew there was no point in persisting.'

'Then she married.' Perez thought of his mother, the fuss she was making about his second wedding. It seemed a child's wedding was a big deal. 'Did you know about that?'

'There was a note about it in a natural history magazine I was reading at the dentist's,' Stella said. 'It had already happened by then. I certainly wasn't invited.'

'But you knew she'd taken up the position of director at the Fair Isle field centre?'

'Occasionally I'd Google her,' Stella said. 'It was one way of keeping track. The field centre has a website. There was a picture of her next to the lighthouse. She looked very happy.' She was staring into the distance. 'I did think of booking myself in as a visitor. Perhaps using a made-up name. But really I had no right to intrude where I wasn't welcome.'

Perez was astonished by the woman's restraint. He tried to imagine Fran in a similar situation. She wouldn't consider the niceties of her daughter's feelings — she'd be on the first plane north. But Fran hadn't run away and left Cassie behind.

'I'd understood from a colleague that there'd been a more recent contact.'

'Angela phoned me,' Stella said, 'a week before I left for Brittany. I was so certain when I answered that it would be one of my friends from the choir that at first I didn't recognize her voice. I couldn't speak. When Angela first broke contact, every time the phone rang I imagined it might be her, but this was a real shock. I didn't know what to say. In the end she became impatient: 'Mother, are you there?' I asked her what she wanted. It was clear, you see, that she must want something.'

'And what *did* she want?' Perez was suddenly tense. He was aware of the workings of his body, his heart pumping, his shallow breathing. Stella's answer might explain the case.

'She wanted to meet. She said she had to be in London to see her publisher at the beginning of November. Could she come on down to Somerset? Perhaps stay the night? This was new, Inspector. When she was a student we met on neutral territory. In restaurants or cafes, at the university. She would never come to my house.'

'You must have asked her why she wanted to see you after such a long time.' What must that have been like? A call out of the blue from a daughter she'd believed was lost to her.

'No, Inspector!' The response was sharp and immediate. 'I asked no questions! I didn't want to scare her off.'

So, no magic answer. Stella Monkton's trip to Fair Isle had helped him understand more about the victim but had brought him no closer to her killer.

The woman continued: 'I'm so grateful for that short telephone call, Inspector. It was a sort of reconciliation.'

She began to pile the plates together as if she expected the discussion to be over. Perez reached across the table towards her. No physical contact, but a way of telling her there were still things to say.

'What?' she demanded. 'What else is there?'

'Angela was expecting a baby.'

She looked at him, horrified. 'Oh no, the poor child.'

Was she talking about her daughter or the baby? He was certain the pregnancy was news to her. For the first time since she'd arrived on the island, she lost control and began to cry.

* * *

By the time they reached the field centre she was composed again. Maurice was waiting for them in the common room. Through the open door Perez saw Fran in the kitchen. Not working, it seemed, but sitting on a high stool next to a workbench, drinking tea. Sarah was there and so was the young birder Hugh Shaw. Fran glanced up and saw Perez, gave an immediate smile then a frown. *Don't interfere. Let me get on with it*. There was no sign of Sandy and that worried Perez. He'd told Sandy to keep an eye on Fran, to make sure she was safe, though surely no harm could come to her in full view of all the residents.

Perez wondered now what he hoped to get out of the encounter between Maurice and his mother-in-law. Not much. No dramatic revelation or confession. Maurice brought in a tray of coffee and they sat making polite conversation, like strangers in a waiting room, passing time.

'Would you give us a moment, Inspector?' Stella said when the coffee was drunk. 'I'd like to talk to my son-in-law alone.'

The description jarred. Maurice and Stella must be the same sort of age. And Perez was reluctant to leave them alone together. After all, he had hoped for some breakthrough in the case from the conversation. But he walked away and stood in the lobby for ten minutes.

Sandy came down the stairs from his room.

'I've tried every bank in Lerwick. If Angela Moore has her own account, it's not held anywhere in town. And I can't find out what she did between leaving the RBS and going into Boots.'

Perez supposed that in a city there'd be CCTV. In Shetland they had to rely on inquisitive people. 'OK,' he said. 'Keep trying.'

Sandy nodded towards the common room. 'How's it going?'

Perez shrugged. He didn't really know. When he returned to the common room he found Maurice and Stella much as he'd left them: polite, distant, formal. He sensed no drama or increased understanding.

It was only when Perez looked at his watch and said he'd have to get Stella back to the airstrip for the afternoon plane that Maurice spoke with any real feeling. He stood up and took Stella's hand.

'Your daughter was a remarkable woman.' A pause. 'I loved her very much.'

34

The autumn was over. That was clear to Dougie as he walked back from the south of the island for lunch. All the birds he saw belonged to winter. A flock of snow buntings turned so the light caught the white under-wings and they gleamed against the grey sky. A straggling line of pink-footed geese flew over, calling, and came slowly in to land on the west side. There would be no more migration, no more rare birds. It was time for him to escape back to the city, to his grubby flat and his tedious work. Perez couldn't keep them imprisoned any longer. Dougie would take the boat out on the following day.

He always suffered a mild depression at the end of the autumn. Winter birding was more predictable and lacked the excitement of the migration season. And it meant leaving Fair Isle and Angela. This year there would be no contact from her to look forward to, no emails, no tipsy phone calls in the middle of the night as she called him for reassurance. You *care about me, don't you, Dougie? You'll always be there for me*. And he would have been. It came to him now, struggling against the stiff northerly breeze, his face scarlet, his eyes and nose streaming, that his failure to make any real relationship with the women at work had been of his own doing. He'd begrudged the time in cinemas and restaurants. What if Angela should call him at home while he was away? She'd controlled his life, just as she'd controlled the lives of her lovers.

Perhaps now he'd feel free to develop other friendships, perhaps even find himself a woman. Someone who liked the outdoors, he thought. She wouldn't be a beauty; it would be unreasonable to expect that. But someone kind. Generous with her time and her body. A simple woman without an agenda.

When he pushed open the door into the field centre, the depression remained, but he felt comfortable with it. At this time of year he would have missed it if it weren't there.

Inside, there was the smell of cooking. After the effort of walking all the way from the Havens, the centre seemed very warm. Dougie hung up his coat and took off his boots. He wondered if he'd come back to the Isle next year. Perhaps he'd have a woman to bring with him; he pictured someone big and soft, in a hand-knitted sweater and a woolly hat, a huge smile. He'd show her the common birds, start a list for her. Or perhaps she'd prefer somewhere gentler for a holiday. It had been years since he'd been to Scilly and he still needed on *his* list some of the American migrants that turned up there in strong westerlies. They could rent a little cottage. She'd cook for him.

John Fowler was in the common room, a laptop on his knee, tapping away. Fowler had made a fuss when the police team from Inverness had insisted on looking at it. 'This is my livelihood.' All pompous as if none of the rest of them had to earn a living.

'And this is a murder investigation,' the leader had said. 'If you prefer I can get a warrant and we'll take it south with us.' Fowler had handed over the machine quickly enough then. Dougie couldn't see the point of paying to go away on holiday if you were just going to work.

Fowler looked up when Dougie walked into the room, logged off and shut down the computer.

'Don't mind me,' Dougie said. As usual, Fowler looked very clean. As if he'd just stepped out of the shower and put on clothes fresh from the washing line and the iron. Hugh had looked very dapper recently too. Who was he trying to impress? Dougie didn't really do ironing and he'd been here so long that all his clothes were dirty anyway. He'd need a trip to the launderette first thing when he got back. He didn't mind the launderette. A couple of back copies of *British Birds* or *Birding World* and he was sweet.

'No problem.' Fowler shut the computer, put it away in the case. 'I probably won't sell it anyway.'

'What are you writing then? A book?'

'No, just an article. A travel piece on the field centre. It seems in poor taste now Angela's dead.'

'I don't see why.' Dougie thought the place would need all the visitors it could get after two unsolved murders. Because it seemed to him that the police were no closer to finding out what had happened to the women. Or were people such ghouls that they'd want to come just to see where Angela had died? He'd done his bit for the island anyway. There'd be birders who'd be attracted to Fair Isle because he'd seen the trumpeter swan there.

Lunch was pizza. Dougie liked pizza and positioned himself on the seat nearest to the serving hatch so he could be first in the line for seconds. Perez's fiancée was there. She'd laid the tables and now she was standing beside Sarah Fowler and dishing out. Because his attention was on the food, it took him a while to realize that there was an argument. Ben, the assistant warden, and Hugh, bickering away like kiddies. Something about mud on the bird room floor. Though it seemed to Dougie that wasn't really what it was about at all. The tension of the situation had finally got to them.

'Didn't it occur to you to clear up your own mess?' Ben, flushed and indignant, half-stood and leaned across the table.

'Hey! You're paid to be here. It's cost me good money,' Hugh said, with the usual bloody smile that seemed to imply that the words were a joke. The smile that made Dougie feel like slapping him in the face, that was calculated to provoke violence. 'In fact, I'm paying your wages.' He looked around the table, in the hope of gathering support and an audience.

'What were you doing in the bird room anyway?' Ben demanded. 'It's not as if you're a ringer. It's not as if you do anything useful.'

'I was using the computer. There was something I wanted to check out.' For a moment the smile slipped. 'If the police can't find Angela's murderer, I thought I'd do something.

We can't stay here for ever. I need to be moving on.' The last words sounded like something from a bad Country and Western song and Dougie couldn't help grinning.

Then Sandy Wilson, the second cop, the one who had been staying in the centre, stood up. He moved quite slowly, but still somehow he captured their attention.

'Just sit down, boys.' He spoke with an easy kind of voice. Like he knew what it was to lose his temper and it had never done him any good, so they'd do well to take notice of him. 'It's a tough time for everyone, trapped in here. But it won't be for long now. It'll soon be over.'

Dougie wondered if he had any reason for saying that, or if they were just words to calm the young men down. He thought Sandy was playing a dangerous game if he had no evidence to charge the murderer, because he was raising expectations and people would be even more frustrated if nobody was arrested. As it was, he supposed they were all under suspicion. It wouldn't be easy, Dougie thought then, to find a kind and respectable girlfriend if she believed he might have stabbed two women.

After lunch, people scattered. Dougie had eaten far too much and after the exercise of the morning all he really wanted to do was rest. He liked to sit in the common room with a field guide and a cup of tea; soon he knew he'd be snoozing. But John Fowler was back there with his laptop and the sound of it, the staccato and irregular tap-tap of the keys, really got on Dougie's nerves. Anyway, if this was going to be his last day maybe he should make the most of it and get out into the field.

He found Ben in the bird room. He was still angry, Dougie could tell. Still kind of smouldering.

'Want some company on the trap round?'

'Sure.' Not exactly welcoming, but that was because of the mood he was in, not because he resented Dougie asking. Ben gave Dougie a pile of bird bags and they went out to the Land Rover. Just driving away from the North Light, they had to pull in to the side of the road to let Perez past. He was in Big James's car and there was a strange woman in the passenger seat.

'What was all that about at lunchtime?' Dougie asked.

'Nothing. Hugh's really starting to piss me off. That's all.'

Fine, Dougie thought. *Bugger you then if you don't want to talk*. He'd always thought the tabloid papers were right when they said prisoners had it easy. A warm cell with a telly and someone to bring you food. What punishment was there in that? Now he thought the hard bit would be keeping sane, surrounded by all those strangers. No privacy. No wonder living in the centre had driven Angela crazy. Dougie had only been stuck here for a few weeks and he was already going mad.

They parked by the double dyke and did the rest of the trap round on foot.

In the gully trap, Dougie walked through the vegetation, pishing and knocking against the stunted sycamores, to push any birds resting there towards the catching box. There was always a chance of something unusual, but today they only caught two meadow pipits that had already been ringed two days earlier. Ben held them for Dougie to see, then let them go.

'Would it have hurt some eternal plan if one had been an olive-backed?' Dougie said. 'I mean, I know we've all seen olive-backed before, but it would have been something, wouldn't it? Something to cheer everyone up.'

They scrambled back on to the road and moved on to the plantation trap. When Dougie had first come to Fair Isle the plantation had been a joke, the name ironic. A few straggly pines planted in a fold in the land, with the trap built over them. Now the trees had grown up, some of them through the wire mesh. Inside it smelled and felt like a real wood. There were pine needles on the floor. Dougie walked through it rustling the lower branches, felt the same expectation, hope and excitement as he always did. The plantation was where he'd seen the brown flycatcher. There was a small bird somewhere ahead of him. He heard it fluttering, just caught a glimpse of movement. Then he tripped on a root that had grown out of the thin soil, fell hard and couldn't stop his cheek from hitting the ground. There'd be a cracking bruise later. He swore under his breath. On the other side of the wood, Ben yelled to ask if he was OK.

Dougie pushed himself to his feet. There'd been a sharp sting on his palm and when he looked, he saw that there was blood on his hand, trickling through his fingers. For a moment he felt a bit faint, then he looked down to find what had caused it. A knife, half hidden by the pine needles. The search team had been on the island for two days, looking for the knife that had killed Jane Latimer. But they'd been on the hill, taking the direct route from the Pund to the field centre, and after that they'd looked along the road. They couldn't have searched the whole island even in two years. It had taken Dougie to stumble on it by chance.

35

'Just an ordinary kitchen knife,' Perez said.

'I suppose it could have been here for years.' Sandy pulled up his collar to stop the rain dripping down his neck. They stood under the only real trees on the island. 'Did you know they take school kids to that copse that they've planted in North Mainland? To give them a feel of what it's like to be in woodland. In the summer they had a teddy bears' picnic. It was in the *Shetland Times*.'

Perez didn't answer the last point. Sometimes Sandy's brain worked that way: he opened his mouth and let out the words without realizing they weren't relevant to the matter in hand.

'The knife hasn't been here for very long. There's no rust. The blade's still sharp.' He squatted to look at it better, smelled the damp earth and the pine, thought it wasn't such a daft idea to give Shetland kids the experience of a forest.

'I suppose any blood on it will be Dougie Barr's. It's typical that the search team has just gone out. We could have got them down here to do a fingertip through the trees.' Sandy had an almost religious faith in forensic science. Fibres. DNA. Perez thought he watched *CSI* on the quiet. 'Do you think it came from the centre's kitchen?'

Perez straightened. 'I think Jane Latimer

would be the only person to tell you that. But probably. If it came from anywhere else on the Isle it'd likely have been missed. And everyone here knew we were looking for a murder weapon.'

He scooped it into an evidence bag, taking care to include some of the soil and debris from the plantation floor. It could go out on the boat the following morning; he'd get Morag to meet the *Shepherd* and send the knife south to forensics.

Perez got the call about the discovery just after the afternoon plane had taken off. Stella Monkton had thanked him in her quiet, polite way, before taking her place behind the pilot, but he hadn't known what she was thinking. On the drive from the North Light to the airstrip she hadn't spoken. After the birdwatchers had come across the knife, Ben had driven back to the centre to find Sandy, leaving Dougie to stand guard. Now the two detectives were on their own. The light was fading and a steady drizzle had set in.

'Why did the murderer leave it here?' Perez said. He was quite certain that this was the weapon that had killed Jane. 'As you said, it would have been easy enough to throw it over a cliff. Then probably, it would never have been found.'

'Does it matter? I mean, if it came from the centre they'd all have had access to it. If they manage to get a fingerprint it'll be: *Yeah, I touched it. I helped with the washing-up*.'

'But it was removed from the scene. Not like

at the first murder.' Perez was still haunted by the second murder scene, saw it again, as clearly as a photograph: the body, the stained sheepskins, the tiny white feathers. He'd missed something. Perhaps it was simple — the killer had removed the knife to replace it in the centre kitchen, not sure if its absence would be noticed, if its loss would be traced back to him. Perez tried to picture the route the murderer would take from the Pund to the North Light. The most direct way would be over the hill, but that was heavy going: a steep climb and bog and heather moorland. Much easier to walk to the road past the house at Setter and go north that way.

'He was scared,' Perez said. 'He heard someone coming along the road and didn't want to be seen. He wouldn't want anyone to know he'd been so close to the Pund once Jane's body was discovered. It would be easy enough to hide in the plantation. Then perhaps he lost his nerve. Jittery. The state he was in, he couldn't imagine walking into the kitchen, rinsing the knife under the tap, putting it back in the drawer. That was his plan but he didn't have the nerve to carry it out. Though he still had the pillowcase in his pocket. Did he forget about that in his panic?'

'Or she.' Sandy was already walking back towards the road. Perez could tell he wasn't comfortable here in the trees. He wasn't used to them. Maybe he felt claustrophobic. 'It could have been a woman. You're the one who said to keep an open mind.'

Perez knew Sandy was right, but he thought

the murderer was a man. The victims were women. But perhaps he just didn't want to believe in a female killer. He followed Sandy away from the trap.

'There was a bit of a ruckus at lunchtime.' Sandy stepped across the ditch and on to the road, then began to walk back to the car. 'Ben and Hugh. I thought it might come to blows.' He opened the passenger door and got in.

'What was it about?'

Sandy shrugged. Perez could see the droplets of rain on his jacket, smelled wet wool. 'Something and nothing. Hugh had left the bird room in a mess and Ben had a go. He's an arrogant bastard though, that Hugh. None of them seem to like him much.'

'A scapegoat, maybe,' Perez said. 'They all want someone to hate and he's starting to get on their nerves.'

Sandy turned his head quickly. 'Like *The Lord of the Flies?*'

Sandy could always surprise him. 'Aye, something like that.'

'We did it for English Highers,' Sandy said. He paused, while Perez started the engine. 'Everyone staying in the North Light knows that one of them is a murderer. They'd like it to be Hugh. He's the loner really, isn't he? I mean, he puts on the charm, but he hasn't got any real friends there.'

Perez supposed that was true. The Fowlers had each other, John's calm and Sarah's anxiety meeting the other's need. Dougie had been coming to the field centre for so many years that he was something of an institution. Maurice and Ben had worked together all season. Nobody knew Hugh. All they had were the stories he told about himself and now his humour was probably wearing a bit thin. *And all I have is the stories he's told about himself*. Perez pictured Fran as he'd last seen her, sitting in the centre kitchen chatting to Hugh. It was time to get her away from the lighthouse and back to the safety of Springfield. He thought he should spend some time at home this evening. His mother would have prepared a special supper. They might even get an early night.

Am I like the other field centre residents? Would I prefer Hugh Shaw to be the murderer? Because Perez realized that he too disliked Shaw; the dislike hit him now with a surprising intensity.

They'd just started the drive north when Sandy's mobile rang. Perez pulled into the side of the road, so he could take the call without risk of losing reception. He couldn't hear the other end of the conversation but he could tell Sandy was excited. 'Sure? Yeah, thanks. You're brilliant. I definitely owe you a few drinks next time we're in town. But keep it to yourself, yeah?'

'What was all that about?' Perez played the game. Let Sandy prolong his moment of triumph.

'I know what happened to the money Angela withdrew from her bank.'

'Well?' It wouldn't do to show impatience. That only made Sandy worse.

'She didn't have another account in her own

name; she paid the cash into a third person's. She had the number and the sort code.' He paused. 'You're really going to like this! It was Hugh Shaw's account. For some reason she paid him two thousand five hundred quid.'

'Why would she do that?' Perez didn't expect a useful answer. Again he was musing to himself.

'Could it be something to do with the baby?'

'You mean she bought Hugh's sperm?' Perez looked up. He found himself faintly disgusted by the idea. 'But we have no evidence that they knew each other before he came to the North Light.'

'They must have known each other,' Sandy said. 'You don't give thousands of pounds to a stranger.'

'He could have been blackmailing her,' Perez said. 'But what about? Not her sexual exploits. They seem to have been common knowledge.'

'Only among birdwatchers and some of the islanders,' Sandy said. 'Maybe the field centre trustees would have been less than pleased to hear she was seducing her younger staff. Couldn't that be seen as sexual harassment? Probably against the law.'

'Only one way to find out,' Perez said. 'We'd better chat to young Hugh Shaw. See what he has to say for himself.' He started the engine and drove too quickly up the narrow track. He remembered Fran and Hugh standing in the kitchen. He told himself there could be no real danger, but he wanted to know she was safe.

* * *

They came almost immediately to the white-washed walls surrounding the lighthouse. Although it wasn't dark, the lights were on in most of the rooms but the curtains hadn't been drawn. Perez sat for a moment in the car looking in, allowed himself a moment of relief when he saw Fran in the kitchen. There was Dougie Barr standing in the common room drinking something soft and sweet from a can. In the flat Maurice was sitting at his desk reading through a pile of papers. Perhaps the routine of running the centre was helping him come to terms with the death — and the life — of his wife. Upstairs, Ben Catchpole looked out from his bedroom, apparently deep in thought. The lives of the field centre residents were spread out before him and watching them as a voyeur, Perez understood why Jane might have been killed. Again he saw a motive of a sort. It was all about what she knew about the first murder. Now he had to replay in his head the events running up to her death. It was the day the gale had begun to blow itself out, the day he'd interviewed the residents in the community hall. The coastguard helicopter had come in to carry out Angela's body. He forced himself to concentrate on the detail; the timings were important. But Angela? He still couldn't pin down the motive there.

'Are we staying here all night then?' Sandy opened the door. 'I don't know about you but I could use a beer.'

Perez sat for a little longer, looking up at the symmetrical squares of light on the first floor of the building, and then he followed Sandy in.

Perez went to the kitchen first. He wanted to see Fran. Perhaps because he knew she'd be back in Ravenswick the following day he was desperate to hold her, to feel her body against his, a lust that reminded him again of his passion for Beata, the German student. What was happening to him? Usually so controlled and measured in his emotions, within ten minutes he'd experienced dislike and desire with equal intensity.

She had her back to him, bending to lift a tray into the oven. She was wearing a thin scarlet scarf to hold her hair away from her face and her neck, frayed jeans. No apron. As she leaned forward, her jersey rode up her back and he could see her bare skin. He waited until she'd set the dish — some sort of sponge pudding — on the middle shelf and closed the door, then he came up behind her and kissed her neck, put his hand inside her clothes. She turned and kissed him on the mouth. Her hands were useless, still wrapped in oven gloves.

'Jimmy Perez, you'll get me sacked.'

'Where's Sarah?'

'She's gone up to grab a shower before it gets too busy.'

'Why don't you go home? You can take my car. I'll get a lift later. Mother will be expecting you home for supper.'

'She'll be expecting *us*,' Fran said. 'I know what you're like, Jimmy Perez. If I leave you here, I won't see you for the rest of the evening. Besides,' she frowned. 'We should talk. Not here. Sarah will be down in a minute.'

'Has she said anything to you?'

'Nothing specific. I think she's scared.'

'Who's she scared of?' *Everyone*, he thought immediately, then wondered if he'd got that quite wrong. Perhaps she wasn't as timid as she seemed. After all, she'd managed to hold down a responsible job until she became ill. He thought that of all the field centre residents he understood Sarah Fowler the least.

Fran paused. 'I'm not sure. They all know I'm engaged to you and they suspect I'm here as your spy. Everything's guesswork and innuendo. None of them will tell me directly what's worrying them.'

'I saw you with Hugh.' He tried not to let her see how he felt about the young man. He wanted her perspective, untainted by his prejudice.

'Yes,' she said. 'He makes out he has secrets of his own. You should speak to him. But he's such a show-off. It's hard to know how much is real and what he makes up for effect.'

There was an unexpected noise in the common room. Thuds and bangs, then Sandy's voice raised in irritation: 'What the shit do you think you're playing at?' Another crash. Perez hurried in and found a scene like a playground fight. Sandy was holding Ben Catchpole by both arms and Hugh had blood streaming from a cut above his eye. It ran down his cheek and on to the carpet. The other residents stood around watching, fascinated, enjoying the drama. Despite the cut, Hugh seemed immensely pleased with himself.

Sarah Fowler walked in as Ben tried to break

free from Sandy's grasp. She'd changed into neat cord trousers and a white shirt, an old lady's navy cardigan. Her voice was shrill and loud.

'Please. Don't do this. Hasn't there been enough violence? I can't stand it!' And she began to sob. The sound unbearable, like nails down a blackboard, tearing again at their nerves. She turned towards John, who took her into his arms, stroked her hair and murmured reassurance as if she was his child.

Perez thought he couldn't keep these people here any longer. The tension was getting to all of them. He'd have to let them out on the next day's boat, even if it meant sending the murderer away too.

They took Hugh Shaw into the bird room to interview him. As they walked along the corridor Maurice appeared from the flat.

'Jimmy, I need to talk to you!'

Perez turned round just for a moment. 'Sorry, not now. Give me a few minutes.'

'Jimmy, it's important.'

For a moment Perez hesitated. Despite himself he always felt sorry for Maurice. 'Really,' he said. 'This won't take long. Wait in the flat and I'll be along as soon as I've finished here.' And he turned his back so he didn't have to look at the man's sad, pleading eyes.

In the bird room, he made it formal, as if this was an interview room at the police station. Perez asked all the questions. Sandy sat in a corner, a notebook on his knee.

Despite the bloody nose, Hugh still managed a grin. 'Shouldn't you caution me, Inspector?

Have a tape recorder running so there's no misunderstanding? I doubt Sandy could run to shorthand.'

'This is just an informal chat,' Perez said. 'But we can ship you out in the boat tomorrow if you prefer. Talk to you in Lerwick. That way you could have a solicitor present. I'm not quite sure what the horde of reporters still very interested in the case would make of that. They might just misinterpret *helping the police with their inquiries*. Your parents might not be too pleased to have your name all over the tabloids.'

'No need for that,' Hugh said quickly. 'Of course I'm only too pleased to help.' He dabbed at his nose with what looked like a tea towel.

'I've always wanted to travel,' Perez said. 'Never really had the chance.'

'You should!' Hugh's face lit up. Here he was on safe ground. The eccentric Englishman abroad, the charmer, the storyteller. 'My favourite part was coming back along the old silk route. Most of those places, they don't see a European from one year to the next. There's something about a desert — '

'But expensive,' Perez interrupted. 'Even roughing it, you have to eat. And you'd want the occasional beer.' He got up and switched on the light. Outside, it was almost dark, the time of day Shetlanders called 'the darkenin''.

'Hey, my parents were glad to get me out of their hair. They thought it would be educational. Money well spent, they thought.'

'Until recently,' Perez said. 'Recently, I understand, they've been less obliging. You've had to look elsewhere to fund your adventurous lifestyle.'

There was a moment of silence.

'Why did Angela Moore give you two thousand five hundred pounds?'

Another moment of silence, then a return of the practised grin. Perez thought he would always be a con man. In the past he'd have been one of those quacks selling snake oil and charms to delusional and desperate people.

'Hey, she fancied me,' Hugh said. 'What can I say? She didn't want me to leave so she offered me money to stay on. Was I going to turn it down?'

'No, Angela wasn't paying for sexual favours,' Perez said. 'You didn't have any sort of physical relationship with her, did you? She took her regular lovers to the Pund and you knew nothing about that. Your encounters were purely business.'

Hugh stared at the detective. He seemed unable to speak.

'What was it?' Perez asked. 'Blackmail?'

'The money was a gift,' Hugh said at last. 'At least, a loan. Angela knew I'd pay her back. We might not have been lovers but we were good mates. She trusted me.'

'You weren't friends,' Perez said. 'And Angela wasn't known for her generosity of spirit or her ability to trust her fellow man. She would only have paid up if she had no choice.'

'You have no proof.' The inevitable smile, forced, more of a grimace.

Perez continued as if Hugh hadn't spoken.

'And she would have hated it. No one made Angela do what she didn't want to. She'd have been determined to find a way to stop you from bothering her further. Is that why you killed her? Because she'd started to fight back? Had she begun to threaten *you*? It wouldn't be pleasant to be known as a blackmailer.'

'I don't have to listen to this.' Hugh got to his feet. 'I'll be happy to talk to you again, Inspector, when you have some proof.' He sauntered from the room, a parody of the old cockiness. Sandy stood up too, and seemed prepared to stop Hugh leaving, but Perez gestured for him to let the boy go.

'What could he possibly be blackmailing Angela about?' Sandy asked.

Perez was saved from answering because his mobile rang. 'Yes?'

It was Vicki Hewitt. 'We've had the results on the DNA analysis on the feathers you found in Angela Moore's hair.'

'Go on.'

He listened to her words and he knew who had killed the two women. A strange intuitive leap that had little to do with logic. A confirmation and at last a motive. He walked quickly out of the bird room to pull Hugh back in. There were more questions that needed answering now. But the boy seemed to have disappeared.

36

Fran was making custard. She was tantalized by the noises coming from the common room, but good custard, even from a packet, took concentration. Although the numbers of residents had declined, she was still cooking for more people than she was used to. She stirred and listened, distracted again by the raised men's voices. The milk started to burn on the bottom of the pan: there was a brown skin on the tip of the spoon when she lifted it out of the yellow liquid. Quickly she reduced the heat. It thickened at last in a satisfactory if slightly lumpy way and she switched off the stove. She would warm it through later.

She'd heard Sarah's screamed plea for the men to stop the fighting and decided dinner was down to her now. No way would the woman be in any state to cook, her nerves were in shreds. As she prepared vegetables, Fran's thoughts turned to Cassie: she wondered if the girl was excited at the prospect of her mother coming home or if Duncan with his treats and his spoiling had seduced her. *Will she love her father more than me?* Knowing it was pathetic, but unable to prevent it. She'd phone Duncan later and make sure he'd bring Cassie down to Grutness to meet the *Good Shepherd*. Next time they came into Fair Isle she'd bring Cassie with her. Mary would enjoy playing grandmother.

There was a sound behind her and she looked round, expecting to see Perez. Hoping to see Perez. It was Sarah Fowler, very pale. Her skin looked blue and translucent as if she was frozen and she seemed to be trembling.

'Don't worry,' Fran said easily. 'I can cope here. Maybe you should have a rest.' *Or a whisky. Do the Fowlers drink?*

The woman didn't answer. It seemed to Fran that she had the frailty of an old woman, that she'd lost weight even in the past few days. Fran went up to her and took her into her arms, felt the bone close to the skin under the clothes. 'What is it? Look, it's been a terrible time. But I'm sure Jimmy will let you go soon. And if he doesn't, you should go anyway. You'll make yourself ill. Come out with me in the boat tomorrow morning. I'll clear it with the police.'

Sarah was still tense and Fran pulled away, realizing that the physical contact wasn't helping, that Sarah was disturbed by it. 'Tea,' she said. 'We both need tea.'

She filled the kettle and set it to boil, hoping the familiar domestic movements would calm the woman down. When she turned back, Sarah was standing just where Fran had left her.

'I'm scared.'

The words were so melodramatic that Fran thought: *She's acting. Putting it on*. 'What about?' Then, with a flash of intuition, remembering the conversation from earlier in the day, she added: 'Is it Hugh? Look, Jimmy's back in the lighthouse now. You're quite safe. Don't worry about him anyway. He's all bluster and showing off.'

'Angela's mother shouldn't have come here,' Sarah said. 'If she hadn't come here everything would have been all right.'

'What's Angela's mother got to do with this? What's going on? Sarah, you must tell me.'

'He'll kill me,' Sarah choked and put the back of her hand to her mouth.

At first Fran thought she'd misheard. Then again thought this was all nonsense, the hysteria of a woman on the edge of a breakdown: 'Sarah, what is this about? You must tell Jimmy what you know.' She felt impatient, wanted to take Sarah by the shoulders and shake some sense into her.

'No!' And the woman repeated more loudly, though still hardly more than a whisper: 'He'll kill me.'

'Then talk to *me*.'

A door banged. The door from the flat to the public area of the field centre. Sarah started, like an animal at a sudden noise, and ran away, through the lobby and out into the dusk.

Fran stood in the middle of the kitchen. In this domestic setting, with the smell of treacle pudding and steak pie, the theatrical quality of the situation seemed ridiculous. Again she found herself irritated. It was like dealing with an irrational, nervy child. Two women had already been killed but surely Sarah was safer in here, surrounded by people, than wandering around outside in the dark. The cliffs north and west of the lighthouse were as steep as anywhere on the island. There were jagged splits in the land that let in the sea. Fran could still hear heated voices in the common room.

She went to the door intending to find Jimmy — he needed to know what Sarah had told her and that she was outside playing the stupid female. But Perez's attention was on Hugh and as she watched he marched the younger man towards the bird room. Then Maurice appeared and insisted with a persistence quite unlike him that they should talk. She saw the field centre administrator through the open door; he was standing in front of the others in the corridor and she noticed the hole in the elbow of his sweater, the beads of sweat on his forehead. What was his problem? Didn't he realize Jimmy was busy? She was tempted to call Maurice to ask him to help her search for Sarah, but he walked away towards the flat.

The bird room door closed. Jimmy wouldn't forgive her for interrupting now. It occurred to her that he was about to arrest Hugh for the murders. Fran looked at her watch. Half an hour until supper and everything in the kitchen was ready. She'd left her coat and boots in the cupboard next to the larder. She pulled them on and followed Sarah outside.

Now it was quite dark. The wind was deceptive, blowing in gusts and swirls around the lighthouse. It was hard to tell exactly which direction it was coming from, but it was cold, so probably from the north-west. Sarah had come out with just the cardigan and soft shoes. Fran swore at her under her breath. *I bet she was spoiled as a child*. Above her the lighthouse beam swung, regular as a metronome. Three short flashes and a long one. It lit the outcrops of rock and reflected on the pools of water.

She found Sarah sitting by Golden Water. This was where the trumpeter swan had come to roost, where the birdwatchers from the mainland had gathered. Now the pond was empty. In a dip in the land and sheltered from the gusting wind the water was calm. Fran spotted Sarah first as the lighthouse beam moved slowly across the landscape, saw her in the flashing light like a primitive cartoon, sheets of paper flicked to bring a character to life. But here there was no movement. Sarah sat quite still. As Fran walked towards her, wellingtons squelching in the sodden ground, the clouds broke and a thin moon partly lit her way. She took off her waxed jacket and put it over Sarah's shoulders. 'Come back inside. You'll freeze to death.' And for a moment she imagined that the woman was another victim and that she'd been killed too, because she seemed quite rigid. Fran remembered the body of Angela Moore, stiff with rigor mortis. *Her* skin had been blue.

'Come back inside,' Fran said again. 'It's all over. Jimmy knows what happened. He's making an arrest now.' *Stretching the truth perhaps, but she was freezing and just wanted to get back to the warm kitchen*.

Then the woman turned her face to Fran and with the brown clouds rushing across the moon, and to the beat of the lighthouse beam, she began to speak. The words spilled from her mouth, the whole story told right from the beginning. Fran shivered and tried to lift Sarah again to her feet. 'Come inside. We'll sort it all out. We'll help.' And along with the cold, she felt almost excited because Sarah had confessed to her and not to Jimmy. *Who's the detective now, Jimmy Perez?* This was her own moment of triumph.

37

Perez ran through the common room, but it was empty. He thought everyone had been embarrassed by the earlier scene and had scattered to their rooms. He stood at the foot of the stairs. The building was quiet. He couldn't bear the thought of marching around the building, dragging them all back like recalcitrant children. *After all, there's no hurry*, he thought. *Where will they go? There's no escape. They'll come down eventually*.

'I'm sorry, Jimmy,' Maurice said. 'I really have to speak to you.' It seemed he'd lost patience and had refused to wait in the flat any longer. Though looking at his watch, Perez saw it had only been a quarter of an hour since they'd spoken. This evening, time seemed to have stretched. So much had happened since they'd returned to the North Light with the murder weapon that it appeared that days had passed.

'Have you seen Fran?'

'She was in the kitchen a moment ago,' Maurice said. His voice had lost something of its neediness and had gained a new authority. 'You have to know what Angela's mother told me. I think it could be important.'

Perez weighed up his options. Could he entrust Maurice to Sandy? Looking again at the centre administrator, he saw that wouldn't do. Maurice would only talk to him.

'Come into the bird room, then. Sandy, bring everyone into the common room and keep an eye on them there. Everyone. Fran included. I don't want her wandering around on her own.'

Sandy nodded.

At the bird room door Maurice hesitated and Perez saw he was thinking about his wife. He'd never thought of Maurice as an imaginative man but the picture of Angela, with the knife in her back and the feathers in her hair, would surely remain with him. *Knife in the back*. The words stuck with Perez for a moment. A metaphor for betrayal, he thought, and he wondered if that was what the murderer had wanted to convey, if like the feathers, a message had been intended. In that case did the killer want to be caught? Did he want the world to know what had provoked the act of violence?

'Stella asked to speak to me alone because she had information that might lead to Angela's killer.' Maurice leaned against the windowsill. The wall was three feet thick and the glass encrusted with salt. His profile was reflected in it, but it was blurred, made him look like a ghost peering in.

'More appropriate, surely, to speak to me!'

'It doesn't show Angela in a very good light,' Maurice said. 'Stella left the decision to me: should we go public and ruin her reputation or keep the information to ourselves and risk the chance that the murderer would go free?'

'And you decided to talk.' Perez could tell that this decision hadn't been lightly taken. Maurice had been in the flat, worrying away at it all afternoon. *But I know already*, Perez thought. *At least I've guessed most of it; Vicki's phone call confirmed it. And anyway, how much of the truth are you prepared to tell?* He felt a sudden distaste and was impatient for the case to be over. Maurice's scruples seemed the worst sort of self-indulgence. There had been too much talk and too much complication. If you scraped away the words and the show, this was all about petty jealousy.

In the lobby he heard voices, running footsteps, the outside door being opened and banged shut.

'I'm sorry,' he said. 'This will have to wait after all.'

He turned and almost ran from the room, leaving Maurice standing bewildered by the window. Perez wondered how he could have allowed himself to be distracted by the man. The story would all come out eventually. Statements would be taken and lawyers would fight over the words. Rhona Laing would buy herself a good dinner to celebrate. But tonight he had an arrest to make and the evening to spend with the woman he loved. And then tomorrow he would go out with her on the boat. He'd spent too long cooped up on this lump of rock. How could he have thought he might make his life here?

There was nobody in the lobby. He rushed through to the common room. Still it was empty, so quiet that he heard the background chug of the generator. The world outside was briefly lit up by the lighthouse beam, then it was dark again.

Perez had a sudden panic. This was the stuff of nightmares; it ranked with the sensation of falling and with being chased by unknown monsters. With chasing evil spirits that vanished into thin air.

'Sandy!' His voice disappeared in the echoing space of the old building.

There were footsteps on the wooden stairs. Sandy yelled down. 'Sorry, boss. It's like trying to round up a herd of cats. They'll be down in a minute.' Routine words, easily spoken.

'Is everyone accounted for?'

'I think so.' But he was trying to please Perez. He didn't know at all. 'I'm not sure.'

'And Fran?'

'I haven't seen her. Isn't she still in the kitchen?'

Perez struggled to control his temper, but understood how Ben Catchpole had come to lash out at Hugh. *Could I commit murder? Could I stab him in the back in a moment of madness? Just because he's so stupid? Didn't he realize Fran was the one person I needed him to look out for?* Then reason took over and guilt. *I didn't explain. Do I expect him to be able to read my mind?*

The kitchen door, which had been open all day, so Perez had managed to catch reassuring glimpses of the women inside, was shut now. When he opened it, the room was empty. There was a big pan of water on the hob, the heat turned off. The smell of cooking: something sweet and appetizing. A pan containing thick custard, with a skin on the top. A big colander half full with chopped cabbage. Everything ordinary. Yet again Perez had the sense of a nightmare continuing. Sometimes, he thought, terror can be in the everyday. He shouted back to Sandy: 'Who exactly did you see upstairs?'

'Dougie and Ben. Ben was covered in blood and Dougie was helping him to clean up.'

'What about the others?'

'I thought they went upstairs. But maybe they came through the kitchen.'

'Someone went outside,' Perez said. 'I heard the door.'

By now Sandy had picked up his boss's panic. He looked close to tears and was perfectly aware of his own stupidity, his ability to cause the biggest cock-up in the world. 'I'm sorry. I was in the dormitory. I didn't see.'

In the enclosed space of the yard, Perez was hit by the cold. There was a faint gleam from a moon half-covered by cloud, and the bright occasional spot of the lighthouse beam. He ran through the gap in the whitewashed wall, ducking the clothes lines on the way, and looked out on the open hill. A thicker cloud covered the moon and suddenly it was pitch black. The sort of darkness you never get in a city. Then the cloud thinned again and he made out the silver line of reflected light that was Golden Water.

A woman screamed. Not Fran. He'd have recognized her voice, even as a scream. Thank God, not Fran. He raced towards the sound, tripping over the heather and outcrops of rock, splashing through the bog towards the loch. He was surprised by a movement at his feet, a slow beat of wings, saw a pair of eyes, yellow in the pale moonlight. A short-eared owl flying low over the hill.

The lighthouse lens circled and there was a brief snapshot before the beam moved on. The pool, a pale backdrop. Very black against it, a man's silhouette, his arm raised. Perez saw the glint of light on metal, like a silent flash of lightning on a stormy night, before everything was dark again.

For a second the old curiosity kicked in: *Where did he get the knife? Did he pick it up from the kitchen on the way through or is it what he was intending all along? He couldn't allow the woman to speak*. The light came back, pulsing and regular as a heartbeat. This time Perez almost screamed himself because now the silhouette was moving; the arm slashed and chopped, mechanical as the engine that moved the reflector in the lighthouse. If the killer had begun as a rational man, he'd certainly lost all reason now. *How could he do that to his wife? The woman he claimed to adore?* More darkness.

Behind him, Perez heard someone yelling. Sandy. Good. It would take two of them to restrain the man. As he ran, thoughts and images rattled around his head. Sandy was the stronger: once they had the knife, he could control John Fowler and then Perez would comfort Fran. He'd hold her and wrap his jacket around her shoulders and tell her she would never have to deal with anything like this again. He wouldn't expose her to more violence or danger. Perez thought he would have to resign now; Fran wouldn't like it, but he'd insist. Despite the chase, the stumbling, the gasping for breath, he felt a sudden and immense relief. How strangely the mind worked under stress! So the decision was made. There would be no more police work. That part of his life was over.

Sandy was younger and fitter and had already overtaken him. He must have grabbed a torch on his way out, because the light bounced ahead of them and captured the three people on the shore of the loch. They were posed like a sculpture. One of those pieces in white marble Fran had dragged him to see in a gallery the last time they were south. One figure was standing, one sitting and one lying. Fowler was standing and his arm was by his side. He'd dropped the knife, which was hidden somewhere in the tussocky grass. His head was bent as if he was praying and he seemed quite calm.

Perez lost his mind for a moment. He heard screaming in his ears and knew it was his own. When he came to he found himself in a frenzy, scrabbling in the boggy water for the knife. If he'd found it he would have killed the man. It was only Sandy's voice that brought him to his senses. Because the sitting figure was Sarah Fowler and the statue on the floor, pale and bleeding, was Fran. Sandy was already bending over her, his mobile in his hand, shouting for an ambulance flight. A helicopter. 'Just get us a fucking doctor.' Perez took off his jacket as he'd planned he would, wrapped it around Fran and held her in his arms.

38

Wherever she'd been, Fran would have died. They said that over and over again to Perez as if he were supposed to find some comfort in it. She could have been stabbed next door to the most well-equipped hospital in the world and still they wouldn't have saved her. The attack was too violent. And besides, the helicopter did arrive very quickly. Perez remembered very little of that. Flying out with Fran's body, knowing that this wasn't Fran, not essentially. Looking down as Fair Isle disappeared beneath them — a scattering of lights marking each of the familiar crofts — wondering suddenly if he'd ever be able to return again. If he'd ever be able to face it.

His father was in the helicopter with him. His mother had wanted to be there, but Perez couldn't bear the thought of her fussing. And now, at this moment, for perhaps the first time in his life, he'd thought he had the right to disregard other people's feelings. His father had offered tentatively: 'I could come out with you, lad.' Suddenly that was just what Perez needed: the taciturn man with the granite face, flawed but still certain. Unsentimental.

Then there was lots of waiting about in an office in the Gilbert Bain hospital. Gallons of tea. Distant noises — the clang of a tea trolley hitting a metal bedstead, cheerful voices. The doctor, who looked to Perez no more than a teenager, repeating over and over again that there had been nothing they could do. He'd been with the team that had come into Fair Isle in the helicopter and in the morning when it was getting light and James was telling Perez they should go back to the house in Lerwick, because Jimmy needed to eat and to rest, the doctor clung onto them. As if he was the bereaved person. And Perez didn't want to go. Because somehow this young man, with his acne and his bad breath, was the last link he had to Fran.

In the hospital they'd offered Perez pills to help him sleep, but he'd refused them. He didn't deserve to sleep again. He sat in the narrow kitchen in his house by the water in Lerwick watching his father frying bacon and eggs. The older man's face was grey. He was exhausted but his movements were deft. He warmed the plates, flipped the oil over the egg to make sure it was cooked. As soon as the meal was over he washed the dishes. 'Why don't you get some rest?'

While his father was lying on Perez's bed, the detective replayed the moments of Fran's death in his head, over and over again, like a film on a loop. Maybe thinking that eventually there would be a different ending to the story. Knowing that was crazy but wanting to believe it.

Sometime in the afternoon Sandy turned up at the house. He blamed himself for Fran's death. Perez saw that as soon as he came through the door. He was shaking. 'You told me to look after her.' He couldn't stop saying that. Not the same words but meaning the same thing. Why did people feel the need to speak so much?

In the end Perez said, quite roughly: 'You weren't holding the knife, man. Give it a rest.'

So they sat in silence, drinking more tea. Perez would have liked a proper drink, but knew that if he started he wouldn't be able to stop.

'We brought all the witnesses out in the boat,' Sandy said. 'They're making statements in the station now.' He paused. 'I wondered if you fancied sitting in. Not to do the interviews, of course. And not Fowler, that wouldn't be right. But it's your case.'

'Worried you'll miss something, Sandy? Worried you might have to take responsibility at last?' His grief was liberating. He'd never been so cruel before to Sandy. Now he felt as if he had licence to do or say anything he wanted.

Sandy's face went very red, streaky as if he'd been slapped and the finger marks still showed. 'Aye,' he said. 'Something like that. But I wanted to give you the chance to be there if you wanted.'

'Sorry. You're right. I would like to sit in.' A lie, of course. He didn't care enough to want anything. But Perez thought it would be better to go with Sandy than to stay here as dusk fell, he and his father sitting on either side of the fire, like two lonely old men, not knowing what to say to each other.

⋆ ⋆ ⋆

In the police station, where once he'd been so at home, he felt like a stranger. He was a different person. He saw Fran everywhere: standing behind the custody sergeant at his desk, laughing with his colleagues in the canteen as Perez walked past. He thought: *Is this how it'll be for the rest of my life? I'll be haunted by her*.

Her ghost hadn't made it to the interview room and for that he was grateful. He tried to focus on the matter in hand in case she slipped under his guard and found him there too. There was a detective Perez didn't recognize, sitting at the desk alongside Sandy. Perez assumed he was from Inverness, maybe even Roy Taylor's replacement, but he didn't care enough to ask. The stranger might as well not have been there: Sandy did all the talking. And he was bloody good, Perez thought, taking a stolen moment of pleasure to think Sandy had been well taught. Perez pulled a seat into a corner. Anyone looking in would have assumed he was sleeping, but he listened, caught up in the stories beside himself. They spoke to Hugh Shaw first.

'Tell us about the blackmail,' Sandy said. 'It'll all come out now. Fowler's talked to us. No point hiding.'

Hugh stared at Perez, but didn't mention his presence. He slouched across the table towards Sandy. He reminded Perez of the cocky teenagers he'd often picked up in the city. No discipline, no work, believing the world owed them a living. But those young men had grown up on sink estates with little prospect of work. Hugh Shaw didn't have that excuse.

'I knew Angela wouldn't miss the money,' he said. 'She was minted. She made more from one TV documentary than a year's salary at the field centre.'

'So tell me.'

'It was all about the slender-billed curlew,' Hugh said. 'The bird that made her famous.'

'What about it?

'It was lies. She didn't find it. The fame, the money, the reputation as a great scientist, it was all built on a lie. She stole another man's research.'

Perez understood why the woman had been so unhappy, why she'd married an older man just for convenience. Her work had been the most important thing in her world and she'd compromised it. She had no pride left. Perhaps she saw the baby as a chance for a new start. Something honest and real. Perhaps it was a biological imperative that had driven her, a desperation to give birth. Fran had been experiencing something of that sort in the last few months. Again, he tried to banish Fran from his mind.

'How did you find out?' Sandy leaned across the table towards Shaw, his elbow on the table.

'There was a Brit in Tashkent. An ex-pat doing something dodgy with the Russians, but also a birder. We sat in the Rovshan Hotel one night, drinking local beer and Johnny Walker Black Label, and he told me the whole story. John Fowler had tracked down the curlew population. Angela was looking for the species. She wanted something big to make her name. But he got there first; he found the birds by looking for the food they took, some kind of insect.'

Mole crickets, Perez thought. Fowler was still trying to interest the scientific world in his story.

There'd been a letter saved on his computer, but none of them had recognized the significance.

Hugh continued: 'Fowler was an amateur lister, in a hired car, wandering across the desert, hoping for the big story to make his career as a natural history journalist. He didn't even have a degree! She had a PhD and a research budget and he beat her to it!'

'But he never got the glory he deserved.' Sandy again. *That's just what I might have said*, Perez thought. *You're just speaking my lines*.

'Angela published first. And who was the establishment going to believe? Fowler already had the reputation as a bit of a stringer. Angela made sure nobody took him seriously again by spreading rumours around Shetland about rare birds he was supposed to have claimed. He became a laughing stock.'

It became his obsession, Perez thought. *At first I thought he was driven by the need to see birds, like the twitchers who piled into Fair Isle to see the swan. But it was about revenge. He blamed Angela Moore for everything that had gone wrong in his life. For the dead baby and the dead marriage as well as all his lost dreams*.

'And you thought you'd take advantage of the situation?'

'I'd always wanted to visit Fair Isle. I'd run out of money and my father refused to give me more.' Hugh looked up and Perez saw an attempt at the old smile. 'Tight bastard. He could have afforded it. So yeah, I thought it was worth a go. I wasn't greedy, only asked for a couple of grand to tide me over. I didn't expect

Fowler to turn up though.'

'That must have been a shock to Angela too.'

'You could say that! Maurice took the booking and suddenly Fowler was there in the common room when she came through to do the log. But Fowler was pleasant to her. Polite. Calm. He certainly didn't give the impression that he was out for revenge. Maybe she thought he was a good man, who wouldn't harbour a grudge. He went to church every Sunday. Perhaps he was into turning the other cheek. She was jittery though. Everyone thought she was moody because Poppy was staying in the lighthouse, throwing her tantrums, but that wasn't it at all.'

'What I don't understand,' Sandy said and there was something steely in the voice Perez had never heard before, 'what I *really* don't understand, is why you didn't tell us about this before. Two women dead and you knew a man had a motive to kill them. We could have had this cleared up days ago. A third woman need never have died.'

Hugh gave a little shrug. 'I didn't know for certain.' He must have been aware that Perez looked up at him, stared at him very hard, but he didn't show it. From the beginning he hadn't acknowledged that Perez was there. 'Besides, as you said, I'd committed blackmail. Not something I was going to own up to.'

'So it wasn't that you considered Fowler another target?' Sandy said. 'Angela was dead, she was no more use to you, but Fowler . . . He'd committed murder. He'd go on paying for the rest of his life as long as he was free.'

The smile returned. 'Really, Sandy, that's guesswork isn't it? Speculation. You'll never ever know.'

* * *

Ben Catchpole had a graze over his eye, covered by a sticking plaster. He saw Perez immediately and made a move to go over. He would have offered his condolences, said kind words about Fran, but something in the detective's manner deterred him. Not hostility, but a new indifference. Perez felt it in himself.

'Jimmy's just sitting in,' Sandy said easily. 'I take it you don't mind.' He spoke in such a way that it would have been impossible for Ben to object. 'What was it with you and Shaw?' Sandy went on. 'Scrapping like bairns in the schoolyard. I thought non-violence was your thing. Eating lentils and seaweed. Saving the planet.'

'It was the tension,' Ben said. 'All of us on top of each other in the lighthouse.'

'But more than that,' Sandy said. 'Surely it was more than that.' He looked up. 'Did you know Angela was carrying your child?'

'It was true then?'

'Who told you?' Sandy asked.

'Not Angela. She didn't say a thing!' The words came out hard and bitter. And Perez thought that was what Catchpole minded most: being excluded from Angela's life, completely disregarded. 'She'd have got rid of the baby without even telling me she was pregnant.'

'So who did tell you?' Sandy was gentle, prompting.

'Shaw. He said he heard the Fowlers talking. Sarah's a nurse. Perhaps she guessed. Perhaps Angela talked to her.' Perez thought then that Hugh Shaw was like some kind of snake, slithering through the lighthouse, listening at doors, spreading his poison. Catchpole looked up at Sandy. 'Was I the father?'

'We think you must have been. It certainly wasn't Hugh Shaw. Theirs was a purely . . . ' Sandy hesitated, ' . . . financial arrangement.'

'He told me he'd slept with her.'

'Aye well, he would.'

There was a moment of silence. 'You never told us,' Sandy said, 'that you'd met Fowler before. He wrote that article for *The Times* about the Braer protest. It confused us for a while.'

'Was that him?' Ben looked surprised. 'I never met the man. We did an interview over the phone. There were lots of interviews.'

'A coincidence then?'

'I suppose. Birdwatching's a small world.'

Like Shetland, Perez thought, sitting in his corner and watching. *By now everyone in the islands will know Fran's dead. There'll be no hiding from their kindness*. The best thing to do would be to move south. He thought with something approaching pleasure of a grey anonymous town, a small tidy room. No clutter, emotional or physical.

Sandy was waiting for Ben to leave, but still he sat there. 'That wasn't my finest hour,' he said.

'The Braer protest. My mother was so proud of me: I'd stood up for what I believed in. She came to court, took me out for a grand meal when it was all over. Paid the compensation order. But when they arrested me, the police said I'd most likely go to prison. Just give us the names of the locals who helped, they said, and we'll put in a word with the Fiscal for you. I couldn't face prison.'

'So you gave up the names of your friends?'

Ben nodded.

Now at last, he stood to go. This time it was Perez who called him back. 'I think Angela was glad to be pregnant,' he said. 'It was planned. It was you she chose. She wanted your baby.'

* * *

At that point Perez decided to leave. Now he knew enough. He couldn't face watching Sandy question Sarah Fowler. It wasn't right that the woman was still alive. She must have known her husband was a killer after the first murder, even if she hadn't realized he'd come to Fair Isle with the intention of stabbing Angela Moore. Perez could understand that Fowler might have nurtured his obsession in secret. He'd dreamed about his revenge for years and planned it in every detail. He'd arranged the crime scene like a theatrical set, each prop with its own meaning. The knife in the back, symbol of betrayal. The slender-billed curlew feather, the one he'd collected in the desert of Uzbekistan, which would be his proof and his ticket to glory, before

Angela had stolen the possibility from him.

But once Angela was dead Sarah Fowler must have known. She'd stood beside her husband in church, singing hymns and pretending to pray. Had she convinced herself that her imagination was playing tricks? That John Fowler was a good man? Or was she so wrapped up in her own grief, the loss of her child, that she didn't care?

Hurrying down the corridor away from the interview room, Perez caught a glimpse of her in the distance. She was wearing a long grey cardigan with a hood, which gave her the appearance of a nun. He supposed she was another victim but at the moment he hated her more than he hated Fowler.

Outside, he was surprised to find that it was still light and that there was pale sunshine reflecting on the water in the harbour.

39

In the house by the shore his father was asleep in his chair by the fire. He jerked awake when Perez came in, looked around him for a moment as if he weren't exactly sure where he was.

'Duncan phoned,' he said. 'Cassie wants to see you.'

Perez lay awake for most of the night thinking about that. He'd agreed to meet the girl of course. Just now he'd have done anything for her. But it was the last thing he wanted. Surely she would blame him for her mother's death. He didn't think he could face that. Or the little twisted smile, that was just like Fran's. The voice. A bit of Shetland in it after a couple of years at school, but still using Fran's words. Words from the south that sometimes they had to explain to him.

They arranged to meet in Lerwick in the Olive Tree, the cafe in the Tollclock Centre, because it was neutral territory and Fran had liked it there. It had been more her sort of place than his. Fancy salads and an arty clientele. She'd said the coffee was to die for.

Perez's relationship with her ex-husband Duncan Hunter was awkward. They'd been friends at school, good friends, despite the difference in their backgrounds. Duncan's family came from big Shetland landowners, the closest thing to aristocracy there was in the islands, and he still lived in the big house on the shore at Brae. They'd fallen out before Perez had taken up with Fran and since then had maintained an uneasy truce for Cassie's sake. Perez worried sometimes when the girl stayed with her father. Duncan drank too much, had a chaotic life of parties and diverse and sometimes dubious business interests. More skeletons in his cupboard than a professor of medicine. Fran had said Cassie needed contact with her father. 'You're not jealous Jimmy, surely?' That twisted grin again. And Perez had admitted that maybe he was jealous, just a bit. He'd be proud to be considered Cassie's father and there were times when he'd wished Duncan lived anywhere other than Shetland, so the three of them could form their own family.

Today Perez arrived at the cafe half an hour early. The least he could do. He wouldn't want Cassie to have to wait for him. He bought coffee. He didn't recognize any of the patrons. They were probably visitors waiting for the ferry to start boarding: the terminal was just down the road. Lifting the cup to his lips he found his hands were shaking. He got up to leave. He couldn't face Cassie after all. Duncan would surely understand and make his excuses. He was standing there, poised to make his escape, when Dougie Barr came in, obviously on his way to the ferry too. He had an enormous rucksack on his back and was strung about with optical equipment.

The birdwatcher saw Perez immediately and stood blocking the door, flushed with embarrassment, not wanting to intrude, but feeling it would be rude just to walk away. Perez couldn't bear his discomfort and gave a little wave to put him at his ease. He heard Fran's voice in his head: *What is it with you, Jimmy Perez? Are you some sort of saint?* Reassured, Dougie approached; he said nothing, but he held out his hand.

'Tell me,' Perez said. 'Did you know Fowler was a killer?' The question had been bothering him. He'd pondered it in the middle of the night. How widely could he spread responsibility?

'No!' Dougie was horrified. 'I'd have said. Honest. I didn't guess about the curlew. I believed the stories Angela made up about Fowler being a stringer. She fooled me too.' He paused. 'I thought it was Hugh. I could tell she didn't like him, that maybe she was even scared of him. Wishful thinking. I couldn't stand the guy.'

He reached out again and touched Perez's shoulder, then turned and left the cafe. He'd find somewhere else to eat before he boarded the boat.

That was when Perez saw Cassie, walking through the shopping arcade. Not holding Duncan's hand, but close to him. Six years old. Small for her age, stocky, brown hair cut in a fringe over her eyes. Enormous eyes like a bush baby's, made even bigger because she'd been crying. She saw Perez and rushed towards him and he swung her into his arms as he always did. Now he clung on to her as if she were saving *him*. He was aware of a couple at a nearby table staring and realized there were tears on his cheeks. The people turned awkwardly away, almost affronted by the emotion.

Duncan bought coffee for himself, juice and chocolate cake for Cassie. Fran had never liked Cassie eating too much junk, but Perez swept the thought away. Let the girl have whatever she wanted.

'I want to go home,' Cassie said.

'I've explained it's kind of difficult.' Duncan looked at Perez. 'We have to sort things out.'

'I want to go to school. I have to go to school.' One way of coping, Perez supposed. Hadn't he gone into work to watch Sandy interview the witnesses? Though now, a couple of days on, he couldn't understand how it had seemed important.

'Miss Frazer will understand,' Perez said. Miss Frazer was the head teacher at Ravenswick, had only been there for a couple of years. She and Fran had become friends.

'I'm in the play,' Cassie said patiently. 'I've learned my words.' Then: 'Jessie will be missing me.' Jessie, her best friend, granddaughter of Geordie, who took the visitors out to Mousa in his small boat.

'Could you move into the Ravenswick house for a while?' Perez talked to Duncan but was aware all the time that Cassie was listening. 'It would probably be good to have things back to normal. I mean as normal as we can make them.' He was still crying, wiped his face with his napkin, hoping that Cassie hadn't noticed.

'Sure.' But there was some uncertainty in Duncan's voice. He travelled a lot for work, didn't really like to be tied down.

'I'll help,' Perez said. 'Any way I can.'

'Fran's parents are coming up,' Duncan said. 'Things will be easier then.'

But only for a while, Perez thought. It occurred to him that they might want to take Cassie with them back to London. They weren't so old after all and Cassie was very fond of them. Perhaps that would be a solution. He knew they wouldn't want to live in the islands. They were city people. But then might he lose contact with the girl altogether?

That evening, back at his small house right by the water in Lerwick, he drank whisky with his father and worried about Cassie. James was still there. Perez had half-heartedly tried a few times to send him home and was always relieved when the older man refused. 'It'll be good for the crew to manage without me.' There was something comforting about the dourness of his father, the solidness of his body and his lack of imagination. Perez had given up his bed to him and slept on the sofa in the living room. It would have been impossible for him, anyway, to sleep in the bed he'd shared with Fran on occasion. He suspected his father knew that. Perhaps he had some imagination after all.

* * *

The next day Rhona Laing, the Fiscal, called Perez to see her. As always when he walked into her office, he felt as though he had mud on his boots, that in some way he was contaminating her clean and elegant space. 'We have to discuss the case, Jimmy. I know it'll be hard but it has to be done.' No mention of Fran, no soft and easy words. He was grateful for that. 'Perhaps you're interested anyway.'

'No,' he said. It came to him that he hadn't tendered his resignation yet and that he should do it soon. If he were any sort of cop he'd have protected Fran; he couldn't be in a position again where he put another life at risk.

'John Fowler confessed.' It was as if she hadn't heard the negative. She smelled faintly of citrus. Expensive citrus. She'd done something different to her hair. Perhaps she had a new man. There were always rumours of the Fiscal's men. 'He was happy to talk but we found a confession on his laptop too. At least, more a series of excuses than a confession.'

'He had no choice,' Perez said. 'Besides, that was what he wanted all the time. To tell his story.'

'You knew it was him?' She'd ordered a pot of coffee and poured him a cup.

'A gut feeling at the beginning maybe,' Perez admitted. He looked up and gave the first flash of a smile. He knew what lawyers made of gut feelings. 'He seemed so uptight. A little strange. And there was the name of his bookshop.'

Rhona looked up sharply. 'Which was?'

'Numenius Books. It seemed a strange sort of name. I looked it up. Numenius is the scientific name for curlew. But it could have been a coincidence and we had no evidence, no motive until the DNA analysis of the feathers. Then I spoke to a few people and found out that Fowler had been travelling in the former Soviet Union at around the same time as Angela. Stella Monkton's confession on her daughter's behalf that Angela had stolen Fowler's research confirmed it, of course. Angela wrote to her about it after asking if they could meet up.'

Rhona leaned back in her chair. 'Why don't you tell me, Jimmy? In your own way.'

Perez was tempted to get up and walk out. *You know already. Sandy will have done a report. Although the spelling and the grammar will be crap, he'll have set out the details*. But he stayed. This was his last case. Might as well see it through for one more time.

'John Fowler was a writer and journalist. Respected. A freelancer, but he did OK at it and made a good living. It seemed unlikely that he didn't know Angela Moore. They're all obsessive, these bird-watchers, and the scientists even more so. Look at Ben Catchpole. They come across an area of research and dig away at it.' Perez found himself feeling his way into the skin of the murderer despite himself. He'd spoken to Fowler's former colleagues; sitting in the kitchen in Springfield there'd been long telephone conversations about the man's state of mind. This was Fran's killer, but Perez had never really believed in monsters. To dismiss Fowler as a monster would be to let him off the hook. It was better to understand him and force him to take responsibility.

'After Angela published the work on the slender-billed curlew everything went wrong for him,' Perez went on. 'He lost his credibility. He tried to persuade a few people that the find was his, but who would believe him? Angela was young and attractive, a publisher's dream. It would be much harder to promote a middle-aged man, with a reputation for claiming rare birds that had never existed. Everyone had a vested interest in dismissing his claims. He gave up work as a journalist and set up the bookshop. He told everyone he needed to de-stress.'

'Did he see a psychiatrist?' The Fiscal looked up sharply from the paper where she was making notes. 'Is he fit to plead?'

Perez shrugged. It seemed to him that anyone who had killed three women could be considered insane. He blamed himself. *I knew. I should have stopped it*.

'He came to Fair Isle with the intention of killing Angela Moore,' Rhona Laing went on. 'It was pre-meditated. Planned. He didn't lash out in a jealous rage. Not manslaughter due to diminished responsibility. They can't go for that.'

But jealousy had been at the heart of it, Perez thought. A slow-burning fury that had consumed Fowler, taking over his thoughts and his dreams, destroying him. Destroying the women who had stood in his way. Was that illness? Luckily it wasn't for Perez to decide.

'Go on, Jimmy,' the Fiscal said, making some effort to control her impatience. 'Let's hear the rest of the story.'

He looked up and for a moment he wanted to hit out at the smooth, expensively made-up face. This was just work to her. Work and ambition.

She'd take his words and use them to make herself seem clever. 'Why? You know already. What am I? Your performing monkey?'

The outburst shocked her. 'I'm sorry, Jimmy. Is this too soon? Do you want to stop?'

He shook his head fiercely. He couldn't bear her pity.

'So, it was all about a bird,' Perez continued as if the exchange between them had never occurred. 'Slender-billed curlew. Some scientists thought it was extinct. You wouldn't think it could generate so much passion. But I watched the birdwatchers come into Fair Isle for an American swan and I saw how mad they could be. Some of them almost in tears when they realized they could have missed it. And for Fowler it wasn't just a hobby. It was his work. It was about respect, proving himself worthy of his job in journalism.'

'So he found this curlew before Angela Moore did, but she claimed the credit.' Rhona looked at her watch. Her sympathy hadn't lasted for long. Perez thought the Fiscal just wanted the facts; she'd never been much interested in the background. *That's what social workers were invented for, Jimmy*.

'He worked out where he thought the birds might be breeding,' said Perez. 'Something to do with the insects they feed on. He looked at the maps, sought out likely search areas. They call it ground-truthing.' Perez had liked the idea of ground-truthing when he'd heard about it, thought it was a useful concept in policing. It was about testing theories, keeping it real. Now he wondered how it could have excited him; it was an irrelevance.

'It must have been galling for him to miss out on the credit,' Laing said, showing some understanding at last. She would understand about professional jealousy. Perez had never met anyone quite so ambitious. 'The woman became a real celebrity as a result of that book.'

'Of course.' Perez imagined Fowler trying to keep his business afloat, but everywhere he was hearing of Angela Moore's success, while he scratched a living taking orders for books over the Internet, meeting up with the occasional eccentric in his shop. 'Angela was on the television every five minutes, warden of Fair Isle, the most prestigious field centre in the UK. Of course it ate away at him. That should have been him. He woke up thinking about it and he dreamed about it at night.'

Rhona raised her eyebrows. Perhaps she was thinking that Perez knew something about obsession. He must wake up thinking about Fran dying in the dark on Fair Isle and no doubt he dreamed about it too.

'Did the wife know what was going on? I still haven't decided how we should charge her.'

'I've been thinking about that.' And it was true. Of all the aspects of the case, this was the one that haunted him most. Sometimes he saw Sarah as a figure like Lady Macbeth, the malign influence behind Fowler, feeding him poison, persuading him with her words and her unhappiness that Angela deserved to die. Had she lured Fran out of the lighthouse, so Fowler could kill her? At other times, he saw Sarah as a victim. 'I don't think she was unhappy when Angela died. She was desperate for a child. They'd been through the stress of IVF and then lost a baby late in pregnancy. Angela was pregnant. Sarah was jealous too.' What a couple the Fowlers must have been, Perez thought. Both of them wrapped up in their disappointment and envy. How did they live their lives? By making small efforts at conversation and normality? Bizarrely, he found himself wondering if John and Sarah ever had sex at the end. There was something almost sensual in the way the women's bodies had been displayed. Another example of John Fowler's odd repression?

'Sarah Fowler knew about Angela's pregnancy?' Rhona's question startled Perez, brought him back to the tasteful room, with the high ceiling and the photographs of old sailing ships on the walls, the immediacy of the investigation.

'I think so,' he said. 'Hugh Shaw claims he heard the Fowlers discussing it. She'd trained as a nurse. And she'd be hypersensitive, wouldn't she, when she longed so much for a baby for herself?' He found himself wondering if Rhona Laing had ever wanted a child.

'Do you know who the father was?'

'Ben Catchpole,' Perez said. 'The timing doesn't work for anyone else.'

'I can understand why Fowler killed Moore.' Rhona reached out and took a piece of shortbread from the white china plate. She seemed disappointed in herself as if she'd given in to a terrible temptation. It seemed to Perez that she had a strange attitude to food. Did she maintain her figure because she was on a perpetual diet or was it all about self-control?

She went on: 'At least, I can just about understand it as an elaborate act of revenge, conceived by a twisted mind. But he had nothing against Jane Latimer.'

'That was to do with survival,' Perez said. 'It was clear from the beginning that Jane was killed because she'd decided Fowler was the killer. I think she was playing detectives. She liked puzzles.'

'A dangerous game.' The Fiscal licked her index finger and scooped up a biscuit crumb from the plate.

'The keys to the lighthouse tower were kept in the kitchen,' Perez said. 'That's where Fowler went to watch people moving around the island. Jane might have seen him take them or replace them. She searched his room. There was the draft of his original article about the possible search areas for the curlew. He'd brought it with him to confront Angela. She'd been reading it in the bird room and was frantic when Fowler took it back. Of course, she didn't want anyone else to read it. It meant nothing to us, but Jane had spent a season in the field centre and understood the implication of it.' He paused. He tried to imagine Jane's exhilaration when she'd thought she'd put together the pieces. When was she planning to tell *him?*

'She wasn't foolish enough to confront Fowler with her suspicions?' Rhona looked at her watch again. How much time had she allowed him?

When was her next meeting due to begin?

'No, Fowler went back to the North Light when Jane wasn't expecting him. I think he saw her searching his things. It was partly my fault. It was the morning Angela's body went out on the helicopter. I sent Sarah and Fowler away from the hall where I was conducting the interviews and told them to come back later. You can see into all the bedrooms as you come into the centre. The ground's a bit higher there and there's a perfect view into the rooms of the first floor. Jane wouldn't have expected them back so soon.'

'He killed her?' Rhona said. 'Just for that?'

'By then,' Perez said, 'he'd lost all reason and all perspective. Perhaps she gave something of her suspicion away. The bookshop name would have intrigued her too and I'm sure she would have looked it up. Perhaps in his mind she was implicated in Angela's betrayal just by being part of the field centre. The fact that the crime scene was decorated with feathers would indicate that. Fowler watched her from the lighthouse tower and saw her go towards the Pund. Jane knew Angela used it as a place to take her men and to keep her secrets. I guess she hoped to find more evidence of Fowler's guilt there. He picked up a pillow from the laundry room, stuffed it into his day sack and hurried over the hill after her. At least, I'm guessing that's what he did. You know more about it than I do. What does Sandy's report say?'

'You're right,' Rhona said. 'Of course you're right. You're the best detective I've ever worked with, Jimmy.' She looked up at him before continuing. 'What happened then?'

Perez thought he knew, but suddenly he was tired of talking. This wasn't his story. He forced out the words. 'He found Jane in the loft. I suppose she was searching for letters, a diary, anything that would give more details of Angela's fraud. That's where he killed her.' Rhona turned over a printed report on her desk and read from Fowler's confession. '*It was very quick. She must have heard my footsteps coming up the ladder behind her, but she didn't even have had time to turn round. I like to think she wouldn't have suffered.*'

'That's not true,' Perez said angrily. 'There were defence wounds on her hands and arms. She fought him off and of course she suffered. I even think he enjoyed that. He didn't have to kill Fran. He must have realized it was all over for him by then.' He paused. 'He killed Jane with a knife he'd taken from the kitchen.'

'You must hate him, Jimmy.'

Perez ignored the observation. He felt drained and he wanted this over as soon as he could. He thought almost with pleasure of his house by the shore, where his father would be waiting with a bottle of whisky and a simple meal.

'Angela had told Stella Monkton that she'd stolen Fowler's research,' Perez said. 'I think Angela did have scruples where her academic work was concerned and she regretted it. When Stella came into Fair Isle she passed on the information to Maurice. He could decide what was most important — to destroy Angela's reputation or use information that might lead to her killer.'

'He decided to tell you.'

'Yes.' Perez looked up at her. 'If I'd listened to him sooner, Fran might be alive.'

'You can't believe that, Jimmy.'

'Oh, yes,' he said, 'I can.' He looked up at her. 'Of course I've decided to give up my job. I can't face this responsibility any more. And every day I'd be reminded of her.'

'What will you do?' She didn't try to talk him out of it. She could see his mind was made up.

'Something useful,' he said. 'Practical. I'll make furniture or keep sheep.' It wasn't as if he needed much money. Now he only had himself to care for.

'You'll always be a detective, Jimmy, in your heart. You're too curious to walk away from things.'

He didn't know what to say to that.

'Will you go home to Fair Isle to live?' she asked.

He answered immediately. 'Oh, no. I'm not sure I'll ever be able to go back there.'

40

Yet two days later he found himself on the *Good Shepherd* on his way home. He still wasn't quite sure how he'd allowed himself to be persuaded. He'd arrived back at his house by the harbour after the interview with Rhona Laing, exhausted. It was as if he'd relived the nightmare days on the island; he felt again the claustrophobia, and the tension hit him as a headache, so fierce that he could hardly see.

His father had greeted him with the small whisky that had become a habit. They both allowed themselves just the one. 'Your mother phoned.'

'Oh, aye.' Mary phoned every evening. She'd been a bit earlier than usual, but that was hardly worthy of comment.

'She wants us home.'

That was hardly worthy of comment either. Mary liked her men around her; she thought they were incapable of caring for themselves.

'You go if you like,' Perez had said. In fact he felt a sudden panic. Left to himself he thought he would sink into a depression he'd never get out of. But in the end, he thought, did that really matter? And his father couldn't live with him for ever. The *Shepherd* crew would need their skipper back and though it wasn't a busy time for the croft, there was always work to do.

'You come,' James said. 'Just for a day. We'll

make sure you get off on the plane on Wednesday. One night. You can stand that.'

In the end Perez hadn't found the energy to fight them. His father drove them south to Grutness in Perez's car. They had to pass Fran's house in Ravenswick, could see it down the bank. Hunter's 4×4 wasn't there. Perez hoped Cassie was in the school close to the beach, that somehow with her friends and her teacher she was coping.

'That's where Fran lived,' Perez said. 'That little house. The old chapel.'

'Do you want to stop?'

'No!' He thought Fran's parents might be inside. He got on with them well enough. They were friendly, intelligent. But he couldn't think what he might say to them. They'd left a message on his phone asking if he'd ring them, but he hadn't responded. He couldn't imagine what might be worse: that they blamed him openly for their daughter's death or that, prompted by their liberal principles, they were sympathetic and understanding.

The *Shepherd* was already at the jetty when they arrived. The crew were loading sacks of mail from the post van, and boxes of vegetables for the shop. They stopped when they saw Perez and one by one, put their arms around him. No words needed. It was a chilly afternoon with a bit of a northerly breeze, but fine enough for him to sit outside on the deck all the way across. James took his place in the wheelhouse and Perez watched Fair Isle approaching over the water with something like dread.

Mary met them at the North Haven with the car. Maurice and Ben were there to unload the boxes for the field centre; Ben had flown back to the Isle as soon as the police in Lerwick had finished with him. He and Maurice were the only people left in the North Light, there would be no more visitors now until the spring. The men had shared the woman who had dominated their lives; now they seemed to have negotiated a way of living together. Perez thought he should ask Maurice about Poppy. Had she settled back into life at school? What had happened with the unsuitable relationship? But he wasn't sufficiently interested to make the effort to form the question. These days he didn't bother if folk thought him rude.

At home, Mary made them tea. She looked as if she'd been baking for days, all his favourites. They took their usual places at the table and sat for a moment looking out over the South Harbour. Perez sensed his mother was building up to saying something. He thought: *Oh, please! Not a speech about Fran. Nor a plea for me to come home to live*. If that happened he'd have to walk away. Otherwise he'd say something he'd regret later. They sat in an awkward silence, until James nodded towards his wife, prompting her to get on with it. This was something his parents had cooked up between them.

'I need to show you this.' Mary set a big notebook in front of him. It was Fran's sketchpad. She'd been working in it all the time they were on the island. Notes and doodles and ideas for paintings. Including the picture of

Sheep Rock she'd planned to make for his parents.

Perez was relieved. They'd found the book and thought he would want it as a memento. Then worried that it might upset him. No big deal. Nothing he couldn't handle. He'd found scraps of her work all over his house. There'd be more in her place in Ravenswick. One day, perhaps, he'd collect her stuff together, have an exhibition in the Herring House gallery in Biddista.

'I was tempted just to throw it away,' Mary said, 'but James said I shouldn't. He said we should leave the decision to you.' She opened the book and turned the pages, put it back on the table again.

It was a page of writing, large and bold and obviously Fran's. Done in charcoal. She'd often left notes for him in the kitchen at Ravenswick in exactly the same form. *Just dropping Cass at Duncan's. Wine in the fridge. Can you make a start on supper?* For a moment he couldn't bring himself to read it. It brought her so close to him, made him realize all over again what he'd lost. And when he did read it he could hear her speaking in his head. Making a joke, but serious at the same time:

To whom it may concern. In the event of my sudden death, for example in that bloody little plane or if the boat should capsize, I entrust my daughter Cassandra to the care of James Alexander (Jimmy) Perez. He thinks of her as his own and I can think of nobody better to look after her.

Then came the signature that Scottish art experts and gallery owners would recognize.

That was it. Two sentences. Perez could hear the gulls calling outside. He said nothing. Had Fran realized that he thought of Cassie sometimes as a replacement for his unborn child? They'd never discussed it. Too mawkish, he'd thought. Too daft.

'I think it's too much to ask,' Mary said crossly. 'To become legal guardian of another man's child. Besides, Hunter would never stand for it. Just tear this up. Who would know?'

For a moment Perez was tempted. This was the last thing he wanted, not because he didn't care for Cassie. He adored her more now than ever; she was all he had left of Fran. But because the only way he could cope with the gut-wrenching guilt was to become dead himself. Not to feel. Not to think. You couldn't bring up a child if you were emotionally dead.

'I'd know,' he said. And he thought Hunter *would* stand for it. He was a pragmatic man, not given to sentiment. He loved Cassie but he wouldn't want to wash her clothes or clean up her snotty nose if she had a cold. And it made sense in another way. The alternative would be for Fran's parents to take Cassie south with them and Hunter wouldn't want that either. It would be a muddle and Perez would have to involve Hunter again in his life in a way that would be a daily penance, but they could make it work. He took the paper from his mother's hands. 'It's the least I can do for Fran, don't you think?'

It was almost as if he'd been in court and a life sentence had been handed down. He felt the relief of reparation, but the pain of facing the real world again. For him there could be no escape into drink or manual labour. No turning wood or keeping sheep. He'd keep his job to provide for Cassie. There'd be no involvement this time in his work though. No empathy. Jimmy Perez the detective was coming back to life, but he'd be a harder, less forgiving man.

Other titles published by
The House of Ulverscroft:

RED BONES

Ann Cleeves

When a young archaeologist studying on a site at Whalsay discovers a set of human remains, the islanders are intrigued. Is it an ancient find — or a more contemporary mystery? Then an elderly woman is shot in a tragic accident and Jimmy Perez is called in to investigate by her grandson — his own colleague, Sandy Wilson. His enquiries uncover two feuding families whose envy, greed and bitterness have divided the community. Jimmy, surrounded by people he doesn't know and in unfamiliar territory, is out of his depth. Then there's another death and, as the spring weather shrouds the island in claustrophobic mists, Jimmy must dig up old secrets to stop a new killer from striking again . . .